DETROIT PUBLIC LIBRARY

P9-CCV-654

*Interactive Press*

CHASE BRANCH LIBRARY
17731 W. SEVEN MILE
DETROIT. MICH. 48235

*As If!*

*Barry Levy is a former South African journalist who moved with his Australian wife and two children to Australia in 1984 because of their abhorrence of apartheid. In 2004 Levy had his first fiction novel published – **Burning Bright**, a story of young love, hate and child abuse, which is currently being translated into Italian. Other publications by Levy include **The Glazer Kidnapping**, the true story of one of the kidnappers involved in the world's biggest kidnap of its time, which took place in South Africa in the mid sixties; a novella **Farewell, Mrs Eels**, in **Scenes From Another Day**, a collection of poetry and prose, and a short story, "The Promised Land", published in **At the Rendezvous of Victory**, a compilation under the title of principal author and Nobel Literature Prize laureate Nadine Gordimer.*

*Levy has been a winner of the Australian Human Rights Award for Journalism—for a multiple series of stories on child sex abuse, domestic violence and homelessness; a winner of the Anning Barton Memorial Award for Outstanding Journalism (Central Queensland)—for a series of stories on child sex abuse (incest-rape), and a Walkley Awards Queensland State finalist—for his series on homelessness.*

CHASE BRANCH LIBRARY
17731 W. SEVEN MILE
DETROIT. MICH. 48235

*The **Literature Series** showcases the best Australian literary talent and is available in digital and print form.*

# As If!

## Barry Levy

*Interactive Press*
*Brisbane*

**Interactive Press**
an imprint of Interactive Publications
Treetop Studio • 9 Kuhler Court
Carindale, Queensland, Australia 4152
sales@ipoz.biz
www.ipoz.biz/ip/ip.htm


First published by Interactive Publications, 2008
© Barry Levy

All rights reserved. Without limiting the rights under copyright reserved above, no part of this publication may be reproduced, stored in or introduced into a retrieval system, or transmitted, in any form or by any means (electronic, mechanical, photocopying, recording or otherwise), without the prior written permission of the copyright owner and the publisher of this book.

Printed in 11 pt Book Antiqua on 18 pt Lithos Pro by Konway Printhouse, Kuala Lumpur.

National Library of Australia
Cataloguing-in-Publication data:

| | |
|---|---|
| Author: | Levy, Barry |
| Title: | As if! |
| Publisher: | Carindale, Qld. : Interactive Press, 2008 |
| ISBN | 9781876819804 (pbk.). |
| Dewey Number: | A823.4 |

*For everyone under there, somewhere.*

*'Twas in another lifetime, one of toil and blood*
*When blackness was a virtue and the road was full of mud*
*I came in from the wilderness, a creature void of form*
*'Come in,' she said, 'I'll give ya shelter from the storm.'*
– from "Shelter from the Storm", Bob Dylan

# Acknowledgments

*Jacket Image:* Izabel Habur, "Urban Teens"

*Jacket Design:* David Reiter

Thanks to Gael for all the years, and patience.

# Contents

As If!

# *As If!*

# 1.

THERE ARE CHOICES IN THIS WORLD. Like bloody shit. Don't let em tell you otherwise. Maybe in some parallel universe. But not here, mate. Not here. My only concession: if I knew it was going to turn out this way, I would have re-scripted the flippin thing. Would have re-painted the wording, would have nailed new bright an glossy chapter headings on it. Sorry to say, we just don't have a bleeding word, not a blimmin letter in the alphabet in these things. Not us. Not us kids. Not us kids like falling stars tumbling and shooting out of the skies, born to no one, known to no one, born only to an arcing mass of black sky, heaven, that everyone looks up to as if the lights that shine from there give direction, show the way as to ships, hold the substance that glues us together as fellow travellers, humanity. And yet I look around me, among all the stars, among all the cheerful, smiling faces, and I only have one person, one single person among all the world, and he is shouting at me, 'C'mon, have a fucking drink. Just have a fucking drink! You'll be fine, mate.' And all about us it is dark, but there is laughter. Loud, possum-like running and screaming and snarling laughter across the carpets and gloss-varnished floorboards, because this is the only day in our lives. This is where it begins and ends. In chaos.

Sitting there in the dark like that, with my big bro Gordon in someone else's home, a drink of spirits cutting down my throat, a much more comfortable place to be than where we just came from. Mum telling Mick to shut the fuck up, Mick telling Mum to shut her gob or he'd shut it for her. Only minutes before Gordon and me in our room, getting away from their drinking noise, sitting there, kicking back on our beds, wondering what was in store. Soon seeing it was Saturday night and maybe we weren't going to watch that video with Mum and Mick like they said like a family — like they wanted us to — watch a movie and eat takeaway pizza like they promised for us.

No, even their buddies, the visitors they said were coming over, hadn't arrived. The laughter of the afternoon, the build up to another Saturday night lost in Mum's yellow wine, the bottom of Mick's brown beer that Gordon snuck one or two of because Mick said he wasn't allowed any, was too young for, even though he was already eighteen.

Mick standing there earlier in the afternoon, scraggy like an old broom, a grey cardigan blowing out his skinny shoulders, promising Mum: 'Hey Ange, we'll get a video and pizza for us and the boys hey, what about that? Just us fer a change, a real family. An Stirlo an Val when they come. What d'ya think, Ange, hey?'

And Ange, Angel, our mum, responding on our behalf, 'Yeah, Mick, that sounds great. Like a real family. The boys'd love that, I know.'

Mick looking so clean for once and pleased with himself. Even his grey, billowy cardigan looking suddenly almost neat and pressed.

Without knocking as usual, Mum curling a long, stiff head into our room.

'Did ya hear that boys? A video an pizza tonight, just for us — an maybe Stirlo an Val?'

'But we're going out,' Gordon spraying back, eyes alert like a private detective.

'Yeah, but this'll be different, just us for a change. You can still go afterwards, Gord. No worries. Mind, just make sure ya leave Grey behind when ya go. He's still young ya know.'

Gordon responding with a smile that breaks the brownness of the room, 'Yeah OK, Mum, that'll be good. Just tell Mick not to leave it too bleeding late.' Me glaring at her like a child shoved against its will into a playpen.

'Yeah, of course,' Mum smiling back like it is a family wedding or something we're waiting for. The only thing missing the caterers.

4

Seven o'clock moving on to seven-thirty no video having arrived, no pizza ordered, Gordon sucking on the last of one of the beers he has stolen off Mick, there is the usual loud smash of a table falling over that seems to announce it. That all has changed. The couple of before-dinner drinks turned into a throat-drowning fountain, the grown-up mind from fuzzy warm to fuzzy bent, and Mick is screaming, 'Gordon's gotta get a bloody job, ya know Ange? He's gotta contribute! He ain't a bloody kid no more.'

And Mum is defending, 'But he already does, when he can, Mick. Give the lad a chance. He's only just eighteen, ya know, and it's not like there's that many jobs in town. He's trying. Remember, he even worked in the supermarket for a while, collectin trolleys and carryin parcels an that for people?' And then she says it, what she usually does, what sets the coals burning. 'Would be nice if *you* got a real bloody job fer a change.'

And Mick, we know, even hidden as we are in our bedroom, looks at her with eyes that have an ancient and unpredictable fire in them, and erupts. 'Say that one more time, just one more time, an I'll smash this bloody fist in yer mug. Trouble with you, Angel, is ya have no bloody respect for me. You just don't get what I'm bloody trying to do here.'

'And what exactly is that, Mick?'

And then, as usual, hell breaks loose. Gordon the first out of the bedroom, to see Mick shaking Mum by the collar, and like a popping bubble of hot coal he yells: 'Get the fuck off Mum, prick! Get the hell offa her.'

And Mick screams back, releasing Mum, 'No, you get the fuck outta here, wool-head. And get a bloody job, mate! Ya not gonna break this family!'

And Gordon's tongue fires back, 'Good one, Mick, good one. So what about the movie an pizza hey? And being nice to Mum an us, huh? Or ya forgotten already?'

And Mick moves towards Gordon who is moving towards Mick, 'Get a flipping job, mate, and then maybe *you* can get the flippin movie and the flippin pizza for a change. Show ya can contribute to this family.'

Mum seeing the two heads about to exchange horns like goats determined to knock one another over, me rustling in my baggy pants for my puffer, to open my lungs, to squeeze the oxygen down my throat, wishing some big hand would appear out of the sky and pick Mum and us up and drop us off somewhere nice and comfortable and safe, away from him.

'Just keep away from one another, Mick. Keep away, for God's sake.' Mum, her wiry frame, her grained face throwing them apart like a boxing referee.

Gordon chewing under his breath: 'Cunt.'

Mick mincing in the spittle of his tongue, 'No, you cunt.'

Me wishing Dad were here. Our real dad. A long time, a long, long time since we'd seen the bugger, but it never got this bad. Never this bad. Well, sometimes. Yeah, maybe sometimes. But at least he was our real dad, like, and we were family. And even most people in town, or on the outside of our place at any rate, thought we were. Now it was all over. Like Dad was all over. There was nothing left. Just squabbles and drunkenness and promises.

Standing there seeing in the white hollows of Mick's dark cut face the times Dad, our real dad, took us out for a drive, a real drive, to the mountains, just us, him and his lads, off to Mt Moon, there, right there, just beyond Ipswich, near Boonah. And coming back again to Mum's cooked meal of chops and mashed potatoes, still smiling and feeling the day warm inside — until the drinking began. Until the drinking began with them, too. Until it ruddy began with them, too. But at least Dad had a job, well, to be honest, most of the time had a job, and somehow the line to the grog — or food — never dried up, was never an issue, like it was now, always. 'Who's going to pay for it? Who's going to pay for dinner? Who's going to pay for the videos? Who's going to pay for the next bloody beer?'

Now suddenly, instead of the occasional visit, it was like the cops cruised by all the time. Senior Detective Constable Watno Thornes and them, cruising round like they were the only ones who cared. Who worried about our safety. But we weren't the only ones in the neighbourhood. The truth was they needed a permanent cruiser, for the entire neighbourhood just about, but they made like they cared, even stepped in sometimes — that's when the fighting stopped, quick like the final whistle on a footy game — and they saw that Gordon and me were big enough to look after ourselves, just like they saw when our real dad was around and we were much younger, even smiled then because our dad, our real dad had a way with the coppers; and then they cruised down the road to the next house, the next neighbourhood, back to the cold safety of the cop station.

I breathe in, struggling to gulp down the oxygen like it is an ice cold thick shake striking straight into the roof of my head, seeing into those times, how Dad always dealt with them, the uncanny warmth between him and the cops, like their skin was somehow of the same colour, like in their eyes they saw and knew one another's homes. And despite all Dad had done, there was a feeling that we were protected, that the streets were out there and we were still in here, in our home, a family contained.

Now it was Mick and Gordon standing toe-to-toe. In the middle of the wobbling living room, neither of them giving way. And Mum, seeing the blood in those eyes, was half whispering, half shouting at us: 'I think you lads better go. I think you better get outta here. The both of ya. Come back later again. It'll be OK then. It'll be OK then, I'm sure.'

'Yeah, listen to ya mum for once, just get the fuck outta here,' Mick screaming, fists in the air, classic boxing pose, squaring up to Gordon's woolly head, breathing out a boxer's triumph, seeing us turning and disappearing out of the front door.

'Shit Gray, ya know I'm gonna leave for good one of these days,' Gordon is saying as we lumber darkly through the black streets.

I look up at him, sort of like a beggar up to a rich man, and he looks down at me, and says, 'I dunno mate. I just dunno what we gonna do about you. You still have to go to school an all that. You're good at it. They all say so. I don't want to spoil that.'

'But it doesn't matter where we are,' I hear a hot liquid spilling in my throat, 'I can still finish school. I just can't... I just don't want to be left with them, ya know, alone like. He's not even our dad. I could kill him sometimes.'

'Yeah, bro, I know,' Gordon is saying. 'Someday mate, someday soon, we'll work something out, buddy. We'll work something out, I won't go without ya.'

The hot, thick liquid in my throat softens, pours, seeing that Gordon is family, real family, seeing Mum left behind in a place where we can no longer see her through the kicked-up, angry dust particles, where we can no longer get to her. Where we can no longer see anything.

'Maybe if it wasn't for that one big fight, Dad would have stayed?' I venture like a sick calf.

7

And Gordon looks down at me. 'Hah, yeah, right. You romantic thick-head. It was more than that, mate, it was much more than that. I think you already forgetting what Dad did to ya, buddy. Maybe you can forget it, mate, but I can't. I mean, just look at ya — walking with a permanently broke pin cause'a him. It's just worse with Mick the prick. I know. Mum's a bloody sucker for punishment. Don't you be one too, mate!'

I look down, feeling my limp like it had suddenly gotten there by some heavenly magic, like I had magically forgotten how I could never forget Dad because of this bloody perverted limp. How, in everyone's eyes I saw without even trying, how no one could forget me because of my limp. My squeaky, uneasy breath. How Gordon and me knew the truth. The darkness in there. And Mum. And Mum too, but she was stuck now.

'I think we can do better than em, mate. Specially you, Grey, specially you.' Gordon is whistling into my face as though into a dark breeze.

We look forward into the night like we are children again, walking quickly, holding hands, afraid of the blackness, knowing that we have to seek out the others.

# 2.

IN THE COLD WIND THERE IS NO CHOICE but for Gordon and me to spend a night with the kids out here, in the stroking but uncaring breeze, while Mick and Mum cool off, sort through another lost Saturday night. Everything so dark and groggy.

We seek them out, our homies, our bros, under the bridge, by the river in the Ipswich dark, and then as if of one large mind, like a single huge brain cell, hungry and in search of things to do we go seeking through the suburbs looking to fill our bellies and have some good, honest to God fun. Scouring the neighbourhood for targets.

And now we are here, all of us kids, in the blackness of someone else's home, afraid to switch on the lights, but warm and comfortable in a way we can't be in our own artificially lit homes. Seeing for the thousandth time that we have eyes that can see in the dark. Yes, it is true. It is the way we grew up. We did not need chandeliers or bed lights or even torches. We were brought up as marsupials. Our lives were the night. We bathed in it, drank in it, shat in it, ate in it. And it gives us a paradoxical kind of freedom. A kind of control. Superiority over our superiors. They say that you need light to dispel darkness. But the reality, we have found, is the other way around. Freedom lies in darkness, under covers, far from the seeing eye, from the light of day. Darkness dispels reality, the imprisonment that day imposes, that keeps you scattered, skulking, out of shit, out of the way. Darkness, as me and Gordon and the rest have found and see now, gives you a bond, like a huge connecting shadow, like right now in this house, in this rich, middle class home, no this palace, this palace filled with security and fermented spirits and chandeliers and books — books that we will never read, books that we can tear out of their shelves and covers and throw to the ground, books that we can rip into shreds without giving it a second thought, books that we can destroy to teach our teachers, our parents, city aldermen, state authorities, government handlers, supervisors, yes, all the supervisors of the world, imposed on us, who think we are just hoons, scum, dirty gravel of the earth.

Yes, we are all of those things: dirty, brown, thick gravel; we have been told so many times, even in the mess of our own grey-brown homes, and yet it is like a song, a requiem, a top of the pops blockbuster, a hip-hop street poem that fires our blood, that lights our minds with neon dreams, this drinking rich people's grog, slinging their books and plates and vases across shiny lounge floors, ripping with pen-knives and bread knives into soft, tempting couches that you want to sleep on, so desperately want to rest your head and sleep on, that you want to spend your entire life on, that you want to die on. Yes, it is like a heavy metal, twisted steel guitar that sings inside you, that makes you feel kind of full, alive. Worth something at last. That makes you dance an Irish fling with Gordon, your brother, who has saved you yet again.

And I am singing, I think even with him hearing me, 'Thank you, buddy. Thank you, bro.'

And he is swinging me round him, like when we were kids, except our own lounge was never quite big enough, right in the thick of this lusciousness, this impromptu Saturday night party that began with the promise of a family night of pizza and videos, and ends with this — me letting him pour a drink of something that cuts like razors down my shaking throat, seeing the curtains in front of me coming down, falling, tumbling on our heads. Ripped loose like falling screws from the walls, eight-foot high, at least, feeling that pure soft satin finish flouncing round my head, the kids in this new covered warmth embracing me in laughter, soft then loud, bowel biting, angry. But close, comforting.

Me, Gordon, Jamie, Kelly, clutching onto one another, hugging like children in movies of Christmas morning, a family, a happy family beneath these drapes. We, a family sheltering in that light that only darkness can bring, that special uninhibited intimacy, the dark glue that casts us together. Brings joy to the world. Lights up trees. And streets. And other people's rooms.

And then rolling out, disentangling, grudgingly falling apart, the dark outside the curtains even lighter now, mouth opening to yet another razor-cutting explosion of vodka going down. For them like juice. For me like barbed wire hooking in the larynx. But warming, freeing inside. Anaesthetising the constantly scratching gravel in me. Little Danno, twelve, a smooth-faced star in the night sky, dancing like a swirling ballerina, screaming, 'Meeee... Meeeee... Meeeeee...' It is his song, the hip-hop song that is constantly in his head. Little Danno's anthem. The song that lives deep inside. 'Meeeeeee...'

No one even notices when Little Danno sits in the middle of the lounge, that pretty, decorated lounge full of swish woven rugs, with his trousers down, and shits, no one even notices. Except me, weak, crippled me, struggling to breathe again, remembering that fist coming out of the sky that not even Gordon could save me from, that fatherly crunch in the jaw like solid rock through water, watching like seeing an orchestra strike up, just for the hell of it, as we sometimes did, watching it strike up on the stone podium in Queen's Park as we rested from the night before, from nothing else to do, from boredom. Watching him now, it is like Little Danno is a conductor with supreme power over his own orchestra, his own big band, his own band of drummers and trumpeters and saxophonists, picking up the baton and then throwing it against this pristine white wall, smudging it with his hands like finger paint, like children do, like sometimes we even did at the city library, under guidance of watchful eyes of course, and in art classes at school. Just smudging the shit all over like a Pro Hart spectacular. Striking long upwards reaching strokes like he is trying to touch the roof, Heaven, only too short, always too short, at age twelve, too damned short, and then arcing down with his spread out fingers, artistically like Japanese writing, until the paint runs out and the design loses touch with its beginnings. Going back for more, to finish the work, to show that inside there, there is design, construction, composition, controlled thought, anger composed and forged in primeval fire, in history, a kind of creative force that comes from the belly, from deep inside, anger and creation, creation and anger, two sides of the same piece of shit. Two sides that I understand. I have seen it with my own eyes. Felt it, the full fist of it, in my own cheeks. And it seems the only thing left I have to thank them for, Mum and Dad, my real dad that is, is forcing me to go to school, not that I liked it, or ever wanted to go. But there were some things there that I even liked, like reading and writing, although I didn't like to overstate it to any of them. Not even Dad, especially Dad, even when the teachers, some teachers, sent home praises. Remembering the time in primary school I won the reading prize and Dad who was so proud of me, but couldn't even make it to the prize-giving because he fell asleep dead drunk. But we always had takeaways those nights, when the teachers sent home praises, not like with Mick, just when they, he and Mum, were too lazy. Which was most nights. And, inevitably, specially on weekends, it ended like now.

Seeing inside Danno before me, muddled thoughts of why it should be him, he of all the invisible spirits up there, that should be tossed down out of the sky. To taste the breath of reality squashed out of screaming, tear-drained thighs. And Little Danno's orchestra, Little Danno's yellow-brown painting, Little Danno's creation grows, a fountain spouting wildly, shooting upwards and then flopping, dragging, and then rising again, a lightshow of candles flickering, bright stars outside, from whence Little Danno came, peering in through the now curtainless windows at their Little Danno's creativity, his great composition. Until… until Kelly, long hair following her twisting head, her hip-shaking dance, like it is a thing, a mop thing on batteries, ends it with her own motherly kind of song: 'It stinks in here, man! It fucking stinks, you little bugger! Go an fucking wash y'self off, kiddo!'

And when Little Danno, a rabbit stunned in torchlight, will not move, as though he cannot believe himself what has happened, the painting he has created, the foul words he is getting for it now, the lack of applause, Gordon steps forward with his broad shoulders that I always wish were mine, his dark brown woolly hair that looks recently cropped like a badly cut Afghan sheep, and grabs him in the thickness of his hands, around the scruff of his long little chicken neck and leads him, in the darkness, like he already knows the place blindfolded, into a bathroom.

The girls, Kelly and Candy, happy to have a real man take over their duties, running around holding their noses, making puking convulsions, hugging one another, smoking cigarettes, stubbing them out on shiny varnished floors, into Persian rugs, pouring dishwasher and Handy Andy and toilet cleaning chemicals all over. Then flying out of the room like ghosts spooked by their own shadows, pirouetting back in a few minutes later, angels blowing powder and squeezing perfume around the lounge, desecrating Little Danno's fired up, God-given inspiration, making the place smell like a ladies house, a hairdresser, a dogs' parlour.

'Little shit-head!' Kelly falling over in laughter, onto the thick couch. Candy swirling around, following, slinking into it, the sheer comfort of it, like daughters, the Hilton sisters, affectionate siblings at home, like they have always somehow been a part of it, this couch, its ensnaring warmth, its safety, its cushiony peace. And then standing up again, taking two massive jumps and leaps, as if something has been forgotten. Stashing souvenirs, things to sell, to bargain with, into their jeans pockets, little silver ornaments from table tops, sliding into a handbag; then entering bedrooms, scavenging for things that shine, that are the nightlights in the darkness: silver necklaces, gold bracelets, earrings, shimmery coins. Tearing apart and throwing cheap looking strings of beads to the glowing floorboards, sliding on them like it is an ice rink, and it is funny seeing them there, the two girls, so free and light-headed, slipping on the floor, onto their backsides, onto beds, in big, luxurious five star bedrooms. Ripping out drawers and laughing like it comes from somewhere deep inside. Now in the main bedroom, six star lush, perfumed sex and kink, opening eight-foot doors, rummaging through huge cavities in the walls, gold-specked drawers, trying on fancy shoes and tops and panties, pocketing glinting pieces of jeweller bent metal. Gordon and Little Danno in the room now, Little Danno in his hot black tracksuit pants with the neon gold stripe down the sides, smiling now, wet and clean like an angel, shouting: 'Meeee… Meeeee… Meeeeee…'

'Ah, shut the fuck up, will ya!' Fat Deano thumping into the master bedroom too now, a bottle of whiskey in clumpy hand, diving onto the bed. Kelly collapsing on top of him, kissing him, rubbing his balls, pretending they are actors in a movie, Nicole Kidman and Tom Cruise, only it's Eyes Wide Open here, bouncing on the bed like it is the trampoline they once had, or maybe never had. Passionate, playful actors; spontaneous, unscripted words, uninhibited, erotic, majestic. A light shining on them, through the window.

Me screaming out to Gordon, 'You see, we don't need em. We can live on our own, man.'

And Gordon screaming back, as though possessed, as though not hearing a word I have said: 'C'mon dudes, for fuck's bloody sakes, let's get the fuck outta here. Now!'

And then we are running, running for our lives. Or in my case, hobbling. And then out of danger, bouncing along the road, a party of revellers, brave in the dark that is so camouflaging, and so freeing.

'What a laugh,' Kelly is saying. 'What a fucking laugh.'

'That little shit Danno. Did ya see the little runt? Painting the walls with shit! Jesus, Little Danno, get a life!' Candy is saying.

Gordon hitting him hard behind the head like he is me, a little brother, and then smiling. 'At least warn us next time, homie.'

Coming to the bridge, near the railway station, in Central Ipswich, home for the night, walking slap bang into Thornes. Fucking Thornes. That is Detective Senior Constable Watno Thornes to everyone else in the town.

'So, what have we here? Do I smell trouble?'

'What d'ya think! We done nuffing.' Candy, affronted, confronting.

'And what if I tell you to turn out your backpacks and bags and pockets, huh?' Turning with a smile to his lanky, Brylcreem-clean looking sidekick.

'Why us, why always us? Why don't ya go an catch real crims?' Fat Deano looks up into the dull-white eyes, equally affronted, squeezing his fat knuckles like a husband ready to defend a wife.

'Well what d'ya think we should do with em, Steve-o?'

'I think we should search em, Wattie.'

'Ha ha — Wattie! Wattie!' Kelly calling out suddenly and then all of us following like a warcry, having not heard that nickname pinned to him before.

'Wattie! Wattie! Wattie!'

'Smart arses, hey? OK, Steve-o, search this street shit.'

And like a lightning fast baseball pitcher Detective Senior Constable Watno Thornes — Wattie — grabs Candy, the nearest to him, by her pencil thin neck and with his boxer-like hands squeezes the back of it until she is white in the face, and Gordon steps in.

'Please sir, all we wanna do is get home. We tired, man. We don't want no trouble.'

'Doesn't look like you don't want no trouble to me?' he stares back into Gordon's wide eyes. 'Sure you fellers haven't just come from trouble?' But he releases Candy anyway, reluctantly, slowly, like he is letting go of a cold beer.

'Yeah, I swear Mr, I mean Sir… Cunstable…'

Squaring with one another now, Detective Senior Constable Watno Thornes' thick, leather shoulders looking down into Gordon's broad but relatively thin pancake shoulders, solid chest into pleading chest, brick-thick face into round, skin-thin face.

'Well, what d'ya think, Detective Constable Steve-o?'

Constable Steve-o nodding, retrieving from his jeans pockets surprisingly thin, delicate girls' hands, as though in readiness. Anticipating an ambush.

'OK, I'll tell you what, we won't search you buggers if ya promise me one thing?' Everyone looking up to the Almighty Thornes, mug-serious, as to a deity. 'If ya promise me you'll all be off the streets and home in bed — wherever the fuck that may be — within the next half hour!'

Staring up into eyes that we know even in the dark are a dull film of blue. Have behind them the thick power of heaven.

'Yeah, we promise, mate,' Gordon says for everyone.

'Well then get the hell outta here — except you two.' Pointing with that dull film of blue, and a short, stubby finger like a cigar end, at me and Gordon. Looking up at him like we didn't hear right. 'Yes you, Mr Morrow, and your scrawny little brother here.'

'See yers,' Kelly and Fat Deano shouting, knowing the plan, and then all of them gone, like flying foxes noisily into a tree, buried in the dark leaves. A narrow escape, thankful. Maybe Thornes not so bad a chunk of juvenile aid copper after all?

Now Gordon and me are standing there alone, uncertain schoolchildren before Detective Senior Constable Watno Thornes and his gel-swept deputy, Detective Constable Steve-o. Between them, a power far greater even than a school principal. Than the sky, than the stars, I am thinking.

Thornes, his huge face, a colourless putty with sun-bleached gravel rubbed into it, shining gloomily under the lamp post we stand beneath, is scanning our eyes like he is trying to see something in there, see somewhere deeper, into places that we can't even see. Like he is a scientist discovering new genes, unravelling them for the first time. His eyes stopping, suddenly, like they are applying brakes, then softening, smoothing like a careful foot off the accelerator. Like a father.

'I don't think you two fellers should be hanging with em...?'

Me, shaking my head nervously, humbly, more than eager to admit guilt.

Gordon replying, 'With who?'

'Who d'ya think, smart arse? With that crowd, that mob of no-good street kids!'

'They just people we know.' Gordon, squaring his shoulders. 'We just having a bit of fun with em, mister, that's all.'

'Well listen to me for a change, Gordo mister. They mean trouble those kids. I know you two lads, we been in this town a long time together. You come from a better home than that. You don't have to be mucking about on the streets with their sort.'

'They just friends, we like em. We don't always hang with em.' Gordon defending with eyes that pour, like you would to a father.

'Listen to me now, Gordo boy,' Thornes flicking holy eyes to his sidekick Steve-o and then back again, 'I'm just trying to tell you, lad, they'll always be no good those kids, they're beyond hope, beyond redemption. Understand?' Gordon nodding, eyes shifting down warily then back up into Thornes' putty face. 'So, I'm just squaring with you, mate. You two Morrow boys will come to no good if you stick with filth like that. You know, I knew your dad, and he was a good bloke. Worked when he could and looked after ya mum like, like she meant something. I know she's with a bad egg now, but that don't mean you have to be like that. Take care of ya mum. That's what you should be doing, lads. You're better than them, these other kids. Listen to me. Keep away from them, get a job... and just get on with your lives. Gordo, I know you're a tough lad, but the only thing you should be doing now is finding a job, earning some bread for yourself, man, and encouraging your little brother here to finish school.' The bulky eyes in his lumpy face sear down like wings into Gordon's face, '...I hear Gray's very good at school, English an things... when he bothers to go... so, listen up, I want you two fellers to make something of your lives. I think you can. What d'ya say?'

Gordon's eyes strike like an arrow, straight up and beyond Detective Senior Constable Watno Thornes' bulky eyes, into the sky, the dark heavens. 'Yes, sir... Cunstable. 'Course, we'll try.

Can we get on home now, dude?'

'Just promise me I won't find you fellers hanging around with that lot again.'

'Promise, dude man.'

'Well *dudes, man*, then get outta here before I kick ya bloody arses and search ya bags. Go on, get the hell outta here.' He shoots his eyes to his lanky colleague Detective Constable Steve-o, finding him already aiming his own crossbows at us.

And then we turn and run and are gone like dust particles abruptly blown away, ourselves now buried in the night. Knowing the plan. Gordon yelling under his breath, 'Pig!'

Me out of breath, echoing, 'Piiii-hhg!'

Stopping.

'For God's sakes, Gray, take a snort on that bloody puffer, will ya.' Gordon ordering.

I get the asthma puffer out of my pocket, my life-blood, my wheeze machine, as I think of it, that I can't remember ever being without, and take two shallow puffs, out of breath, feeling the pipes in there open and declog, wishing I had one of these machines permanently affixed to my jaws. Seeing for the thousandth time, life's not like that. Difficult to breathe in. Looking to Gordon to breathe for me.

Within half an hour we are back on our path, our original path, sliding, running, slipping down the embankment under the bridge, across the road from the railway station, in the dark blanketed cosiness of the bridge, on the banks of the Bremer River, the darkness making the water look like a stream of floating tar, all of us hugging and laughing. More arriving. Bottles of gin and whisky making the rounds, the smell of a bong on fire, the world becoming transformed, lighting up, darkness making that quick transformation to radiance again, hard to soft, deadly silence to drum-bashing noise, coldness to warmth, fear to joy.

Little Danno twirling around in circles just like a spinning top, looking like he is tripping. On what? Who knows? Glue? Gin? Chasing his own tail, 'IIIIII... Weeeee... Meeeeee...' Next moment he is bent over, so far, you can't even see him for the ground, puke gushing out of him like a too quickly turned on garden hose. His guts mixed into the Bremer soil, his little life prostrate now, hugging his skateboard, fast asleep on his cold, damp mother, crusty earth.

Kelly and Candy operating on three hundred volt batteries propelling them into a jig, tugging each others arms and throwing themselves around, Kelly's long hair flinging behind her like a skirt, Candy's short hair teased back like a dove, and then shaking their hips, hip-hop Public Enemy cum Britney Spears style. Burn, Hollywood, Burn. Shake it, baby. Shake. Fat Deano, next to tall, acid-speed-thin Jamie, his baggy skateboard pants sitting around him like a low hanging dress, glugging unquenchably from a bottle, sitting there, all laughs, eager, he and Jamie like an audience at a live show. 'Go! Go! Go! Yo!' The river an airplane landing strip in the background, drops of falling light, a fairy's tarmac going who knows where? Where do rivers go? Deep underground back to the whales? More certainty in that dark liquid runway, where it is going, than any one of us gyrating on that embankment.

Stunned with alcohol, lying on my back on the slopes of the embankment I can hear Gordon's groans, as I have so many times before, groans that sometimes arouse me, sometimes sicken me, sometimes make me see green, always leave me feeling empty, like we are all really running on some low octane gasoline, needing to be sparked, constantly fired up, lungs, mine the sickest of all, clogged with uncertainty, hearts and liver and bowels the mechanics we do not understand, winding on and on, our heads doused with that feeling of always asking for directions, without ever being told where, of having maps, internal organs we cannot read, stopping at roadsides and hospitals we do not know the names of. Looking for parents who do not exist. Wondering who it is this time beneath him, squirming, squealing, grunting, wheezing like me. Knowing that day, brutal light of day will reveal all, the smell of parched eucalypt leaves dampened by night dew sticking in my nostrils like suffocating wet dust.

# 3.

WAKING UP LIKE A SLOW MEXICAN WAVE, one at a time, two at a time, sun already a piercing knife on the flesh, in the eyes, lolling around, hanging about, moving down river, up river, shaking muzzy heads, wondering at our own ugliness, that in the darkness was so beautiful, smooth, milky faces, removed of pimples, blackheads, bruises, cuts, dirtiness. Seeing the brown muddiness of the river, like our skin now, unable to be seen through, reminding us of the embankment, our beds, hard sodden earth.

Who it was beneath Gordon this time I do not really want to know, do not care, though I suspect, from the sounds I have heard before, was Candy, her swinging, rocking, hip-hopping, battery operated body no doubt out of steam now. Does it matter? Friends in the darkness, half-eyed drunkenness, a twinkle of lightness in the storm, that is all that counts. Just Gordon and me now, on the embankment, watching the mud that is the water, that is the mustard-brown of the river slowly floating by, little ripples sometimes silver, sometimes even golden in the pounding sunlight, our chests inside, beating placid, somehow calm. Next to Gordon, a small, shining silver DVD player.

'Where's that come from?'

'Granty. Ya know Granty? Lad from Gailes, had it with him last night. Give him fifteen bucks for it. And he was happy, man. Happy as Larry. Not bad, hey? Gonna give it to Mum.'

'To Mum?'

'Yep, she needs it like ya know, mate. Never had one of these in the house, a DVD player. An the ol' cunt would never buy her one.'

I nod. The 'ol' cunt', our stepfather, Mick, had been with us almost just as long as our dad now; me since I was just past ten, Gordon since thirteen. Jesus Christ, stepfathers! Not that Dad was so great, when you thought about it — hadn't seen him in six years, since the day he left without a hug goodbye. My own dad that Senior Detective Constable Thornes knew about but knew shit about. Like Gordon and me and Mum. But stepfathers! She would have been better off without anyone, without any fucking ratbag come and cause chaos in her life — 'An that's the way I'm gonna stay,' Gordon would say, often, 'on me own, mate. Just me an myself, and maybe you, mate.'

'Fuck it!' Gordon slaps me on the thigh. 'It's the least we can do, bro. I want her to have this.' Using my thigh as a lift-up, he presses down with his heavy, glove-like hand signalling that it's time to get on home now.

Walking through Ipswich Square, the shortest cut home, surrounded by a wall of perennial sales and penny-cent shops, vacant windows, for lease signs, everyone smelling so fresh, of perfumes and showers, big men with grey Mohawks, small men with long Ned Kelly beards, fat, dumpy, short-skirted women wheeling prams, sometimes two or three kids to a pram, looking so sparkly clean now, up past the Police Beat, stupidly. Fucking stupidly. Square-bodied, battle worn intergalactic transformer stepping out into the sunshine in front of us: Detective Senior Constable Watno Thornes.

No howdy do-dees, no how's your day been. Just a 'Where d'ya pick that up, Gordo? Thought I told ya to stay at home, off the streets?' His thick, square shoulders steadying in uniformity with the bulging, laser-staring blue eyes.

'Fuck it, man! It's ten in the morning. Aren't I allowed to walk around me own city?'

No response, just film-thin eyes beaming into Gordon and what he's holding.

'I paid for it, dude. It's mine.'

'And how much exactly did you pay for it, dude?'

'…A hundred bucks.'

'A hundred bucks, eh? Can I see the receipt?'

'There's no receipt. I bought it from a buddy.'

'You mean a homie, who stole it?'

'No, a buddy who just wanted to sell it 'cause he needed the bucks.'

'And where, Gordo, did ya find a hundred bucks?'

'I been saving up, mate — me Centrelink money like. And I had a job… in the supermarket, like, collecting trolleys for a while.'

'Well, I'm glad to hear you at least had a job for a while, Gordo. But you know what?' We both shake our heads, even though Thornes isn't even looking at me. 'I don't the hell believe you.'

'Believe what you like.' Gordon's woolly hair perks up like it can think. I can see he wants to muscle his way past Thornes, but Thornes stands, chest puffed, not moving a centimetre, shoulders spread like massive transformer wings, neck thick like a steel brace, and flaring.

'Both of you, in here. Now!' He aims his eyes at the Police Beat office door.

'But… please… sir, Cunstable…'

'I said in here… both of you twerps. Now! Yes, you too, Gray. You fellers won't the hell listen to me, will ya? You don't want to see I'm really trying to help you; you don't want to take my free, helpful advice, so now I'm gonna teach you lads a lesson.'

Marching into the Police Beat, Gordon, his brown baggy skateboard pants that hang so low off his waist they look like they could fall off his bum at any second, the bottoms worn and stringy, dangling over his hard-toe worker shoes like car rags, leads the way, me sliding along in his jet stream in my own torn black jeans, real rips and tears that I am proud of, carrying the backpack full of goodies from the night before — that Gordon, thinking fast, knowing it is more likely that he will get searched than me, has just swiftly handed to me as we enter the Police Beat door. Following just behind us, the thumping giant robot, the transformer Thornes, wearing a tight fitting cheap black suit without a tie, now carrying under his own bulking arms Gordon's sweet silver gift that he had purchased for our mum.

The interview room at the back of the Police Beat, despite the fluorescent light shining down, has a darkness to it, not the kind of darkness we liked, rather the kind of darkness that is like school, or home, the darkness of something being foisted on you, of thin curtains pulled on sunlight, of something unexpected about to happen, like Mick, our stepfather, suddenly beating up on Mum. Not that much different really to the days when Dad was around.

But at least Dad would give us the occasional smile and mean it. The hug on our birthdays. The kiss goodnight when he was blind drunk and didn't know whose bed he was climbing into. And in his old Holden Camira, green and rusted, mostly rusted, would drive us up to the Moon, Mt Moon that is, just me and Gord, the three of us like brothers. He would park the car on the dusty sand road somewhere and we would walk up the path, like Gordon and I walk up ourselves now, through the farm gates, into the brush, through the green trees that looked so solid and lush; especially from a distance, it was like the green felt on a pool table, only thicker, and higher, and filled with things.

And when Dad thought we were far enough out of sight of the farmers out there, from other people, not that there were ever any other people there, we just sat there, the three of us, in a row, Dad, Gordon, then me. Gordon and me watching, or rather pretending not to watch, as Dad rolled a smoke. Knowing what it was he was smoking, even though he never told us. And then we would just sit back or lie there with him—feeling wanted yet strangely cold and distant—and dream dreams in the shade under the trees that sometimes became sunlight.

And he would say to me: 'Gray, you know, you're getting to be a big feller now, and I know you're clever as hell, so if there's one thing I want ya to promise me, it's that you go to school. And Gordon, lad, I want you to promise me one thing, too… you make sure he does.'

I would smile, and feel the sun on my cheeks and Gordon would nod like an old uncle.

'Gordon,' Dad would go on, 'I am afraid for us it's different, mate. We don't need school. We just not like other folk. We gotta make our money other ways.' And I could see Gordon beam, like the sun and the shade and the trees belonged to him.

And then when we had slept and dreamt too long and he wanted to go, Dad would wake us, and it pierced into us, for a moment paralysing us, remembering all he had done to us and Mum. All this—the pain—in the gloomy light of the Police Beat room, dragging through my fish net head. Just the big fish, the big events remaining stuck in there. Without hugs or kisses. But it was happy times. When the sun was light on the brain and the trees a dark shadow on the flesh, the coolness of the breeze licking our faces like kisses. We did not say much, did not say anything much at all, but it was about as close as you could get to Dad.

22

'Gray… Gray! Will ya the hell wake up, lad!' Thornes' trombone voice rises and booms like he is standing in a pulpit; only the parishioners are animals, pigs, sows, goats. Us. I nod, looking up and then down at muddy canvass shoes. Mine. 'OK now,' he says, 'all I want is the truth fellers,' voice softening. 'And Gray… hey feller, I'm talking to you, too!'

I nod, but it is Gordon who replies.

'Think what you like, man, I paid for the flippin thing.' He says it with a self-righteousness that is hard to cross.

I begin to lose breath and take out my puffer.

'Now listen here, I like you fellers, I think ya know that?' We both look down, ears perked to Thornes' stale breath. 'Or at any rate you might finally be getting the idea. Well I hope so, anyway… if you still remember last night?' We nod and look down at a whistle clean table, the opposite of the dirty, paper filled desks in the movies, "CSI", "Law and Order" style, a cleanness that makes us wonder for a second if he is a real cop. 'Now then, listen carefully,' he says, laser eyes fixing into us, 'because I am not going to repeat myself again. Gordo boy, you especially, you especially should listen very carefully…' He raises a fat finger to the fluorescent light. 'If you want to save yourself and your brother a lot of bloody trouble, mate, and you, being eighteen and an adult now — a man in the eyes of the law remember — don't want to end up sitting in a bleeding gaol with faggots foraging up your arse, you have to tell me the truth, mate. And that's all I want. It'll save you a lot of trouble, mate. Now, where the ef did you get this spanking new DVD player?'

Gordon looks up at him, worms receding coyly into his eyes, slowly unfurling. 'I'm telling the truth, dude, man! I paid for it with me own bread, man. You can ask anyone.' Gordon's fiery brown eyes meet Detective Senior Constable Watno Thornes' laser blue ones. Sword against ice.

Thornes, staring ice into Gordon's eyes, takes a step closer to Gordon and places a lumpy, heavyweight champion hand on his shoulder.

'I'm going to level with you, Gordo, if I take this further you know you're in deep shit, mate? And if you don't get done for theft I can assure you, lad, you'll get done for receiving stolen goods. And with your record, mate, that will mean one thing — a walk inside. So, see what I mean, I'm only tryin' to help you fellers. If you or Gray—Gray, are you the hell listening to me, mate?' I nod quickly. 'Good... well then, if you or Gray tell me the truth, you can leave this machine, just leave the machine here on this desk, make a clean break and just walk outta here. Scott free. Bob's ya uncle.' His eyes dance, intergalactic laser like, between Gordon's two eyes, soften, then speak again. 'You know, fellers, maybe you don't know this, but there was this one thing about your dad, he stood on principle. If there was something he didn't like he walked away from it. And if he done wrong he told the truth about it.'

Gordon bites his lower lip and shakes a hand through his thick hair, his fingers like earthworms in his sunburnt, coffee-brown locks. He looks up like he once looked up to Dad.

'Take the fucking thing!' he says. 'I didn't really want it anyways. I was just helping out a buddy and getting something for Mum at the same time. I don't think it'll fit in our TV anyways.' Gordon breathes into Thornes' face like he is taking a breathalyser test. Thornes steps back and removes his hand from Gordon's shoulder. 'Even if you never believe me, man, I paid for it with me own bread—twenty bucks—from one of the homie kids. But I don't know where the frig he got it.'

'Now that's better,' Detective Senior Constable Watno Thornes' laser eyes soften and spread like a fan, 'that's what I like to hear, Gordy. Honesty, just like your dad was once honest. That's what I expect from ya. Just a bit of truth. That's all. I told you before, and I'm telling you again, you're better than most of these other kids around here. But you've got to keep your arse out of the Ipswich toilet bowl. Understand what I mean?'

Gordon bites his lower lip, not for the first time, and nods, eyes sweeping the ground.

Thornes punches a right laser eye right into my forehead. And stops there.

'Yeah... 'course,' I mumble and nod as well, sunburnt eyes quickly following Gordon's to the ground like a dustpan.

'OK fellers, just take this as a warning. Just take it as a severe warning. ...And I definitely don't want to find you on the streets again!'

We nod, struggle to look into his laser eyes, and then he comes up behind me, real close, placing one of those lumpy, heavyweight hands behind my head, and then squeezes until it feels like he is digging cement nails into either side of my neck. My face bloats red like a kid's rubber swimming tube and my eyes water. 'Because if I do, I'll break both yer bloody necks. Understand me?' Gordon nods; I try, but just feel my neck block, being squeezed like it is soft plastic in a steel vice. He isn't even looking at me anyway, just Gordon. 'We got enough scum in this town without the Morrow lads adding to the filth. I'm gonna be watching you fellers from now on, very, very closely. I have eyes and ears everywhere, you know? Look,' he says voice smoothing, fatherly again, iron-hand releasing his grip very slightly on my neck, 'I'm just afraid I see the possibilities for you two fellers running out, you know. And I want you to know that. I also want you to know this: if I didn't like you lads, you'd be in the bleeding watch-house right now. You following me?'

I yelp, involuntarily, and Thornes lets go of me with a final squeeze that feels like an exclamation mark.

'Now get the bloody hell out of here, the two of you. And keep off the bloody streets!' His colourless eyebrows jut like awnings on the front of a Queensland house; you feel yourself cool in their shadow as they follow you out of that dark interior.

We slouch out of there, Gordon mimicking, *'You know your dad stood on principle... If he done wrong he told the truth,'* and we laugh, walking into the thin, flat dazzle of sunlight that spreads like a water spray through Ipswich Square. Even more shoppers milling about now, completely oblivious of our ordeal, some straggling, some striding in and out of glass shop doors, some talking lazily in circles, all like tiny dots of colour in my eyes, like coloured vibrations rather than people, cracked-faced men with long hair and red beards that we all want to be like, the Ned Kelly dads and fat and thin leathery skinned mums doing the shopping with the kids we go to school with; everyone looking for treats and bargains, quick cash from the Fast Access Loans and Penny Wise exchange shops. It seems to me right now the poorer you are the more you want of everything. And the more you want of everything the less you get. I look at Gordon, eyes set and determined; it's like someone, somewhere, has it all worked out, and is tricking us. And everybody wants to break through that unknown law and be just like The Kellys.

'Fucking Thornes,' Gordon grinds his teeth. 'I guess Mum'll never know now. Probably would of kicked our arses out with it anyways.'

25

'Fucking Thornes,' I agree. 'He thinks he's our bloody dad.'

Gordon looks down. 'That's what I don't like about the prick,' he says. 'He's fucking with our heads. And then, one day, just like that, he'll beat the shit out of us, I reckon.'

I look up at Gordon, feeling small, like a tiny bird, seeing that fist coming my way. That unpredictable fist that was Dad's.

'C'mon, buddy, let's get outta here, go for a spin,' he says.

I nod. Happy to be going anywhere.

# 4.

WE WALK TO THE HOUSE, our little weatherboard railway cottage with the rusty brown corrugated iron roof in Sadliers Crossing that is not so different to every other house in the street. Neat rows of them huddled together like blue collared workers down a coal mine, only sterile, without touching. Paint-flaking. Wanting. On the wispy, overgrown front path our black garbage bin lies on its side like a derelict trying without success to reach the street. Garbage day, no one has bothered to bring it back in. Gordon picks the bin up like he is taking a man by the scruff of the neck and drags it into the front garden.

'Bloody Mick,' he snorts.

Now we are standing on the small porch, knocking on the paint-flaked front door, to see if anyone is home. Mum had taken Gordon's key away. She didn't want us coming in and out any longer whenever we wanted, she said. 'You gotta learn,' she said. 'Behave like gents first. And then I'll give you back your key.'

Mum answers, little black and purple streaked tufts of hair poking up like horns on her head, looking like she has just pulled herself out of bed. She hugs Gordon and then me. She sometimes does that, and it feels good — despite the skeletal thinness, the wire-coldness in her face. Like warm, thin white bread toast wrapping around you, that's what it feels like. In the background, behind Mum, Mick stands in puffed out black boxer shorts that make his legs look like strands of chicken wire. He is standing there, arms crossed over his little convex stomach, without a shirt, his thin torso filled with smudgy tattoos and dancing strands of straight black hair. He looks at us, suspiciously, like it might be burglars, and does not wave, just stands there, in still motion.

A sour smell, like a dish of cat's milk gone off, hits in the nostrils as we enter the lounge. Except we didn't have a cat — well, not for a long time. Mum got us one once from somewhere when we were small. Dad used to kick it and say it was on heat and eating us out of house and home. He kicked it whenever he saw it. One day it never came back. Bastard-d-d! I actually loved that cat, felt closer to it than I did to him, most of the time. It used to sleep on my bed, like family. As we enter the lounge Mick turns his back on us and then, as if changing his mind, sits in the couch in front of the TV, already on and shining dull images and sounds filling in our world.

Angrily he lights a cigarette. Scowls, 'G'day,' putting the match in the burnt village of stubs and piles of ash that already exist in the big glass ashtray on the coffee table in front of him. He takes a deep drag, sucking in the smoke like it is breakfast juice. 'Aren't ya even going to tell ya worried mum where yers have been?' Smoke sits around his head like a lamppost in fog, and he sneers at us.

We look at Mum, both of us, and Gordon says, 'We just been out with the kids, like, having some fun an that. Slept over at Deano's. You can even call his mum if you wanna check...'

She eyes us, but not uncomfortably, not in the shadowy way Mick is eyeing us, I think just happy to have any explanation, Mick off her back, her eyes in the dark morning light of the lounge like black shrouds bearing the weight of generations, above and below. Also lighting a cigarette now, licking in the smoke deeply, like she is eating from the same breakfast table as Mick, only wallops of smoky bacon, lazily lolling her eyes over to the TV to see if any sense is coming out of it. She turns back to us.

'Gray, you must go to school this week,' she says. 'Be a good lad for once. Show Gordon. Show him school's not so bad.' The smoke is burning through her nose like a laser beam show as she talks.

I nod and Gordon glowers. 'Have I done something wrong?'

It's Mick who replies. 'Just let ya mum know where the fuck ya are sometimes. I'm the one has to cop the shit.'

Gordon winces, but does not reply. Looking instead at the TV, vacantly rummaging through the never ending saga in there, the

28

bright American faces and gymnastic voices that wind up the players — us — in the room.

Gordon taps me on the shoulder and I fall into step with him, following him to our bedroom which almost adjoins the lounge it is so close to where we are already standing. There is nothing in it, but at least it is still here. Sometimes we just have this feeling, I know Gordon has it too, something we never actually speak about, but we just both know we have it, that some day when we come home the bedroom will be locked, just locked and barred with wood and banged shut, and we'll never be allowed back in.

'They ever lock us outta this fucking bedroom I'll burn the place down!' Gordon once said. Out of the blue. He had that unbreakable grey frosted glass look in his eyes that you see when he gets angry. Like grey-red worms. That appear whenever he has to stand up to Mick. Actually, the bedroom isn't quite empty. There is a narrow cupboard with a peeling mirror on the door, a mirror that in the dark sometimes looks like a witch. I feel lucky I share my room with Gordon. I am safe with him. The cupboard leans to the left and you cannot shut it. Gordon has tried, many times, when he has wanted to hide small things he's stolen in it. The door just always snaps open of its own accord. Even when you think it is shut and locked and have pulled out the key, it just snaps open. You come home and think you have been burgled or Mum or someone has been through your personal belongings. You, well Gordon, kicks up a big fuss, but nine out of ten times it's just that the door has snapped open. It's haunted, that cupboard, I'm convinced. Now Gordon never even tries to shut the door. I still keep my journals in there, my secret little notebooks I write and record things in, right at the back; door open or closed no one bothers to reach right in; so I think they're safe. One day I'll put them all together, my ramblings, to make sense of our lives, I keep telling myself. I see Gordon now standing there emptying the contents of our backpack into the pockets of an old jacket that hangs in the cupboard.

'Safe-keeping. Investments for the future,' he says.

On the wall above Gordon's bed which is bowed so far in the middle it looks like a swimming hole in the middle of it, there is a large Rambo poster, frayed at the edges, but somehow still sticking to the grey-white fibro wall. Gordon loves the movies, the entire Rambo series. And we watch them whenever we have the chance or the money to get a video. Mick likes Rambo, too, so that helps. It's a time of peace in the house, even when Mick and Mum are drinking heavily, when Rambo movies are on. Blaring so loud we have to shout at one another to issue instructions. Those are the good times. They are few and far between, and seem to be getting fewer and further between. Below that, below the Rambo poster, on a piece of purple paper, there is a saying that Gordon picked up about a year ago from somewhere, or from someone — maybe even a house he broke into? — Who knows? — and put a thick black felt pen border around it. He is so proud of it. It reads:

> When a man finishes
> he is only beginning
> and when he stops
> he is as puzzled as ever

I have never quite followed the words, what they are really saying, or why Gordon has taken to them so, but I suppose they have that kind of 'lone wolf', Rambo feel to them, man against the world, man unsure of why he is always under attack, why life can never be straight, and just when it becomes straight something happens to make it all crooked and confounding again. We never speak about it. I think Gord just takes it for granted I like it just as much as him. There is another thing Gord keeps in the room, behind the metal bed frame, at the top end of the bed. It is a small stone from Mt Moon. There are lots of them out there, all kinds of old and volcanic looking stones, but this one he always keeps and takes with him places, especially whenever we go on one of our jaunts up to the mountain. The stone is shaped like an ancient pyramid, rugged with cracks in it, smooth on the underside. It is on the red side of ochre, sort of electric pink, like you sometimes see when the sun is setting behind folds of grey-white clouds. And this is the best part of it, I suppose what makes it so special to Gordon, it has thick sunburnt orange, streaking pink and blood red lines that look like they are shooting off beyond the stone, into who knows where. It is like a precious stone, that you see sometimes in the money exchange shops in town. I don't know why Gordon holds onto this one in particular; maybe it's because of the way the lines shoot off into the beyond? But I actually think he holds onto it because our dad, who, come to think of it, never gave us that much, gave it to him one day. Yes, I'm sure, during one of those talks they used to have on the way back to the car.

Just him and Dad, walking in front of me, while I limped behind, trying to catch what they were saying. Once thinking I heard Dad say, 'I don't know how much longer it can last, mate... your mum and me...' To me the stone, the shooting lines in it, are like that part of the words on Gordon's wall poster that say 'puzzled as ever'. It's like everyone, even Detective Senior Constable Watno Thornes is caught in Gordon's rock, shooting off somewhere. Gord holds onto it like it is gold, and yet I know he never liked Dad that much.

Gordon kicks his legs into the air and jumps off the bed. He stretches then picks up the stone. Says, yawning, 'OK, buddy, let's get the hell outta here before we stuck in here forever, mate.'

I jump off my bed, kicking in the air like he did, hearing the mattress springs creak, and follow him into the smoky lounge.

'Just going for a bit of a ride, Mum,' he says to Mum, sitting in her nightie, by herself, a glass of wine at her side.

'Is there petrol in that thing?'

Gordon nods.

'Take care. And look after your little brother, mate. We only have one of him, ya know. And make sure he gets to the hospital during the week. He has to have a check up and get his puffer prescription thing.'

'Yeah, OK Mum, don't worry, we'll be around. We just going for a quick ride, hey. That's all.'

She takes a sip from the yellow looking wine, and it strikes me it is the same colour as her eyes. I think they are very, very tired, and there is also a dampness in them.

Outside, Mick, still in his baggy boxer shorts and no shirt, is hammering at a wooden box with that sort of concentration like he is actually doing some meaningful work. He has a pair of bright yellow thongs on his feet and is standing near the rotating washing line, nothing on it but old, coloured pegs and an old muddy towel no one has touched in months. I look down at his canary yellow thongs, thinking they must be Mum's, and see the black tattoo on the side of his shiny, hairless right calf. It is of a long-haired, ink-blotched, naked woman with her hands behind her head. Now all he can get is Mum, I think. With her hair so short cropped and purple streaked she looks all wired up like a punk type, only much older, maybe even like a punk guy? I shiver. Thinking, Jesus Christ, that's our mum.

'Cheers,' I call out to Mick, trying to be friendly, show my manners, as Mum is always on at us about. But he just carries on hammering his box and says nothing. Until Gordon heaves the bike out of our flaking, leaning garage, and begins to kick-start it like a racing driver into motion. When finally it takes, Gordon revs the bike, loudly, on and off, on and off, because it has not been started in weeks.

'Shut the fuck up with that thing, will ya?' Mick shouts out, angry, wiping sweat from his brow with a hairy forearm. Which only makes Gordon rev higher, which only makes Mick shout out again, even louder, which makes Gordon continue to rev when we could have really already been out of here, which makes Mick put down the box he is working on and stride up to us, long steps, hammer held above his head like a Red Indian about to come down on us with a tomahawk, which makes me jump on the bike like an acrobat as Gordon shows Mick a stiff middle finger. We ride off just as Mick comes down with the thick steel hammer, the tattoo on the back of his blue-veiny palm, a cross with a naked women nailed to it, bearing down in my face.

And then we are racing out of Ipswich, in a growling noise of engine and smoke, over the bridge past Leichhardt Park, and on our way into the open, free, free country.

I love getting to Boonah where the fields are like English hillsides in sprays of greens, like in pictures you see in magazines of England, where Mum says our family comes from. Some of them rich now, she says. But we've never met that side of the family. And they've never called around. So, I don't know. Someday, says Mum. But I'm old enough now to ignore it.

Seeing before us now the small mountains abreast one another, Mt Alford, Mt French, and the one that is our 'home', the one that our dad used to take us to, Mt Moon. It is covered in a green forest of dry yet sweet smelling eucalypts, and at the base of the trees, standing up like a tightly woven village of little people, is a green brush so lush it is like a bed to us. Riding, or rather choking the bike as far up the gravel road as it will take us, Gordon and I jump off, throw our badly scratched helmets beside the bike, and walk upwards, opening the farmer's steel gates and walk on until we, or rather Gordon, feels like stopping. Then we dive in, scrambling like two children into the forest, letting the thick brush tickle our hands and faces, until we, or rather Gordon, is tired, and then we sit back against a tree, lazily gazing up at the sky, imagining that it is Heaven, that place we were told we come from. Sometimes, like now, we even wrestle a bit, Gordon always letting me get the better of him, because he knows I am so much weaker than him. Which is a darn sight better than Dad ever was, or Mick, or even Mum, letting me get the better of them. Dad, even with Gordon, used to always make sure he was the winner. And the game never stopped until one of us was crying. Usually me. It used to make Gordon so mad, he swore one day he'd show Dad. He'd get him. Dad left before he could. And I always scream, like now, 'You're just lettin me. You're just lettin me.' And he screams back, 'Ah bullshit, man, Gray. You're strong, mate. Bloody strong. If only you knew it, little bugger, stronger than a bull.' And then, like now, we lie back and just let our tired, begging eyes take in the mountains around us.

'I don't know, I just don't know…' I hear Dad's voice ringing through me in a cicada-driven haze. It was something he always said out here with Gordon and me. Like he was always 'puzzled' like in that poster of Gordon's. But then we would be walking back to the car and Gordon and Dad, as usual, would go a bit faster, a little ahead, and talk as I limped along not ever really knowing what they were saying, my old broken leg that never healed, that Dad, I do not remember, do not remember properly, fixed good and proper in a fit, seeing only myself, pleading eyes, looking up to him, his face black and prickly, curving into a punishing sun, reaching up from my strewn position in the dirt of our backyard, feeling like it had snapped, snapped again like when I fell out of the tree, just three weeks before; Gordon pulling him off, pulling Dad off me, intruding into his anger, crying, getting a slap through the face for his trouble, but succeeding, eventually succeeding. My lesson: learning never again to sneak into the neighbour's house and steal fruit off the kitchen table. Fruit that looked so good, so fresh, I can still taste the succulent juice of it in my mouth. Fruit that Timmo, the boy next door, that I was friendly with, never offered me. Learning that a Saturday morning with a groggy head from beer the night before is like fireworks to a father's head. And then a few days later, like the sun is shining again, he would take us up here, to Mt Moon, and we would just sit up here and sleep and dream. And he would tell me I had to go to school, if there was one thing I ever did, I had to go to school. And that was as close as we ever got. Well, except on the bike. The bike Gordon now rides, the 500cc Yamaha that Gordon and I thought was stolen because it was always hidden in the little tin garage at the side of the house, kept under a blanket.

Sometimes, when he was in the mood, when he was clear-headed, or even not so clear-headed, he would take us for a spin around the corner, along the road out of Ipswich, and we would get to hug him then, because he would insist that we hold him tight around the waist. And we would take it in turns to have rides, and lean our heads against his muscly back. Or all three of us, just for the fun of it, would ride together sometimes, Mum screeching that it was fucking dangerous, one of Dad's hair-brained ideas, and he was crazy and would kill us, and it was like being at a fun park, well close as we ever got to a fun park, except the Ipswich Show, once or twice, for one or two rides; and we sat on the bike all warm and close together, me bridged between Dad and my best person in the world, Gord. And then he left. Dad left. It happened one day after a fight between him and Mum, a fight that grew so bad Gord, angry and agitated as hell, eventually climbed out of our bedroom window, because Dad had locked us in, and snuck back into the house. There he saw Dad like a factory machine raining blows down on our Mum, Angel, the woman he used to call his Angel, who fought back with a string of dirty, high-pitched words and fingernails that dug deep into a face already bleeding like a river. Gordon flung himself, all of his twelve year-old weight against Dad's shaking, out of control factory hammering body, and by the time I too managed to get out of the room and back into the house there was blood everywhere; it looked like someone had been murdered, and they were all just running around like cowboys and Indians, no one claiming victory, no one falling over in defeat. And the neighbours were banging against the kitchen windows screaming they were going to call the police.

No one spoke for the rest of that day, not a word, and the next day he just left. Not even a hug goodbye, not even a breath farewell. For months we all just sat in a kind of stunned silence, Mum, me and Gord, singing his praises. Like we'd done something wrong. Each of us, in our own way, feeling guilty. And when he did not come back for eight months or so, Mum said to Gordon, 'I s'pose it's yours now, when you're old enough, the bike. We'll sell the blinking car, that's all we have.' And then Gordon, from that day, began to look after the bike like it was a baby, cleaning and greasing and starting it, just to hear its engine vibrate, just to hear if the growling engine would ever purr, until Mum said he was old enough to learn to ride it. Threatening that because it was not licensed, would never be licensed, he should never go far on it, should never ride around town with it. And at least for about a year there was peace, a kind of peace in our house — until Mick the prick arrived.

We did not know where Mum picked him up, but one day we awoke to Mick, whose dark face was like that evil Sykes guy in the *Oliver Twist* film we saw sometimes on video and TV, only more cut, even more sliced and jagged looking, like he was walking around in a permanent cloud of anger. It wasn't long before he took charge and started to restrict Gordon and me from going out, Mum from seeing certain friends, started bringing his own family and friends around and Gordon and me sometimes had to share a bed. And then the fights began and he screeched at us to get out, like he owned the house. And Mum, sometimes cowering, sometimes crying, sometimes just with moist, yellow eyes eventually slid in behind him, like she was paralysed. And there she sat goading him. Saying we had to listen. Mick was always right. He was family now.

School seemed to end for Gord then, while Mum begged me to stay on because she said I was good at it and could make something of myself someday. Just like Dad had said. And just like some of the teachers told her, she said. Sometimes I even got good grades on my reports, I knew that, and was told that I was of above average intelligence, especially in English and things like that. And Mum would say: 'We're relying on ya, Grey. You're the one who's gonna get us out of this mess some day.' But for Gordon it was over. He went to school less and less, was out of the house more and more. Some nights he did not even stay at home any more, and started taking me all over the show, to new friends, even girlfriends, to the crowd that hangs under the bridge, to Ruth's Place. Come to think of it, especially in those days, we spent a lot of time in Ruth's Place.

'One day, I swear, I will live in a place like this,' Gordon breathes, sitting up in the grass, looking out into a winding river of trees, rubbing his precious Mt Moon stone like maybe, just maybe, a genie will spring out of it and grant his wish. 'And there'll be room for you too, mate. And your bloody family. If ever you have one.'

'And how will you afford it?'

'Don't worry, Gray, it'll just happen. It'll just happen, man.'

I laugh.

'Don't laugh,' he says. 'I'm telling you, man, it'll happen. I can just feel it. Sometimes a man just feels these things in his bones.'

And then we lie back down again and dream, dream some more, until it is time to go — to break the cicada-filled silence with the loud growl of the bike and head back to Mum, to home, like we'd promised. On the bike we watch the fields recede, the rainbow sprays of greens, wanting to attach ourselves to it, those fields, and then as we are approaching Ipswich, I feel Gordon tense against my flesh, knowing what he is thinking — about the way we had left, Mick attacking us like a Red Indian with a hammer, Gordon giving him the finger, and he turns off the coughing engine until the bike hums and comes to a standstill.

We jump off the bike and Gordon wheels it, I can see, not wanting anyone to hear us, up the road, up the old driveway, and into the even older falling down tin garage. I can see he doesn't want any confrontations with Mum or Mick, who he knows, you didn't have to be a magician to guess, will have put more drink in them by now than they will have food or water, who will maybe even be fearlessly drunk, especially since it is the weekend, the sunset of the weekend, the last effort at numbing themselves before the weekday guilt of not working.

In the garage Gordon covers the bike with a brown sheet, very quickly, not giving it the usual affectionate baby pat he always does when he is putting the machine to bed, and then we run back down the drive and when we are a few houses down the road we slow the pace, begin to breathe easy, and I know for sure, as we turn the corner at the railway crossing, we are headed for Ruth's Place. For sanctuary.

# 5.

THE THING ABOUT RUTH'S PLACE is that it is no hotel. Not even a motel. Nothing like it. Not that I know what a hotel is like. Though once or twice with Mum, and with Mum and Dad, even with Mick, we have stayed in a motel, whatever the difference is. I guess you don't get breakfast in bed? And it's all on ground level or something? Either way, as Mum always complained, cost a fucking heap. So, no, Ruth's Place certainly is no hotel, with bedrooms and huge dining rooms and snooker rooms and games rooms for kids and things like that. But it sure is a place you can at least go to hang out in. And even if you have more people to share with than in your own home — there are always tons of kids around — it is better than home, most of the time. And at least the kids there, well most of them anyways, are kids like Gordon and me. Only it definitely, definitely isn't like the homes you see on TV, the big American homes with plenty of ornaments and wooden stairways and shiny lamps and chandeliers and playrooms and things. But at least you know when you go there, no one is going to chase you out or make you feel like you shouldn't be there. Well, unless you mess up real bad and come in so drunk or drugged up that you are violent or abusive or swearing like crazy or something. Then Ruth Hannah, the wise old sheila whose place it is, will take you by the ear in her pink-peeling, old lady fingers and sling you out. And no one, no one I ever knew of anyway, ever fought back. Not even Gordon.

That is the thing about Ruth Hannah. She makes you feel like you have a place, but she sure as hell lets you know it isn't a place for putting your feet up or anything like that. Some of the kids there are even younger than me, sometimes even eleven and twelve years old. You can stay there as long as you like, if there is room, or until you find some other place, move on, find work, or go home as Ruth is always encouraging people to do — with the help of God, who she only, thank bleeding Christ, ever really mentions at mealtimes, with us all clumsily holding hands like stupid children. And that's another thing, she guides everyone with her quotational posters that she keeps pasting around the house like they are her personal message boards. So, there are always new faces there. Most of them asking for answers to questions they can't even write. Some eventually become like that themselves, what Ruth wants, what I suppose you call Christians. You know, accept Jesus and Holy Spirits and stuff into their hearts. I don't know how long it lasts, because you never seem to see them again. So maybe it is forever? Yeah, right.

Ruth Hannah, a woman with white hair trying to get messages across. I guess that's where Gordon got the idea of putting a quotation next to his own bed? It wasn't one I'd ever seen at Ruth's Place, so I'm sure he didn't rip it off her — it didn't seem Christian enough anyways. Too confusing. I don't think Ruth would have liked it.

Tonight, as we lumber into the house, Ruth says in that sort of singing voice of hers: 'Just in time, lads. There's potatoes to be peeled and a kitchen to be swept.'

We look down, trying to squirm out of it, but Ruth Hannah has a way of prodding you with her white, prickly eyes, and soon we get to work, irritated, expecting to put our feet up, not standing in the kitchen cutting and peeling and sweeping. But it is worth the ultimate peace. Actually, there is something so clean about Ruth's Place, it is almost cold, even in this end of winter heat. It smells like Ajax or some supermarket cleaning agent or something, so bright and shiny hospital-white sometimes you just want to ruffle everything up and throw things against the walls — anything: banana skins, muddy balls, eggs, cigarettes, potato peels, just to make the place look more like home. Of course no one ever tries anything funny like that, except in a wild, unexpected tantrum. But we speak about it sometimes among ourselves, laughing. Fuck, if only she knew.

With the potatoes peeled, by Gordon and me, sort of sitting there grim-faced, peeling, peeling, peeling, and then that part of the kitchen swept and dust-panned up by me—because Gordon says, as he usually does, 'It's your turn, young fella'—we slink into the living room where one of the kids, Bazza, who we know from previous visits to Ruth's Place, one of the longer term residents, is strumming a guitar. Slowly everyone sits around him, Ruth and a couple of the girls left in the kitchen now, doing the cooking, and we just sit there and listen, a couple of kids singing along. Behind Bazza the guitar player stands Little Pumpy, just eleven, and so white and clean looking. I guess he's just had a shower. But he always has that look. Unlike most of the others, he always looks so angel-clean, like an altar boy. Behind him, on the wall directly behind his little frayed-white body, a poster reads: *Forgiveness is the fragrance the violet sheds on the heel that has crushed it – Mark Twain*. Actually I have heard of Mark Twain because my last English teacher used to often say I should read *Tom Sawyer* or *Huckleberry Finn* or something like that, but when I saw how many pages there were, I nearly freaked out. Sort of just looked at the covers, but when I tried to read it, you know, page by page, I actually enjoyed it. It was like running with real children, well in those days type of children, like running with the wind. Sometimes an ill wind. But it's so big I doubt I'll ever finish it. Like Charles Dickens, who I am trying to read as well. Maybe one day… if am still alive I will finish them. Luckily they are school books, otherwise Mum—definitely Mick—would ask me what the dickens I'm doing with such crap and throw them out.

Tonight, for some reason, we seem to know everyone in the room. Well, except one girl. She sits on the lounge floor, cross-legged, Buddha style, in a corner of the room, near where Gordon and I settle. Eyes yawning and lips moving sluggishly slow, she is telling one of the other lads her story, how she has come to Ruth's Place. Her hair is furry, almost spiky at the top, like a crown, otherwise it rushes straight and dull blonde down her neck; she keeps running freckled hands through it and sweeping it out of her eyes. Her skin is so light in colour it looks like all the blood has drained out of it, like when you're about to be sick.

'Yeah… God, shit, fuck man… just sooo off me face, like ya know, trippin out of me fucking tree, hey… Couldn't even the hell move. Just sitting there like on the side of the road like… when this freaking van pulls up… I think, shit, like hey, some fuckers out to cause trouble, ya know, or the frigging cops in a unmarked car or something… an I look round, hey… an there's this frigging white-haired woman standing there like she has a massive light round her… ya know, round her face like… all bright an glowy like the sun… but I'm so fucking smashed, hey… an she looks just like one of them church paintings, ya know, ol' shiny red cheeks… an all she does is fucking smile. Smile! Fuck, I nearly die.… There I'm expecting it to be the coppers, ya know, or some feral pricks like, an there she is just staring down at me like no one's ever looked at me before.… Anyways, instead of being chucked in the back of a van, it turns out to be Ruth, an I ride, still outta me frigging head, in the front of her van like I'm a queen all the way here to Ruth's Place. Fucking Christ! Anyways, that's yesterdee, an I was still fucking off me freaking face this morning, man, so yers can imagine, hey.'

My eyes switch to Gordon, seeing him taking her in, breathing her down, but not like he does other girls, a momentary flicker of want, arranging in his eyes a time and place. No, more like maybe it's not so much him breathing her in as much as he allowing her to breathe him in, sip him down, if you know what I mean. Sort of take him in, for real. And I can see his eyes, all glassy now, like they are filled with cigarette smoke, losing himself in her dull blonde hair, her small, mousy eyes, her dry, cracked lips. It is like, to him, she is somehow the refrain, the tune behind the rhythm of the guitar Baz is still playing in the background.

Once I thought I saw him looking at our mum like that, and she slapped him and told him to get to bed. I don't know why. I never found out. I think all he wanted was a hug. So I'm not quite sure what the look means only that there is something going on in here. Behind her, behind this new girl, there is a poster that says: *If the other person injures you, you may forget the injury; but if you injure him you will always remember – Kahlil Gibran*. I can't even pronounce the fucker's name that wrote it – K'hill Gabran or something? And I know, at reading and writing, I am way better than the rest of the kids here, some finished school already and they still can't even read or write properly. Not even a recipe. Or even these frigging posters. Clean as Little Pumpy looks, and always looking like he is doing his homework or something like it, he can hardly read a word. So much for cleanliness.

The freckled girl sweeps her hair back, swallows some spit, bites her lip, and half cranes towards Gordon, who says, 'Hey, chick, I'm Gordon an this is me little bro here, Gray. Ya got a name?'

She sweeps her hair with her fingers again, like she had not at first noticed Gordon there, and squinting her little pink eyes, says, 'Dusty... Dusty Jones.'

And now he is reconnoitring Dusty Jones and she is reconnoitring him like they are both on drugs or something, their eyes sort of swimming right into one another, like there is going to be a collision.

'Why, Dusty?'

'It's me hair,' she says shyly, stroking her hair out of her eyes. 'Promise ya won't laugh, mate...' Gordon eagerly seesaws his head, 'me real name's... promise ya won't laugh...' Gordon's head seesaws again, '...Dawn.' Gordon giggles and abruptly stops, so does she. He nods sorry, she reddens and continues anyway. 'No one calls me that, though. It's Dusty now, ever since I were small like, and everyone used to say me hair wasn't quite white or blonde or ya know like brown — but dusty. So, that's me name now.'

'Fuck,' Gordon says. 'Dusty, hey.' Looking down, almost shy. 'Where're ya from, Dust? How come we never seen ya round here?'

'Mum moves round a bit, ya know. We used to live in Sydney, Darlinghurst like. But we been in Brisbane a few years now.'

'So, ya gonna stay here? At Ruth's?'

'Yeah, kinda, well naa, I'll go back... soon. Home to me mum. It's good here, I'll... it's just not good now... me home.'

'An why's that?'

She looks at Gordon as if to say, 'Do you really want to know, dude? What's so good about you?' But Gordon nods with kangaroo-wide eyes, like he sometimes does with Mum and she will just let him off the hook for whatever it was he'd done wrong, and in the same way Dusty now opens up and says, 'Well... OK, it's goes like this — me mum's got this new boyfriend like, ya know. Actually, he's been around for a frigging while now, about a coupla years or more; ya know, in an out, fuck knows, home for the night, weekend, quick bang an goodbye; but lately he's been sticking round, an he comes over with his mates and it's just like no good, hey. I just had to get outta there. They fight like fucking crazy. Throw things an swear at the top of their frigging lungs at one another. So, I get off me face, not even knowing where in shit's name I'll land up, an here I am. Thanks to Ruth. I think she's a blooming angel.'

Gordon's eyes are set on her like microscopes, peering into her like he is dissecting an ant, or maybe reading that quotation by his bedside, or even one of Ruth Hannah's posters, trying to fathom the words. He is seeing, I can see, knowing Gordon, something in there that maybe no one else can see, like he is trying to savour something from it, for another time. Seeing something beneath the anaemic freckled flesh, maybe in the blood flowing through the invisible veins?

We are called to dinner and the guitar strumming stops. Ends abruptly like a string breaking. We all sit round the large table, about ten of us, squeezing in at the corners, and Ruth, her white hair, stiff and matted like coir, dishes up and passes around the food. Everyone waits, unlike home where you just dig in immediately. When it is all passed around, Ruth scans everyone with lukewarm hazel blue eyes that you can see maybe once had the guys running, but now look more like they are caked with flour, or icing frost. And I suppose, in a sense, still have the guys running. As she scans the table, as though receiving a message from above we all lift our hands and clasp them together. Ruth can be warm but inside there is this draughtiness. You feel it, even at the opposite end of the table. Sometimes she will speak, say thank you for this day and looking after us and that sort of stuff, but mostly, thank heavens, like on this occasion, she says nothing, and after a minute of absolute silence we open our eyes again, and I see Little Pumpy blinking his eyes like crazy. I suppose to get used to the light again?

We begin to tuck in, plates and cutlery clinking suddenly like broken instruments in a loud bush band, or like you saw it in that Oliver movie in that home Oliver came from. At least we can always ask for more here, no worries. Although most times there isn't any. Another thing I noticed when I opened my eyes, Gordon is sitting next to Dusty. They speak throughout the meal, even laugh, but I am way out of range and can't even begin to hear what they are saying, even though I keep trying. I sit there wishing I could be like him, like Gord, my big bro.

After dinner, and everyone has sucked their fingers and licked their lips, Dusty helps to clean up and wash the dishes in the kitchen with one of the other lads Ruth has assigned. Gordon and me, having done our duties, lounge on a small couch in the living room and mess around with the other kids. Mostly we rag Little Pumpy because there is nothing much else to do and Ruth has a rule that says we have to wait another hour, until eight, before we can switch on the TV. The idea, as Ruth has explained a trillion times, is so that kids who have homework can do it then, or if there is no homework we can all read. But usually we just get any old book out of the bookshelf, don't even look at the title, and just speak and muck about like we're doing now. Little Pumpy is a good target, though, because he is genuinely trying to do some homework, sitting at the dining room table as soon as it is cleared off, trying desperately to read and write something in a pad.

'Don't be such a grump, Pump,' one of the kids says.

And that seems to set everyone off. 'Here, can I help you?' one of the girls says. And peering over his shoulder before he can even say no, squeezes her lips like a teacher, 'Oooh, trying to write stories, hey?' She passes his homework book around. The passage, smudgy and hard to read, is about a boy who's lost his mum in the supermarket. 'Scared'a losing ya mum, huh Pumpy? Don't ya know ya way home, hey? Where's ya mum anyways? At the supermarket, huh? Or the pub? Shame, don't ya mum love her Little Pump? That why ya lost in the supermarket?' Everyone laughs. Loudly.

Until Ruth appears. 'Leave Pumpy alone, for God's sake! At least he's getting somewhere. Like you all should. Like you all should be doing. Your homework. Reading. Getting somewhere.' Her eyes burn coals, and everyone scatters leaving Little Pumpy to his schoolwork.

It is the way they treat Little Pumpy, why I will never show anyone my own scribblings, my diary, or diaries rather, that I don't even show to Gord anymore, even though he knows I have them, the small notebooks that I keep hidden in the cupboard at home, that blinking haunted cupboard that will never close, small notebooks stolen from Woollies, that I write in usually in the darkness, or at school, during journal time, because I don't want to be discovered. I bag Little Pumpy, too. But I know what it's like. Even Gord. I used to show him some of what I was writing in the

43

beginning, but then he just became like all the rest. 'Writing things down will get ya nowhere, smart arse,' he'd say, just like the rest of them. 'It's for kids who think they smarter than us.' Words are dangerous, I saw then. They only get you in trouble, at home, at school, on the streets. So you swallow them, or hide them, like me. I know how Little Pumpy feels. But I also know how everyone feels about fucking words and trying to be clever.

Dusty slinks like a dull white cat out of the kitchen and you can see restlessness revving in Gordon's eyes. He just wants to get out of here. Out of Ruth's lounge. Be with her. And I see him, shoulders bent, coolly stepping up to her, telling her of a good place he knows where they can smoke cigarettes to their hearts content, chill out and just relax, without all these commands and instructions and order at Ruth's Place.

'Ya coming?' He winks at me, giving me the command to follow, and I immediately slip into his footsteps, behind him and Dusty.

'Ten o'clock, and it's lights out, remember?' Ruth looks ruffled, like we, well Gordon, is being disobedient. Turning her orders upside down. Like we're 'stealing' Dusty, who she has just saved, from under her nose. 'She can do with the rest, you know? She needs a good night's sleep, poor lass.'

Gordon nods, fatherly. 'Don't worry, mum, we'll take good care of the lass. Tuck her in nice an early.' He winks at me again, and I blink both eyes, red-faced. But it seems to be enough to assure Ruth. Not that she can really do anything about it.

'OK then, take care, children.'

'Sure, 'course we will,' Gordon calls happily and breathes into his neck, 'fer fuck's bloody sakes.'

Dusty puts on a little shiny blue peaked cap, more like shiny electric turquoise-blue in colour, that she wears at an angle over her right eye, fringe streaking out like a comb. It is unexpected, the shiny leatherette hat, at this time of night, but cute, really cute. Just the angle it hangs at. I think Mum's mum would have called it a Jean Shrimpton or a Barnaby Street hat or something like that. And then we are out, in the streets, under the lamp posts, in the darkness that we know so well. I don't know why, just jumping and twirling around like butterflies or something. Like we've been freed from a prison. And it isn't even a full moon. I look up into the sky to make sure, because some of the kids go funny, actually a bit crazy when it's a full moon and we're all out on the streets.

# 6.

WE END UP, AS GORDON AND I OFTEN DO, in familiar sandy, bushy surroundings, under the bridge, near the railway station, meeting up with the other kids, Fat Deano and the girls, Kelly and Candy. And the others, of course, even Little Danno, still around. A carton of wine going around like it is an after dinner dessert, and we just sit there, on the embankment, in the darkness by the Bremer River, seeing the river running still, like it is an empty tar road before us, hearing the cars above us passing over to their happy, comfy homes... g'doop, g'doop, g'doop. Everyone, except me, of course, is smoking cigarettes, and look like little fire-glows in the dark.

A boom box arrives. It is too early to crank it up loud, we know that at this time of night it will only attract passers by above the embankment, and sure as hell mean the cops—before we've even begun. So it is kept soft, for now, and we just sit in a group, in little huddles, and smoke, drink, begin to laugh. A bong suddenly comes around like a precious stone being passed along for viewing, which we must examine, weigh its value, and then put a bid on. Everyone is inhaling deeply, sucking in like hard-working vacuums. They know more might not arrive, well not that soon, and every speck of smoke counts. Only me, with my asthma, I have learnt to keep out of the way, to avoid being ragged, called a 'homie baby', if not just a plain 'homo baby'.

The music is getting louder, the kids braver. Some are singing to the music, and now Fat Deano is doing cartwheels, or trying to do cartwheels to a rap song, on the grey cement path right by the river that no one ever walks along. His stomach is hanging out of his black t-shirt like a band of crinkly pink rubber, and his baggy pants are up at his knees like a girl's dress falling down. Everyone is laughing at him, like he is Bozo the Fat Clown. Little Danno, with his black beanie almost falling into his eyes, has a new skate board from somewhere, that he insists is a gift from an uncle visiting from Melbourne, and he is riding up and down the cement footpath, in the dark, like a rabbit through a warren. And as he rides along, bent down, touching the ground momentarily with his fingertips and then jumping up off the board, only to land back on the board again, he is screaming his own rap song, 'IIIIII... Meeee... Weeeeee...' Smiling and waving his arms whenever someone calls out, 'Go fer't, Little Danno. Yo! Go fer't. Let it all hang loose, man!' It is like his whole family is suddenly watching, checking out his talent at work. He has the smile of a winner at the Commonwealth Games over his dark face.

Then one of the kids sees me. Sort of muscles in above me.

'Make Gray have a smoke,' he says. 'See what he's like stoned, hey?' There is general agreement from the huddle that has found its way around me. And not just general agreement, a kind of glee, like little boys making a kid pull his pants down in front of everyone else or something.

I want to run, not a good option, because then sure as hell they will brand me a scaredy-cat, wussy homo-boy forever, and anyway I know I will not get far before I run out of steam. And when they catch up with me I'll get a thumping, too. So, I just sit there, smiling, pretending not to notice, bracing myself. They laugh, more a kind of girly giggle, and bring the bong up to my lips, forcing the plastic milkshake straw into my mouth. I am desperately thinking of ways to breathe in without really breathing. Wishing I were an alien from Mars who breathed through my ears. That would fucking get em! Looking around me for an alien ship to spirit me away, thinking of jumping in the river where I know they will never follow me, but then I will probably also drown, wondering where the hell Gord has suddenly got to with his fucking Dusty Jones. I know he would swim after me. Seeing out of the corner of my eye Gordon and Dusty just like they are some ordinary folk on the river, enjoying themselves, talking, sucking in the peace, looking into one another's eyes. Shit!

I breathe in shallowly, letting the smoke loll and then roll on my tongue, and they all shout, 'Breathe, mother fucker, breathe!'

I let the hot smoke circulate in my mouth for a while longer and they scream again, 'Breathe fucker, breathe. Deep. C'mon deep.' I know I am going to choke unless I breathe the tongue-blistering smoke out—out into the black night air that Gordon and Dusty are enjoying like everything is just so dandy and fine. But then they will only force me again—to have another drag. So I swallow, swallow the smoke like thick spit, and the smoke gets caught in my throat like a fish bone, only coming up again through the top of my mouth, my thin little nose, and I begin to do the only thing my body is aching to do—cough. And cough. And cough. And they begin to laugh and now they are really getting the fun they came for, screaming, 'One more time, homie, one more time,' and I have to go through the whole entire ritual again. Only this time the smoke seems even hotter, like there is much more of it in my mouth, and as I swallow I feel it is not just choking my throat like a fish bone but strangling me like fingers across the outside of my throat, tough, stubby fingers like Senior Detective Constable Watno Thornes', and I cough and then sneeze and fart at the same time, and they all laugh their fucking heads off. Tears, I feel heat tears foaming in my eyes, through the hot fog in my eyes seeing a grey Gordon shaped cloud rising above me. I reach, like a blind man in the dark, into my pants pocket for my puffer, and when finally I find it, begin to take deep breaths like it is a hospital oxygen tank or something.

'What the...? OK which one of youse is the fuck behind this shit? Who made him?'

The kids are sitting in a circle around me, all quiet now, one or two having managed to slip away. They all look up at Gordon, like he is a cowboy blown in from the west, and no one answers. And then the kid who started the whole thing, seeing Gordon and his wild west puffed out chest, begins to laugh. He is a big kid, one of the bigger kids, bigger I would say than Gordon, even broader shouldered, more solid, only maybe squarer in the shoulders, thinner necked, and he says, 'So what the fuck ya gonna do about it, sheriff?' And everyone laughs.

Gordon just looks down at the kid and doesn't even reply. He just sort of unwinds, or maybe I should say winds up like a spring and smashes a rock-like fist into the kid's face, fully flat into the middle of it, a fist held so tight you'd think he had precious metals rolled in it. We all, pretending to be tough, unmoved, feign dispassion as our eyes follow like jet-balls the kid's head bounce back and then forwards followed by a fountain of liquid maroon bursting from the middle of his face. The kid immediately brings his hands up to his head and bends into the middle of his knees. You can see the blood drizzling between his fingers.

'Cuntface! I'll get ya for this!' he cries into blood-soaked hands.

And one of the girls gives him an old rag to wipe his face down; someone else passes him some wine. After that everyone leaves him and he just sits alone, sullen, excommunicated, on the embankment. And life returns to normal, the boom box revving up again, much louder now, screaming words from Michael Franti. Fat Deano not doing any more cartwheels but dancing like he is a hip-hop star now, a couple of the girls dancing with him. 'Rock the Nation, baby. The truth will come,' Michael Franti assuring us. Yeah, right, as if.

Gordon puts his arm around me and leads me down the embankment to Dusty, who says to Gordon, 'What the hell?'

'No one messes with me little bro,' he says and looks as if it is a warning even to her. And then those wide brown eyes of his soften. 'They should fucking know, dickheads! The kid's a bloody half cripple and got asthma bad.'

I laugh. 'I'm not a cripple.'

'The fuck yer not,' he pushes me, and then lets me fight back until I have him pinned to the ground, and he is screaming, 'OK, Gray, OK, ya not a fucking cripple. Ya not. I was only fucking joking, man. I swear.'

We all lie back now, me Gord and Dusty, listening to the music and the noise of the other kids in the background, and Dusty says, 'You guys got it good here, mate.'

Gordon turns and looks at her, like she must be a freak, like maybe she doesn't know what good is or what she's on about.

'In Brisbane,' she explains, her little mousy eyes earnest, 'we just mess around the streets, ya know, mainly in the city, in front of City Hall like, by the fountain. But there's always so many straight people around and the police forever fucking hounding us. No one thinks to go down to the river like this. Well, not often. I mean like it's peaceful here. It's real good.'

'Fucking coppers hound us here too, no different,' Gordon says like they are suddenly having a real adult conversation. 'All of us. 'Specially Thornes... specially ol' dickhead Thornes — this youth

48

dickhead copper — ya know Juvenile Aid Bureau — who for some reason thinks he owes something to Gray an me. Or maybe it's the other way round, he thinks we owe him something? Dunno the fuck why, but he's just forever fucking on our case, man. More than anyone else. He's like a freak, man, always tellin us how we better than the other kids, how we can be something one day, an crap like that. Always the same.'

'Maybe it's 'cause you guys are better,' Dusty says unexpectedly, and both Gordon and I blush.

'Naaa, fuck,' Gordon says.

And Dusty goes on, just like a real adult. 'Just sitting here like this, ya know, at the river, it's kind'a like maybe life's worth it, not so bad, you know. Like maybe things can change one day.'

'Yeah,' Gordon says. 'One day they will. One day me an Gray — and if you're around, hey, you can come along too, man — we're gonna be living on a property surrounded by mountains, far away from the city as possible, outta sight of everyone. Outta all this shit. Just us and people we wanna be there. Just enjoying ourselves, doing nothin but enjoying ourselves. No shit.'

'Hey, ya know, I think we from the same planet,' Dusty says, and I feel rather than see Gordon putting his arm around her, pulling her towards him, until she is cuddled into his shoulder and the three of us are under the bridge, looking out from under there, at the few stars between the clouds that flicker like naughty children from behind a curtain, like maybe there is another kind of life somewhere and it isn't that far out of reach. Maybe.

A sharp hammer-like blow in the ribs wakes me up into a piercing sunlight. Behind the pain in my side, a black boot. Above the big black boot is attached a super heavyweight sized leg. And it belongs to no one less than him — the man himself — Detective Senior Constable Watno Thornes. He is standing above us, like some giant tree out of Lord of the Rings.

'Thought I told you fellers to steer clear?'

'We... we...' I struggle to breathe.

'We're just having a bit of a rest, for fuck's sake,' Gordon rises, shaking his groggy head, finishing the sentence for me. And to Dusty I hear him whisper, 'This's im, the fat piggy.'

'What? What did ya say?' Thornes juts his head like a boxer daring an opponent to take a strike. 'Get up!'

49

We slowly pick ourselves up, unwinding, dusting ourselves off, Dusty pulling down her shirt, which she suddenly realises has pulled right up above her bra.

Thornes stares at her, a dart to a bull's eye. 'And what have we here? Plannin a family, are we, Gordo?'

'Just leave her alone. We told ya, we were just having a bloody rest.' Gordon looks around, all the other kids have gone, nowhere to be seen, either long gone or scattered when they saw the detective prowling along the river.

'So how come I never seen ya around, girlie?' Thornes lowers his tone to an elongated trumpet wheeze.

'I'm up from Brissie like, visiting friends.'

'Oh, and what friends might they be? — These two?'

'What's it your bloody business?' Gordon steps in, chest heaving, worms ringing round his eyes.

'It's plenty my business, Mr Morrow.' Thornes stares Gordon down, the awnings over his bulky eyes set like steel. 'I'm the one, matey, who has to walk these streets, remember? I'm the one has to keep these streets clean, remember? Has to protect the public from the likes of you, I think you'll remember? So, you see, it's plenty my business, Mr Morrow.'

'Actually, sir... mister... Cunstable,' Dusty presents a shield before Gordon, '...I... like... I'm just... you know, at Ruth's Place. You know, Ruth Hannah's place?'

'Ah, the beautiful, indomitable Ruth Hannah. Well then, why are you here and not there?'

'The boys are just showing me the river, sir... an... we kinda lay down and fall asleep like.'

'Ah, how romantic. So, I am right, you *are* planning a family, Gordo?'

We all just smile, because really there is no reply and really it is quite funny. The intergalactic robot just standing there. Enjoying his assumptions.

'Well, maybe I am,' Gordon finally says. 'But you sure as hell ain't invited to the weddin.'

Dusty and I laugh.

The detective puts a clumpy hand on Dusty's shoulder, but lightly, just very lightly, while Gordon and I are left to consider the size of his tree-branch fingers. He bends a little, to her height, which is far down his barrel chest, and sets his eyes in a squint, like he is squaring with her.

'You see… ' he looks hard at Dusty, and waits.

'Dusty… Dusty… Jones,' she offers.

'You see, Mzzz Jones… these fellers here have always got an answer to everything, that's why much as I think they are capable, and much as I try to keep em off the streets, I believe in the end they're going to disappoint me.' He looks at all of us, eyes spinning like tennis balls between us, yet slowly, in slow motion, like a father teaching his sons the greater lessons in life, like there is something in those eyes that cares. 'Now, my only question is,' he leans his hand more heavily into Dusty's sleeveless shoulder, '…is what's a lassie like you—and I mean that in a good way, nothing bad intended—what's a lass like you doing with fellers like these, who wouldn't listen to anything if you blew a bloody foghorn into their ears?'

'They really OK, sir… Cunstable, really… really good blokes.' Dusty looks straight into the jutting, creviced stones that are Detective Senior Constable Thornes' eyes. 'They don't want no trouble, sir. Honest.'

'Yes, but in the end, in the end, Mzzz Jones, I don't think they're going to do you any favours either. Ask them.' He looks at Gordon and then me, 'I've given them lots of warnings, I can tell ya. Now, I'm just telling you this once,' he moves up to her, like a confidant, like a big brother rather than a policeman, 'keep away from these streets and you'll be OK. It's not a lot to ask… and it'll save you a lot of trouble in the long term. And if these two lads want to lead you back onto the streets, you just say no. Understood?' Dusty swings her head smoothly up and down, pushing a white hand through her hair, swishing it out of her face, half smiling at Gordon. 'Because I'm telling all of you, right now, I don't want any more dirt on my streets. And I think deep down inside you also want to see em clean?'

Following Dusty's lead, Gordon and I nod, the three of us like a row of mice in front of a big black cat.

'C'mon now, fellers,' his eyes spring a soft punch into Gordon's and my downcast eyes, 'show the good young lass here you can make something of yourselves. For once in your bleeding lives do the right thing.' Gordon and I nod, our hearts pounding. 'And remember this, fellers, always remember this, God helps those who pick up after their selves. Now clear the hell outta here, the lot of you—and stay the hell outta these parts!'

We blink into the stone of his eyes and he lets his clumpy boxer hand slide off Dusty's shoulder, real slow, like a heavy tree, like a final warning, and then he turns slowly and walks off. As soon as he turns we just look at one another, wide smiley, but feeling pinched, deflated, hollow inside, like, without saying it, we all see we don't have much power against this man that is judging us. Then, spontaneously, we poke our tongues out, stick our middle fingers up in the air, and there is a kind of relief, the kind of lifting release that comes from suddenly knowing you all feel the same, but can't quite express it—except through one pointed hand signal. There is a bond between us now. Like big, strong arms embracing, and inside me there is this sliding feeling that Thornes has climbed in, is right there in the middle of us, ripping that bond.

# 7.

GRIM-FACED, FEELING LIKE MUD, we meander through Ipswich Square back to Ruth's Place. We are sauntering like three refugees on an island that doesn't want us, the world already at work, well those that do work, and the others, like us, drifting as though on a ship adrift from anywhere rescuable. You can see the ones who are refugees like us, only mostly older, men and women, dressed like Salvos advertisements, slopped up in coloured flannel shirts and pants two sizes too big or too small, their sunken cheeks grey and black and prickly. Or in some cases, massively bloated. They struggle along in threadbare, calf-high Ugg boots.

Hot, sweaty, crapulent and still gauging the day, even though it seems like half of it has already been dragged away from us, as soon as we get to Ruth's Place, Gordon apologises, cap in hand, but of course with no cap in hand, not even a gesture of the hand, just a flick down of the eyelids, apologising that we didn't come back the previous night.

Ruth, Ajax clean as ever and glistening in the face, grunts, says: 'I'm not a policeman, you know; I'm not here to tell you what to do. But if you take advantage you'll be out. Hear me? There're plenty of kids like you who'd love to be here. And *she*,' pointing with magistrate's eyes at Dusty, 'needs a rest. I told you that.' But in the end, she lets us in, adding only, 'And take a shower — all of you.'

Gordon makes to smell under his armpits, and then pulls a face, and we all laugh under our hangover breath except Ruth who just says, 'God, you kids!' And then we do go and have showers, with me last as usual, getting the frigging cold water.

It is Monday morning and we are the only ones in the house, sitting in the living room, just sort of kicking back, resting, Gordon and Dusty on opposite ends of a three-seater couch and me in an old armchair, digging with my now clean right index finger into a hole in the material just to the side of my bum, reaching into the foam, unconsciously spading little globular, snotty feeling bits out onto the dark wood floor, feeling bleary-eyed and thick-headed.

Ruth walks into the room like Jesus, if he were a girl that is, like she has suddenly remembered something. Or is about to enact a miracle. Her frosted, hazel-blue eyes spiralling with things magic.

'Shouldn't you be in school?'

I gasp; it hasn't even really crossed my mind, well, except in a very slight, dream-like way.

'I got to go to the hospital today,' I say, breathing and swallowing as though munching on a bone, 'to get me puffer prescription fixed up and things.'

'Well then, shouldn't you go then? You of anyone should know how long you have to wait at the hospital?'

'Yeah, I guess,' I say, eyes swinging hard right to Gordon, who says, 'Don't worry, Ruth, Mum's already told me. I'll take care of him. Get him up there—in a little while.'

Ruth nods OK, sceptical, wiping her eyes across my body. 'And get your finger out of that hole, please!' She turns away jerkily, each jerk of her body making a statement, like the miracle or whatever she had in mind has gone astray.

When there are at least two plasterboard walls between us and Ruth, Gordon says: 'Ol' duck, she's only trying her best, ya know. C'mon then.'

And Dusty and I follow him out of the front door, Dusty first grabbing her little electric turquoise-blue cap and sitting it on her head at that cute angle.

'So, where to?' Dusty sings, or sounds like she's singing when we're out of the house. 'Ipswich Hospital?'

'Naaaa, fuck that for now, we're goin for a little ride,' Gordon says, all serious, like our father sometimes used to look when he wanted everyone to listen to one of his crazy brainwaves.

'A ride?' Dusty screws up her eyes just like Mum.

'Yeah, just follow me an Gray, an you'll see.'

We walk, or rather saunter again, only with bigger, more

determined strides than before, Dusty a pace behind us, up the road and around the corner, back across the small steel railway bridge crossing, past the big old white grammar school where the rich kids go, and on to our little housing commission home in Sadliers Crossing.

As we enter the roughly whipper-snipped driveway, grass sticking up everywhere like badly bonsai'd bamboo shoots, Dusty says, 'So, where's this?'

'This's our place. Gray an me.' Gordon sticks a stiff finger across his lips, as if to say shut up now.

She whispers, 'Why the fucking secrecy?'

'I don't want no one to stop us—an make Gray go to school and that, alright?'

Her head seesaws up and down, and she follows, bending like we are now, so that we can't be seen under any of the windows. As if. But we do it anyway.

In the garage, Gordon, like a famous bullfighter in a dazzle of sunlight and cheering crowds, except it's almost black and empty in there, uncovers the bike—and Dusty squeals, 'Wow!' And then he throws the cover into a greasy corner, heaves the bike off its side leg, and begins to push it down the drive, where once again following him, we all bend low, like World War Two spies, sort of crouching behind the bike so that it looks like it is moving of its own volition, and out into the street. We walk with the bike well out of earshot of our house, Dusty and me following at Gordon's side, taking up most of the road.

'So how far we going to walk this thing?' Dusty says.

'Not far. Not far now, duckie. Any rate, you'll dig where we going.' Gordon's eyes roll up like those aluminium remote control garage doors that bundle up into big round cylinders at the top and says like he is waving a wand: 'We're going to the Moon.'

'What? The moon? Are ya crazy?'

'Naa. Not *the* moon. Mt Moon! It's a mountain. Just down the road like. It's kinda like our place. You'll love it, Dust, I'm fucking telling ya—it's Only fifty k's from here.'

'Fifty k's! I'm not walking. No ways. Not with this fucking thing!' Dusty swishes her hair out of her face like she is suddenly precious, like a ballet dancer on a stage. Now she knits her fingers through her hair, beneath her cap, glaring down at the old bike, and Gordon.

'Hah, don't worry, chick. We'll all fit on, it's OK, serious.'

It is true, aside from on a few occasions with Dad when we were small, and Mum looking on shouting and yelling, we had done it before, taken the odd buddy, usually a girl, one of Gordon's 'chick-bitches' on the bike for a ride out to the mountain, always making sure the chick-bitch was small enough, like Dusty, like most of his other chick-bitches always were, so we could all fit on the seat.

'And the coppers?' Dusty says.

'Naaa, we never been caught, I swear. And if we are, we just hop off the bike and you say you're hitch-hiking to Boonah and we just been carrying ya a little bit of the way like. If we keep a straight face, they'll give us a warning, that's all. Promise. Or I'll cop the shit, hey. No worries. I swear.'

She laughs, I can see very uneasily, and then Gordon begins to kick-start the bike. Only, as usual, it's not exactly a Grand Prix getaway. About ten kicks on, when Gordon is about to smack his beloved baby and curse the thing in a string of purple and black, if not plain throw it out with the rest of the rubbish into the black bins on the side of the road, it splutters into its usual cough and then groan and then Gordon keeps revving just in case, so loud even the crows, which in these parts wouldn't move out of the way for a crashing Boeing 747, fly for their lives. Dusty, now kind of encouraged and full of daring and adventure at the same time as she is biting her lower lip, climbs onto the bike behind Gordon, his leg stretched out like a crutch onto the road, straining for balance, I think almost about to buckle. But his thick, heroic leg holds even as I climb on behind them, used to the gymnastics of being last one on, the up-jutting back of the seat digging like an anthill into my bum as I try to slide down into the seat. It is worth it, I see straight away, as I have to slither in behind Dusty, squeeze and clutch onto her so that I don't fall off.

I think, like Gordon, I have already become, I don't know... stirred by her. She doesn't say anything. Just slides further and further forward into Gordon who is now squashed up against the bulging, red testicle-like petrol tank. I notice he doesn't even use that bitch word with her. Like he does on others when he's squashed so far forward. He is also the only one without a helmet on because he knows his hair already looks like a Viking hat and you wouldn't really notice it. Me, I'm happy as Larry and a half.

She's thin, sort of bony, but not thin and bony as Mum, and you feel yourself sort of knit into her rough-sewn, silken finish. It's warm and cosy and I lie my head against her narrow shoulders, naked except for the stringy sky blue vest she wears, wondering if she is noticing the rainbow strips of green as we pass into Boonah country and beyond, finally feeling the bike smoke its way up the gravel road to Mt Moon. And then Gordon switches off the bike engine and all is silent. He holds the bike up with his rhino-muscle leg while we demount, like cowboys, except I fall over, and Gordon laughs and Dusty says, 'Shame, poor Gray.' And I am proud that she has noticed me.

We throw our helmets to the side, in the thick bush next to the bike, and Dusty retrieves her electric turquoise-blue hat, dug into her pants at the waist. She angles the cap exactly right, and for a while, as we all walk up the gravel road I feel like I am with two exotic birds: they laugh, twitter, chirp, sing; Dusty in her electric turquoise-blue cap and sky-blue singlet jigging up the path like a shot of mistaken colour on a thick green canvas; Gordon stout and woolly, brown against the green.

'This is like... wow, so much better than Bris Vegas,' Dusty almost croons. 'Awesome man. Like that movie, ya know... *Lord of the Rings*.' She takes out a cigarette for her and Gordon. We stop momentarily as she lights up for both of them, leaning a little cupped hand over a sky-blue plastic lighter that matches her singlet, and then hands one of the cigarettes to Gordon like it is the sealing of a bond. They inhale deeply and we continue to amble and weave up the steepening gravel road, the smoke from their cigarettes almost invisible in the electric blue light of the day.

Gordon stubs his cigarette out, and for a moment it is like he has seen something, something remarkable, unworldly, something great, and he makes a dash off the road, diving into the bush, Dusty and I looking at one another and then, like we're caught in his breeze, follow through a stream of trees, through dry yet lush thicket, until Gordon slumps over and gratefully we slump next to him, looking up through the cool shade, into thick, crayon green rivulets of trees drifting down the mountaintop across the way. Mt French or Mt Alford, I think. And I watch Gordon and Dusty wrestle with one another, the way me and him usually wrestled, but I don't mind, it is just so waveless, tranquil; it is like we are family, like we have known each other since childhood.

57

Gordon and Dusty lie still now, and I slip in next to them, into the honeydew smell of their bodies, wishing it can always be like this. Like the juice from that rich, ripe fruit on Timmo's kitchen table, which I can still taste on my tongue, that my dad smashed me over, that left me broken forever.

Dusty suddenly says, 'It's like a painting, ya know? Sort of like someone's painted us into a painting.'

Gordon wipes his nose with the back of his hand. 'Actually, Dust, it's more than a painting, because we can walk round in it like. Be free, ya know, talk, jump, bounce, swear in it. Fuck! Fuck! Fuuuuck-ennnnn 'elllllllll!' he shouts out to prove his point. 'No one can hear us. No one could give a fuckin monkey's out here. No coppers, no parents, no teachers, no dickhead bosses.'

And Dusty looks into Gordon's chest and unexpectedly, just like a teacher, says: 'Where do you think you'll be in five years from now, Gord?'

'Fuck,' his eyes swirl in his head, like in a cartoon on TV. 'Damned if I know, chick. What a question, Dust. …But one thing I do fucking know, one day I'll have a place like this. A house in a place like this. That I know.'

And Dusty says, 'Well, that's more then me, Gord. Shit, you know, I don't even know where I'll be tomorrow. At least you've got a dream, ay. I just see nothing… one day hitting into the next. Like thick clouds. Like the fucking clouds up here, colliding and butting up against one another, one cloud shoving up against the next; I can see nothing through it.'

'Fuck Dust. Jesus, chick. I'm telling ya, we can do it. And not 'cause Thornes fucking says so. We can get beyond this. We can make something for ourselves.' Gordon looks across her white, freckled face, which looks so old right now, sort of like a forty year-old mother with a bunch of stroppy underage kids. And she strokes Gordon's rough face with a white, thinking hand, her turquoise hat at her side, a bright dot of paint in the dulling brush.

That's what's so good about Mt Moon, I am lying there next to them thinking, it gives you that feeling that anything is possible. Like we can touch the clouds. Like we can even part them if we need to. That we can part them for Dusty. And you can tell, seeing her lying there, stroking Gordon' s face like there are a trillion tomorrows, despite what she says, it has pricked into her, too.

58

That feeling. It is there in her fingers, her tickling nails, her dusty blonde crown, the hair hanging down her face. Yes, lying there, you can see she is not like the others who come up here, get bored after five minutes of looking around and cry out for a drink or a cone to release the pressure.

And so the three of us just lie there, without a thing to eat or drink, until the late afternoon and the sun deepens in colour, a dirty crayon yellow now that falls through the clouds like it is trying to make its way out of Dusty's painting. Gordon sits up suddenly, like he has remembered something, frantically digging through his baggy jeans pockets. A few seconds later, smiling like a prince with a sword, he comes up with it, his stone, his precious Mt Moon stone. He pushes out a clumpy hand and shows the ochre rock to Dusty. She lifts it, examines its pyramidic shape, places it in her hand and rolls it round, looking at the shades of red and orange and electric pink that shoot in lines through it, like it is a diamond.

'Wicked. Fucking wicked,' she says.

It is like a signal from God to Gordon who runs wildly, like a savage, down the hill into some thick bush below. Dusty and I look at one another, like he's suddenly shot through in the head. A few moments later he is lumbering up the hill again, baggy pants and woolly hair leading the way. He sighs, out of breath, and sits down next to Dusty, leaning on her thigh like it is a watchmaker's workbench.

'Check this out,' he says, and like a knight from Prince Arthur's Round Table, he hands her a dark grey stone. It is circular and almost smooth. On the outside it has charcoal and dark brown lines running through it like the rings in an ancient tree.

She rolls it round in her hand like a princess, then looks into her prince's eyes and squeezes it like she is making a wish.

'It's yours,' Gordon says.

'Yes, I know.'

'No, I mean the wish,' he says, and then she jumps on him and squeezes him and they embrace, and even though I am not touching either of them I feel I am right there in the middle of them, feeling their warmth. And it feels bloody awesome.

The sun behind us now, a burning pink prune at the edge of the sky, we run down the hill to the bike like we have been re-energised, forgetting we have not eaten for most of the day. We climb onto the bike, and like the three amigos we arrived as, swing our arms in the air and ride away from the setting sun, trying to beat that burnt prune and the gas pink waves it is shooting across the sky through the clouds to Ipswich.

Sputtering into the outskirts of town, crossing the Bremer at Leichhardt Park, we come across some of the kids, Kelly and Candy, and Fat Deano, and a young scrawny little kid we have seen around but don't know at all. We stop the bike and laugh and chortle about nothing. Past deeds. The night before. Old hunting grounds. Places to sleep. Gordon's famous bike. Realising we are all feeling that familiar cut in our stomachs, dry spit falling on nothing. We are hungry, even us invulnerables must eat. We decide on pies or some garage hamburgers if we can afford it. But between us we can't raise more than six dollars.

And that's when the new young kid Reno says, 'Hey, why don't youse come over to me old place. No one's there. They away for a couple of days hey.'

Fat Deano takes over and explains what he means. What he means is that his last foster parents, who live in the area, are away from home, on vacation or something, and the kid knows how to get in. Which means we have a kitchen to raid, which means we can fill our empty wells. Which is heavy bad. Heavy bloody awesome bad.

# 8.

A STRUTTING, BENT-SHOULDERED KING PARROT, about fourteen, proud to be at the helm, Reno leads us to his old place that he has just told us about. The three of us, Gordon, Dusty and me are on the bike, going ahead at times, falling back, falling off, laughing, but slowly keeping pace with our little top dog and his bunch. It is already dark when we reach the single storey brick house in the new housing estate that we know straight away is not rich, just new. And sanitary clean. We also realise we have immediately been spotted by the prim, straight as an aeroplane landing strip neighbours, mostly returning from work, so we just mooch around the estate, pretending to be going through the neighbourhood to some place else. About an hour later, our stomachs clawing deep for food, we park the bike down the road, at the end of the street, and move in on the house.

Reno, small and wiry, like a miniature Houdini, climbs through a bathroom window at the back of the house, a yabby swallowed into the sand colour of the brick, and then lets us all in through the kitchen door with the confidence of someone who owns the entire estate. He heralds us in with a big, white smile. The first thing we do is go around the house like we have been let into a new hotel room, our eyes accustoming to the dark, getting our bearings, opening drawers, checking out ornaments, looking for the bar, and money. Taking in the fresh, Glad-clean smells that make us feel dirty. In this house I feel like the Bremer. Like I bathe in the river; in mud. We all feel like that, like our nails and hands haven't been cleaned in years.

By the time we rejoin in the kitchen no one has found more than a few dollars and some small change. So we decide to eat there and then, and then trash the place for yielding so little. For smelling so repulsively clean and fresh. Reno says he doesn't care what we do. He didn't like these foster parents anyway.

'Don't owe em nuffingk,' he says. If anything, he moans, 'Had em fucking long noses stuck up their arses in em clouds.'

So we pull out sliced bread from a fancy wooden bread holder and grab a great big hunk of cheese from the fridge, which we break with our fingers, and place on the slices of bread. A couple of us start munching straight away, the rest making cheese sandwiches and grilling them in a spanking new, shiny silver toaster. Or at any rate it looks spanking new. It makes a big cheesy, burnt smell as we try to squeeze the thick toast out of the polished, silver machine, eventually like workmen on a construction site having to dig the toasted sandwiches out of the toaster with knives. Kelly yelling, 'Ya better switch the fucking thing off before ya all land in hell.'

Kelly throws some eggs into a frying pan and just starts cooking as many as she can. We grab some salami and tomatoes and just start chunking into them like we are hungry mountaineers returned from Everest or somewhere. What we don't want in the fridge or don't like, which includes a big slab of butter, we just spit out or throw over the kitchen floor, and laugh. Reno sets a good example by throwing a couple of eggs against the white walls, and screams, 'Take 'at! Take 'at, mate!' each time one smashes and drips off the wall.

The butter we use to spread and slide up and down the kitchen floor on our shoe heels like we are ice-skating. Dusty and I have a great time swirling around one another like we are on a celebrity show, in front of TV cameras, and are performing for the world. The world is naturally going crazy and applauding us. Until Gordon pushes me out of the way and does some of his own ice-skating with Dusty. Fuck him, I think, we have already been judged the best in the world, and walk away. Now it is tomatoes as well that splatter against the walls and floor, and milk that has gone off, and soft fruit, thinking we are making one of those huge Pro Hart paintings that you used to see him slapping up in a jungle of squishy foods and sauces on the floor in those ads on TV.

'Oh, Mr Hahrt!' we hear the fat, foreign maid scolding in that ad, but we just go on and on. Our tummies are full now, full to the point of belching and farting, so we go searching the place for alcohol, coming up with one single bottle of wine that Gordon opens by pushing the cork into the bottle with a sharp knife that he hammers with the bottom of his fist. The lack of alcohol makes Fat Deano really angry, he smacks Reno over the back of the head and then goes around the house toppling furniture, first in the adjoining dining room, then in the lounge. We all follow him, through to the bedrooms, like businessmen or real estate agents being shown a floor plan. Only we're not really looking at the bedrooms, except to notice how neat and large and wonder-white clean they are, and we are immediately inspired to turn everything in them over. We make sure to throw chairs at, and smash, the stupid fake antique shades hanging from the ceilings. We throw shoes at the smart, delicate bedside lights. Glass shatters everywhere. The girls, Kelly and Candy and Dusty, are going through the cupboards like they are in a department store, trying on shirts and pants and skirts and belts and even pantihose. They are smiling and pulling model faces and whirling around in the gear. Reno goes and grabs some big black bin bags from the kitchen and we start throwing the things we fancy, sort of like a colony of Santa Claus's, into the big bags.

Gordon, Dusty and me have one bag, and I notice Fat Deano, Kelly and Candy are also sharing a bag. The kid Reno doesn't bother, he just stuffs things into both bags. I guess feeling sure that somewhere along the line the stuff will catch up with him, and he can take his pickings. Yeah, like as if. But he doesn't seem to give a screw. I just stand there thinking we'll hold onto whatever he throws in, except I notice he's throwing in some pretty stupid things, like these little white jogging socks with no ankles that nobody in their right mind would wear, and old baggy undies and shiny ties that absolutely nobody in the world would even dream of wearing, so I push him aside and tell him to piss off and put his stuff into the other bag, or get his own bag. Except he doesn't piss off and pushes me back, obviously not seeing Gord, or realising Gordon is behind me. Or knowing Gordon. So, as soon as he pushes me back and I nearly fall over, Gordon steps up, and tells him to fuck off otherwise he won't have no teeth left between his little rosy lips. That seems to do the trick, and he starts assigning his shit to the other bag until Fat Deano tells him to fuck off as well, so he goes and mopes in the kitchen, and we just hear things smashing in there. It is also beginning to smell in there, like maybe he is doing something else. One of those paintings? But none of us care, as long as he is out of our faces. Then like a convocation of elders, Gordon and Fat Deano digitalise through one another's eyes, burp, and decide time's up.

'Let's get the shit outta here,' Fat Deano says, already following Gordon, but yelling to let the girls know as well that it's time out.

'C'mon, Reno, ratbag!' he yells at the still sulking kid, who is spitting aimlessly onto the floor, and stinking like shit. Reluctantly, Reno unpastes himself from an egg-basted wall and follows us out. We feel like ladies and gentlemen gliding out of the front door, except for surly Reno, who looks more like the spoilt, ruin-everything goddamned Richie Rich kid. The only thing that seems to be missing is the stretch limo to pick us up. Kelly gives the final burp at the front door, as though a release from some evil. And for a moment, to anyone watching, we are nothing but satisfied dinner partiers, well, except for the big black plastic bags filled with clothes and electric clocks and jewellery and CDs and things that hang over Gord's and Fat Deano's shoulders.

As we glide merrily through the front gate, a neighbour spots us and calls out. Reno catches such a fright he immediately cuts and runs, which makes us all jumpy. Our eyes bounce and bump from one to the other in the dark, and immediately we are all running down the street, flinging our plastic bags filled with treasures into neighbouring houses. Someone is chasing after us. Kah-thud! Kah-thud! Kah-thud! We hear feet slapping down on the tar road behind us. At the end of the road, where Gordon has the bike parked, we jump on, the three of us, Gordon, Dusty and me, almost at the same time, like we are trying to get on a horse, only we all fall off and have to try to mount again, me out of breath and Dusty almost just as breathless, calling out, 'Shit, shit, shit, this is all I fucking need. C'mon, for fuck's sakes!' The man giving chase has another neighbour with him now, and instead of climbing onto the bike, Gordon having ordered Dusty and me off, is struggling to kick-start the thing. No fucking go. One of the men is actually on us, actually grabbing my shoulder when Dusty pushes him backwards, hard, and Gord by some miracle gets the bike started. It creates such a noise and so much smoke, I think from sheer shock the man stays away from us, sort of cowers a bit, and the second man goes to help him rather than even try to stop us.

We all hop on the bike now, Gordon using that rhino might in his legs to hold the stodgy thing up and we move forward, seeing the two men thankfully receding into the dark background of their prim new estate. Somehow Dusty and I have our helmets in our hands, proudly hanging there like the victims of a slaughter.

As we head into Ipswich, we realise it is way too late to go back to Ruth's Place — she doesn't like you using her in that way — unless it's desperate — just arriving at any time after dinner. So we decide there is no option but to head for the bridge. We park the bike across the road, out of sight in the Ipswich Square cinema car park, and walk across the empty street outside, over the steel pedestrian barrier on the other side, to the bridge. And then meander, our hearts pumping like hoses, down the familiar embankment, and walk along the black tar river and then sit for a while, catching our breath.

An hour later, in the darkness, we find Kelly and Candy and Fat Deano sitting a little way up from where we usually sit. They are sipping wine from a bottle they bought with their few remaining dollars. They are like clowns in the night by the river, laughing and patting one another, recounting events — saying how the 'shit-scared little wuss' Reno ran off and never looked back. But they couldn't give a fuck. He was a useless little turd anyways, they concur.

Which doesn't really solve our next big problem.

None of us, well none of them — because I'm still in school — has any money until next Thursday when their Centrelink payments come through. And we all, well except me, need cigarettes, but we will all sooner rather than later need something more to drink and eat, most likely in that order, and Gordon is saying how the bike is already running on empty.

So we hatch a plan. Which is not really a new one. Because it's already been tried and tested. Well at least a couple of times. Kelly is best at it. Not that she is so pretty, she has sunken, stale fetta coloured cheeks and pimples all over her face. But in the night you can't see that, the darkness hides all the blemishes, brings out a smooth peachiness in her face, and she looks striking, a world famous model perhaps, especially her trim body with its, well, weighty bazookas.

The plan: she'll wait outside a city pub, her shirt half unbuttoned so that it shows her naked bazookas almost to the nipples, and pretend to be a prostitute. Not that hard for Kelly really, and she is happy to play the star role. Everything else will follow, just as sure as day follows night, just as sure as the Brisbane River, with its pitch-brown mud, flows into the Bremer, with its pitch brown mud. Everyone nods and agrees it is a good plan, yet again. Even Dusty, who only moments ago looked disinterested, wasn't that keen, and said she would rather just go to sleep or try her luck back at Ruth's Place suddenly looks animated. After all, we need the money if we want to go out to Mt Moon again.

We kill some time first, thinking the later the better, and allow Kelly to suck in some courage from the wine bottle. We talk and make endless plans about nothing in particular. Going to other cities. Sydney figures big. As well as Melbourne. And Mt Isa. And Cairns, where it's summer all year round, and essentially you don't need no shelter. We talk about how long it would take to reach the sun? Was it possible? At what point would your spacecraft begin to melt and disintegrate? Or enter a parallel universe? I suggest. Did they even exist - parallel universes? People like us, living our lives — somewhere else? How could anyone live this life at the same time, on another plane, any other fucking planet or plane for that matter? I say. This *exact same* life? Who would be so fucking bashed in the head to devise a plane like that? Not even God. Not even God, I am thinking. No one seems to argue, but they still think there could be a parallel universe. That there are people just like us somewhere out there. At about which point Candy says she's feeling dizzy and has other plans, and cuts out of ours, like something kooky in her head has been emphatically zoned into that other universe. Her thin little denim skirt lazily just covering her arse, she waltzes off up the embankment.

Everyone shrugs at her disappearance. More for us. At about ten-thirty, a sleek silver fingernail moon hanging in the black Ipswich sky, we amble over to the chosen pub in upper Brisbane Street. And there Kelly, pretty as a centrefold picture in one of those bikie magazines, succulently sexy in the half light of a street post, stands, legs apart, arms folded beneath her half naked bazookas, while the rest of us hide around the corner in a black alleyway, squatting behind a row of garbage bins, waiting for her to attract some prey.

# 9.

EXPECTING INSTANT ACTION WITH THE SAUCILY HALF-NAKED Kylie Minogue way Kelly looks, a mercilessly slow half hour passes by without even a nibble. The only break from the boredom and smell from the rubbish bins we are hiding behind, occasional giggles and jokes about what happens if Kelly gets kidnapped instead of luring a normal bloke, or, worse still, finds the Prince Charlie of her dreams—and ends up marrying him? And just leaves us stranded here forever in this stinking black alleyway?

Just when we are getting so irritated we are thinking of turning it in, and Dusty is anxiously saying it would be better—and simpler—to fucking break into a house, Kelly turns the corner with an old bloke following like a rickety walking stick at her side. Even from where we are, you can feel his heart, or maybe it is his pacemaker, pumping in his stiff mouth, expecting to get what he wants for a quarter the price you'd normally pay: Kelly—Mighty Bazookas—Bargains Galore!

Deep in the alley, right near where we are perched bird shadows behind the big black bins, Kelly leans back against a wall and positions the walking stick man directly in front of her. You can see the tip of his tongue hanging, his eyes pink and hopeful he can bargain downwards, maybe even something for free? Kelly slaps her hand out like a checkout chick in a supermarket, only minus the smile and the 'How's ya day been?' instantly putting paid to any such cheap thoughts. Reluctantly, like his arms have suddenly developed severe arthritis, the man fumbles somewhere in his old grey jacket. Eventually he heaves out a heavy leather

67

wallet like he is guiltily retrieving a biscuit from his mum's cookie jar, eyes darting up and down the alleyway in case Mum spots him. Kelly whispers something, pouting her lips like a fish, and the man peels a twenty-dollar note out of the wallet. He places the note in her mouth and she spits it into her hand in disgust. We laugh and, I think hearing us, she laughs too, and puts it in her back pocket. With effort, he places his wallet back in his jacket and Kelly opens her shirt fully now, slowly, like a stripper, like a real live stripper, like she has been doing this stuff since she was a little kid. Her stuff pops out into the open like torpedoes loading into their black submarine encasements. She adds to their size by sticking her chest out and holding her hands beneath them like they are a mighty fruit platter or something. His tiny pink eyes open wide, an antique statuette waking in the dark. His mouth stiffens like a bird and he rubs a hand over his zipper. Fumbling, he starts to unzip his pants and Kelly puts her little girl hands out to help him. At last a smile forms on his lips. Staring into the smile on his drunken face, Kelly wrestles with his pants. His bedazzled head gazes upwards now, into space, finding that shiny fingernail moon, and as his long, baggy pants fall down to his ankles we know it is time.

He doesn't even hear us, or maybe he thinks it is some celestial sounds, some ringing of the city's cathedral bells across the street, because he does not even flinch or twitter as we steal up from behind the bins and move in behind him, Gordon and Fat Deano suddenly rushing at him, rugger style, propelling him forward, hard up against the wall. Now their positions are reversed and he is the one leaning back against the wall and Kelly is the one leering into his drunken mug.

Fat Deano retrieves a stick, an old heavy plank from behind a bin, and stands behind Gordon while Gord squashes the man up against the wall. Gord keeps squashing even as the man struggles to pull up his pants. Kelly and me, like trained bank robbers, immediately begin rifling through the man's pockets, fighting with his stiff hands as he tries to stop us and pull up his pants at the same time. Dusty is standing a little away from all of us, keeping guard, biting her nails, busy adjusting her electric turquoise-blue cap.

A strange, dog-like look of glee fans through Kelly's face as she finds the wallet deep in the man's old grey jacket. But the wallet is thick, so she is pulling at it with difficulty and her smile and laughter soon become a breathless frown. As she struggles, almost retrieving the wallet, the man lets out a sudden, unworldly shriek that seems to chase even that speck of hanging fingernail moon from the sky. The Martian sound sends the wallet slipping out of Kelly's grasp, back into the old man's pocket, and we all stiffen in fright. A cat wails up the alley and Fat Deano catches such a fright he drops the stick, and the old man seeing Gordon turn around to see what has happened, somehow manages to squirm out of his grasp, bend over and pick up the stick Fat Deano has dropped. The old man is strong, or obviously in his day was strong, because he goes beserk like he has lost all his marbles, and he strikes Fat Deano over the shoulders with the stick. And he strikes him again and again. Fat Deano slips and falls, and as he hits the ground Gord and Kelly, like a tag team, run at the de-brained old man and tackle him, pushing him wide of a cringing, begging, dazed Fat Deano. Gordon wrestles the plank from the old man's hand, not that hard given Gordon's strength, and throws it heroically, like a wild and famous wrestler, to the side.

'Ya wallet, that's all we want, old bugger, and then ya outta here, alive and breathing,' Gord pants hoarsely.

The man just gawps, I think unable to speak. Fat Deano recovered now, but smarting like a spoilt brat from a parental beating, takes the man from behind and squeezes his neck while Kelly begins again to chug at the wallet in the man's jacket pocket. While she struggles away, Gordon's chocolate eyes light up like he has spotted something and he grabs the man's left wrist. What Gord is looking at is a big, shiny silver watch that he proceeds to delicately and carefully unlatch from the man's hand. When the watch is in his hands, Gordon quickly takes a second look at it, smiles with pride, and then drops it into his own pocket. Finally Kelly's little girl fingers pick the fat wallet from the old man's jacket pocket and the man squeals, but not loudly this time, more a wet cry emanating from his neck that is being tightly squeezed by Fat Deano.

'...Fucken ...slut!' the old man manages to eek between his old, yellow teeth.

Everyone looks up at him surprised, but willing somehow to let him have his final say.

Except Fat Deano. It is like he suddenly snaps, like he is suddenly seeing something in the old man that no one else can see, and he grabs the plank from the ground and rushes at the old man with it. Fat Deano is like an enraged gorilla you see in the wild on TV: with stunning strength he bashes the man across the head with the plank, once, twice, three times. Then faster and faster, like he has finally found his rhythm and cannot stop until the song is over.

The old man's legs start to give way, begin to bend, and he goes down with his hands held up towards the sky. But Fat Deano shows no mercy, he just continues on his gorilla-wild path in a kind of jungle reverie, slamming the wood down on the old man again and again. Blood pours from the top of the old man's grey head, a leaky pipe bursting through the crust, and the man tumbles flat on his back, his arms at his sides, like they are paralysed. But Fat Deano just sees it as chance to pummel the man in the face like his head is a fat coconut that we will soon drink from and enjoy once it is cracked open wide enough. The man's lips burst with colour now, like a child has painted them a deep maroon.

I pitch baseball-fast eyes to Gordon, and see him digging into his thoughts, so much so that his head looks like it will blow sky high if it does not find some solution. I am hoping my eyes, the thoughts behind my eyes, are reaching him. His nose flares and in his eyes I see those grey-red worms I am familiar with. He has made his decision, I can see, and bursts forward, I think at first to stomp on the man with his boot and maybe put an end to the misery. But it isn't that, instead like a rugby league forward he smashes his body against Fat Deano and drives Deano's shaking, bulky flesh into the alley wall. While Fat Deano gasps for breath Gordon grabs him by the shirt and starts kicking him, just kicking him, everywhere and anywhere.

'Shit, man! Shit!' Gordon is screaming in a hoarse voice. 'For Christ's bloody sakes, man! What the bleeding fuck d'ya think ya doing, man? Get the fuck outta here! Just get the fuck outta here!'

Fat Deano, white in the face, bent over and defending himself like a panicked bird with wildly flailing wings, bounces on his heels and stands against the wall, sweating profusely.

'I want me fucking fair share — and then I'll get the fuck outta here, dude!' he shouts.

'Piss off!' Gordon says, shoving him back against the wall.

And it is like the mastery of Gordon's shout is like a blow to Fat Deano's head and he seems to just give up, allowing himself to be pushed about, finally hanging around like a dust particle in the dark by the bins where the momentum ends, where the mad reverie is broken.

Gordon bends over to the old man, a snapped walking stick lying in the black alley, his face and ragged clothing painted all grey and muddy and purple and maroon.

'Fuck!' Gordon stares up at us all accusingly. 'Bugger's hardly bloody breathing. Shit! Fucking Fat bloody Fat Deano! Prick!' He looks up at Fat Deano, still skulking by the bins, a little boy in his round red cheeks, and then Gordon's eyes roll to Kelly standing directly above him, head down, holding her shirt tightly folded over her naked bazookas like they have suddenly turned cold and embarrassed and are badly in need of sanctuary.

Gordon puts his ear to the old man's wet face and it is like he is suddenly in bright orange overalls working for the local SES. He looks up and shouts at Kelly: 'Get on ya fucking mobile, will ya? Dial triple-O, for fucks bloody sakes! Get a fucking ambulance!'

And then Dusty, everyone forgot she was even there, is shouting, 'Coppers, dudes! Coppers!'

We don't even turn, we just flee, fragmenting like a clay ball splattered with machine gun fire. Behind us a voice is screaming: 'Get back here, you little bastards. Get back here, you bloody scum!'

But it is all just noise in the back of our clogged heads. We can't even hear our own grunting as we scatter through the dark town.

# 10.

ONE THING WE KNOW, THERE IS SO MUCH BLOOD on and around the old man that not even the police will bother giving us chase until they have called an ambulance. We have spread in so many different directions we have confused them anyway. And if there's nothing we know better, it is the streets of our city. It would be like looking for a brown shoe in the Bremer River coming after us, unless there were about three thousand of them.

Knowing Gordon's thinking, relative to where we were, out of breath and half running, half limping by myself now, I head up to the very top of Brisbane Street, near the Grammar school, by the steel railway crossing. It is all dark and shadowy at the crossing, and out of the shadows, as I expect, Gordon and Dusty step.

'You right?' Dusty is asking me, seeing me heaving, wrestling for breath, searching in my baggy pockets for my puffer.

I cannot even reply.

'Just give him some space,' Gordon says. 'He'll be right. Give him a few seconds, otherwise we'll get him down to the hospital, hey.'

My chest is like a ship at sea on a black night, lightning crackling through the centre of it; I can't hear them properly, can hardly see them through the dark, finally just managing to bring my puffer, like it is a heavy rock, to my mouth and take a couple of weak inhales. My lungs are closing in, tightening like thick ropes around me, and Gordon sits me down and then lays me out on my back on the pavement. He loosens my shirt and pants and just softly massages my chest. I am on a cloud and there is this

73

ball of cold air coming up from my stomach. It is spreading to my chest, turning to liquid under Gordon's warm hands, those strong fighter's hands which have fought off our dad, fought off Mick, which have fought off everyone on the streets, even teachers, yet can be so delicate, so like a mother's. I take a breath, a deep struggling breath, feeling something like pipes, like long, cylindrical church organ pipes in me begin to widen, the ropes to loosen. I am floating down a river, but it is not a red, muddy river, it is refreshing, the water below me clean as ice in a new freezer. Slowly Gordon and Dusty, both of them kneeling above me come into focus. They look like altar boys, and I just want to lie there, on the street, like it is a caressing river. I don't even care if I die, I am so happy seeing them above me. I am breathing in rhythm with them, it is as soft as a gently flowing river to my head.

Gordon is lifting me now, standing me up, saying, 'C'mon, Gray, c'mon, mate. Ya going to be right. Ya going to be right, mate.'

And when I am up on my feet, swaying a little, but upright nevertheless, I am saying to Dusty, I don't know why, 'I'm sorry, I'm sorry.'

And she is saying, 'It's OK, Gray. Just relax, mate. Everything's fine. Ya done nothin wrong, mate. It's not your fault.'

Although light-headed, I can stand on my own now, and after a brief discussion, with me mainly listening and not saying anything, it is decided the best place to head is home. The bridge right now would be like walking into the local cop shop and giving ourselves up. The cops are probably already there right now, swarming, frisking everyone in sight.

Luckily Gordon has the wallet. We look in it. It's huge. The man's wages or TAB winnings or something are in it. It is like we have won Gold Lotto. Our hearts are pounding and we pour over it like kids over a chocolate cake. Five hundred dollars and some change. No wonder the old codger was holding on so gallantly, I think.

The only thing is the bike, which we had parked in the Square. Gordon convinces us, without much trouble, we have to get to it before the police find it and he never gets it back. It is our source of freedom. It is like Christ, like church organs to us. Another decision we make, or rather Gordon makes, we will tell the others the money in the wallet is four hundred bucks. Our bonus for the trouble caused by Fat fucking Deano.

We sneak like creeping shadows through the back roads of the city to the bike in the cinema car park. We walk it out, back onto the street, knowing the thunderous noise it would create in an empty cement car park. It would wake the entire Ipswich, never mind the dead. In the distance, coming from the bridge, we are sure we can hear yelling. We think it could be the cops harassing kids, but of course it could be just any of the kids just having fun.

A block later Gordon starts up the bike with a single kick. Amazing how things seem to start so easily when you're not in a hurry. We also get onto the bike more easily now, sort of glide onto it like we have suddenly been trained in gymnastics or something. We ride through the empty town, slowly, not to make too much noise, though it is almost impossible to miss the asthmatic splutter of that engine. I don't even look, just hug onto Dusty as she hugs onto Gord. I am smiling; my breath has not felt so even for a year.

About a block from our house Gordon switches off the engine and we walk again, pushing the bike up the road and into the garage. Gord carefully pulls the cover over it this time, pats it like a father putting a child to rest, almost cooing.

'I'd say she's pretty well empty now,' he says.

'What's ya mum like?' Dusty is standing next to him, holding onto his arm. 'What'll she say?'

'Screw her,' Gordon snorts. 'Anyways, Mum's OK. If it weren't for that stupid ol' Mick boyfriend of hers.'

'Will it be OK? I mean me just pitching up like… at this time?'

'Yeah, 'course it'll be fucking OK, Dust. She can't do nothing to you anyways. It's our fucking home, too. Just stand behind me when I knock on the door, she won' even notice ya.'

I see Gordon taking a deep breath before he knocks on the front door. And then knocks again. And again. He looks up into the sky, as if praying, or gulping.

'Aw fuck.' He knocks again.

It isn't until about ten minutes later that someone, Mum thankfully, comes to the door.

'Fer Christ's bloody sakes,' she says, 'what the effin hell's going on here? Where's yer key?' Her hair, though short, is like Gordon's, all woolly now and sticking up all over the place like coir.

'Remember, you took it from us, Mum? Said we can't have it back till we act like gents?'

'Jesus. Well get another one cut for Christ's bloody sakes! Yers are lucky ya haven't woken Mick. Ya know what he's like. Was in another one of them moods tonight.'

'Well, we're sorry, Mum, can we get in now?'

'Yeah, 'course ya can,' she nearly smiles, and then startled, like a cat suddenly frightened by human footsteps, gasps, 'An what the hell is this?'

'It's Dusty, Mum. Dusty Jones. She just needs a place for the night like. Just tonight, Mum.'

'Bleeding hell. Mick'll throw a fit. What d'ya think this place is? Well ya better get ya tired arses in here.'

Dusty stands there, slightly round-shouldered, neither quite cringing nor quite embarrassed, like she has been here before. Her electric turquoise-blue hat, mercifully, dug into her armpit.

Mum groans something under her breath and we head straight for the bedroom, Dusty in between us, like we are still trying to shield her. When we get to the bedroom, we don't even bother to put the light on. Just go straight to bed, Gordon and Dusty, like nature bequeathed it, flopping into Gordon's bed, and me into my bed, thinking of the blood that has flowed tonight. Blood like I have not seen in a long time. Our room seems to lack air tonight, like there is a pump in the middle of it, sucking out the air.

# 11.

BREATH HEAVING LIKE MAULING POSSUMS, coming in yawping gulps and drags wakes me up. I know what is happening. Gordon and Dusty are doing it, making out together. I think for the first time. There in the bed near me. Yes, it arouses me, as it always does when Gordon has girls, on their backs, or straddling above him like famous rodeos, on the odd occasion even allowing me to reap some of the desserts, the only way it seems I can ever get anything. As a favour. When everyone is absolutely drunk or stoned off their faces, or both, it makes no difference anyway.

And now there, near me, in our house, with Mum and Mick a thin plasterboard wall away, the long breaths are turning into quick ones, raspy and gasping, an ambulance siren urgency about them, only this time it is different. Not like with the others. Wham-bam, thank you ma'am. I feel it in the electricity that runs like firecrackers through me. There is a different feel in the room this time; it is like two freight trains smashing into one another, unable to be disentangled, blood and juices intermingling like hot glue. My body feels like it is going to burst.

And I hear Dusty, hoarse and intense, 'You come. I want you to come.'

There is a silence, a tension, and then deep, rich laughter, breathlessness. My world is just being created, a river in me flows, and I love Dusty for loving Gord.

I close my eyes, pretending to be just waking as I see Gordon and Dusty sit up, Dusty covering herself, or most of herself anyway, with a sheet. And then Gordon, in the nude, his sweaty, naked body glistening in the morning light, leans over and draws something out of his baggy brown pants pockets.

With it in his hand he kneels by the bed, before Dusty, like one does in a church, and says, 'Hey Dust, for ya.'

I can see now it is the heavy, silver watch from the man we robbed in the alley. It twinkles in the morning light, and he places the watch around Dusty's wrist much more gently even than the graceful way he took it off the frail, old hand. Awesome, the word strikes through my head. Bloody huuuge. And I see Gordon leaning over her, slightly olive skinned, oily, glowing like one of those marble smooth ancient Greek sculptures of discus throwers. She looks at the watch like it is an engagement ring, a big white diamond, startled like a child putting on her mother's high heels for the first time.

'Heeeyyy, mate,' she says, and kisses him on the forehead and then the lips, and then they are laughing and cavorting on the bed like old friends, like old wrestling mates, and I feel happy to be alive.

Pretending not to be in the room, I scavenge through the cupboard for some clean clothes to wear.

Now we are in the kitchen, dressed for the day, pouring Crunchy Nut Corn Flakes into an oddment of bowls chipped around the edges like mice have been nibbling through the night at them, and then we stand there pondering the white, rusted fridge. Opening the peeled silver door handle to the brown inner chamber, a dragnet of green and blue looking oddments stares dolefully back at us. And I am ashamed. The ice tray looks brown like the Bremer. I take out the grease-fingered milk carton, and immediately feel it is so light there will never be enough to go around. In the end Gordon just winks at me, and I add water to the mixture because no one feels at this minute like walking up to the shops to go and buy more.

Dusty looks cuter than ever foraging in our little kitchen, her shiny turquoise-blue cap once again clamped on her head like a long eye-lashed sixties doll. We all stand there now leaning back against the sink and the small kitchen table, hungrily sucking the breakfast cereal down.

Mum walks in, wraith-like.

'Make yourselves at home, why don't yers.'

'G'day, Mum,' Gordon says. 'This's Dusty. You met her at the door last night, if ya remember?'

'Dusty, hey? Looks a bit like it to me. Not from round here, I take it?'

'No,' Dusty says. 'From Brissie. Just visiting some friends for a while. But I like it here.'

'Yeah, I can see that. Well, I hope you've enjoyed your stay, because we can't feed no extra faces round here.'

'Mum,' Gordon says, 'For Christ's bloody sakes, act civil. We can look after ourselves.'

'The way you've looked after young Gray here?' She throws out a thin, rangy hand towards me and then walks up to me and puts an arm around me, but not in the way I want, in a way that is treating me like a child. I feel my face pumping wet and red and move away from her. I stand there wishing I could win Gold Lotto and turn life around, put the fat back in her raggy skin.

Mick walks in. He stands there, no shirt, eyeing us in his shiny royal blue boxer shorts that have glossy yellow Tweeties and black and red Sylvesters chasing one another around. His naked, wiry frame, except for the little gut, is surprisingly firm. I guess from the physical labour he once did? The smudgy navy blue tattoos that hide beneath the black mat of hair across his chest are etched like the front of a dirty vest that needs to be washed. Red Sylvester, naughty smile, claws poised, is hanging over his crotch.

'So, what do we have here? A breakfast par'dee?'

No one answers.

'An the slag?'

Gordon drops his bowl on the sink and goes straight at him. Mick puts up a hand to deflect Gordon's blow, with some unexpected speed and adeptness, and as he does so Mum steps in between them. It would have been nice to see Gordon bash him, I think.

'Please, not now Mick,' Mum says. 'Just let them have their breakfast and get on their way.'

'What d'ya think this place is?' Mick says to Gord, who is standing back now, against the sink, next to Dusty, glaring.

'Home, Mick. This is me home!' His eyes shoot torpedoes at Mick, and Dusty holds his hand, but I think not out of love, but rather feeling that he might make another lunge at Mick. Like Mum, she's acting just like a mum.

'Well, it's also me flippin home ya know,' says Mick. 'And I think ya should know ya mum, Ange an me aren't runnin no sleepover joint here. If you gonna come an use the beds when it suits yers and eat our food when it suits yers — with ya lady friends — ya can also bleedin contribute.'

Mum looks at Mick, like Tweety looking out from under Sylvester's shadow on his boxer shorts.

Gordon bursts. 'OK, for Christ's bloody sake. If that's what ya want, why don't ya just say!'

Gordon digs angrily and deep for a while into a baggy pocket that hangs down to his knees. Finally his knuckly hand comes up with a fifty dollar note — from our share of the loot. He looks at it like it is filth and throws it on the small green vinyl kitchen table.

'Now ya talkin,' Mick says. 'An I'm sure Ange will appreciate it, too.' Our mum nods. But Mick leaves the money lying on the table, like it doesn't mean anything to him. Like it *is* filth. 'Guess I better not ask where it comes from?'

'No, thanks, ya better not!'

'Just as long as we don' have no coppers crawlin round here,' Mick says. 'Like that Thorny shitbag, hey?' Mick looks up, the pink glare in his eyes softening. 'Ya know, he's been round here, Thornybag, telling ya mum an me what good lads ya could be. If ya only done something about yourselves.'

Gordon just shrugs. I feel something in me flicker, like a missed heart beat. I look up at Mick, surprised. Almost embarrassed.

'Well we don't want no ratbags like him round here for the wrong reasons, understand? So keep your noses outta the shit.'

'Screw you, too,' Gordon says, and pulls Dusty along by the hand. 'This is me digs just as much as yours, Mick.'

Mum reaches out a hand to Gordon as he passes out of the kitchen, touching but unable to grab him. Mick just lets Gordon and Dusty glide by.

Seeing them slip through the kitchen, I feel dragged along like a magnet and follow them into the dense lounge air.

'Hey Gray, where ya going, mate?' Mum calls behind me.

'With them, of course.' I stop.

'An what about school, mate?'

'Shit, what about it?'

'Ya have to go, ya know. I don't want ya to be like Gordon, lad. You're the only one in this family's made it all the way through to Grade 12. I want ya to finish, lad. Then ya can do somethin. Somethin decent like. Get us all out of this dunghole, hey?'

I shrug my shoulders. Thoughts are flying all over the place in my head, smashing into my cranium that is growing hot and sweaty under my long hair, especially thinking about Dusty and what she must be thinking about me. Right now I don't want to go back to school ever. There's too much happening. But I look into Mum's pleading, yellow eyes and I can see there's no choice. My eyelashes begin to flutter and I grow red.

'OK,' I say. 'Whatever.'

She smiles. I can see she is really happy. 'And brush ya bleeding hair before ya go, for God's sake,' she says. 'It's nearly down to ya flippin shoulders ya know. You've got beautiful hair, Gray mate, but it's beginning to look just like ya blinkin no-good dad's.'

I shrug my shoulders again. 'Yeah Mum, whatever ya say.'

Mum reaches out and puts that raggy arm of hers around me, and it is strange, even though she embarrasses me, I feel like the circulation is coming back into my body as her arm squeezes damply around me. She pulls back and studies my face like my eyes, my mouth, everything is unreal. She flicks the long hair out of my eyes, I think just to confirm there is something there, that I really exist.

'That's me lad,' she says. 'I know ya can do good, Gray. I know it. And don't ya worry about Mick — sometimes he can be good to me, ya know? At least he has a job... most of the time.'

Mick snarls from a distance. And I see both Tweety and Sylvester marching like drunken soldiers out of the kitchen into the lounge while I quickly uncouple from Mum and separate from Gordon and Dusty and head for kids' gaol.

# 12.

LIKE EVERYONE IS BIGGER THAN ME, I feel just like a little nipper again, black leather shoes squeezing my toes, grey flannels handed down from Gord hanging off me like a garbage bag, white shirt fraying at the collar that Mum picked up from the Salvos squeezing into my armpits like it is stuck with Blu Tack in there, tie throttling my neck. School. Christ!

My head is spinning just being here. Sitting at a little wooden desk with a bunch of bleeding idiots who look just like me. Sitting here, alone, without Gordon. Already wondering what he — and Dusty — and the other kids are doing. Caught between two worlds, that's what school is: safety from the cops on the one hand, prison on the other. Like one of those old prison boats on the Thames we learned about... but just for kids! No wonder we can't be sent to gaol until we're seventeen — because they already have these gaols for us before then. Life — that's school. Just ask Gord. Soon as he was finished Grade Eleven he was out of here. And it's done him no harm stopping. Just less to whinge about. We manage quite well to count our money without bleeding school. Jesus, in our house, with Mick and Mum around, even in the days of Dad, actually especially in the days of my real dad, we had to count every cent. That was maths — real maths — every bloody day maths. Putting our five cent pieces together to buy milk and bread and cigarettes and things. And petrol, shit, you needed dollars for that. But we found a way — and we knew how to count em.

Dickens that's what I like. Books by Charles bloody Dickens. Well, especially videos by Charles Dickens. Like *Oliver Twist*.

But there's that one, along with *Tom Sawyer* and *Huckleberry Finn* that the teacher keeps for me to read — *David Copperfield* — that I have been reading for about a year now. It's just so bloody big and long. Like *Huckleberry Finn.* But I like it. I like the words. Like Shakespeare, I never thought I'd like that kind of thing. But the teacher gave us some Shakespeare stuff once; said just try it: 'Experiment like.' Like it was drugs or something. As if. As bloody if. But I liked it. I didn't understand what the shit he was on about, but I liked the words, Shakespeare's words; sometimes individually I liked the words, sometimes in sentences. Like when Shakespeare says, 'All the world's a stage, And all the men and women merely players.' As if. I mean who could imagine such shit? If you were from where me and Gord live, you'd see there ain't no acting. No bloody stages or anything. It's real. Like the time Dad smashed Mum's nose, like the time he smashed my leg like I was a little chicken, that was all real. No actors. No stages. Like cutting yourself with a knife. Like my limp. It hurts and bleeds like shit. But still I like it, those words, just the idea, the world is a stage and we are all merely actors upon it. Maybe? Some day? Who knows? That's why I like to write for myself, keep my diaries, because of words like Shakespeare's — you don't always have to agree with them, but they can sound like the wind. Or be like big black clouds. Or can make you feel like a crow about to swoop without your being able to fly or even see. Well, that's the good part of school. Reading. But it's still like reading in a prison. Everything tied to a bell. Like we're cows or something. It's not even like that at home.

At lunch break I hang around in the playground with the other kids who, like me, don't have any lunch. We sit around on a bench in the shade, just mainly talking rubbish and imagining things. Like how good it would be to be loaded with bucks, and we mean big bucks like, like hundreds of thousands of bucks, or to be famous rock stars with lots of girlfriends and big houses and endless supplies of grog and drugs and stuff. We paint our own silver and gold colours over Lamborghinis or even Porsches that we even occasionally see running around our own streets. But always the subject comes back to school, how good it would be to get out of this blinking kids' gaol, which is what we're raving on about when one of the lads turns as though to a wall and says out of the corner of his mouth like he is smoking a pipe: 'Hey, check it out... there, ol' Thornebag.'

I feel myself stiffen. 'Flip. Where?'

'Just there, at the gate, drongo. You can smell im a mile away.'

I half get up and crane my neck, and there he is. Right in front of me. Taking up my entire vision like he is the only thing between me and Heaven. The big heavyweight champion of Ipswich in a suit without a tie, just standing around at the gate speaking to the headmaster. I think his square baldhead looks my way and immediately I look the other way.

'What's up?' the kid next to me says, reading my movements like he is reading his own breath.

'Naa, nothing,' I say, turning, real casual like. 'Just the usual shit with Thornebag.'

'Fucking cocksucker!' we all say in a kind of church choir unison.

And Thornes turns from the principal like he has heard me. Fuck, I duck, like someone has hurled a steel ball at me. I pretend to tie my shoelaces, and after a minute or so when I look up he is gone.

After lunch, in English, my favourite period, I am told by the teacher, with a big smile on her face that I have to go and see the principal immediately. She looks at me in that way like the principal, Mr Goss, is going to give me a certificate or a medal or something for good work. My stomach tenses and I feel like making a run for it—just sort of flying out of the window like a bird, but I know it's impossible. Gingerly, like an old woman with rheumatoid arthritis or something, I rise behind my desk, everyone's eyes on me, all of them already wanting to know the story. What shit I am in.

My blood is pumping, but hoping like hell, hoping against all the odds, I am maybe dinkum going to get a medal or a certificate or something for good work, like the smile on the teacher's face implies. But I've hardly been to school in a week, so I know it can't be that.

Head buzzing like a million cicadas screaming at one another in the bush, unable to catch my thoughts let alone my breath, I make my way bit by bit, like a one-legged spastic, across the tarmac courtyard into the school office area. Casually leaning against the counter, I tell the principal's secretary I am there. I speak very softly, in the politest way, my breath caught in my nose, but she immediately eyes me like I have done something wrong.

Mr Goss, like he has a psychic connection to his secretary, almost immediately pokes his thin sparrow nose out of his principal's door. With a curling finger and a tense smile he calls me in.

I sit down, sensing immediately there is no way I am getting a certificate or a medal for good work.

'Young Mr Morrow,' he says, still with that tense smile, 'where were you last night?'

'Just hanging, sir, you know, like,' I jab, but slowly, like a big, nose-beaten boxer seeing double vision. 'That is to say, uh-hem,' I clear my throat, thinking quickly, 'hanging with me brother, sir… and his girlfriend… Dusty… Dusty Jones.' Despite everything I am proud to say her name. It is like a spark of light in the darkness. But it doesn't seem to make a dot of difference to the dead straight human structure of tense and vertical flesh and bone in front of me.

'And what were you doing while you were *hanging*?' He waves his sparrow nose like he is wiping the air of dirty words or something.

'Just hanging, sir, you know, like we always do.'

'Where — *hanging* — exactly, like you always do?' His sparrow nose nods towards me, like it is thirsty.

'You know, sir, near the station, and by the bridge, hey.' I feel my fingers jumping.

'And what about outside a pub in upper Brisbane Street — *hey*?'

'No sir, you know, sir, I'm too young to go to pubs.'

'I mean hanging out in an alleyway *outside* a pub?' His eyes prod me like they are sharp sticks.

I look him straight back in those sharp-stick eyes, my guts jack-knifing like a semi-trailer all over the tarmac, my heart thumping like a burst water pipe. 'Naa,' I say as casually as I can, 'why would I want to hang in a alley, sir?'

'I don't know, Gray.' His breath is like an industrial strength fan in my face. 'How should I know why you would want to be hanging anywhere?' He looks at me like he is waiting for me to blink, or look down.

But I know better than that. I have trained my eyes, trained them through the years. Something I learned long ago with my real dad and even Mum, to train my eyes not to blink, just stare straight forward, never blink. Then they think you're telling the truth.

'Well I wasn't there, sir,' I say without blinking, clutching at my jumping hands.

'Well that's a funny thing,' he says, 'because a man was found half dead there. Yes, Mr Morrow, don't look at me like that! ... Lying in a massive pool of blood, minus an expensive Seiko watch and a wallet filled with hundreds of dollars in it. And the funny thing is, Mr Morrow, a couple of eye witnesses say they saw someone with a limp—like a cripple—running out of the alley into the darkness...'

'Well I don't know, sir.' I feel my breath shudder in my throat like it is a blocked pipe trapped in there. I force my eyes to meet his, feeling hot sweat dripping from my locked hands. 'It wasn't me, sir. Ya know I'm not the only one with a limp in Ipswich?'

'Aaah. A clever lad, hey?' He stares at me. 'Well, I'm just trying to find out, Mr Morrow, because I don't want to hear you—or anyone of my students for that matter—were involved in this vicious attack. Do you understand that? ...Hey,' he sticks those sharp eyes into me again, 'are you listening, mate?' I immediately nod. '...Good! ...Because all I want you to know is that this is your chance to come clean—if you know anything about last night.'

With a half smile, and still clutching at my jumping fingers, I say, 'I don't know anything about it, sir, I swear.' My heart is spurting out shots of blood like someone is doing a quadruple bypass in there.

'Well, you better be telling the truth, my friend,' he says, eyes stabbing even harder now, like in that film *Psycho*. Schhwiiiish!-Schhwhiiiish!-Schhwhiiiish! 'Because whoever is behind this crime is in big trouble. *Biiig trouble*. And I just hope it's not you, Mr Morrow—as the police are implying. I don't want to see you, especially you, Mr Gray Morrow... are you even listening, lad? ... Good... well, I don't want to see a lad with your promise starting out life with a crime like this.—Hey, are you listening, mate? Are you bloody listening?' I give a definite nod this time, and stare straight back into his hard eyes. 'Well you better be! Because to be frank, just thinking of this crime sickens me to the pit of my stomach; I hope you understand that? It could even end up as a murder, you know...?' He takes a sharp breath. 'For God's sake, man, stop staring at me like that, will you, Gray!' His voice comes out like panic-driven bat's wings, shuddering all over the room. I bolt forward and for the first time look down, realising how I have been dead-on staring at him all this time. 'Are you following me, Gray? Are you following me, Christ!'

I nod my head vigorously, turning my eyes to the side of him, noticing for the first time a picture of the Queen behind him, in big white frilly dress and white gloves that looks a bit like a cartoon from *Alice in Wonderland.*

'And that's another thing, Gray,' he stares at me. 'While we're on the subject of you and your brother and crime — do you know anything about a break-in at a new estate around Leichardt?'

I just stare at him, well just to the side of him, and shake my head stiffly like he must be off his head or something.

'Do you want some good advice from me, Mr Morrow?' he smiles tensely.

I nod my head this time, look up, but just a little. Trying to avoid the prim, cartoon-glare of the Queen at the same time as I narrowly avoid his eyes, because of what he said about staring.

'Well, this is my advice. Don't let your brother be your keeper, mate. Gordon will only bring you trouble and darkness, mate. I think you are better than that, Gray. You deserve better. You are better.'

I nod my head hard like it is a bell in a church or something and half smile, looking down again, purposefully, because of that staring thing he spoke about. Wishing I could punch him in his sparrow face for what he has just said about Gordon.

'Remember, Gray, God helps those who help themselves,' he repeats words I am sure I have heard somewhere before, that I seem to be forever hearing these days. Like someone decided it should be a new kind of greeting or something — Yo! God helps those who help themselves. Praise the Lord!

'You know, from what I've been told,' his voice lowers and softens, '...from what I've been told by most of your teachers — when you apply yourself, Mr Morrow, when you really apply yourself that is, you're not just a good student you're actually a brilliant student.'

Fuck! I can't believe it. I am actually chuffed. Like he has dinkum just handed me a medal or something. I feel like shouting out: Yo, bro! Give me five! Instead I say: 'Yes sir, thank you sir.' I look him straight in the face. Well, into the tip of his straight beak nose. Still afraid to look him in the eyes.

'OK, you can go now, Gray,' he says, looking at me down that steel sharp nose of his. 'But if there's anything you want to tell me …remember my door is open.' His smile is more rounded now, like it is a relief to be rid of me.

'Yes sir, thank you, sir,' I say, without dropping my head, keeping my eyes on his sparrow nose. And then I turn, dropping my shoulders, and shuffle slowly out of the office, my shoulders and head rounded like I am concerned for his sake. For the school's sake. Funny how people above you always think they know all about you. Like they can see right through you. Like you are transparent and they are not.

Outside, by myself in the school courtyard, I feel my stomach burst like the nerves in there have suddenly gone wild. I just want to run to the toilet, and puke. But most of all, I want to get to Gord as fast as I can and tell him to run for his life. Tell Dusty and all of them to lie low, get out of town, hide, *do something*. In the end, because I cannot face going back to class, I meander to the toilet. I lean over one of the rusty brown toilet basins and wipe some cold water over my eyes, like I am trying to wake up. My stomach is swirling like a wave about to spill a surfer, so I rush for a toilet. Nothing will come out, so I just sit there. I can't face the idea of going back into class. Maybe we can all camp out at Mt Moon for a few days? I am thinking. Start living there—from now? My entire body is braced in electric shock waves. Eventually I know I have to get off the toilet and head for class.

I am not even in the class yet, and already I feel every kids' eyes spiking me like flick-knives for the story. But I say nothing. Just pretend like it was nothing, or even smile to myself at times, like maybe I did get a special medal or certificate or something from the principal. Of course they know I am bullshitting. Something's going down.

And then there is still after school, when the final bell suddenly sounds like a Christmas clanger and we get to shout out with happiness and break from our prison cells. Only today, of course, for me is a bit different. Unable to avoid my close buddies that I hang out with at school and even after school sometimes, as we walk together across the tarmac, I look them in the eye like I did in the beginning with Mr Sparrow-nose Goss until he shouted at me for staring like a dumb-ass at him, only unlike with him, after a while I feel I have no choice but to tell them the story. Well, that is, all I think they need to know. So, I tell them of the serious assault in the alley of the night before, and that I know something about it—but that I don't the fuck know why Mr Goss or the police are on my back about it—except that maybe my brother is the notorious Gordon Morrow.

'They just like to hang shit on Gord and me,' I announce heroically.

I feel like a leading actor as they stand, ears pricked, gathered around me. Like maybe the world is truly all a stage. When I say I have to get the hell out of school and let Gordon know what's going down, they stand aside, and let me go. Like I am Superman. And can fly. I walk through them, calmly, but as soon as they are out of sight, I run. Run, like a loony tune to spread the word.

# 13.

IPSWICH SWEEPS PAST MY EYEBALLS IN A DULL MONOTONE GREY as I half sprint, half hobble through the centre of town praying I will not get a breathing attack, praying that I will see Gordon before I even get to the bridge. But there is no sign of him or Dusty or Fat Deano or Kelly anywhere on the streets.

And when I arrive at the bridge, it looks deserted. Just washed out dirty yellow concrete, high above me, under the base of the bridge, the silver, black, gold tags and scrawls — *BERP; GMSO Mc1996; ONWARDS; GRAFFWARS; Burn Crazy* in fancy comic book writing; plus others like *Ron-Ron IPPY-Boy 2005; I want to suck dick so call me now 28381246; SLEEPLESS;* and the indelible sign off: *B'cawz we'll prevail.* Showing people, different, but with normal pumping blood and feelings have been here. I dig my dirty black school shoe into the gravel and curse, looking down into the dull red Bremer. It is like a lump of badly painted concrete that moves ever so slightly, almost standing still. And then I hear a whistle, like a sharp call rather than a songful bird, and I know it is one of them. I run along the walkway, and behind some brush I find Gordon and Dusty sitting together, sort of leaning into one another. Sitting with them, deep in thought, is Fat Deano who looks, I don't know why, but like a big clown when he is thinking. Kelly, beside him, also deep in thought, looks pretty when she thinks, like a woman, a real grown up woman, maybe like one of those Royals, only definitely not the Queen. She is changed out of her prostitute clothes from the night before, and is now in black jeans and a black shirt that looks three sizes too big for her. You can

91

see all of her white swelling breasts when she leans. Her pimples struggle against heavily applied base to get a whiff of sunlight.

I stand there, out of breath, hands motioning frantically, trying to convey my urgency. But they just sit there, in their same state, like mesmerised Bremer River swamis or something. Saying nothing. Not even smiling.

Seconds tick by. A minute. Two minutes. No one says anything. No one budges. Then, eyes kicking like a Kung Fu expert, Gordon turns to Fat Deano.

'Fucking thick idiot!' he says. 'Fuckwit!'

'Fuck you,' Fat Deano shouts back. 'Get nicked, bro!'

'Don't tell me get nicked, prick. We the ones getting chased down 'cause of your stupid fucking crack-head!'

Fat Deano sits back on his hands, scrunching them into the gravel like he is trying to control a burning fire in them. The back of his khaki pants are spread over the ground like an extra layer of soil. He scratches his wide forehead. It is sweating.

'I'm sorry, bro,' he finally breathes. 'I'm sorry, man. I fucked up like. That ol' codger just made me mad, hey, calling Kelly a bleeding slut like that.' He looks up at Kelly, who looks down her shirt like she is still protecting her mighty bazookas. He looks back at Gordon, blinking. 'Fucking arsewipe! I just snapped, hey. I know, I fucked up, man. Just couldn't hold meself back like. Really, man. Really, bro. Even if it was me own old feller I would've done the same. Fuck it!'

'OK! OK! Don't panic,' Gordon says, glaring sharp spikes at Fat Deano like he's the world's biggest dickhead. 'We'll find a way outta this fucking mess. We'll find a way.'

He thinks for a while. We all sit there thinking, our eyes rolling like worms down the embankment into the concrete river like maybe, just maybe the answer will punch up out of there like the Lady of the Lake or something. Of course nothing stirs. The river just looks back at us, dull as concrete.

'I think the best thing, dudes, is we all split up,' Gordon finally says, taking control again. 'We just all gotta keep separate like. Otherwise they'll hit us all at once. Bag us together like. Then we all got no chance hey.' He eyeballs Fat Deano with the sagging eye of a mafia boss giving out commands, expecting to be obeyed immediately. And when Fat Deano just sits there, hands still worming in the warm soil, he hits with a more direct angle. 'And

Deano, bro, you better be first to get your fat bloody arse outta here. Like right now, man! Just bugger the hell off to somewhere where no one's gonna find ya for a while, man. 'Cause if anyone's in it deep, mate, it's you!'

Fat Deano leans back on his chunky hands, looking back at Gordon. But still he doesn't move.

'And I fucking mean now!' Gordon raises his voice. 'Right fucking now, homie!' He turns his mafia boss eye to Kelly. 'And I think ya better split, too, Kell.' She shakes her head, a little Royal unwanted. She also doesn't move. 'Just find somewhere, for fuck's bloody sakes, just find somewhere the two of yers.' Gordon turns to Dusty like he is appealing to her to intercede. So she looks at Kelly, girl-to-girl, in that unspoken way that nobody understands between people, and Kelly starts to rise. Her big naked breasts hit me dead centre of the eyes like a wet slap as she gets up, and I feel sorry for her.

Fat Deano stands up after her, brushing down the back of his pants that are now damp and brown with soil. His bulging stomach eyes the concrete river. 'Fucked up place this, anyways,' he says. 'Get yers later.' He looks down, but not at anyone in particular, and then as he turns, a replica of the Big Hulk about to unchain himself, his rough, whiskey voice groans like a drill in our ears as he dishes out his parting words: 'Know this, dudes, what my nan always says: "…The river does not swell with clear water."' And then he climbs the embankment, followed by Kelly, who grabs his hand.

'Fuck you, too,' Gordon says when they are out of earshot, and Dusty and me just sit there looking straight ahead at the river like we are waiting for it to swell, waiting on Gordon for a move. Near us, there is a birdcall, and another… and above us a train of cars calls back, ga-dump, ga-dump, ga-dump.

Finally Gordon stands up; only this time he is Napoleon.

'To the moon!' he commands.

I breathe out, so bloody relieved I could hug the bugger.

93

# 14.

LIKE THERE IS A STRONG WIND BLOWING AGAINST US, we slink through town keeping well away from the centre, from Ipswich Square, not walking fast so that it does not look like we are in any hurry, and mostly looking down. At the top end of town, at the top of Brisbane Street, near where we had mugged the old guy and Fat Deano had near clobbered him to death, I see Dusty, I am sure unconsciously, touching with her little freckled fingers the watch Prince Gord has given her.

She gropes for Gordon's hand and he lets her little pink hand slide into his. They double their pace while I limp behind, glad that whatever trouble we are in has had this effect: it has bonded us.

We reach home and it is, luckily, only Mum there. The door is open and she is sitting alone in the lounge, the air grey around her.

The first thing she says is, 'What's wrong?'

'God, is that all you can say?' Gordon says, as though offended.

'It's written all over yers.'

'Christ, can't ya just for once bloody trust us?' Gordon says.

'Yeah, mate, I'd like to. But I think Mick's right. Ya only gonna bring trouble here. I think youse're already in it, thick?'

'Fuck Mick! Prick!' Gordon says. 'Tell him to stick his beak in his own bleeding business and treat ya... Ah, just forget it! Whatever! What fuckin ever. Think what ya like. We just come to get the bike for a bit of a ride like — till the sun goes down proper.'

And before she can say anything, which he sees she is about to, he says, 'Can't ya even say g'day to Dust?'

They just look at one another, Dusty and Mum. Like two women seeing not people but a continuum, something I, nor I think even they, can understand. Mum's short-cropped hair this afternoon looks like it is the top of one of those tough straw backyard brooms.

'Well ya always know what's best, Gord,' she says looking halfway down his body. 'Just make sure Gray's home for school t'morrow.' And then she says, 'That dickhead cop Thornes' not going to come poking his snout round here, is he?'

'No, why should he?' Gordon's eyes slide quickly east to west. '...But if he the Christ just happens to, Mum, tell him... just tell him... you haven't seen us today. Please Mum.'

'Yeah, yeah, right... God. You kids! Just get the hell out of here before Mick gets in, and don't let me find out y've done anything wrong.'

She looks up at me from her position on the couch, like her black eyes have water from the Bremer running in them.

Feeling I have to say something, I say, 'Everything's good, Mum. Honest. We done nothing... bad... wrong.' It sounds weird, strange, and I wish I could swallow what I have just said. Breathe it back in. Gordon just looks the other way.

'Gray,' she says out of the blue, 'give yer mum a kiss before Gordon steals ya completely.'

And I feel so red-faced and embarrassed in front of Dusty, it feels like my forehead is blowing up in welts. I turn around as if I don't hear what she says and turn to leave with the others. In the back of my mind, as we head out of the room, I see Mum sitting there, a cigarette and a drink the size of a water tumbler in her hand. She is just this thin floppy bag of flesh and bone.

Just getting out into the street, on the bike with Gordon and Dusty, is like entering another plane, where people actually live and breathe.

At Mt Moon, on the gravel road going upwards, we get off the bike, or rather nearly fall off, my flesh peeling like glue away from Dusty's. I don't want to feel her in this way, already missing the closeness of her warm skin. And I look at Gordon, but he is already pulling her hand and running up the hill and into the green bush.

And in that lush Mt Moon bush we just lie there, in among the trees, in the long, tall grass, the three of us, breathing in fresh, airy fantasy. And for no reason at all we all laugh. Just lie there and laugh. And Dusty touches me on the stomach as I laugh and I feel like my head is spinning. And then the three of us are embracing and touching and prodding one another like small children, in the ribs and the stomach and the chest, just laughing and screaming and then screaming and howling and screaming some more. A pack of wild wolves. 'Fuuuckyoooouuu. Fuuuckyoooouuu. Fuuuuckyoooouuuuu,' we scream at the top of our voices at the darkening sky.

Gordon and Dusty smoke the night away… the only inhale I take, as the night grows darker and colder, is from my puffer. But when my body begins to shiver, to physically shake from the cold on the hard damp ground, thinking I may not even make it to morning, Dusty pulls me over, into their warmth, hers and Gordon's, allowing me to squeeze up to her… and it feels like I am sure Mum once felt, like I often dream she felt, and I almost feel like calling Dusty Mum then.

We awaken into green reality… shards of golden fan-like sun that have already warmed and dried us piercing through the green brush. But still we do not open our eyes or get up, not until the sun is hopping like cane toads on our foreheads. Then we struggle to our feet, dusting ourselves off.

After a while Gordon sits down, as though collecting himself, I can see wondering what to do, thinking about a plan. Finally, clicking his tongue like he has run out of ideas, he takes out his ochre Mt Moon stone and rubs it in his hand like it might somehow reveal the future, open up some new way. And Dusty sits next to him and takes out the grey stone he had given her the time before. Smiling like children, they rub their stones together as though two stones can reveal more than one. I look around and find a round brown stone and bring it up to theirs. They laugh like I am funny, but let me touch their stones with mine anyway as they hold theirs up in the air, higher and higher against the gleam of the sun. I feel like I am somehow on top of a very high mountain doing cartwheels.

Suddenly Gordon brings his stone down and shoves it in his pocket, and says, 'I don't know about you guys, but I'm bloody starving.'

Nobody had thought to stop to buy food or supplies, not even to get us through one day. We look around and suddenly the shimmery blue that stretches around the yellow dot that is the sun, looks grey. We feel it in our stomachs.

'Let's get the hell outta here,' Gordon says. 'We can't stay here. Not like this. It's fucked up. We'll drop the bike at the house and get on to Ruth's Place, hey.'

'Are ya sure?' Dusty says, and not even waiting for his answer she grabs him by the pants and we begin to walk through the bush. In no time the bike is drowning out the silence of the mountain, bouncing us like a trampoline down the hill.

We stop at the first roadside garage we pass, fill up with petrol and buy a huge packet of chips, a family size Coke, and three pies that look just like the gravel road on the way out of Mt Moon. But it smells so good, and we sit outside the shop behind the bike grazing like rabbits until we are full, stuffing our mouths with chips and pie and long sips of Coke. In the end we even throw some of the chips away, burp one by one, Gordon's the longest burp of course, and climb back onto the bike. We see some people in the shop laughing at us like we are not real, or like we are clowns, three kids trying to be funny on a bike, two with helmets, and one slim, diminutive girl in the middle, a shiny electric blue cap on her head turned to an angle like she has just come out of a fashion show or something. We couldn't give a stuff, we are full again and we are heading somewhere.

# 15.

BY THE TIME WE HAVE SNUCK THE BIKE BACK INTO THE GARAGE at our house and then walked to Ruth's Place, which is not that far away, it is well after lunch.

Ruth comes to the door, as always spring clean and sparkling like she has a silver halo round her head, her white hair dignified like the Queen's, and says, 'Ah, look what the heavens blow thither.'

'Can we come in?' Gordon says.

'Now, that's a funny thing, Gordo, you've never asked before. Are you in trouble?'

Gordon looks a little surprised and embarrassed. 'I dunno. Maybe. Can we talk to you?'

'You know my door's always open to the Morrow boys,' she says, 'but I'm glad to see Dusty's still in one piece.'

'What d'ya think I am?' Gordon spits, affronted.

'Don't worry, mate, just joking. But you know I have my sources. This is a small town. There's not much that gets by ol' Ruth Hannah.' She smiles like she is sitting on a perch high in a tree and leads us straight downstairs into her study.

She sits behind a large old wooden desk that has a computer and phone on it, and we sit in front of the desk, in a straight line, on old wooden kitchen chairs that squeak when you move. The poster on the wall behind Ruth says: *Start treating yourself as if you are the most important asset you'll ever have. After all, aren't you?* It is signed, *Anonymous*. I don't know, I really don't, when I think about it, that's the way Mick and Mum think about themselves—all the time. Everything always about them. I wonder what Gordon thinks.

Ruth eyes us for a while, I can see trying not to look like a magistrate, but when nothing is forthcoming, not even from Gordon who asked for the talk, she says, 'You know, Detective Senior Constable Watno Thornes called around last night — asking for you, Gordon?'

'Shit,' is all Gordon says.

'He says you and Gray may know something about that attack in Brisbane Street that everyone woke up to in the papers yesterday morning. They say the old man's next to death.'

'Fuck,' Gordon says.

'Now, now,' Ruth says. 'You know the rules.'

'Sorry, mum,' Gordon says.

'Well, is Thornes onto something? Tell me? Or is he just barking up the usual trees?' Her marble eyes roll over all our faces, coldly, from one face to the next, until she gets to Gordon where she stops and squints.

'Can we trust ya?' Gordon suddenly looks up at her, but like a priest rather than a sinner.

'You wouldn't be here if you couldn't.' Her halo hardens.

Gordon takes a deep breath, braces his thickset shoulders, Dusty and me following suit as though we are part of a choir and we are all going to sing at once. But it is Gordon who talks, who proceeds to tell Ruth the whole tale, from fun-filled desperate beginning to bloody end. Only, knowing that neither Fat Deano nor Kelly ever come to Ruth's Place, even bag Ruth's Place as 'a place for wussies and homos', he adds a simple little twist to the story. That we were with Fat Deano and Kelly earlier in the day and we knew what they were up to. But we did not want to be a part of it. Even tried to talk them out of it. Later that night, when we were walking up the street on our way home, we spotted something going down in the alley — that is Fat Deano, plank in hand, kicking and smashing the shit out of some old codger. And that if it weren't for us, the three of us using our strength together to pull the maniac Fat Deano off the poor old man, the poor old man probably would be done already. Dusty and I dart proud eyes at one another, impressed like shit with Gordon.

'I see,' Ruth says. 'The gods work in mysterious ways, don't they?'

We all just nod our heads, looking her straight between the eyes, except Dusty who looks down after a while, at the computer.

'Where did you get that watch?' Ruth says, suddenly turning to Dusty.

Self-consciously, Dusty fingers the watch nervously, looks up and then down, and says, 'It's me step-dad's, mum. He give it to me as a pressie, like. I don't always wear it.' Her face is shining pink and she turns the heavy silver watch, gleaming in the strong artificial light of the room, so that it faces down, under her wrist.

'OK,' Ruth says, 'I know thousands wouldn't believe you fellers, but I do. Yes, I do.' Her clear, royal blue eyes drive into our tired, dirty eyes like she is trying to read guilt or maybe even sorrow in them. She breathes out. 'If my thinking's right, mates, it doesn't matter what your involvement, you dudes are in a lot of trouble.' She breathes in like Gordon and Dusty inhale their cigarettes. 'What I suggest is you just lay very low for a while. Even get out of town for a couple of days. Are you listening to me? You are? Great! Because I think you should be. What I think you should be doing is let the dust settle for a bit... give them a chance to find Fat Deano or Kelly, get the truth out of them first. Because I think they are key... from what you are saying?'

Gordon just nods, and Dusty and I shrug.

'Anywhere you fellers can go for a while? That's *not* in Ipswich?'

And Dusty immediately says like an excited child, 'My place, mum, Ruth. We can go to my place in Brissie.'

Ruth looks genuinely confounded. 'But I thought that's why you were here, darling, trying to get away from *your* place?'

'Yeah, I know, you right,' Dusty looks saddened, disappointed, looks up, 'but I think it's probably OK again now, Ruth mum. It's just sometimes, ya know like... and then I have to get away.'

'Absolutely sure?' Ruth says again.

'Yeah, yeah,' Dusty smiles at Gordon, hopeful. The freckles on her nose redden, she is as excited as a little girl.

'OK, OK then, sounds good to me,' Ruth gives her judicial consent. 'If Detective Thornes calls again, I'll just say I haven't seen the three of you in a while. Heard you gone on holidays.'

We all laugh. It is all beginning to sound just like a real holiday to me. Huuuge.

'Just you're not going anywhere until you've showered and washed your clothes, that I can promise you!'

Happy with the plan we say nothing and head for the shower.

Sitting on the toilet, waiting for the shower, on the back of the door I read Ruth's latest poster: *We are all travellers in the wilderness of this world, and the best that we can find in our travels is an honest friend – Robert Louis Stevenson*. Shit, Robert Louis Stevenson – *Treasure Island*, I think. I want to tell Dusty and Gordon to come and read the poster; I am so excited to know the author of this one. But when I start to tell Gordon and drag him to the door, he doesn't even bother to enter, just pulls back and says, 'Pah, fuck Gray, you've left such a fucking stink in here,' and walks away.

Ruth lends us some old clothes from a pile she always keeps spare, and we wash our clothes in a washing machine that Ruth has to show us for the hundredth time how to use. We know we will have to wait till the next day before we can leave, so that our clothes can dry. Also, Dusty insists she will not wear any clothes but her own. *Well, ain't she just snooty*, as my mum would say.

That night, just before dinner there is a loud banging on the door, and one of the kids shouts out, 'Fuck. Thornes!'

Gordon, Dusty and I look at one another, eyes speeding like pinballs off pin cushions, and we see Ruth Hannah taking a deep breath as she rushes out of the kitchen with an apron on and screams to us, 'You three, quickly – get the hell out of here. Into the study. Now!'

We race off like children caught with our fingers in the chocolate spread.

'All I want is to have a little chat with the buggers,' we can make out Detective Senior Constable Watno Thornes' boom-box voice bursting from just inside the front door. 'I assure you, Ruth, Madame, Royal Protector of all that is evil in this city, I have absolutely no intention of doing anything to them – not yet, anyways.'

'I told you, mate, they're not here,' Ruth insists. She can be very assertive. It is the thing none of us like about her. Except at times like this. 'They've gone out of town, with Gordon's girlfriend, I believe... you know, Dusty... Dusty... something or other... who pitched up in town recently…'

'Don't bullshit me, Ruth!' Thornes' voice booms back into her face that must sit at least two-feet down from his. 'I can make your life a misery, ya know?'

'Believe me,' Ruth says, 'that's what I've been told, Detective. And anyway, listen here mate, I may help them out, but I'm not their bloody keeper you know. These kids were grown up long before you and me were even born. No one can tell them what to do.'

Dusty and me are standing just behind the door in the study, all ears, while Gordon is in Ruth's chair, flung back like he is the boss of a big factory or something.

'OK… OK,' Thornes says as though finally caving in, 'but if they're here… or… if you just… just by chance… happen to see em… let em know I'm desperate to speak with em. Actually, let them know it'll help them to speak with me. But sooner the better. Maybe then this town can sleep in peace again.'

'Cunt!' Gordon shouts out.

'Quiet!' Dusty breathes out. 'Are you crazy?'

'Maybe we should just leave forever?' he says.

Yeah right, as if, I say, but to myself.

'Bloody pisshead Deano, fat bloody mother,' Gordon says. 'Got us deep in it this time. Brissie here we come!'

# 16.

WAITING AT THE STATION FOR THE TRAIN TO BRISBANE, I really do feel like we are going on a summer holiday now, not that we are any ways fugitives from the law. I can see Gordon thinks differently, though. He is sitting next to Dusty, agitated, while I stand excitedly peering down the tracks to see if the train is coming. Now he and Dusty are holding hands, but mincing their hands round and round like they are worry beads, Gordon turning his head every way it can turn, looking like it has springs in it. You can tell, anxious as he is, he does not want our 'getaway' — my summer holiday — derailed by cops.

Finally we are on the train; I gaze out the window at Ipswich receding into a grey whirr, and I cannot help but scream out aloud, 'Wooo-hooo. Wooo-hooo…'

Dusty and Gordon laugh and rest their feet on the seat where I am sitting alone opposite them. Dusty has long canvass-like boots on with three inch thick plastic bottoms, a bit like an alien from Mars, and Gordon is wearing, as always, hard-toed worker's boots. I lean my head against the train window surveying the little white weatherboard houses passing along the rail tracks with their dirty red and green and blue tin rooves that sit on their frames like little boys' school caps. Dusty and Gordon are cuddled into one another now, her shiny electric turquoise-blue cap resting in her lap like it is a holy man's hat. She turns it round and round with her fingers.

Underground, at Brisbane Central Station, it is so crowded, like all of Ipswich is piled into one dark place. Everyone getting off trains and jumping onto trains. Only they seem to know exactly where they are going. And they are dressed much smarter than in Ipswich. Which is about when we realise we have, all of us, fallen asleep, and long missed our stop, which Dusty said was Oxley Station – and which we will now have to get a train back to.

'Shit!' Gordon and I say, but I don't really care. I'm happy as a wombat in a hole to be in a real city.

For some reason Dusty starts saying that maybe we should just spend a bit of time in the city, looking around, before we head off to her place.

Gordon says 'Shit!' again like he's massively disappointed, his eyes roving around him like we are being watched.

But I cannot contain my excitement. 'Yeah, let's walk around,' I say. 'Look at the shops an things.'

'What happens if the Ippy cops have passed on information about us?' Gordon says.

And Dusty says, 'Naa, they won't find us here so easy. C'mon, Gord, it'll be fun. Some of me friends hang round here; I'll show them to yers. I just don't want to get home too early like. It's not that I don't want to go. Everything'll be great hey. It's just I don' want to go right away.'

Gordon nods, crankily. And we follow Dusty.

Outside the darkness of the station, people are walking and racing around. It makes me feel even more like I am on holiday; because unlike any of them I am in no rush. We follow Dusty down to the Queen Street Mall and amble past Jimmy's on the Mall, Gord and me immediately attracted like little puppy dogs to the smell of rich food and alcohol. It is not even mid morning and already we are licking our lips. We stroll casually up to an outside menu and stand for a moment, noses in the air, emulating the appearance of the people we see around us in their Cucci or Cuggi, or whatever you call them, suits and shirts and ties. Then we bend over and study the menu, Gordon is just in front of me, his hip-hugging pants showing a thick band of dull white flesh that is the crack above his arse.

'Shit,' Gordon says. 'I'm not the fuck paying sixteen bucks for a steak sandwich.'

I look down the list for cheaper things.

'Fuck,' Gordon pipes up again. 'Seven dollars for a flippin beer. We could buy a flippin half-dozen for that. Or a bloody slab for...' he thinks for a while, gives up the maths in his head, and says, '...for not the fuck much more.'

We turn up our noses, agreeing. 'This place is shit.'

We walk around some more. Up the wide brick mall, right up through the middle, caught in sunlight at last. It seems, aside from a couple of wino types on benches, it is only us who have all the time in the world. Everyone else is hurrying like the place is about to be hit by a comet. We look in the large shop windows which are so bright they make your eyes sore: David Jones, Myer, Table Eight, Jacqui-E, Country Road, Cotton On, everything looks so filthy clean. My eyes feel like they are dripping. Dusty keeps sighing without even knowing it. 'Coool man,' she says, 'Wicked.'; 'Bloody awesome.' Her eyes, like mine, are dripping.

Gordon says. 'This is crap, I don't wanna look at bloody clothes shit.' He looks around him with that goose bumpy feeling, like we are being followed.

'OK, OK,' Dusty's upper lip curls accusing Gordon of being just a guy. She drops her shoulders like she is giving up a free ticket overseas, and says, 'Right then, let's head up to the fountain. You'll like the dudes up there.'

She pulls Gordon by the shirt while I follow entranced by the cafes and restaurants and ice cream shops.

The fountain that Dusty leads us to is just up the road from the mall, in front of the old, squat, brown-looking Brisbane City Hall.

As we reach the nearly still fountain, someone calls out, 'Hey, bitch!' and immediately we are sitting next to some kids on the grass to the side of the fountain. Dusty doesn't say who they are, just, 'This's Gordon and his little bro, Gray. From Ippy.'

'From Ipswich?' a boy about Gordon's age, with dull, long brown hair, a bit like mine, says.

'Yeah, dude,' Gordon says.

'Crap place, I spent a bit'v time there once,' the boy says.

'It's OK,' Gordon says. 'Better then this heap'a junk concrete.'

The boy looks around himself, pulling his fingers through his dirty hair, surprised at what Gordon has just said, like he has never perceived the place in that way. It is the end of their conversation.

A couple of the kids who have skateboards start riding them on the pavers around the fountain and are screaming at the thrill of swinging their way inwards and outwards, narrowly missing the oncoming traffic of suits and ties.

Dusty has her turquoise-blue cap back on and is leaning backwards on her hands talking to a couple of the fellers and girls.

'Hey bitch, don't get crap-ass with me...' the hip-hop words reach through Gordon's ears and make their way into his eyes. He knows the words are pointed at Dusty. Immediately he is up and at Dusty's side.

'Who said that? Who's callin' Dusty "bitch"?' He is like a boxer about to enter the ring, all hyped up with springy ankles.

Dusty immediately stands up, pulling down her little frayed canvass skirt, and says, 'He don't mean it, Gord, he's just showin off hey.'

'Yo!' one of the kids hisses. 'Just calm down, Ippy boy.'

Gordon winds his clumpy hand into a fist and Dusty puts herself between the two boys. She starts fingering Gordon's t-shirt like it needs attention. 'Relax, Gord, please man, they don't mean no harm, mate. Cool it.'

Gordon sits down, eyeing everyone like they are prey. He looks like he could throw a bomb at them. The strange thing is they look away and then back again with a kind of respect.

Now everyone is cool, sitting or lying back watching the fountain, talking music, telling tales of being stoned, getting pissed, getting trashed, getting thrashed, cops running them down, and Gordon and me are excitedly saying that Ipswich is no better, only smaller than this concrete shit-hole. Maybe the place to be is Sydney? Or Melbourne? Everyone agrees.

By the afternoon, to Gordon's relief, he still looks like his eyes are twisting around him for invisible coppers, we have moved off from City Hall and are sitting on the embankment in the old Roma Street Forum, in the parklands there, above the Roma Street railways, half in the sun, half under trees in the shade, a bottle of vodka going around. A little later another bottle comes from nowhere and then a bong is snaking its glow around and everyone is sitting and laughing. Suddenly everything is alive and familiar: the park, the trees, the grey-blue air. Everyone is in such high spirits it is beginning to remind me of the good times we have under the bridge in Ipswich. No different.

Now some of us are standing, dancing, shouting, air-guitaring with the wind. By the time night comes we are all brothers and sisters. 'Yo, bro'; 'Yo, chick'; 'Hey, sister'; 'Yo, homie.' We're all so high, it dinkum feels like we are on a stage. I love it. Not surprisingly Gordon has a crowd around him, telling them how there is only one way to live—in the country, deep in the scrub, where the rest of the world can get nicked. Just lying back with a bong.

Later that night I hear, as probably everyone else does, Gordon and Dusty, their loud, coarse breathing, Dusty's sudden screams, almost animal like, and I feel jealous, not of them but that everyone else should be able to share them like this.

Bleary-eyed, the piercing spikiness of reality hits us next morning. It is like the sun is a knife. It stabs us. Another day to get through.

'Let's get some Maccas. I'm bloody starving,' Gordon says, brushing back his thick hair with his fingers; I don't know why he bothers, it just springs back into its normal coir mattress state.

Dusty nods, placing her cap delicately on her head like we are going out dining.

'Then we can head out to Mum's.'

'So early?' Gordon says. 'I thought yesterdee when we got in here you were saying it's too early, ay?'

'That was yesterdee,' Dusty says, curling her lip. 'Today... it's better to get there early.'

Gordon shakes his head at the logic.

We say goodbye to everyone in the park like we are saying goodbye to best friends for having us over at their place for the weekend and head straight into the city. Dusty sucks in, almost with desperation, like smoke from a bong, as much of the fashion as she can as we pass by the big shop windows. I look mainly at the computers and toys and things, Gordon, still adamant, stares straight ahead, his eyes, I can see, still peeled for coppers. We walk past Jimmy's on the Mall and almost as one scrunch up our noses. We head just across the way, down some stairs, into the underground, into McDonald's, licking our lips.

Full to the brim on whoppers and double cheeseburgers and chocolate thickshakes, we enter the dark underground of Brisbane Central Station, uncertainly, like it is sweeping us into dark, swelling waters.

# 17.

A SMALL, SINGLE STORY CHAMFERBOARD COTTAGE WITH HUNGRY grey wisps of long brown grass growing up its dirty white sides, at least Dusty's place is near the station, only about two blocks away. It is surrounded by soiled white, double story weatherboard Queenslanders that have no plants or flowers in their gardens, only khaki grass squares that look like rows of brush-cuts. Just like Ipswich, I think.

At the door, Dusty's mum, not that old, not as old as we were expecting, in fact quite young, definitely not as ragged looking as our mum, actually quite pretty, greets us.

'God blimmin Christ, well guess who?' Just like Mum. A parallel universe? She is strong and wiry looking, like she may have done kickboxing or jujitsu or something some time. Her dyed jet-black hair is brushed back with long sideburns, a bit like Elvis. She looks like one of those tough girls you see in kick-boxing videos. Her face is like tarnished leather, like Mum's, only younger, fleshier, more kissable.

'Mum, this's Gordon and his little brother Gray. This me mum, Jean.' Dusty looks incredibly shy, a gorgeous little girl with long golden ringlets and rosy cheeks in one of those American TV shows.

'Well, I guess you better come on in.' She looks at Gordon as if to see if he is suitable for her daughter. Scratches her face for a moment and then stretches leathery fingers that are darker than her face through her black Elvis hair. But says nothing.

We walk through a short hall into a lounge where two old couches face into a small TV in the corner of the room, just like in our house. The TV, on and blaring something inaudible, stands on a wooden box with a white cloth thrown diagonally over it. A bit of style? Behind one of the couches there is a green vinyl kitchen table with four or five green vinyl kitchen chairs neatly positioned around it. The table is exactly like ours at home, which is in the kitchen, only much larger. What's mainly different about this lounge from ours is that at the head of the large vinyl table, bent over, sits an old man. He is grey and unshaven, and although he doesn't have a big beard or anything close to one, he looks like he hasn't shaved for thirty or forty years or so. Grey, gaunt and tired looking, like he is wedged in a hospital bed or something, he looks up at our movement in the room without actually concentrating an eye on any one of us, and neither Dusty nor her mum even bother to introduce him. On a little wooden sideboard on the far side of the room, in a badly scratched see-through plastic vase, hang two dead flowers that look like they have been trying to escape for years. Then we are being introduced to a very fat young woman, a Tonka size bulldozer in fact, who has just entered the room, and who immediately plonks herself on the far end of one of the couches. The cushion at the other end flies up as she sits. Two children dash out from the same direction she came from and hang around her soccer ball knees. They are a boy and girl, aged about three and four. You can hardly see their eyes behind the woman's thighs, which they seem to purposely use to hide themselves behind. With a big, wide smile, Dusty introduces us: it is her aunt, her mum's sister, Cress or Cressy or something.

'Ay Dust, don't worry what yer mum says, ya look bloomin good, gal,' Cress or Cressy's lumpy hand fans thickly through the grey air. 'An I like what I see with ya, hey.'

Dusty smiles shyly, takes off her electric blue cap and strokes a hand through her hair, fluffing the fuzzy crown.

Jean, her mum, looks at Gordon. 'I hope you been looking after our Dust,' she says.

'Don't need no looking after, I can tell ya that,' Gordon says in a way that is not meant to be cheeky, only complementary, but seeing Dusty's mum's eyes flicker, Aunt Cress or Cressy quickly intervenes, 'I think Mum's just tryin t' say it's not always been easy fer the young lass.'

'For Christ's sakes Mum, Aunt Cress, can't ya just shut it for a minute? Let em arrive?' Dusty's lips are curling like that gorgeous little girl in the TV show when she is upset.

After that, Dusty's mum sits down on the couch and lights a cigarette, and Aunt Cress turns to her two children. The older one, the girl, is digging her fingernails into her mum's doughy thigh like it is a sandpit, the other, a little less in hiding now, has his index finger foraging right up his nose like his finger is a fat worm desperately looking for a hook. But no one is saying anything about it.

Her aunt just says proudly, without looking at them: 'These are me two little brats, Georgie an Dylan. Little buggers!'

Dusty's mum sucks in a thick curling tongue of smoke. 'I s'pose you're hungry?'

'Naaa, actually we're full, Mum, just had some burgers an stuff at Maccas.'

'Ah well, good, because I can tell ya there's not much food round heres, not till Thursday, when our Centrelink comes through.'

'We can take care of ourselves, Mum,' Dusty says, and tells us to sit down.

Dusty sits down with a large smile between her world's fattest aunt and her wire-thin mum, forcing Gordon and me onto the other couch. For a moment Dusty looks like a child showing off, sitting there between mum and aunt, like a snug, overgrown joey in a pouch. Her mum puts out her cigarette and immediately lights another one.

'I s'pose you're going to want beds as well?'

'Yeah Mum, that'd be nice, if we can?' Dusty's says.

Dusty opens a cigarette packet from her shirt pocket. She looks surprised when she sees it is empty and asks Gordon for one. He lights two cigarettes and hands her one, like it is already a tradition.

'Well, I s'pose your boyfriends could move in with im,' Dusty's mum blows out a long, plank of smoke. She doesn't even point to the old man, just says it like he is an old display in a Lifeline window. 'Or they can sleep on the floor out here hey; we got a couple of spare mattresses in the laundry.'

'That'll be fine, Mum. Just fine. They won't mind neither way,' Dusty says. 'Where's Pete?'

'Got some work today,' she says. 'Helping some bloke move houses. Good hey?'

Dusty nods. 'That's great, Mum.' She smiles at Gordon and me, and asks Gordon for another cigarette. He lights up for both of them again, and offers Dusty's mum one.

'Got me own, thanks love,' she says, and takes another cigarette out of her own box.

Aunt Cressy, with her stout hands, fishes around in a deep canvass shopping bag and finally pulls out a mobile phone that is so small you can hardly see it in her palm. She begins to tap away at it. She looks like she is crushing it.

About five o'clock, a tall, wire-thin man walks into the house. He looks sort of like a long branch with hundreds of cracked brown nodules on it, and on his head he wears an upside down bowl of hair like a grass tree, only bleached blonde. He is carrying a cylindrical, old-fashioned tog bag across his shoulders. It turns out to be Pete, Dusty's mum's bloke. He smells like a horse and it is obvious he is in a good mood. A bit like our Mick, I think. Only he looks much friendlier.

'Well, well. Look who we'z got back hey, the beautiful, untouchable Dusty,' he half smiles and half groans. 'And to what do we deserve the honour?' And without waiting for a reply, adds, 'Shit, babe, it may be winter, but it's bleedin hot out there. Just troi movin some furniture. Jaysus Chroist, ya'll know ya worth yer bloody sweat. Never moind, never moind,' he says, slapping a twenty dollar note into Dusty's mum's lap. 'Hundred bucks in the hand's a hundred bucks in the pocket.' He pats his top pocket and puts down his tog bag where he stands.

Dusty's mum tucks the note into her shirt. Down in her bra. Just like Mum sometimes does.

Pete strides through the lounge and out into the kitchen and out the back door like he is surveying the territory. A minute or two later he clomps back in again, only this time he re-enters showing off a six-pack of Fourex beers.

'You fellers just help yerselves, there's plenty where this comes from,' he says to Gordon and me, pointing with his eyes to the small kitchen that virtually adjoins the lounge we are sitting in. 'Cheers fellers,' he says. 'I hope ya took good care of our Dust?' and before Gordon, who is opening his mouth, can reply, Pete clomps his way back into the kitchen. A few moments later he emerges with three small water glasses filled with white wine.

'Fer the ladies,' he says, winking at Aunt Cress, and handing a glass to each of the girls. He doesn't even look at the old man, who seems to be trying to wave at him all the time. Freaky.

His beer quickly scoffed down like a badly needed cordial, he burps, long and tunefully low. 'Never moind, never moind.' Uuuuurph, long and low again, and then clumps back into the kitchen to fetch another beer. Then he is standing in front of the evening television news, in front of everyone, planning a holiday: In a caravan, he says, somewhere up north, like Bundaberg, which he says is possible, soon as they get their Centrelink cheques and if he gets just one or two more moving shifts. Dusty's mum looks excited, smiling bashfully like a little girl, as does Aunt Cress, whose stubby fingers are back on the mobile like they are spreading the good news to everyone all over Australia.

Pete looks down at her and says, 'Just fer me an Jeannie this time, Cress, no one else, ay. Just a little holiday fer the little lady an me. Won't that be noice?'

Aunt Cressy curls her lip and stops pumping the mobile for a while.

It is getting dark outside, the sun sinking just like the light in the room, which is now a tepid teabag brown. But nobody is bothering to switch a light on, although Aunt Cressy has gone to the kitchen to fill the wine glasses again and even puts a light on in there. Pete stomps out of the room, only this time in the opposite direction of the kitchen, down the passage, and returns a couple of minutes later, still in his sweaty overalls. This time he has a pack of Rizzlas in his hand and some tobacco. He sits down at the kitchen table, right next to the old man, and without even a flicker of acknowledgment, rolls a cigarette. Then he gets up, goes back into the kitchen and comes back with a metal ashtray. He switches on a light at last, sits down next to the old man again, and begins rolling his Rizzlas again. When he is finished, he lights it, takes a deep inhale, and now he has two cigarettes burning. Only, after a couple of puffs on the second cigarette, already made black by his greasy hands, he passes it on to Aunt Cressy who takes it shyly, darting a quick look at Gord and me, and then begins to inhale as well.

Gordon and me just look at one another, seeing the joint lost in Aunt Cressy thickly folded lips, and Gordon winks, saying softly, 'Coool man, bro. Cool.'

We sit back wondering what Dusty's problem is. Leaving

a home like this. Shit! She must have a screw loose. Nobody is allowed to smoke weed in our home. Well, not in front of us.

The house seems to be growing warmer all the time.

Dusty sips her wine, partakes in the joint, but she is the only one who holds back on the laughter. She sits there, cheeks bloated pink.

Seeing my reluctance when it comes to the joint, Dusty's mum says, 'It's OK hey, Gray. A good lad, hey Cress? Maybe you can learn something from this one, Dust?'

And Pete standing, trying to foist the joint on me, says, 'Ya never refuse a joint son, or a drink, loife's too short, lad, believe a man who knows. … Never moind. Never moind.'

'Ya mean too long,' Dusty's mum says.

'Na, I mean too short.'

Na, ya mean too bleeding long.'

'Na, I mean too bleeding short.'

'Yeah, when yer pissed out of yer skull and stoned like a magpie,' she puffs out short barks of cigarette smoke.

'Hey, who's pissed outta their skull, Little Miss Jeannie Lady? — Why don't ya just shut yer gob fer a change?' He smiles.

'Why don't ya shut yers,' she says, half smiling at Gordon and me, I think trying to apologise for Pete's behaviour.

And then, miming, he makes a flat hand in the air, as if to smack her with it. He laughs, and says, 'What about some tea, hey? Or ain't we gonna be eatin tonight?'

And Dusty's mum looks him between the eyes like she is aiming with a catapult, 'You so rich now ya worked one day — why don't you buy us some tea?'

''Cause I did the work m'lady, and now it's your turn,' he breathes out and you can feel the temperature in the room shooting down.

'I'd shut me gob right now if you want anything to pass your lips at all tonight,' she lets a spray of spit from her lips moisten the air, but gets up nevertheless, followed by Aunt Cressy and Dusty, the three of them like Chinese soldiers on a march, into the kitchen.

The two children, who had been asleep, wake up and come running out into the lounge, groggy, hair shooting all over the place, like little drunken midgets. As soon as they see Pete they start crying.

'Fuck yers,' he says, and leans back.

A few moments later the children are shyly gaping through the side of the kitchen door with bread and butter sandwiches squashed in their hands. The little boy is scratching his nose with his sandwich. He is looking at Pete as if to say, 'Seeee.'

In the background the old man at the table crinkles a smile. Suddenly there is a smell in the room, like hot packaged chicken just being aired.

'Ah, fer Christ's bloody sakes,' Pete says half turning to the old man, waving his hand under his nose. The old man waves back with a scrunched smile.

By the time the food arrives, Pete looks like he could eat the entire house. Dusty's mum dishes up for all of us, including the old man. For a while I was wondering if they fed him. The food is lots of thickly buttered white bread for Pete, mashed potatoes and a couple of black-fried chops. The rest of us, including the old man, get lots of mashed potatoes and scrambled eggs, but no chops.

After dinner, Dusty's mum smiles all friendly like, and says, 'Can you clean up, Dust?'

Dusty curls her lip like that little blonde American girl and grumbles under her breath, 'Christ!' She smiles at Gordon like they are at their in-laws or something.

Aunt Cressy immediately hits the mobile again.

'Hey, can yers shut it for a while. It's "The Biggest Loser", case yer interested!' Dusty's mum suddenly screams out.

We all shut up, even Pete, who watches intently as well. In the first ads he is off to the kitchen for more beer. Just before he comes back out, a stifled voice pitches, 'Leave me the fuck alone, will ya!' It's Dusty's voice. From the kitchen. Gordon cranes his neck a little, but he can see nothing.

The old man at the table, at just this point, lifts himself from his seat by pressing onto the table, grunts, and then slowly makes his way in the direction of the toilet, which is outside, just by the kitchen.

Pete sits down with his beer and lights one of Dusty's mum's cigarettes.

Dusty's mum, taking a sip of wine, says, 'You're not startin are ya, Pete?'

And he just says, 'Jaysus. Ya can't even talk to Miss Almighty Jones anymore, she's so flippin uptoight.'

I look at Gordon and see the worms wriggling in his eyebrows, brown, ugly worms. The worms tell me he is trying to sort through his dope-filled head into the latest turn of conversation. We are both looking into space trying to work it out.

'Just leave her alone, mate,' Dusty's mum says.

'Jaysus, I was just troiyin' to tell her it was toime to get a flippin job like. Ya know, help round the house a bit. ...Did ya eyeball that watch on her wrist, hey? Pretty smart fer a young lass... wouldn'ya say? Says young feller Gordy here give it to her.'

The worms in Gordon's eyebrows are making their way into the corners of his eyes, sitting just above his nose.

Dusty's mum quickly says, 'Why don't you just mind your business instead of thinking yer such a hero 'cause ya worked a day for once in ya blinking life?'

'Hey, I work more than you flippin do, or anyone else round here fer that matter,' his lips tighten and then loosen. 'Never moind, never moind.'

'Ha. As if. As frigging if,' Dusty's mum says.

'Well, if ya call pole vaulting, er, I mean, pole dancing work, then maybe the fuck ya do.' He is looking at Gordon rather than at Dusty's mum, as though for support, only Gordon has those brown-red worms swimming in his eyes.

'Brings in the bread an butter, don't it? When you can get a shift these days.'

'Yeah, well, no wonder Dusty's the slag she is.'

I don't have to look, I can feel Gordon rising from the couch, but he doesn't have to, because Dusty's mum is already up and slaps Pete, where he is sitting, through the face. She is wearing a hexagonal gold ring and the blow scrapes his thin nose so that the skin opens very slightly and blood trickles.

The temperature in the room has dropped to zero.

Pete bends down into cupped hands for a second, his thin, scraggy hair falling like the wet cords off a mop. Then he lifts his head quickly, as though a decision has been triggered. He eyeballs Dusty's mum like he is shooting pellets into her forehead. Then he gets up lethargically from his seat and presses, in slow motion, a handful of white, bony knuckles into the side of her head. It merely pushes her Elvis head backwards a bit. It obviously doesn't hurt, but you can see it enrages her like a wasp. Like a spring she stands up and kicks him with a black ankle high boot in the right shin.

He looks vacant for a moment, his strawberry sized Adam's apple in his narrow throat turning blood-red like his nose, and then he gets up and does exactly the same again, presses a fistful of bony knuckles in slow motion into the side of her head. Only this time he does it a little harder.

Immediately, almost falling over, Dusty's mum gets up and, just like that, hits a fist into Pete's unbelieving lips. I see even Gordon wince as Pete's lip seeps purple. Pete wipes the blood with his dirty blue overall shirt sleeve and looks at Dusty's mum casually, very calmly, as though a line has been drawn, as though considering whether it should be crossed. He looks to Gordon, but Gordon just stares back. Slowly, almost mechanically, he bends over to where Dusty's mum has fallen back on the couch and grabs her by the collar of her black shirt. It rips, and Gordon and I roll round marble eyes at one another at the appearance of a naked breast. Pete brings his face down to her now, right down to hers, so that they are almost like two puppets in a children's show kissing. For a moment it looks intimate. Almost funny. Like the mood in the room has grown warm and close again. Then he pulls back and a head of bony white knuckles sprays into her sharp-boned Elvis Presley nose. It canons like a ball of lead right into the middle of it. Blood spurts like it is coming from an invisible pipe and she falls over, but slowly, like she is swimming, with just enough time to shoot into his eyes: 'Fuck yer! Piece of dog shit!' As she hits the floor, he begins to kick her, wildly, drunkenly, eventually falling over himself.

Dusty, who has been watching from the kitchen door, and Aunt Cress, who has been sitting there like a crane stuck in mid-hoist, scream out together, a kind of sharp, long, olden days ambulance sound; the children shriek in the background like they're not sure if they're really awake or still dreaming, and run for the kitchen door. They hide behind it, peering out, eyes wet and shaky. The old man, it must have been an hour ago, returns from the toilet and just walks past the kicking, disorganised mess and sits down again. Dusty sprints, or rather springs out of the kitchen now, and together with Aunt Cress they start covering her mum with their bodies. Pete, up on his feet again, kicks away at the body on the floor like he is stoned and dancing wildly to The Rolling Stones or something, hitting everyone in his way. Aunt Cress, losing her balance, falls right over now, squashing Dusty's mum, who yawps like an old dog, and the children, thinking they are going to see someone dead for sure, run further into the kitchen. They are both screaming and breathing in yelps. Gordon looking as confused as I do, shakes his head and burps. It is absolutely psycho in here, and he is even more confused when Dusty's mum suddenly shrieks out: 'Leave me alone, ya little slut bitch! Leave me alone, ya little fucking slut. You the bloody cause'a all this wicked shit!'

'Fuck you!' Dusty bellows, banging her mother with a fist on her bent, crouching shoulder. Heavy, syrupy globules of tears pour from Dusty's eyes. 'C'mon, let's get the fuck out of this insane fucking house,' she screams at Gordon.

Gordon is up like a shot, and within seconds, almost flying up the walls and banging into one another, we have rounded up our bags and things and are on our way out.

Behind us, we leave images of Aunt Cressy and Dusty's mum writhing like pythons on the floor in front of the blaring telly, with Pete still drunkenly kicking away.

And then we're out on the street again. Behind us, suddenly, Pete is at a window, screaming like a maniac: 'G'boi to bad fuckin rubbish! G'boi to bad fuckin rubbish! Bunch'a mongrel dogs!' And Dusty is begging Gordon not to run back and carry out his threats 'to beat the fucking living daylights outta the sadistic prick.' She cries and begs and holds him back, seeing neighbours peering out of their windows like stiff-lipped royalty.

For a while, walking the streets, we feel lost, disoriented, empty. We don't know what to do, or where we are going. In the end, sort of symbiotically, it is Dusty suddenly taking control again, and even Gordon is happy to follow as we find ourselves walking to the Oxley railway station, waiting for a train back into Brisbane. All the time Dusty is biting her nails, sort of madly under her breath, spitting, 'Fuck em. Fuck em all. I hate em! I hate em!' And she will not even listen to anything Gordon says, who is trying to hold her, soothe her, trying to reason with her, saying, 'It'll be OK, Dust, everything'll be right, mate.' Nothing seems to make any difference.

I just wait around in the semi dark of the open-air station feeling a strange electricity passing through me, burning in my neck, knowing we have no idea where to hide ourselves, or where we are going to end up, seeing Gordon's eyes still crazily roving for the cops — or Dusty's lunatic stepdad.

# 18.

WE FOLLOW DUSTY'S ANGRY, SWISHING LITTLE BLACK SKIRT and walk from Brisbane Central Station, through the emptied city night streets, past the neon coloured fountain outside City Hall, where a male voice shouts out: 'Hey Dust, bitch,' which makes Gordon go stiff, but she doesn't stop or allow Gordon to stop, until we are back in the parklands at the Roma Street Forum, tucked under a tree, where Gordon feels safer from invisible eyes, and then she orders Gordon to go and buy a bottle of something.

'Just get me a drink, will ya?' she says. 'I need a fucking drink, dude. I want to get smashed outta me brain.'

He looks at her, seeing there is nothing more to say, and walks across the park to a bottle shop in a hotel across the way. There is very little light in the park, except from the odd lamp post, and Dusty is curled into herself, tense, stiff, her long, dusty blonde hair hanging over her head like a veil out of *Psycho,* her electric turquoise-blue peaked cap upside down on the ground like a child's toy that has been dumped.

I look across the park seeing the city lights fiercely jiving like they have no knowledge of us, don't really care, and on top of that embankment in the park it is like we are on a stage. And then I look through the shroud of night into Dusty's misery and the stage falls away.

Gordon arrives back, a bottle of vodka as ordered in hand. It glimmers in the shadowy light of the lamp post. I can see Gordon is broody.

'Here!' he says opening the bottle and thrusting it at Dusty.

She looks up, her hair flinging back over her shoulders, showing a face half-muddied like a child's neglected painting. She puts the bottle to her lips and drinks from it like it is a fizzy drink. Then she pulls the bottle from her mouth and begins to cough and cough so that I think she is going to throw up. But in the end she does not, and Gordon takes the bottle from her hand, harshly, still brooding, like a volcano is brewing in his head. With no urgency, no urgency whatsoever, he takes a slow sip, like he is drinking from a river, and then hands the bottle to me. I take my usual half drop, a mere smidgeon compared to Dusty's long, thirsty gulping. Suddenly I feel I cannot breathe. I pass the bottle back to Dusty and reach for my puffer. I inhale deeply, opening my closing lungs, watching Dusty drinking from that gurgling river of vodka again, passing the bottle back to Gordon with a sigh, a long cowgirl sigh, her eyes opening properly for the first time since we have been at the park, like suddenly she is seeing the world again. Everything is floating past us in a bubble, protected.

And Gordon says, 'So what the fuck was that about?'

Looking up at him as though recovering from a hospital bed, her eyes black and swollen, she says, 'What?'

'You know what I mean,' Gordon bites on his teeth.

Dusty, in turn, bites her lip, hard, like she is punishing it. 'What d'you mean? You seen for yourself how it is. Why everything's so fucked up.'

Gordon shakes his head like the worms in his eyes are crawling again, like they have electricity. 'I mean what did your mum mean? What did your mum mean when she calls ya a slut? An says it's all your frigging fault?'

Dusty refuses to look up, it is like the damp grass beneath us is her world, a safer, blacker, better world.

But Gordon isn't letting go; he takes another sip from the glinting bottle, and this time does not hand it back to anyone. Just holds it between his legs.

'Well… what the fuck did ya ol' girl mean, hey? C'mon, c'mon for fuck's bloody sakes, I want to know. Or are you the fucking slut they say you are? Is that why they all call ya bitch?'

This time Dusty lifts her head, but like it is a slow moving crane, and then she locks her eyes on Gordon and breathes unevenly. 'You just like all of em, mate. Just a bloke like all the rest.'

The worms are slicing fire across Gordon's eyes. 'What d'ya

mean, like all the rest? You just a fuckin slut, aren't ya? Getting what you can from Gray an me, aren't ya, slut!'

Like her mum now, like her mum had turned around and done to her step-dad, she lashes Gordon's face with a slap that manages to claw a nail into his nose and rip open the flesh.

'Fuck! – Fuckin bitch!' he swears, refusing to touch his ripped nose.

Instead he stares vacantly for a moment, past her, right way past her, just like Pete had done to her mum, and just like Pete, as though looking into the distance, seeing something none of us can see, he draws back like he is pulling an arrow, a long, straight arrow, and unleashes a force from his knuckles that is so stonily hard it pierces her through the cheek and she actually lifts, for a second lifts off the damp ground, and then falls over. And then she just lies there, just lies there like a doll without life, blood-red hands around her head so that I think she will never get up. Will never be able to walk again. My stomach shrinks inwards, spins, my eyes stare. I look up, only to see Gordon take his fist again, that strong, clenched fist that has done the damage and make to strike again. Only this time he slams it like it is a shovel, a big, heavy shovel, into the earth beside her, flattening the ground.

'Fuck you!' he screams. 'Fuck you!'

I rush over to Dusty, touching her gently, shaking her, calling her name, seeing Gordon beside me, like a madman, continuing to pound the ground, until I can see, even in this dark light, his knuckles are glowing red and raw, and he takes another sip of vodka like a hungry man, a grieving man, and then simply drops the empty bottle onto the grass and hangs his head between his knees.

It seems like hours but it must be only minutes when Dusty, responding to my shaking, finally tremors back to life. She is shivering like it is bleak winter and sits up groggily, a discarded rag doll, but she does not take any notice of me. Instead she reaches out a trembling hand to Gordon, placing it round his bent thighs and pulls him to her.

'I'm sorry,' she says. 'I'm sorry, mate, I am just a slut. Like ya say. That's all I am.'

And he lets her hand just hang there, around his thigh, like it is the limb of a drowning person trying to attach itself to a passing boat.

'I don't understand. I don't understand,' he says.

She pulls him to her with that drowning, hopeless hand. Only this time he allows himself to be pulled, allows himself to be attached to. Now they are leaning against one another and he has a hand over her hand that is still dug into his thigh. He is sucking in the city that looks like if you shake it upside down black snow will fall on us from the sky.

And then he says, 'It's the same... it's the bleeding same for all of us, Dust. Exactly the same.'

And Dusty says, 'Yeah... yeah. The same but... different like.'

'D'you mean what ya mum's referring to?'

'Yeah Gordon. Yeah. 'Course,' she says. 'You should just know the half of it, mate.' And then, after a moment of studying Gordon's yellow, gritty face, she says, 'I think you should know about me Gord, I think you should know the whole bleeding story, mate, just what a slag I am.'

Gordon nods, head staring into the ground. At nothing.

'Only are you sure, mate, are you really sure ya wanna hear the all of it?'

Gordon looks at her, studies her soiled, bloodied face, and nods again.

Looking down into the soil like she is speaking to the grass or the worms in there, like they understand better than any of us, she tells us about her dad, her real dad, how she remembers him. 'Ever since I was seven or eight, dude,' she says breathing stiffly, 'maybe earlier, maybe much earlier, I don't know, I don't remember anymore, but I remember me dad, me real dad that is, clear as any movie on your TV screen, coming to me.' Gordon studies the muddied face next to him like it is a painting waiting for restoration, but chooses not to touch it, just stares into it. 'Sometimes late at nights like, sometimes in the afternoons when Mum is asleep or not around, ya know, doing her pole dancin thing, which I didn't know anythin about then, or maybe just drunk in the bedroom, which I did know about, which I had a good bloody idea about, he would come in, an tell me to... ya know... ya know like, touch him, you know play with him like. And he would touch me and say I was his best little girl, that I felt nice and soft like silk and tasted like honey. "This is the way daddies love their little girls," he would say, "daddies who really-really love their little girls."' She looks up at Gordon. There is a glow of water, thick like syrup in her eyes, and Gordon looks at her, his eyes wild, pressing her to go on.

'Later, I dunno, some time later, maybe like when I was twelve or so, he like, like you know, begins to do more things hey,' her voice goes soft like the grass, 'ya know... like... put himself in me like. He always smelled of beer an rum and would tell me how much he loves his "little Dust", his "one an only little dusty-blonde haired girl". I even felt proud for a while. Like I was special. Chosen out of everyone in the whole world to be his best girl. Chosen before me brothers. Before Mum even. Who I know were all jealous, because they would treat me more an more like shit, just lash out at me like, like I was shit. And, knowing our secret, I let him do it.'

She looks at the city, now turned upside down, covered in dirty brown snow.

'Dad...' she says it like there is still a warm, mysterious chord that runs between them, 'would say I was just like Mum, only sweeter, softer, easier to be with.' She looks ahead, suddenly away from the city lights, towards the railways, the derelict back side of Roma Street Railway Station below. 'An he used to stroke me hair an make me feel real good an pretty like, telling me I was the most precious thing in the whole world.' She takes the back of a hand and wipes slowly forming glows of syrup from her eyes. 'If I told anyone, he used to say, all the magic would disappear like, and Mum an me brothers, and Aunt Cress an grandad — the man ya seen at our house — me dad's stupid dad — would just disappear.' She breathes in loud and snottily, wiping that wet syrup from her eyes, telling how once she had this teacher in her first year at high school — who she trusted, who liked her — and because she was so proud to be liked by her teacher she told her dad how she wanted to tell this teacher, who would understand, about him and her, share their secret. How proud it would make her. To tell her teacher how much her dad loved her.

'I thought me dad would be proud, too, hey,' she sniffs. 'I should of known... should of known. Instead he takes a fist, a real hard fist like he is a magician or somethin, and like your own fist, Gord, tough like blimming nails, smashes me right in the face. I hated him then, hated him with all me bloody might. Suddenly it was like I saw the light. What was really happening. But all I could do after that was swear to him I would tell no one. Else he'd rip me apart, he said.' She looks up, glazed, talking to black air. 'I was stuck then, ya know, like in hard cement.' She heaves in a breath like she has no more breath in her, like she could do with my puffer. I feel like offering it to her, but then change my mind; I don't want her to think me silly, childish. Anyway Gord suddenly finds a use for his hand and puts it round her shoulders, which seems to help her breathing. The city twinkles on merrily at our side.

'And then... are you sure ya wanna hear the rest of this, Gord?' she asks again, eyes blinking, peering up, but as though to a policeman.

'Yeah Dust, yeah chick-babe, of course,' he says like a real boyfriend, like a real friend, and in the darkness of Dusty's tale I feel strangely elevated.

'You really sure, mate?' she says it again. 'You sure?'

''Course, Dust. Yeah of course.' He says it without blinking.

'OK then... don't say ya didn't ask for it,' she smiles, childish, a smile almost to herself. '...At about this time Dad starts bringing friends round to the house. We living down the road in Inala then. He would let me sit and watch while Mum was out, and even sometimes when she was there, as they sat there and drank and laughed and smoked cones an the like.

'Then one day he calls me aside and leads me downstairs, under the house into a little half closed off laundry like, and then he calls in this man I never seen, an says, "This's Uncle Ray here. Uncle Ray'll show ya what t'do. Just listen to im." Dad, me own dad, looks at me with sharp, icy eyes, like he'll bash me daylights again if I don' listen. I am trembling hey, sweating hot in the neck and in me thighs like. But Uncle Ray was gentle... I s'pose in his way gentle, an... he shows me what to do like. I never swallowed again after that. I swear...' She looks up, the night sky a low, black boundary that can yet never be breached. 'After that... after that it happened often like.'

With the backs of her hands she wipes more of that glowing syrup from her cheeks. 'And once,' she catches her breath, 'once, there was this younger bloke, in his early twenties like, who stayed over at our house, and sometimes in the middle of the night he would sneak into me bed like an tell me how he was going to take me on holidays to Sydney an things, to see the Sydney Harbour Bridge, and Bondi Beach, and the Blue Mountains an things. And this man, Uncle Chris, was allowed to take me out, just me an him, and he would take me to Sizzler even sometimes, and buy me sweets an fancy looking bracelets an things. And even me dad left me alone then.' She looks up at Gordon, 'I know ya not gonna like this, Gord, but the truth is I loved him; I loved Uncle Chris. I'm sorry, Gord. But I did.' Gordon smiles stiffly, like he has a blister on his gums, and she looks at him as though through a movie, like she doesn't want any of this to be real, like she wants it to just be part of that guy Shakespeare's stage. But she looks down into the railway yard and it is like everything is set in concrete and steel.

'One day,' she goes on, her breath short, 'one day when they all in the lounge drinking like, Dad an Mum, Aunt Cress an Uncle Chris an all of them like... a real fight breaks out, I don't know why, and have never found out, but I peer through my bedroom door where I was laying down asleep to see me dad being kicked on the floor by Uncle Chris. Uncle Chris's teeth were gritting like a mad dog and he was acting like I never seen him before, and Mum an Aunty Cressy were screaming an trying to pull him off. But it is only when he puts a boot into me dad's cheek an splits it open like watermelon that he runs out of the room, packs his bags, an runs out of the house...'

'And I couldn't help meself, Gord, I just couldn't, and I ran into the street after Uncle Chris, screaming I want to be with him, but he just pushes me off and screams back at me that I'm nothing but trash an stuff. "Git off'a me ya piece'a no good shit!" he screamed and yelled, and eventually I let go of him and walked back to the house and I never seen him again. Never.' The syrup is like soapy bubbles in her eyes now dropping down her face in little dark globes.

'Satisfied? Ya satisfied now?' she says, angry, red and angry, looking up at Gordon.

'I just wanted to hear everything,' Gordon says. 'Everything, Dust. I don' care, mate, I still wanna hear everything.' Gordon's face is tight and his jaw is gritting.

She looks up and then down, the syrup from her eyes dropping onto the soil.

And she goes on to tell us that her dad left her mum then, not even a week later. Six months later, she nearly smiles, she tells us they heard he was in a bad car accident, up in Mt Isa, and he is gone. 'Just like that. Enda story,' she says. 'Child-fucker back in the dirty messed up soil.' Despite her anger, there is that mysterious line of sadness, of grief in her face as she says it.

'Only it's not really end of story,' she looks up at Gordon, 'because then along comes Pete.'

She starts studying the black soil around us like there are a thousand different ways you can read it, telling us eventually how there was peace for a while in their house, peace for a while until one day they all got so smashed and Pete started to beat up on her mum for the first time and things changed after that. 'That's when the real shit seemed to start,' she says. 'Because Mum starts going to bed early like and playing hard to get. And one day the prick starts coming on to me, like. 'Cept I know he is lonely and I sort of feel sorry for him hey, an this isn't easy to say, Gord… you sure ya can handle all of this, mate?' Gordon nods his head and looks into her mud-stained face. '…OK, well then, I guess ya know it already, I'm a fuckin slut through an through, mate, so ya may as well know I'm a fuckin idiot, too. I let Pete take me to the bedroom, and slowly, like, he starts doing things, see. 'Cept… 'cept Mum fucking walks into the room and all hell breaks loose. Like ya can imagine. Knowing me mum.'

She looks down to the cold ground. '…I was chucked out of home after that. Went to a couple of shelters an stuff an lived with friends like, an didn't come back for a year or so. Then I asked Mum if I can move back in like, and she let me. But Mum can never really forget. As ya seen. As ya seen for yourself. I s'pose I can't blame her really. But the dickhead's never stopped wanting to touch me after that. And sometimes I would just have to move out and let things cool off and then come back again. And that's how I come, like ya already seen, and Ruth Hannah seen, off me fucking face on drugs ya don't wanna know about, to Ipswich.'

She looks at Gordon, suddenly all coy, wiping her nose with the backs of her hands like a child, the city in the background, turned upside down, sending down dark-coloured pitchforks.

Dusty had never told anyone her full story until now. And suddenly Gordon knows something else, what she shows him now, what we've seen before without saying anything, what she moves the heavy silver Seiko watch she is still wearing to show him — the shiny blue scars on her wrists that are like half-bangles; the thick razor slits that mark her history. We know what those shiny blue bangles mean. In the last year, two have gone all the way. Kids we knew. Below us my eyes draw in Roma Street Station, dark railway lines lit by grey-yellow lamp posts that cast not light but something lonely and desolate. It is the nature of railway lines.

The mood next to me is black, like someone has pitched a dark tent around us. I even fear, I don't know, maybe because of his temper, that Gordon might hit her again. Might just get up and walk away, and I will have to follow him, something I don't want to do.

But in the end he just looks past Dusty, and says, 'Fuck it, mate. Fuck it. What are we doing here?'

And she cranes her head into his shoulder and says, 'Will you take me back now?'

Not really turning to her, as though unsure himself, his eyes rolling forward, he says words into the black air between them that I think I will never in my life hear again: 'I love ya, Dust. Honest, I love ya, I do, mate.'

They laugh now, really burst out laughing, and she pokes him in the ribs and he pokes her in the chest and they are both lying down on the damp ground, wrestling and tumbling down the hill like an old showground candyfloss stick, growing fluffier and fluffier. And I feel like jumping for joy. I feel something so deep in me it's weird. I have never felt it before. It is like I imagine pure snow.

The next morning the day is surrounded by grey reality, and Dusty is saying, 'What now? What the fuck now, Gord?'

Gordon shakes his wild bush of hair which only bounces and then stabs back into his head like bent forks. He looks around, saying we need to think, he needs to think, wishing we could be back home in Ipswich, under the bridge, or at Ruth's Place. Some place he knows. Where if the cops are following us, at least he knows they are.

'Everything is mud. Shit-brown. Nothing's ever clear,' he is saying to Dusty. His words strike through me, hurt in my chest. It is like last night counted for nothing.

Dusty looks down and takes some sand from the ground. She throws it into the still, crisp morning air like she is a little girl waving sparkles from a wand. 'See,' she says, 'it's clear now.'

We laugh, even Gordon laughs. Yeah, right, I can see he is thinking.

'Let's get outta here... before it's too late,' he shakes his head.

# 19.

'JESUS CHRIST! WHAT HAPPENED TO YOUR FACE? It's blue and swollen,' is how Ruth Hannah greets us at the door as soon as we arrive at Ruth's Place; she is zoning straight in on Dusty.

'Walked into a door at me mum's,' Dusty responds with some confidence.

'Ask no questions, hear no lies,' Ruth breathes out, heaving.

'It's no lies!' Gordon raises his voice, stepping closer to Dusty.

Ruth merely breathes out again. 'OK then, but get yourselves into showers for God's sake. Then we can talk downstairs in the study.'

'I'll put more base over it,' Dusty volunteers, turning.

'Yes, you do that, dear,' Ruth says. 'Specially if you're going to be looking for work sometime soon.'

All cleaned up and gleaming we sit on the wooden kitchen chairs in front of Ruth Hannah's desk, Gordon leaning right back in his chair, so that Ruth has to say to him, 'Gordon, sit straight please, you'll break my chair.'

'Sorry,' he says. 'Whatever.'

He grabs hold of Dusty's hand, a very un-Gordon thing to do so upfront, and Ruth looks at him for a few moments, really examining him, sort of looking right into his chocolate eyes and says, 'Do I see something here?'

'What?' Gordon says. 'What d'ya see?'

'Love?'

And he untwists his hand out of Dusty's, and Dusty says, 'He's shier then ya think, mum.'

Gordon, sort of regathering himself like a soldier caught in an ambush, catches his breath, and says, 'Whatever. Say what ya like.' He blinks. 'You wanted to talk to us, mum. What's up?'

Ruth breathes in like she is swallowing useful information. 'Well, I have been thinking about it,' she says, 'and maybe the best thing you fellers can do is just go to the police and tell them everything. Be straight. Go to your old mate, Thornes, you know; I don't think the truth will go astray with him.'

None of us respond for a while and then Dusty looks deliberately at Gordon, like she is trying to talk through him, and he says, 'Naaa, I dunno, mum.'

'Well, you can't just carry on hiding for the rest of your lives?'

And Gordon breathes uneasily, shifting creakily on his chair. 'I dunno.' He looks down like there's so much thought in his head his eyebrows are going to explode. 'I just dunno…' he shakes his head and then looks up. 'But… yep… maybe you right, Ruth, mum.' He stops suddenly, looks down again, considers with his eyebrows, and finally looks up at Ruth again. 'But if Thornes bloody wants us, he must bleeding come an get us, we're not going to him like. We didn't do nothin wrong.'

Ruth considers Gordon for a while, says nothing, and then lets her eyes glide over to Dusty and me. She prods us with her white eyes like she wants to see if we have anything to add. But Dusty just shrugs her shoulders and chews on some invisible gum. I do the same, making sure I am looking straight at Ruth.

'OK,' Ruth says with finality like she is poking our chests. 'It's your decision, fellers. I can only protect you so far. Especially you Gordon, you're eighteen now, and you Dusty, you're even older, nineteen. A woman. So you fellers have to think carefully about what you do.'

I knew it, I say to myself, I knew Dusty was older than Gord. I'm not so sure what's so important about it, except that I always wanted her to be older, more like a mum. And then something else dawns on me, what I noticed in the train back from Brisbane. Dusty's electric turquoise-blue cap is missing. Must have left it behind in the park, or lost it, I think, thinking she is pretty even without it. But I liked it on that special angle she wore it, its electric shininess like competition for the sun. Without it she looks plainer, a little more sallow, dry. Maybe she has purposely left the hat behind? Abandoned it like an old toy one grows out of? I must mention it to her, I say to myself, knowing I will forget or more probably, won't even have the courage.

'OK then,' Ruth says with assertion, like everything is a done deal. 'You can have a few days here, to get yourselves settled, but Gray's got to go home.' Her white eyes fire over to Gordon, catching and then locking into them. 'And he's got to start going to school immediately.' She takes a breath, more a heave. 'He's still young, mate, and has a chance of doing well.' She stares at Gordon until he nods affirmatively, and then says, 'And I think you and Dusty should try to find somewhere of your own. Speak to Centrelink, mate, they'll help you out with a deposit and stuff — or I can help you if it comes to that. Think about it.'

Gordon and Dusty look at one another like they have never considered such a possibility — living in an apartment, together, alone. They are beaming — I can see ideas of playing mum and dad and throwing big parties and things running through their heads like electric radio waves. Only I can see nothing they are thinking includes me, and I feel a sharp arrow passing through me. How do people know when they're in love? I feel the thought bow through my brain. For a moment I am bitterly jealous of them. My hands start to pour sweat and I find myself wringing them in my lap.

Looking away from Ruth I become aware of the poster behind her, and see it is a new one. It says: *When you like someone, you like them in spite of their faults. When you love someone, you love them with their faults – Elizabeth Cameron.* Jesus, I think, those blimming words are a bleeding con. I love Gordon and Dusty but right now I don't love em at all; they seem so full of faults. I sit there wishing Ruth would include me in her plans for them. But not a word is said about that. I feel like mugging em, the whole lotta em.

# 20.

LATE THAT AFTERNOON, IT SEEMS, OUR LUCK is about to change. There is a visitor to the house — and it is none other than the famous heavyweight champion of Ipswich, Detective Senior Constable Watno Thornes. He doesn't have to knock on the door because it is already wide open, and so he just sort of pops in, his wrestler shoulders, his thick neck, his packing box frame, dressed in a jacket and tie, suddenly appearing through the scratchy wooden door like an intergalactic agent. He eyes me, those large, frog boulders falling on me, seeing me crossing the lounge on my way somewhere, and immediately he is shouting at me, why I am not the bloody hell in school. I catch such a fright, for a moment I cannot move, and then I grab for my inhaler. I run down the stairs to the computer room and scream out for Ruth.

'Looks like we're having a few problems, are we?' he says to Ruth as she chugs gingerly up to the front door, in no mood for smiles.

'Yes!'

'Don't blame me,' he says. 'I support what you do. What I don't support is when ya hide fugitives from the law. When you protect kids who should be in school — or custody!'

'OK, what do you want?'

'You know very well what I want — the Morrow boys and their little girlfriend.'

She pokes him with her breath. 'And what are you going to do with them?'

'Don't panic, Mzz Hannah, well not yet. All I want is to have a little chat with em. I know they're here.'

'OK,' Ruth says, 'I definitely wouldn't lie to you.' He smiles, and she calls out to the three of us, turning back to him. 'You can go downstairs now, to the office, have your little chat with them there.'

In Ruth's office the air is so thick it feels like it is made up of wooden dust particles, not oxygen. My throat is tight, scratchy. Thornes does not sit; instead he leans back against Ruth's large wooden desk, the back of the computer sticking into his spine like a large misshapen toothpick, while we, the three of us, not sure what to do, stand in front of him, beside the three wooden kitchen chairs. It is like being called into the principal's office, only this is worse, much worse, it is the cops. Gaol? I struggle in my throat, feeling it click for breath, keeping an eye on Gordon, to see what he does, how he reacts. He and Dusty look relaxed, but I think they are used to it, this kind of thing, much more used to it than me.

Voice low, a bit lower than those alto-falsettos or whatever they call them, and hoarse, real hoarse like, the harsh, streaking lines in Thornes' muddy blue eyes turning soft, friendly, straying casually into Dusty's reddening face, he breathes, 'Hey lass, I'm thinkin ya cheek looks a bit purple an swollen, hey…? Don't tell me… ya walked into a door?'

'How d'ya know!' Dusty's little eyes twinkle with astonishment.

'That's what I'm paid for,' Thornes says. 'To know these things. Ya think I'm just a pretty face?'

We all just look up into the swollen air.

'She'll be right, it's none of your business,' Gordon says.

'Well that's true, matey, but this is. This damned is. I'm going to be straight with you…' and his eyes roll over all our faces, from the one to the other, 'so I want a straight answer. In fact that's all I want. Nothing more, nothing less.' We all nod like we are more than happy to oblige. 'Were you… were you with Dean Valenti and Kelly Baxter on the night of that bloody near fatal mugging in upper Brisbane Street?' Thornes' mud-blue eyes spin like the point of a top right into the middle of Gordon's eyes.

We all shake our heads at the same time. And say nothing.

Thornes prods his intergalactic head forward like he is waiting for something to leap at him. But nothing happens, not a word is breathed, so he pulls his head back and slowly, in that very hoarse tone of his starts to repeat what the principal, Mr Goss, had said to me. That someone saw me running — 'hobbling like a breathless freak from the alley,' he says.

I clutch my baggy pants and again we all just look at him, sort of more like gawk stupidly like parrots at him, like he has sprung completely into the wrong tree or something. Then suddenly, to my surprise, I see something in Gordon's eyes tally like a cash register, like some new discovery or something has dawned on him, and in a low, quiet voice he proceeds to let his dry white tongue unroll. To my amazement, and I think Dusty's, too, what it unrolls is everything — everything about that stupid night. Only, as soon becomes evident, what Gordon's tongue unrolls is sort of like the truth he had told Ruth. That yeah, we saw it all going down, but yeah it was also us who rescued the old bugger from Fat Deano's madness. And, the fact is, we were no ways a part of any of it.

'I swear, that's the whole story an the whole bleeding truth,' Gordon says.

Thornes considers Gordon, carefully chewing the thick particles in the air with his mouth like his brain has somehow slid down inside his fat, cracked lips.

Finally, like it is his frog eyes breathing in the air, he says, 'Well, well, very interesting Gordo, ol' lad. I must say. But somehow, somehow, matey... a little birdie in me head tells me you're not telling me everything, bud.' His mouth makes to whistle or breathe out like there dinkum is a little birdie in his head, and after a moment of loud breathing, me still sweatily clutching my hands into my pants, he says. 'Well, OK then, lad. OK — who am I not to give you fellers the benefit of the doubt?' We all look up into his intergalactic head and feign a smile. Darkly, he looks down at us. 'But just remember, just remember this — and think about it for a moment. I've given you a chance, a good bloody chance to come clean... and now... and now if I find out you're lying — that you were a part of it, Gordo ol' boy, any part of that bloody disgusting cowardly assault and robbery, I'll see to it that you are put away, mate. Yep, that's right, gaol mate. Inside! I hope ya followin me?' He nudges Gord with his eyes and I see Gordon nod, sort of quietly, very humbly, breathing heavily, like you see Catholics kneeling down on TV in front of Jesus.

Thornes just looks through him. 'You're an adult now Gordo. Commit a crime now, lad, and you go directly to gaol. You know that. No passing go anymore, mate. No collectin any Centrelink or expensive goods or anything like that...' He breathes in, a Martian funnel of dust particles passing into his lungs. 'So, if you wanna come clean, matey, ya gotta do it now. Understand?' I don't know why, but right then, just then, I notice that Thornes' tie has Daffy Duck on it. Sort of like our Mick's shiny Tweety and Sylvester boxer shorts.

Gordon shakes his head and says, 'I don't care what ya say. I'm telling the truth, man, I didn't do nothin.'

Thornes' large robot body casts a laser eye at Gordon and then swerves right and falls on me. I feel my stomach pinch, like it has just taken a bullet. But I try, whatever I do, to look him straight back between the eyes. He takes in a breath and after a few moments turns away from me again and I feel the relief of his passing gaze rifle through me like a sharp wind down my ribcage.

Now he turns those laser eyes to Dusty, and before she can even wince, says, 'I definitely, definitely, don't want to hear that this fine lady here was any way involved.' It is hard to make out the borderlines of his thin beige hair for the amount of naked flesh that sits like a washed potato on his head.

Dusty just looks up into that head and then quickly down and clicks her tongue at him like you see those African village women do it on TV. Sort of like, 'You don't have to believe me, but I'm telling the truth, man. And who the hell do you think you are, anyway?'

'I think you'd do well to look at me when I'm talking to you,' he eyeballs her.

Dusty immediately looks up at him again, her lower lip curling. We all look up at him, and wait. There is an arcing moment of silence, it is like a midnight darkness, like a church confessional you see on TV, and then he goes back to that very soft tone of his, only this time more sort of alto-tenor, like he is trying with all his might not to give affront, like he is nothing but a mate in a pub. And like a mate in a pub he steps up to Dusty, places a clumpy hand on her thinly strapped pink-freckled shoulder, and says, 'You know, fellers, I think Dusty here's a good lass. A real good lass. I know all she's doing is trying to come clean, make good with her life. But you lads have got to show the lady some respect.'

I see one of those worms crawling right across Gordon's eyes, it is the yellow-red squint in them, like he is about to take out a six-shooter. Spotting this, I am sure spotting this, Thornes' eye steadies, slow and dense like a slow motion bullet through the air.

'And you do that, Gordo — and Gray — you do that,' his voice rides on that bullet, 'you do that by setting the good lady here a fine example.' Gordon looks at Thornes like he is already shooting bullets at him. 'You do that,' Thornes repeats on his own slowly turning shot, 'by doing one thing — and it is this... by showing leadership, mate. By showing that you are not afraid to turn down a bong, that you are not the hell afraid to say no to robberies and muggings. You definitely do not show it by beating to near death weak old blokes in the street and stealing their hard-earned cash!'

'We didn't beat no one!' Gordon shoots directly at Thornes, looking straight into his eyes.

'OK... OK. You know what's best, my friend? We'll leave it at that, Gordo. That's what's best.' Thornes blinks, shoving that intergalactic ray-gun of his back into its holster. 'For now, OK, we'll leave it at that, mate. But I want you fellers to do something for me.' We look up at him, alarmed, like he is going to ask us to join the police or something. Instead he just says, almost like an uncle, like an old, loved uncle. 'I want you fellers to turn the corner, for Christ's sakes. Just turn the bloody corner. Make something good of yourselves. Try walking down a different street. And for heaven's sakes be a good example to the little lady here.' He massages Dusty's spotted, pink shoulder, and I see the worms, red and yellow, wriggle through Gordon's eyes.

We all stand there, and now there is this silence, this long curling silence, a silence that seems to climb the walls, that presses the dust particles down like a weight on the chest. It is like Thornes has climbed into our skin or something. And for a moment I feel like I almost like him. Like maybe he could be an uncle.

And with this new-found friendliness he starts mouthing rhymes at us. 'Hey fellers,' he says, 'it's not like I don't know lads, I know young fellers, ya know that, I know lotsa lads like you, and of me own little buggers at home I have two. So don't get me wrong, fellers. Don't get me wrong. I don't wanna spoil that. What you three have between ya is fat and I don't wanna get in the way of that. But I also don't the hell want ya to get in my bleeding way either — understand?' We nod as though one. 'You do? Well, good-o. Very, very good-o. So now, listen up, I'll be fair with youse if you'll be fair with me –' And now Gordon and I wince as we see him press his heavyweight fingers deep into Dusty's near naked shoulder, as though to stamp home his point. Dusty, startled, just looks up into his smoothing mud-blue eyes; you can see by the suddenly sprinkling pink moisture in her eyes that she is smarting like a child taking a parental clobbering. In Gordon's eyes I see only worms, deep and brown.

'Yes sir, Cunstable,' she says between her teeth, and his wide head bears down into her forehead.

'OK then, tell me this… were you there with these fellers on the night in question?' He digs even deeper into her shoulder.

'Ow! — No sir, course not!' she spits back quickly, in pain, as though affronted. She turns a squinting eye towards Gordon, who looks like his head could explode.

'So, you never saw anythin?' He lifts his hand off her shoulder like he is going to let her go, and her face immediately lightens, but then instead he puts his hand back even more heavily on her shoulder, squeezing now like his hand is a claw digging deep into loose sand. I see Gordon's lips swell. '…And ya never ever accepted any money or stolen goods either?'

'Ouch, man! — Naaa, naaa… 'course not… Cunstable,' she grumbles, a low, painful mumble, her eyes shooting directly to the shiny silver band of the watch that she still wears face down since Pete, her mum's lunatic de facto questioned her about it.

'Well,' he breathes smoothly, 'don't let me find out any different young lady…'

'Don't worry yaself, ya won't,' she says, and glances down at Thornes' pressing robot hand.

'Well, I'm just warning ya, warning ya all now.' He looks into the worms screaming in Gordon's eyes and squeezes into Dusty's shoulder as though for spite, as though telling Gordon that if he won't take proper care of Dusty he will. He breathes in, dust particles shooting like fencing pickets up his nose. 'Just do as I say, fellers — just act like bloody normal, reasonable adults for a change — and then your lives as well as mine and this whole bleeding town's will be peaceful again.' He smiles.

Gordon just glares, Dusty winces, and behind that intergalactic, world heavyweight square frame, behind the smiley Daffy Duck tie, I bring sweating eyes to yet another of Ruth's posters. It says: *The day the child realises that all adults are imperfect he becomes an adolescent; the day he forgives them, he becomes an adult; the day he forgives himself he becomes wise. — Alden Nowlen.* It is too much for me to take in at one gulp, specially with the interplanetary agent standing there squeezing like Darth Vader Dusty's shoulder in front of me. I try to read the words on the poster again but Thornes moves sideways and gets in the way of it. I look up to see him finally remove his hand from Dusty's shoulder with the extravagance of an executioner letting a crook off the hook, and then he slowly leans back against the desk again, allowing the back of the computer to stick into him again like it is a special machine for massaging the small of his back. Dusty stands there, the colour returning to her face, half looking at Gordon, seeing those red-brown worms still wriggling in his eyes, and half looking at Thornes, who is smiling down at her. She is flushing red and white at the same time, standing there stiff like a statue.

'I'm sure we'll be talking soon?' Thornes whips his eyes across our faces. 'But in the meantime, Gray,' he looks directly at me, but not accusingly or with any malice, 'I want you to go to school, mate.'

'But it's already too late, sir,' a voice just seems to barrel out of me from nowhere. 'It's like half way through the morning already, sir.' I feel like I am falling off a stool.

'Don't worry, it'll be OK, my friend.' He says it to me like I am a son. 'I've already told Mr Goss that after I see you, I'll send you straight back. So, they're expecting ya, mate. They understand more than you think.'

I shrug my shoulders, thinking, It's all frigging bullshit. All pure bullshit.

'And another thing, Gray,' Thornes motions his head towards me, throwing his heavy, boulder eyes directly into my chest, 'spend more time at home with ya mum, OK?' It is strange, but what he has just said kind of shakes me inside. I don't want to think about it, so I just eyeball him back and say nothing. 'Now off ya go,' he says to all of us, no longer looking at me, but rather at Gordon. 'And act like bloody adults.' He pats Dusty on the shoulder like an old gym friend, like he is sorry for beating her, which almost makes Gordon spit, and then the three of us turn, lazily, sort of bumping into one another as we walk out of the office door.

141

As soon as we are out of the door, Dusty and Gordon look at one another and their cheeks bloat like they are going to faint. Their cheeks are so full it looks like they have sucked in a bowl of hot soup, the skin on the outside is all pink and see-through and their eyes are nearly shut and spilling hot moisture. For a moment I think they are going to be physically ill or bawl their eyes right out. But once we are out in the tiny back garden of Ruth's Place, out of earshot, like a blustering wind that they can't hold back, they burst into howls of laughter — and then laugh and laugh some more. Each time they look at one another they cackle and hoot and snort, louder and louder, turning and tapping one another, and then suddenly they fall and lie on the sandy grass, wet-eyed, sort of shivering, and light cigarettes. I look on at them and all I can do is smile, jealously. For me there is no laughter; I know that at least by tomorrow I will have to go back to bloody school — and that means only one thing: day-gaol! And the reality still remains, despite Gordon's and Dusty's loud, blaring laughter, no one, not one of us, is off the hook.

# 21.

EARLY THE VERY NEXT MORNING WHEN EVERYONE IS GETTING READY for school and jobs and things, one of the kids picks up the local paper from the front lawn to give to Ruth, but although none of us ever read the paper, even he can see who is on the front page: it is covered in a huge colour picture of her. Our mum. Ruth Hannah. He goes screaming around to everyone to come and see how famous Ruth is. It doesn't matter that the picture of Ruth isn't a smiley, happy one, and that it looks like she could be throwing bricks at the photographer: her mouth is scowling in that way when her lower lip sometimes drops, involuntarily, at the end of serious speeches like to Gord and me, and the lines on her face are stretched downwards in vicious slants like she could kill. The story is headlined: *Ipswich woman of the year a fake.*

No one can quite understand what that means. Not that we don't know what a fake is, but just that we can't believe there can be any connection between Ruth and that word. Our eyes bounce from one another like spinning tennis balls dipping just over the net—trying to believe there is still some chance of real fame in the story. And maybe that there is just something wrong with the headline. Like they say, newspapers always talk shit.

Ruth pokes us with that lower lip of hers, and scowls: 'Well go on someone, read it.'

Everyone looks around as though some foreigner might appear to do the reading, but no one arrives, so I put my hand up, lay the paper out on the dining room table and begin to read.

'Louder. Louder, we can't the fuck hear ya,' a couple of the older kids call out.

And Ruth says, 'Now-now, don't be rude. And no swearing here! You know the rules.'

I start again and read through the entire article.

It seems Ruth, who had earlier that year been honoured with the prize of the state's 'Woman of the Year' for her work with youth and street kids — yep, us — has been conniving everyone. She does not hold a masters degree in social work, or a masters in psychology, as she apparently always claimed, not even a degree in either of them. Actually, although she had started university at one time many years ago, it seems she had never completed a bachelor of arts even, and has no qualifications whatsoever, not even any TAFE diplomas or certificates that qualify her to work with kids. She had lied. Bullshitted everyone! In fact, her supposed days at university had been spent in a hazily stoned daze, which maybe, it crosses my mind, explains the thin, yellow amphetamine lines that run down her cheeks and the grey bagginess under her eyes.

Suddenly Detective Senior Constable Watno Thornes' words to her of the day before — 'having a few problems, are we?' — and her more than usually curt responses hit home. She must have known something was up, and I suppose didn't say anything to any of us, hoping for the best. I guess she didn't expect to land up on the front page like this. But to us kids, whatever the situation, we not only don't follow why she has lied, we can't understand why she even needed to — and we all look at one another wondering if it can really be so important. Why such a big fuss is being made over it, that her picture, almost as big and smudgy-ugly as the page itself, is right there on the dining room table staring at us like it could commit blue murder. 'As long as it don't hurt nobody,' that's what we were always told about lies. But somehow the front page of the newspaper is showing it like it is the most important thing in the world and everyone should know Ruth Hannah is a liar.

Ruth stands in front of us, drained looking, the amphetamine lines running down her face looking wider, deeper, turning grey, her cheeks the colour of three week-old tea bags. Her lips are so tense they are dancing.

'Well, it's true,' she looks up at last like she is about to address the nation on TV or something. 'I didn't tell the truth. Well, not the whole truth.' She looks down, the way someone who has lied lowers their head. 'I don't know why. I... I... to be honest, I just don't know why.' Then she stops and thinks for a few moments, casting her eyes lightly over all of us as though we might be able to help her out, but none of us, not even Gord or Dusty have anything to help out with. We are all silent. Like in a big church. No one saying a thing. She looks up, above our heads, like maybe she is seeing angels or something. 'Well listen up now, this is the truth... you may as well know it, be the first on the streets to know it... I do, yes I do know why I didn't tell the truth. I just thought... just... thought... winning that prize was the most important thing in my life.' She looks at us to see if there is any reaction, but we are all just standing there like dull-eyed wombats, still struggling to understand. She goes on as uneasily as before, 'It... I just thought... it... winning that prize would give me recognition, show the stuck-up people in this neighbourhood and around the area who hate this house, our house, our place, who despise me for taking in you kids, that I'm at least doing something for other people's benefit. That I'm helping. Not just sabotaging the ruddy price of real estate for the sake of seeing it crash around here!' We all look up at her, to a kid, like she is one of those high priestesses or something from Indiana Jones and the Lost Arc or has just appeared from the burning bush on Mount Sinai or something. She goes on, eyes wide and spinning, 'And... well, the truth is... I thought faking those qualifications would push me... would somehow push us... ahead... would make the people who choose these prizes take more notice of people in towns like this. Not make it such a bloody effort each year to apply for funding.' She stops for a while, looks at our staring, confused, gob-smacked eyes, and says, 'And yes... this is another truth maybe you should all know: To do this work, I could not have anyone know I didn't have even one real qualification. I knew they wouldn't respect me.'

'When a man finishes... he is only beginning... and when he stops... he is as puzzled as ever.' A low voice — Gord's — suddenly shouts out from the middle of the room like a priest from one of those American loud-mouth churches you see on Sunday TV.

We all just stand there, me included, totally confused. But say nothing. I feel like we are in a convocation of Jehovah's Witnesses or something.

'So what?' Gordon says further. 'That's all I'm sayin... so bloody what?'

And everyone sighs, as though they understand a little better now.

'Yeah,' one of the older girls says. 'So what?'

And Dusty says, 'Will they put you in gaol, mum?'

Ruth laughs, but more to herself, the colour streaming back into her face. 'No, they'll probably just take the prize away, but with it will go the funding. The house may have to close down. Without government funding we're done.'

'But why — what did ya actually do wrong?' says Little Pumpy. He is biting his nails, eyes crossing like he is trying to make sense of a moving spiral.

'You heard,' says Ruth, 'the paper said it all. I did what I told you fellers never to do — I didn't tell the truth. I made up stories. I lied.'

'So the fuck what?' Gordon shouts out again. He slams a fist on the dining room table and it sounds like it could have even cracked. Everyone jumps back. 'Ya haven't killed no one, have ya? And... and we all like ya, mum. We don' give a frig about the bachelor stuff.'

Ruth, flustered and reddening, says, 'Thanks, Gordon. Thank you very much, mate. But just try to calm down, please, everyone. And mind the language.' She shuffles her white eyes across to each one of our faces like she needs to know we are actually there. 'Whatever you think, the fact is I have done wrong.' She looks up just above our heads. 'The goddamn truth is... I'm just as unqualified as any of you. Yep... and the truth is I had a drugs problem when I was young, like some of you, and so if you don't want to be here, if you don't trust me, if you think I'm no good, a liar, a thief, of no use, you're free to leave, as, of course, you've always been...' She stares, but into herself, piercing with a fork. 'What I mean is now you're free to say what you like about me, to anyone, to leave and complain to the authorities, and never come back again.'

Mel, an awkwardly long, thin girl with one eye that is smaller than the other, says, 'Naaa, Christ mum, we like it here. It wouldn't be the same without ya.'

'Yeah we... we... love ya... Ruth. We do, mum,' Dusty says.

Everyone looks at Dusty, knowing it is a hard word to say, because the truth is no one really loves Ruth. As if you could. She is too distant, too aloof, too... well, too well-spoken and knowledgeable with all her sayings on the walls and always being right about things. But the truth be known, like I think Dusty is saying, we have feelings for her, strong feelings, that are a kind of love, but in another way, like for just always being around, for always standing by us, good or bad, truth or lies. We even like her for not trying to stuff Jesus and things down our throats, like some do. And, yes, we love her for being consistent. She doesn't just suddenly shoot off her rag at you for no good reason. Like some others do.

'Yeah Ruth, we do love ya… like a real mum,' Mel spoons Dusty's words deeper into the house, and no one moves or so much as stirs or makes any motion to go anywhere.

A yellow colour is pumping into Ruth's face at a million kilometres per hour and the harsh lines in her face seem to fill and soften with an orange drizzle. It is moisture, I see, that is falling from the corners of her eyes. It shines in the shallow light of the room. Everyone stands around her now, amazed, feeling fuzzy. No one ever saw Ruth cry before. No one ever thought she had tears in her.

Between breaths that make her sound like an asthmatic like me, she says, 'Let's… let's all… just hold hands… and give thanks.'

And without thinking, even enthusiastically, we do that, making a huge circle in the lounge, and all the girls in the room, all four of them that are around, start to bawl and bawl and bawl some more through the whole, long five minutes or so of silence, at the beginning of which Ruth whispers: 'We stand together here, Lord, in this circle… in gratitude and with humility, begging forgiveness,' and only at the end, the very end of the five minutes or so, she says, 'Your will be done. Thanks, every one of you… each and every one of you for making this crooked little house look so straight. I am astonished at your love.' And then she squeezes the hands of those next to her and opens her eyes into a showery wetness.

The reality is that all of us here at Ruth's Place will leave, and new ones will come back if Ruth is able to open the house again. It suddenly runs through my head right now the words from that Robert Louis Stevenson poster… *and the best that we can find in our travels is an honest friend…* It seems to me, at this moment, I have many honest friends… Ruth mum, all the people in the house at this moment, and of course Gord and Dust. I feel very, very lucky. I feel like I want to be hugged. Like I want someone, lots of people, to hug. But of course, I don't. I know it'll be read the wrong way.

'We'll get ya at the bridge,' Gordon shouts as I make my way out of the house on my way to school.

And at the front door Ruth is standing there, I guess to make sure I go. 'What's the matter, Gray Morrow?' she says. 'What's so bad?'

And I whisper, looking down, 'No, nothing, Mum.'

'It's always better to tell the truth,' she says. 'Take it from me, Gray. It's too tricky, just too complicated explaining stories and reasons why when they are not true; it just brings trouble. I hope you know what I mean.'

I look into her white eyes, into the white halo of hair that tufts around her head and nod, thinking I do understand, but understanding it more from what her twisted body is conveying now in its doughy outpouring rather than from her words. I walk out the front door and in front of me it is one of those bright blue days that stick hard in the eyes. So bright that it canes. On the side of the sky, I see a wild forest of grey cloud gathering, knowing that slowly, mercifully, the blue will eventually be swallowed.

# 22.

SWEAT DRIPPING DOWN MY BACK LIKE THE SUN HAS IT IN FOR ME, instantly after school I head straight to the bridge and find Gordon and Dusty there, and one or two of the others. The rain that the sky promised in the morning seems to have vanished and the day is still caning hot. But I see no sign of Fat Deano or Kelly, thinking they must have taken Gord's warning seriously. That's something. And when I ask, Candy, depressed and bored looking, says they have left town, gone interstate, she thinks to Sydney. She has tried to call them on her mobile, but theirs is always switched off or out of range or something. Or lost. Little Danno, it seems, never went to school, already skateboarding up and down the cement walkway, singing hip-hop songs to himself, but all sound like nothing more than his usual squeal: 'Meeeee... Weeeee... Meeeeeee...' as his skateboard rattles along like a midget's boat on the cracked cement path.

We sit down on the embankment and eye the river, like it is something alive. Especially Gordon. I know he loves to watch the river flow, slowly, as it always does, carrying its mud downwards in an endless stream. But I know he likes to watch it too because it kind of, without his saying it, calms him, while his mind can fly and dream. Sometimes in that state it is hard to talk to him. It is like he is way stoned, right off his face. I don't mind, I like him like that. Just me, him and the muddy Ipswich river below. And now Dusty Jones sitting at his side. Between us.

'Do you believe in God?' he turns to her, just slightly. Ever watchful on the river.

She thinks for a bit, looking at him, and says, 'Naaa. He—or She –' she laughs at her own cleverness, 'never done nothing for me, mate. If there's a God He—or She –' she laughs again, 'sure don' think much'a me an me family.'

'You know God is here,' Gordon says, and she smiles, unsure, 'right here in the Bremer River.'

'Yer bullshitting me, Gord, tryin to make fun of me?' she says.

'No, I'm not. I'm serious. I mean it. God is down there, right there, in the Bremer.'

'C'mon, Gord. Be serious.'

'Yeah, he is.' Gordon looks at her and then directly down to the river. 'Serious, Dust. God *is* the river, anyways that's what I believe, the mud in the river, that red-brown colour. That's God. God is just the same as this river, all brown an muddy like. That's the God we see and know. But underneath, far down, on the other side like, that we don't see, at the bottom, it's clear, it's all light. It's like everything, you, me, Gray, everybody exists on the surface, but beneath it, below the surface, far below, it's light, everything shines, is see-through. We just can't see it like. It's like… the light that sometimes, ya know, on bright days, glistens on the river, above the mud. Only it's always there, underneath, below the surface.' She looks up at him, blinking, like he is shining silver foil in her eyes. 'Not everyone sees it,' he says. 'The light below…' He stops to ponder and then says, 'You know, I think Ruth… Ruth Hannah, mum, sometimes seen it though.' She looks up at him. 'I really do. You can just see she's been there, in the mud and slime an that, right there down at the very bottom of it… only she come right out again, all good and shiny like. That's why she knows, that's why she knows us. You can see it in her eyes. The way they look inside. Wattie… ya know, Cunstable Thornes, *thinks* he seen it. But he's still like us, no different, oinkin round in the thick of it. Much as he claims to know, he knows shit. I think, like us, really man, he's swimmin in it hey.'

'Gordon ya sound, I dunno… like a priest when ya talk like this,' Dusty smiles nervously, grabbing onto his arm, like she is grabbing onto gravity. 'Like ya seen a ghost or something. Ya scaring me, Gord. Have ya seen it—what ya talkin about?'

'I wish,' he breathes. 'I wish.' And then almost as though he is actually going to cry, he says, 'When I look at the river, Dust, that's what I see inside of me, that's all I see: mustard-brown mud. One day when we have a place of our own like, out in the country, the mud will clear.'

'I dunno how to say this...' she says, '...but you know I sometimes write poetry?' She whispers it like a confession to a high priest. 'D'ya wanna see one?'

'Yeah, 'course Dust,' he says, eyes half-spinning, distant.

'Ya only saying that,' she says. ''Cause it's me.'

'I'm not. I'm serious,' he smiles.

'You see, you're smiling already. Ya havin' me on.'

'OK, please your fucking self then,' he says.

She turns to me.

'D'ya wanna see me poem, Gray?'

'Yeah, yeah, of course!' I say. I'm over the moon enthusiastic that Dusty is even asking me. That someone like Dusty is even interested in writing anything. For a moment I breathe in, withdraw, nervous in front of Gordon that I have reacted to Dusty so enthusiastically, like I am some kind of computer nerd that you see on TV, like you see one or two of, even at my school.

'You see, Gord, Gray's serious. That's what I call serious. Really meaning it. You're just kiddin, Gord, that's all.'

I feel my face bloat in a ball of red, wondering how Gordon will react. Will he punch me? Both of us?

'Whatever,' he says, then as though relenting '...But I do, Dust, of course I wanna see your bloomin poem. What d'ya think I am, just a pretty face?'

They laugh and she fishes around in a shoulder bag that she has next to her, taking a long time, like it must have drawers and shelves and different layers or something in it. Finally she pulls out from one of those drawers or layers, a very neatly folded piece of A4 paper. There are words scrawled all over it in blue ink, and she hands it to me to read — first.

Shyly, I look at Gord, I guess sort of asking permission if it is alright that I see it first, but he just looks away, into the river, fishing, still fishing in there, and I begin to read the scrawl silently to myself.

**Making it on the Streets**
*by Dusty Jones*
Does anyone really care
About all us kids stuck out here

> Our parents say they care but throw us out
> Thinking, no doubt, we can survive on our own two feet
> We're only living people too
> We all have problems we need to work thru
> How d'you xpect us to keep outta strife
> When we wanderin the streets on cold lonely nights
> And to protect ourselves we have to fight
> We walk the streets and vandalize
> Everything that stands before our eyes
> We stand an yell at people too
> Cause we alone and have nothing to do
> People think we bad kids
> And never realise until a car hits the skids
> Theres a kid under there thats dead.

'Wow,' I say, shocked, thinking, Brilliant! And hand the poem to Gordon.

He reads it slowly. As though chewing over each word, as though looking below river surfaces, and then says: 'Fuck me! Yeah, fucking yeah! Good one, Dust. It's like the bloody Bremer. Just what I'm saying. No one realises. About anything. It's all bullshit on the surface. You should write books, ya know. You could be famous some day. But then you'll probably just drop us like wet turds.'

She punches him on the arm. 'Shit, Gord, you have to spoil everything, don'ya? Of course you know I wouldn't.'

She looks crimson, even the freckles on her face are deep electric pink, and her usually white, drawn cheeks are bright rosy. But at the same time she also sits straight up, proud, her little blue eyes drawing a line from her petite, upturned nose directly up to the thin sheet of turquoise sky above.

She folds the poem neatly and puts it away in one of those drawers in her bag.

'Dinkum good,' I say again. 'I mean it, Dust, bloody good one.'

I see her beam a million kilometres back into that bright turquoise sky, and her face looks so shiny. I feel too shy to tell her about my own journals, thinking that maybe one day I will show them to her. Yes, maybe one day.

And then one of the younger kids we haven't seen in a long time, Shooter, comes running down the embankment, almost falling over his own two feet. He is out of breath, saying to Gordon and me, his eyes sort of avoiding Dusty, 'Look what I got dudes. Look what I got, homies.' He drags out from his dirty linen shirt pocket a small roll of fifty-dollar notes. 'Five hundred fucking bucks, man,' he says. 'Five hundred crisp ones.'

We look at him, and then talking fast as spit, maybe faster, which is exactly where his nickname comes from—Shooter—he proceeds to tell us how he came by the layers of money.

'I rolled this guy, hey,' he sputters without breathing. 'Me, all by m'self like, dudes. Like there I am out of money and smokes by meself hey an I see this ol' dude taking bread from a ATM like. He's the only one there and there's no one in the street like, so I sorta walk up to him hey, like I'm gonna make me own withdrawal and I watch him puttin in his pin an password hey, an after he takes out his twenty dollars or whatever, I follow him for a few steps an then like just push him to the ground like, ya know, an then kick him in the face an punch him good a coupla times just to make sure he don't scream out like, and then I grab his card like an run away like fuck. Soon as I get to the centre of town I hit the first ATM I see an draw out this bread, man. Just look dudes! Isn'it like fuck, hey?'

'Here,' Gordon says calmly, like he doesn't believe Shooter, that the money is real. 'Let me count it for meself.'

Shooter hands over his crisp new notes and Gordon counts them like a gangster rather than a bank teller, flicking them one by one, from the one hand to the other.

'Yeah, you actually right mate,' he says to Shooter. 'Five hundred smackeroos,' and then peels off two fifties and puts them in his shirt pocket, and says, 'But now it's only four hundred.' He winks at Dusty and me.

Shooter's face falls, sort of like a passion fruit with the fruit squeezing out of a hole at the bottom of it, like he has just learnt something never to do again, trust anyone. Definitely not stronger dudes, like Gordon.

'I was gonna give ya guys some anyways,' Shooter says, still thunderstruck.

And Gordon says, 'Now just keep the fuck away from us, mate, we're in enough shit as it is.'

And Shooter starts to persist, like he wants or needs our friendship despite everything.

'Will you get us some grog then Gord, dude,' he finally says as a way in. 'They know me man, an they won't let me into any of the bottl-o's round here.'

Gordon looks at Dusty, and then says, 'OK mate, so long as you gonna share?'

'Of course, man. Of course, dude,' he says.

Gordon turns away from Shooter, back to the river and stares into it, while Shooter continues to stare at him, hopeful. Gordon finally shrugs his shoulders but says nothing more, his body receding into the embankment. It is like Shooter's intrusion is a mere fly on the back of the neck, a momentary irritation, and Gordon is still too intensely trying to clear out the mustard-brown mud from the river and come up with a way through.

Gordon never does get that kid, Shooter, his grog, and we leave the bridge just before dark, Shooter still hanging around us like a fly. Just as we leave, we see some of the older lads arriving and know they will gladly help out, make sure Shooter works through his now four hundred crisp ones as quickly as possible.

# 23.

IT IS DINKUM LIKE THE LAST SUPPER—that Jesus thing at the big table—when we arrive back at Ruth's Place. Yep, all sweaty-hot and uncertain, we dive through the door just in time to help with the final setting of Ruth's table for dinner. Ruth looks utterly deflated, like one of those white cotton pod plant things when they have been stamped on, her bottom jaw, usually quite square, set in a droop like it has suddenly been squeezed flat and long by the thick, wooden air. Everyone else, though, is in high spirits doing what they can to assure her everything is OK, telling her for the umpteenth time that after all, like, it is in their eyes that it all really counts, not the cops' or the stupid city council's or the even denser state government's, or the even thicker still universities'—who can all go to hell, and stuff it up themselves.

'Instead of accusing ya, mum, they should come an seen what ya done,' one of the girls calls out.

'Thanks, my little courageous angel,' Ruth says. 'I'm afraid it's all in God's hands now. We'll see.'

Dusty suddenly mashes frenetically around in her shoulder bag, like she has lost something extraordinary that might help turn everyone's life around. Her hands eventually come out of the bag unfolding a piece of paper. Guess what? It's another poem.

'I wrote this for ya, mum, today,' she says proudly. 'Shall I read it, hey?'

Everyone is staring at Dusty before she has even begun the first line, like she has discovered gold, amazed that anyone can actually write something of their own—and then read it out aloud. And it's not even in school, where you're forced to do these things. What's more, unlike under the bridge, showing Gordon and me her poetry for the first time, Dusty looks confident-rosy, straight-off proud as a girl on her wedding day.

Ruth nods enthusiastically. 'Of course, angel. Of course, sweetheart. Read it.'

The fluorescent light above her in the dining room, where all this is going on, is gleaming above Dusty's eyes, sort of glowing bashfully around her face. Gordon is sitting on a seat next to her side, legs spread apart like a drummer in a band, smiling, also proud, like he doesn't normally show himself to be.

'It's called "Our Way",' Dusty breathes, and then sneaking a quick, coy look at Gordon, begins to read — slowly — pronouncing each word like a teacher to her pupils, only with a lot more stumbling and faltering, like she can't read her own writing properly, with lots of 'ums', and lots of apologies like 'er, um, woops sorry.' Her chest is blown out like a little girl's at a school concert as she reads:

> ...If we not on our own... think...ing ...what's — what's —
> in't for us out there
> Or why... should... we... — 'um' — why should we... bother
> if no one... cares
> We're walkin the streets break... break'n into shops
> Or get... gettin into trouble with all of the cops.
> All we want is for peop... for peop — 'er, um, woops
> sorry' — people to... realise
> That there's... some... something... on the... inside
> Call it what ya like... but we call it... Pride
> They just see the rough... — 'um... er, woops sorry' —
> rough... ness on the outside,
> An they always tak... — 'um... woops sorry' — takin us for a
> ride.
> On the surface all... all... all ya see is a... mouth,
> Loud an blar...in' ...screamin... an swearin
> If ya look on the inside — like our mum... like our mum
> Ruth does,
> Y'd see that we... 'um... woops, sorry' — we're... we're
> really quite carin
> And some... and sometimes wish people would care... for
> us, too

For this... for this... whole world is so short of love
That the one with the most... the most—'um, er'—...the
one with the most... is the one... the one... we know the least
The one... up above.

Dusty folds the paper to signal the end, and they're all suddenly looking at her like she is a silver-shiny celebrity on a TV show or something. Her eyes are floating like she is on a stage and a warm pinkness invades my eyes and I feel like crying. Even Gordon puts out a hand to Dusty in front of everyone and squeezes her forearm. It is like Dusty has been invited to be in a film or something. Like she is wearing a real gold crown with great big shining diamonds in it. Her hair is not dull any longer, it is glowing. Even the spiky top is like shards of gold. We all look up at her and then clap like she is our queen. Dusty, our Poet Queen.

'You'll be right, mum. Don't worry,' Dusty strides up and hugs Ruth. It is a Royal gesture that is followed by all the girls. All of them crying now.

Ruth sits and smiles at the head of the table, a little white halo of her own around her yellowing teeth, as though, no matter what, she is still the State's Woman of the Year. And Dusty looks on proudly wearing her crown.

After dinner we sit in the small back garden, everyone smoking cigarettes and puffing away like they are creating a huge barbecue or something; I am the only one reaching for my puffer instead. Wild-eyed, Gordon inhales hot, burning smoke deep into his jowls like he is swallowing some of the cool, black night sky into a cave in his mouth, which will eventually explode. Instead of explosion he breathes out a cool, upwards bound stalagmite of solid white smoke and shakes his head of woolly hair. Next he considers his dry knuckles, then looks over to Dusty standing smoking next to him with a hand tucked into her hip, and through all this sees me with my puffer, and says: 'Shit, dudes! Shit. We have to get out of town. Fast. We have to get out. Make plans. Maybe...' he scratches deep into his thick curly hair, 'maybe even head out after Fat Deano an Kelly in Sydney like? But just... just whatever we do, we gotta get the frig outta here.'

His words are like sunlight on a cold day shooting through my body. I am mercurially, unbelievably, head-over-heels happy we are planning again—and school will definitely be off the cards. Way t'go!

Dusty just says: 'Up to you, mate. I'm with ya — whatever.'

I nod vigorously, like a co-conspirator. I'm not sure either of them even notices my nod, let alone my enthusiasm.

In the end, letting out an involuntary smoke ring, Gordon announces: 'Tomorrow — at the Moon — we'll talk it through.'

Dusty puts her thin arm through his thick one and holds onto him just like you see normal couples do, sitting on park benches, walking in the streets, sitting on busses, boyfriends and girlfriends, husbands and wives, mums and dads. It is beginning to suit them, I think. Makes something in me spin and I feel dizzy. You'd think contentment means calm, still. It doesn't, I see now, it means dizzy.

Next morning, at breakfast, Ruth makes us link our hands around the table — another last — The Last Breakfast or something — and again loudly thanks God for everything we have enjoyed together and for blessing Ruth's Place. Then she says, like a sermon, a real sermon: 'There is no God other than belief and faith; that's where you will find God, in belief and faith.' The thought spins across my mind, and I open my eyes quickly to see most of them, specially the girls, squeezing their eyes so tight — like they are trying to capture this belief and faith. And then everyone is as usual at breakfast time, running around fending for themselves, pushing and shoving and cursing one another, especially those of us who have to get to school. I pretend to be in a big hurry, like I am going to school, knowing I am going with Gordon and Dusty to the Moon — to plan the rest of our lives. Faith doesn't figure at all. Only us and the future.

# 24.

WE FIND MUM AT HOME, ALL BY HERSELF. Thank God.

She lets us in, saying as she often does: 'Well-well. Look what the kitty-cat's dragged in.'

She is her usual self, looking yellow-eyed, dressed in old jeans and a white t-shirt that clings to her body like a vest, and very sarcastic. It is obvious she's been drinking all night. It smells heavily like it. Compared with Ruth's Place, like a pub at closing time in need of a hosing down. Two ashtrays on the floor are filled with butts and mounds of rough grey ash. The ashtrays look like mini garbage tips, still smouldering. She sits on the couch, above the ashtrays, dragging in smoke like she needs the shock of nicotine at the back of her throat to convince her she's still breathing.

'So where's Mick?' Gordon asks.

'Where you should be—work,' she says. 'An what about this one?' she says turning to Dusty. 'When are you gonna find ya dollar's worth? Or ya just gonna hang around this place like a hungry table cloth?'

Dusty opens her mouth, I'm not sure to say what, probably something like, 'If ya don't want me here...'

But Gordon butts in, and says, 'Hey Mum, that's unfair, Dusty's got just as much right to be here as Mick.'

'Like living Christ she has!' Mum says, curling her lip. 'Anyways, ya room's been taken up fer now. Mick's got a coupla rellies down from Mt Isa, and they stayin in there. So, there's not much space.'

'Thanks Mum, thanks a fucking lot,' Gordon shows his teeth, gritting them, like if she were a piece of food he would smash her in two.

She looks up at Gordon from funnels of smoke pouring like straws through her nose and mouth at the same time. And then softens.

'It's not my fault, Gord. You boys are never home like, an I can't keep saying to Mick, that's me boys' room, hey. I'm sorry.'

Gordon looks down and she looks at me.

'Come here, ya little devil,' she says with some new found zest.

I walk over to her and she grabs me by the hand.

'I just wanna hug ya, ya know, like when you was little. Gordon's too big, I know he won't let me now. Not in front of his girlfriend, at any rate?'

Gordon just looks up, clicking his tongue at the paint-flaked ceiling. She pulls me onto her lap like I am a carpet or something, and as I fall forward I look at Dusty, reddening. Mum hugs me, awkwardly, as I half kneel, half bend over the couch into the force of her pull. I am surprised to see tears in her eyes. It makes me feel embarrassed. But briefly, just briefly, for a moment I don't mind; I feel my flesh turn liquid, like someone has run a match over it; it has been a long time since Mum has cuddled me like this, so that I get the hot and cold shivers. I look around and see Dusty looking soft-eyed, sitting down on a chair like she has just walked into a moment in a movie when no one knows what's going on because they have not seen the beginning, but anyway fall all warm and silent into the moment because the music and the atmosphere are so overwhelmingly thick.

And then Mum, eyes swelling, says seriously, 'Get your blimmin self off to school, mate, before I start howlin.' She gives me a slight shove.

My stomach hollows like a tennis ball and I just look at her.

'Well ya going, aren't ya?'

'Yeah, of course I am, Mum,' I say, looking directly into her dented, panel beaten nose. 'Just Gordon said he'll give me a lift on the bike like, so I don't need to hurry much.'

She looks over to Gordon, as though to test my story. And Gordon does something I would only expect a dad to do, or maybe even a child in the movies; he walks up to Mum on the couch and

160

squeezes her, real hard. Then, as he lets go of her, she hits him over the shoulder with a happy flat hand like slap-happy sports people do to one another after a game.

'There'll be a bed fer yers whatever happens when ya get back, I promise,' she says.

'It's not serious, Mum, I just want a change of clothes like,' Gordon says like it is nothing, like he suddenly doesn't really mind either way. He flicks his head and Dusty follows him into the bedroom. I follow them like a magnet.

We feel like strangers in our own bedroom, seeing beds unmade, old clothes, not ours, lying all over the beds and the floor.

'Fuck,' Gordon says. 'Fuck.' And begins to get new clothes out of the cupboard while Dusty sits on Gordon's unmade bed and reads aloud the half-ripped poster on his wall, trying to cipher it.

'I guess that's all of us,' Dusty says, 'Puzzled as ever?'

'Yeah, whatever,' Gordon says. 'Let's just get the shit outta here.' And I see him take his ochre Mt Moon rock out of his old brown pants pocket, where it has obviously been for a while now, and transfer it angrily into the new baggy black pants he puts on. He doesn't even look at it; he is too angry.

And then I just say, I suppose more to Dusty than to Gordon, 'Yeah, nothing's ever bloody clear, is it? Always turns out like shit.'

Gordon turns to us then, and like a general or something says, 'No longer, mate. No longer. I promise, no more. If there's one thing we gonna do, it's find a way through.'

I love it when Gordon talks like this. It gives me so much faith. I feel tall.

And then we are standing in the lounge, ready to go, and Mum says to me, 'Where's your school bag, mate?'

'I… I…' I nearly lose my breath and then force myself to look her straight in the eye, 'I left it in school, Mum.'

'Well, I hope ya haven't lost it?'

'Naaa, 'course not, Mum. What d'you take me for?' My eyes go down a little, staring into her hammered nose.

'OK, get on then, the lotta yers.' She pushes herself up off the couch like she has just risen from a week in bed, and pecks me on the cheek, almost falling over. But it is like a real mum, a real mum sending her boy off to school, like you see in some of those ads on TV. Only I don't have the rosy red apple.

'Remember what I always say to ya, Gray, ya mustn't just follow yer big brother here, act on ya own, mate, stand on ya own two feet.'

My face is swelling balloon-shaped with redness now, and Dusty, I'm sure, seeing this as an opportunity to crack the ice with Mum, says, 'Gray's a very clever lad, ya know, Mrs Morrow, very clever an mature.'

Mum eyeballs her like she has sworn. And we leave.

# 25.

ON THAT NOISY BIKE AGAIN, this time we stop on the way — Gordon suddenly being practical, just like a dad — to buy some sandwiches and crisps and a big Coke, which we stuff into Dusty's shoulder bag. Only after we buy the stuff at the garage in Boonah, I am told I have to wear the shoulder bag; it is heavy and uncomfortable. I wonder what the hell Dusty keeps in it. Real rows of tight-packed drawers and shelves and things? Packed with poems?

At Mt Moon we do what we normally do. After dumping the bike, we duck into the nearest bush, and as soon as we are out of sight of the road we choose a cushiony spot and laze around, and sleep.

Today it does not take long before Gordon and Dusty announce they are going for a walk, and I should stay with the lunch in case ants or rabbits or worse still, rock wallabies come along and try to steal it. I know what that means.

They don't even bother to go that far and I hear them giggling like small children rolling or tickling one another in the long grass; and then everything goes eerily silent, followed by a bit of laughter, silence again, and then there is a sharp shriek. Strange? I perk my head up, but can't see them, and just sit down again. Hoping they aren't having a row and Gordon hasn't slapped her or something. Then I hear giggles again and that makes me feel better, followed by a strong half shriek, just like in scary movies, which makes me worried again, and then I hear Dusty's voice, singing: 'Take me! Oh shit, oh shit, fucking take me!' I shudder and feel excited for a moment, hearing that yearning voice, wishing one day someone will shriek for me like that. A few moments later there is a loud whooshing sound like air being punctured out of a tyre, followed by very loud giggling and laughter again. Seconds later, after a brief silence, a kind of wolf noise pierces the mountain — 'Aaaaaiiiwooooo… Aaaaaiiiwoooooo!' which I know is Gordon, baying like a mad wolf; I guess telling the world how proud he is.

Pink and puffed in the face, they straggle back from where they were, and although it is nowhere near lunchtime yet, Gordon rips open the family size pack of chips and he and Dusty graze on them like they haven't eaten in a hundred years. I have a few, when I manage to get my hands in the packet. When the packet is finished, Gordon covers his mouth with it, taps the bloated bag and makes sure that every last crumb lands directly on his straining tongue. And then they open the family size Coke and nearly finish it completely before they even offer me a sip. I have the last few sips, thinking of leaving a sip for the sandwiches that are still to be eaten, but then see Gordon eyeing the bottle and just drink it down. They are like two little kids, and watching them something in me pops open. It is like a shaken Coke, gushing and fizzing. I am floating. Just happy to be around them.

Gord and Dusty take out their stones, Gordon's ochre stone and Dusty's charcoal one. They examine them against the sun, like they are part of a jigsaw they are starting to put together. And just as I think that, Dusty says: 'And with this rock I thee do wed.'

I nearly fall over.

Dusty says, 'Make a wish.'

I close my eyes and wish that this circle, this triangle, this line of ship's rope between the three of us will never be broken. I open them to see Dusty was not talking to me, but to Gordon. And see them both with their eyes still closed, facing the sky, like their wish is not for one thing but for a whole list. For hundreds of things. When finally they open their eyes Gordon jumps on Dusty and pins her to the ground, digging his knees into her biceps so that I can see it hurts. Then he prods her in the chest and ribs with his tough, stubby fingers, so that she is wriggling in giggly laughter and pain at the same time. She is screaming for Gordon to get off and for me to help. Dusty's eyes nudge me, and seeing Gordon is enjoying his superior strength and has no intention of stopping, I take a deep breath and dive in, smacking Gordon right off her. As

I have him on the ground under me she joins me. We both struggle to keep him down, poking him in the chest and ribs while we can, just as he had done to Dusty. I see him squeezing his crooked teeth together, doing his best to show us that we cannot make him laugh, that nothing we can do will make him bend to anything. And when he has had enough, looks like he is actually about to burst out in pained laughter, he tenses his face like a wrestler, grits his teeth like a footballer, the brown stains at the bottom of them biting together, and with one heave like a weightlifter throws us off him like we are mere butterflies, and we go flying in opposite directions. After that he just lies there, on the grass, sort of like Sampson, with satisfaction, like he has just conquered the world. Dusty creeps up to him like a little animal and cuddles into his armpit.

Feeling left out but determined, on all fours I crawl up to them and snuggle in behind Dusty, as I love to do on the bike. She takes my arm and pulls it over her waist, so that it is over her and partly touching Gordon. He doesn't mind. And I think of our dad and how we sometimes even did something like this at home. With him and Mum. All of us on a big bed, laughing, like their bed was a sun-warmed trampoline and the day would stretch forever. But even when we were up here with him, we never lay like this. Mt Moon was our secret. But there was nothing in between. Just a kind of hollow wind blowing around us. Now I breathe in the eucalypt smell around us; it is so chewably sweet, I feel I can touch it.

We sleep and wake hungry and ravage the sandwiches. Gordon and Dusty curse that we never left any Coke or crisps. I look at Gordon and Dusty with a face that says: 'I know.' She pokes a thin, pink tongue at me; I look down a little apologetic, and then she throws out all the rubbish into the bush around us.

'Don't! Don't!' Gordon says. 'This isn't the Bremer, or the bridge, ya know. We may need this place one day. This is our place.'

He picks up the garbage and shoves it in Dusty's bag. Red in the face, she pushes it further down, like it landed in the wrong drawer. We sit there for a while, sniffing in the day, rocking on our backsides, talking about nothing in particular, and then stroll down the hill to the bike, having planned nothing.

# 26.

HEADS FULL OF COLD MT MOON AIR AND BIKE FUMES, instead of returning home we head straight for the bridge where it is party time — on Shooter's stolen bucks. There must be a dozen or more people hanging out, many of the usuals like Candy and Little Danno, but some fairly new faces, too. A couple of the younger kids, about fourteen or fifteen, are climbing the steel framework on the underside of the bridge, stoned out of their brains. They are like monkeys, stealing from one steel step to the next, from one steel girder to the other, in their pockets the bulge of spray paint, so that when they are at the point of their endurance, they can mark their claim to having made it. To having been around on this planet and put their tag on the heavy cement underbridge that will mark them for posterity like one of those war memorials.

Down at the bottom of the embankment, near the walkway, some of the kids are listening to a ghetto blaster, some just nodding their heads smoking cigarettes and singing under their breath. A couple, like Candy and a new girlfriend are dancing together, while a couple of the lads emulate rap stars they've seen in music clips, twisting and turning and rolling on the cement over their shoulders and spinning on the tops of their backs, mainly unsuccessfully, laughing and then starting all over again. One of the fellers is even doing it with a cigarette in his mouth. And Little Danno, as usual, is skateboarding up and down the walkway, only now with a can of beer in his hand, taking sips as he pushes himself along, bopping up and down like a cripple, sort of like me, drunkenly screaming out his anthem: 'IIIIII… meeeee… weeeeeee…'

Shooter is no longer angry with Gordon, and almost as we arrive he slaps Gordon's hand like they are old friends, and takes a beer out of a carton and foists it on him.

'Hey bro, what about Gray an Dusty here?' Gordon says.

And Shooter dips straight down again, coming up with a bottle for each of us. He points to a bottle of rum, hidden under a small backpack. 'Go fer it, homies,' he sings.

We have our beer and then another, drinking quickly. Gordon retrieves the bottle of rum, takes his usual, fish-like gulps, and then passes the bottle around. We are soon joined by others and a fresh bong that is swirling through the night like a newly ignited glow worm. Gordon's eyes look greedy, they are like vacuum cleaners, nothing getting passed them, and his mouth is taking the most of whatever comes his way. There is a look on his face like it is the last night on earth. Even the red worms are trying to escape out of his eyes. Soon he is laughing his head off and shouting wildly, toking on a long joint.

Candy and her friend are really gyrating their bodies now, looking in our direction, and showing their stuff like they are professional pole dancers or something, but, of course, without the poles. Candy's friend leans over and puts her head down between her legs, her shirt lifting over braless breasts and over her head. She pulls her shirt down a little and stares at us for a while, swinging her backside as she gawks at us upside down.

'Hey, Gray, keep your eyes on that little one. I think ya could score tonight,' Gordon says. Obviously joking.

I know the girls are eyeing Gordon, wondering what Dusty, the new chick, is forever doing at his side these days.

'Fuck, these Ipswich chicks are weird,' Dusty says.

And Gordon says, 'Yeah kinda, I guess, just like everywhere else.'

Gordon starts to roam, stopping to talk to everyone, and Dusty is left sitting beside me, which is really beside me and Shooter, who has suddenly appeared at our side like a lost child, but cackling like an old woman at everything, and getting close in on Dusty, probably thinking without Gordon around he has a chance with her.

But Dusty just sits there, taking no notice of him, staring outwards, over to the river, saying, 'Ya know, Gray, I think I prefer the river at night, with the little bits of light from the streetlights shining down on it like. It's kinda golden in places, not all brown an muddy like in the day.'

I gaze out with her, nodding, but not saying anything, Shooter just cackles on at whatever Dusty says. Until finally she says to me, 'Why don't ya just tell this little weirdo kid to piss off hey, Gray?'

I look at her. Trying with my eyes to tell her I am not Gordon. It isn't what I do. Tell people to piss off — even if I think it a lot. With my weak leg and asthma I never trust my strength enough to confront anyone. Not even Mum, really. Just standing my ground, keeping my eyes dead straight with the school principal is a big deal for me. I breathe in, hoping she isn't seeing how I have to pluck corners in my mind I haven't found yet, to garner the strength in me to face Shooter. But I do, somehow in front of Dusty I do, and I blurt into his face, 'Hey dude, why don't ya just the fuck piss off!'

And the most amazing thing is he doesn't even look me back in the eyes, just sort of shakes his head, looking away to the river, and says, 'OK mate, take it easy, homie bro,' and stumbles off.

Dusty ruffles her fingers through my hair and I feel that liquid warmth run through my flesh that gives me the hot and cold shivers that I love. I feel like Superman.

Down at the bottom of the embankment, against the backdrop of that river dappled in golden tinsel, Gordon is dancing with Candy and that other girl now, touching them all over. And letting them touch him. Pulling them towards him and thrusting them away. Like it is a dirty dance game. Then, sweating excitement, as Little Danno comes skating by, he summarily pushes him off his board so that Little Danno falls over and spills his beer, and then Gordon yells out at the top of his voice for Dusty to watch him. As she turns to him, he pushes himself off on the skateboard, glides along like a smooth tightrope walker for a few metres, comes to an abrupt halt and then jumps on the back of the board to flip it up into his hand. Only he is obviously so drunk and stoned that the skateboard hits him in the knee and he falls over on his back, his bushy hair like wild ostrich feathers around his head. Everyone laughs, including Dusty. But he just gets up and tries the routine again — and again, until he finally gets it right. Then he does a bow, gracefully — for Dusty — and carries on dancing and playing his game with the girls.

Some of the kids have some pills which they are openly popping, and which also make their way down to Gordon and his dirty dance partners. A little later I even hear there is some coke going around, and I see Gordon leaning over a piece of silver paper sniffing — though the chances are it's probably just powdered mandrax or Panadeine Forte or something like that mixed with Johnson's baby powder. As Gordon sniffs he bursts out coughing and grabs for a bottle of whatever is near him. He guzzles on it with that greedy hunger, like it is the last night on this planet.

Every now and then everyone looks up to see what the taggers have achieved, and the more stoned you are the more amazing and cool and 'wow' it is. They are like Michelangelo up there. Or Muhammad Ali. Or General Paton. If only the world could just cement itself in this state. I tried to get up there once. About half way up Gordon had to bring me down.

I bounce my eyes, tennis ball like, between Dusty and the faintly sparkling water, where her eyes are set solid, as though stoned out of her tree. She doesn't look that good. Her face is always white and freckled but now it is yellow, and her freckles are white. Her cheeks look like they are sinking into her tongue. With each toke, with each sip of alcohol she only looks worse. More yellow. After a while I just have to admit something is wrong. She looks worse even than that first night when we met her at Ruth's Place, when she was coming down from being smashed off her face and was totally disoriented and lost.

When I ask her what she thinks now of the crowd at the bridge, the Ipswich homies, she just says, 'Weird man. Crazy. Same old crap.'

And when I ask her what she is thinking, she stops and flicks her flowing hair out of her eyes, rolls a handful of fingers through one side of it, and says, 'When you're in it, mate, you're in it good. Makes no fucking difference where you are, what ya think.'

'What d'you mean?' I ask.

And she just says, 'Maybe Gordon's right, mate? It's all just crap on the surface, sparkles and mud. It's below the water where ya have to look. Where ya have to go to find it. Where it's real like.'

I ask if she's feeling alright, and she says, 'I feel like shit.'

She puts a hand on my shoulder and tells me to hold her. It is something I want to do more than anything else, but always feel

170

embarrassed in front of Gordon. He is off with the fairies right now, down by the river, still dancing with Candy and her friend. I put my arm around Dusty and feel on top of the world.

'I think I'm gonna hurl,' she says.

Like I am not there, she signals to Gordon who is still fooling around on the walkway. Eventually she starts shouting out for him, and finally one of the girls punches Gordon on the shoulder to bring his drunken attention to it. As soon as he sees Dusty signalling, he hugs Candy's friend and then runs up the embankment. My hand is still around Dusty's shoulders; it feels completely limp and cold as soon as Gordon arrives.

'I feel like crap, I wanna go,' she says.

'Just stay, things're good here. Lots t' drink an smoke an things,' he says. 'We can't piss off now. Have a sleep, you'll feel right again in a while.'

'It's women's stuff,' she says. 'I really need a place, Gord, where there's a proper toilet an bathroom like…'

'Ah fuck, ya wuss,' he says.

But then he looks at her again, like he is actually focussing on her for the first time, and she stares back at him in that way that I have sometimes seen Mum do, that tells you not to argue. Even if she may be wrong.

'Suit ya self,' he says and falls slightly to the side. 'I'm stayin, chick… I'm stayin. Where ya gonna go, anyhows?'

'Ruth's Place.'

'Like ya are now? She'll chuck ya the hell out.'

'I'll straighten out, like. She won't notice by the time we get back.'

'OK, whatever,' he says, looking a little sullen, angry, like he is losing his grip on her; like that's the only reason she is sick, I see his stoned mind ticking, so she can reject him. I see those red worms drunkenly spiralling in his eyes.

He looks down at me, my arm still around Dusty's shoulders. I am sweating now, my armpits hot and gluey.

'An what's this, hey?'

'I, I…' I start to say, wanting to convince him how even I have noticed how sick she looks, but nothing will come out fast enough.

'You just wanna piss off — with him!' he says, and all over his face I can see a mask that pumps paranoia, but I can't get myself to say anything.

And she says for me, 'Shit, Gord man. I'm sick, I'm really dizzy like an sick all over.'

'OK, well then piss off,' he says. 'Do what yers like!'

'Fuck, Gordon, ya don't have to get weird on me, man. I'm telling ya, I'm sick, mate.'

'OK whatever. Suit ya self,' he says again, like his mind is made up. Convinced he is being left altogether.

'OK then, I'm goin,' she says. 'Maybe I'll see ya later? Or tomorrow hey?'

I remove my hand from her shoulders, and before I can even stop myself, I say, 'Hey, I'll come with ya.'

Gordon's face changes colour, even in the semi-darkness you can see it turning blue, red-grey worms glowering in his eyes.

'That's it. Thaaat's fucking it!' he shouts. 'You prefer him, don't ya? You just wanna fuck with someone you can control. With nice little ol' Gray here. Don't ya? Don't ya?'

She shakes her head, flicks the hair from her face, looks up. 'Shit man, I don't believe this. I don't believe this man.' She looks like she might hurl over him, and the twisted worms strung through Gordon's eyes say she is sick of him.

'Fuck ya!' he says, 'Fuck ya then! Fuck ya good!'

Her eyes trickle downwards, down to her jaw.

Gordon turns to me. 'Ya wanna screw her, mate, don't ya? Ya just wanna get into her little panties like ya been tryin all along? Ya think I don't know? Ya think I haven't seen? Ya think I don't bleedin know what's in ya little crippled head? OK, well then yers can both bloody fuckin fuck off then! Just get the fuck outta here! I don't wanna see yers again. Neither of yers. Little fucks! The pair'a ya!'

Her pink eyes trickle further down, like vapour, below her jaw, onto her chest.

And I say, trying to look Gordon in the eyes, 'No Gord... please...' without being able to finish, seeing that wild paranoia ringing in his eyes like it does not belong to him, is someone else's that he can't get rid of.

Dusty tries, too, 'Please... Gord, for Chri...'

'Just piss off! Just piss the fuck off, will ya!' He spits. 'Go fuck ya selves! Cunts! The two of ya. Go fuck ya selves dead! I never wanted ya anyways... Dusty... Bones! Go fuck ya self with me crippled little fuck up brother! Go fuck ya brains out together.

Cause ya ain't got any anyways!'

I turn to Dusty and see that old syrup swelling in her eyes. I want to hold her but know I cannot while he is around. Not while he is in this state. He is out of his tree. Completely off his face. I haven't seen him like this in years. He'd kick my head off if I put my arms around her again. And I blame Mick and Mum and Dad and everyone who has ever passed through our house and our lives for his state.

For a moment Gordon's eyes waver, emptily, and he falls over. But instead of getting up, he just lets himself roll, without trying to stop himself, in fact pushing himself on, until he is at the bottom of the embankment again, where he picks himself up, walks around groggily for a minute and then grabs hold of Candy's friend's hand and carries on like he was before. Like a crazy man, spinning around and dancing his head off. And screaming and shouting.

Dusty gets up by leaning on my shoulder.

Her hand feels so small and soft and something breathes out of me, 'I'll take care of you, Dust. I'll take you wherever you want. I'll look after ya.' I don't know where the courage is coming from to say these things, but it slides like a sand-warm liquid up from my gullet.

'Thanks, Gray. Thanks, mate. God will be good to ya one day,' she says.

I swallow like there is steel caught in my throat.

She grabs her shoulder bag off the cold, damp ground like it is all she has, and doesn't even like that.

As we walk off, she says, 'What's happening to him, Gray? I never thought I'd ever see your brother like this. He's gone bloody weird. I just wanna get outta here. I just wanna get outta this bloody life.'

# 27.

TOWN AS USUAL ON A WEEKNIGHT IS DEAD at this time of night. A ghost town of derelicts and drunks and bums and the odd smart suit returning from an important meeting, usually aimed at reviving the town. But if anything we want to avoid people, keep away from smiling eyes, any eyes, so as far as possible we walk up side streets, out of the shine of streetlights. Dusty's eyes are glazed with tears. Her face is so white it is like her freckles have been bleached into her cheeks.

'Hold my hand, Gray,' she says. 'I think I'm gonna be sick.'

But she walks on, steely as ever. Like those eyes are leading us somewhere.

I enjoy holding her hand, even though it is hot and sweaty, glad to be the one at her side. It is like there is some hidden thought in her palm. Like she needs a kind of warmth to fill it and I am glad to think I am the one giving it to her. It is a cool night and there is a slight breeze, the temperature suddenly dipping like a desert, leaving you suddenly wondering why you still have a singlet on at this time of night, like Dusty has. I have a short-sleeve shirt on, too, but the sleeves are longer, down to my elbows. Dusty is cold but her palm warms me, makes me feel brave against the cold, brave against everyone.

We round the corner at the back of the pub at the top of Brisbane Street, the alleyway where Fat Deano went berserk and nearly messed up everything, perhaps still has messed up everything, and there he is before us, right there, standing right in front of us like a dark looming shadow out of a Phantom comic. Taking up the entire alleyway. Senior Detective Constable Watno Thornes, standing right there, thickset, gritting his teeth like knife edges, his shadow a huge castle gate banged shut.

'So, so, finally. I knew I'd eventually catch up with ya without ya smarty-pants, too big for his bleeding boots boyfriend.'

He is a shadow straight out of Oliver Twist. Just like the movie. Dark, grim and cut-faced. He isn't even looking at me. It is like I don't exist. Dusty clutches my hand hard. I can feel sweat from my palm pour back and mingle with hers. I like the moist feel of it. I wish it could just be the two of us here. Sitting on a bench, leaning into one another. Gazing up at the moon.

'And now we're with the little cripple brother, are we?' He laughs.

'Get nicked!' Dusty curls her lip. 'It's none'a ya beeswax.'

'Get nicked, none of my beeswax, huh? You're the one's gonna get nicked, girlie.' His eyes fall, dangerously, like a dropped cannon ball to our tightly woven hands. 'I see you've got a lovely little man's watch there, too? Very nice. Nice watchstrap, too. Can I see it?'

Dusty's hand stiffens in mine. I know she is sick and scared, but I love what her hand is doing, my fogged up head still wishing we were alone, somewhere perhaps in the shade, by a clear lake.

'What's me watch gotta do with ya?'

'Just let's see it,' he says. 'Turn it round. I'm interested. Or can't ya let go of the little spastic's hand?'

I feel her tense again, like she is a mum protecting me, see her lip twist like she is going to slap him, and then she lets go of my hand. I curse Thornes for destroying everything.

'Well?' he says.

She turns the watch face up and lifts her hand in the near complete darkness of the alleyway into mid air. He takes her hand into his, but not harshly like I am expecting and I think so is she, but rather delicately, like a gentleman taking the hand of a lady as she steps out of a carriage in one of those olden days movies about England. He considers her hand for a moment, like he is surprised at its smallness, its velvet softness. For a moment he lets her fingers dangle in the thick of his palm that frames her hand like rough dough. Then he lifts her hand even further upwards, again not harshly, not like he wants to hurt her, but more like the gentleman in that old English movie, like the gent is about to pop the question to his lady. The heavy, silver watch glints in the small amount of light in the alley, and he brings her hand and the watch closer to his eyes. His eyes strain now like a jeweller examining a delicate gem under a microscope. But it seems without magnifying glasses he is not really, in the darkness of the alley, able to see what he wants to see.

'Yours, is it?' he finally says, looking down at Dusty, still delicately holding her hand.

'Yeah, 'course,' she says.

Like in a dance now, a slow ballroom dance at a wedding, still holding her hand in the air with one rough, doughy hand, with his other he retrieves a small penlight torch from his jacket pocket. He lowers her hand then and shines the torch on the watch.

'Pretty good watch, hey? Or do you only wear Seikos these days?'

'Gordon give it to me,' she hisses.

'Oh, so he was there?'

'What d'ya mean?' She looks genuinely baffled for a moment.

'I mean robbing and beating an old man to near death in this very alley here?'

She shakes her head vigorously, shivers. I can feel in my stomach and throat the sickness passing through her body.

'Dunno where he get it,' she says. 'He just give it to me like a gift. Said it was a pressie from his dad once, and he wants me to have it.'

'Likely story, very likely story,' Thornes smiles, thin upper lip spreading, thick lower lip forming a heavy quarter moon, his bulky frog eyes staring into her withdrawing face.

'Ask Gray if ya don't believe me. You can even ask Gray here.'

'Ah, Mr Morrow. The other Morrow. Gray Morrow.' It is like he is awakening from a dream and realising I am there for the first time. 'The other young… never mind. Never mind. Now listen up… this is the deal. You know what I'm going to do, Gray? You know what I'm going to do to ya?' I shake my head. 'I'm going to break every bone in ya scrawny, crippled little body if ya ain't out of me sight by the count of three. You understand that? And I'm going to start counting now. Right now.' His eyes light up like Ash Wednesday. 'One… two… three.'

At the count of three I look into his eyes, and then into Dusty's. They are saying to me, 'Go. Run! Save yourself!' And I turn and run as fast as I can, like I am never going to stop running. And then as soon as I am out of sight, not that far down from the entrance to the pub, I stop and turn back, slipping back into the alley, knowing how dark it is in there, how lost Detective Senior Constable Watno Thornes is in his interrogation of Dusty. I want to be near, I want to protect her, something is just driving me, too. This is a terrible thing to say, I know, but I also want to be a spy for Gordon, see what she tells and does not tell, see that she does not say too much. That I know what she does say, so that we can stay a step ahead, Gord and me, so that we can know what Thornes' strategy is. I want to be Gord's henchman.

I can sense it from a mile off already, Thornes is going to do everything in his power to befriend Dusty, maybe even, if she will not succumb, threaten her, perhaps bribe her, but at any rate use her in some way as bait to make us confess, possibly even to lure Fat Deano and Kelly back into town. I hide behind the row of bins that we hid behind on that bloody, disastrous night, coldly camouflaged behind their darkness, their rotten smell that bites into my shaky nostrils, that makes me reach for my puffer. I inhale air and stink in that darkness, as I listen to the throaty calm in Detective Senior Constable Watno Thornes' voice.

'...Thought I warned ya not to hang with those Morrow lads?' he says, his eyes gleaming down at her, part father, part policeman. Protective yet severe.

Dusty doesn't respond. Just looks downwards at his feet. She looks white as a ghost.

'Look at me when I'm talking to you,' he raises his voice slightly for the first time.

She looks up, a reluctant ghost-white eight year-old.

'Those lads are no good for ya, Dusty Jones,' he says, all father. 'Listen to me. Listen to someone who knows. I mean especially Gordon. Specially him. Are ya following me? I'm only trying to help here.'

She swallows, hard, like there is a piece of metal stuck in her larynx. She bites her lip, but says nothing.

'Look, I'm gonna square with you,' he says. 'I know this watch, I know exactly where it comes from, lass. And I have this strong feeling you were there, too.'

She just shakes her head and keeps it raised while beaming downwards with her eyes. At her own alien boots.

He is still holding her hand, or rather her wrist now, like it is an object he is in charge of, a piece of evidence in a court case, not letting go until the object has been satisfactorily displayed and identified. I think I see him squeeze her wrist now; at any rate I see her blink like it pains, but I can't be sure. In the little bit of light there is in the alleyway it is difficult to pick up such small detail — even though like Gordon, like Dusty, like all of us homies under the bridge, I am a bat so used to seeing in the dark, even scrawling my thoughts in the dark.

Now he puts the torch away, back in his jacket pocket, and places that hand, his torch hand, on her naked shoulder. He is still holding her wrist at the same time, and I see her shiver in the darkness. If I did not know them, was looking at them from afar, a passer by, I would think they were close friends, lovers perhaps, young subterfuge lovers dancing beneath the moonless night, unable to find anywhere else to meet.

'You're a good lass, Dusty,' he says now, again, all father. 'I can tell these things. We... us coppers, that is... we have a sense of these things. But what I also know is that life can change, lass. I've seen it happen, life turn around, and that's all I want for ya, I just want to give you that chance. You deserve it, Dusty. Of all the girls I've known like you, you deserve it, mate. Just believe me, you're not going to get anywhere with Gordon Morrow.'

She looks up at him, biting her lip.

And it hits my forehead like one of those old bombs falling on Gallipoli or somewhere that she has succumbed, has been sucked in. That he will offer her a deal, offer her a new life if she tells him the truth. Dobs us in. She hasn't said anything yet, but you can see even from where I am, you can see it in the sorrowful way she looks up at him, the way he rests his hand on her, how she allows him to without even trying to shrug it off, like they are somehow now flesh entwined, like he has succeeded with her where he has failed with Gordon and me. I know that feeling of wanting to trust the giant shadow in front of you because suddenly he looks like he knows where he is going, where he is taking you. Knows life's direction.

And there she is now, saying to him, 'What d'ya want from me?'

His baulking eyes, yielding and spongy, peer down at her. 'Dusty... Dusty Jones... you see, the truth is, I know a lot about you. Even all about what really happened in this alley—Mzz Jones—and who was involved, ya know?'

'F'k,' she says like there is a pip caught in her throat, and it is growing.

'But I'm willing to give you a chance, Mz Jones... I'm willing to give you a last chance... if you will just listen to me. If you will just listen... I am not joking when I say there are some people in this world who deserve better... so I'm going to give you this one chance... but it is up to you. Completely and utterly up to you.'

And I can't believe it, he puts his thick, lumpy, world heavyweight champion hand on her face, caressing it, not like a boyfriend but like a father caressing a small child, and I think I can see a glint of golden syrup in Dusty's little elfin eyes. There is one good thing about the dark in this alley, you cannot see the gravely holes in his face. In its bloated way, it looks as smooth and normal as a boy's right now, almost shiny smooth, like Dusty's. And with that normal face, that swollen but normal looking face he is petting her wet, syrupy cheeks with those boxer hands of his. Wiping the tears away, just like a caring father would, stroking her head full of dusty blonde hair; and she looks up into his soft, bulking eyes, heedful, a little girl knowing the wrongness of her ways.

And she will be exonerated. She can see that. And in that darkness they are lovers. They look so warm and protected, like they are meant to be together. You can almost hear their hearts beating in tempo, like a dull song. Like Gordon was merely a boy on the way to this reality. Forgotten now in the wisdom of maturity.

Through the bins, the stinking, putrid bins, I see this so clearly, how the darkness holds its own fascinating truth. That will last, I know from experience, until daybreak, when another truth will climb through the skin of the dark. And it is this truth that I want her to see, the truth of daybreak. It is this truth that I am urging her with all my psychic powers to see. Because it is, I realise now, a much more stark and real and powerful truth. But it is like, to her, I am not there, and I suppose in reality I am not. And in that darkness, in the harmony of it, in the truth of it, she squats now like she has given up, has perfectly succumbed to the moment, the great wisdom of it. And it is like, standing there above her, he is about to baptise her. It is freaky man, real, real freaky. But there is nothing, absolutely nothing I can do.

'I just wanna take care of ya like Gordon can't,' he says.

And bending down she looks ahead, intently, like she is looking into the great magnificence of the blackness in front of her, the luminescence of it, the light we see under the bridge in the great shadow of it. It is a dark stage she is staring out of. A stage she can see from but cannot lift herself down from. Her hand reaches up to her head and she strokes her fringe away like she wants to see better, and then she brushes the rest of her long blonde hair back, behind her little fairy ears. She brings her hand to rest on his pants, or maybe it just falls there, an accident? But she lets it linger there anyway, because that is all there is for it. Nothing else for it to do in that darkness but feel the cloth. I breathe in deeply, wishing Gordon were at my side, seeing that cloth grow, hearing something shooting down like a quick siren, like it is a complicated operation, bringing forward a pink torch without much glean, whose batteries are going flat. And that little velvet mouse hand that had held mine is fumbling with that torch now, like it is trying to switch it on properly, bring the glow back to life. Yes, in that blackness, it all looks so perfect. So unblemished and perfect. And he is standing there, giant Phantom shadow, melded into the darkness, bringing the doughy plumpness of his hand behind her head, pressing it towards him. Her little lips that always look so pink and thin when they do not have bright orange or purple lipstick on them, opening now, accepting into them this faint torchlight. But it is like the torch is too big for her jaws and she is struggling to breathe in the light her mouth wants to consume. Still, I see her straining with those lips, hungrily swallowing the grey beam, her head springing now like a child's toy, up and down, squeakily, an olden days doll at a carnival, bobbing and swallowing like it needs torchlight to operate, to shudder into motion. And he is looking up, a giant shadow almost perfectly one with the blackness above, beaming his thoughts up to an even higher night, his lips biting gratefully to the heavens above for making the world so calmly the way it is.

I feel like I am looping right out. I cough involuntarily, softly, muffling the sound, and reach for my puffer, my breath like a lump of stone in my throat, feeling dizzy, confused by this same world that Thornes is finding so calm and exalting, taking a deep inhale, what is left of it, reminding myself, as my mother has so many times, to go to the hospital to get a new prescription.

I don't know what it is, but in front of him now, still down there, at his knees, I see sharp white teeth like cat's claws light up and then strike into that thick, dull torch. Once in there, it is like the claws have become stuck and cannot let go. There is an amazing moment of silence, absolute silence, like the whole town has completely shut down, and in the back of my head, ringing right way in the back of it, like it is my mother, or Gord on Mt Moon, there is this scream, or maybe, yes, this depraved wolf's howl— '*Aaaaaaaaiiiwooooo*'— yes, just like Gordon's, only charged with a shrieking pain and a hysterical deflation of breath, and my eyes shoot over to Thornes, seeing his thick neck suddenly crinkle like a fat wad of paper, his face squashed and anguished looking, like it has fallen with the crinkling of his neck deep into his shoulders. A second passes and then a brown liquid sprays into the air like a council pipe that has been accidentally pick-axed and water from the Bremer River is flowing through it. In the darkness now I see it is coming from Dusty's lips, from behind those white cat's claws, from deep inside her throat, like her throat is a big twanging arrow that is shooting at an enemy position. There is a second burst of the brown liquid and I see it is actually coming from somewhere even deeper in her, from right in the middle of her, from her shaking gut; and you can see it, that brown, lumpy liquid shivering up her body frame like snake venom, and then out it comes, again and again, blanketing the front of Thornes' perfectly black pin-striped pants that he is holding in grimaced pain like he is waking up in the middle of an operation gone wrong.

'Bitch! Fucking dirty slut bitch!' A voice barrels from his stiff neck, bent like a backward facing trombone. 'Nobody but nobody does that to Thornes. Bloody animal!' And it is like his beastly voice is waking up the whole town.

Wiping her lips, she stands up, falling backwards, and as she looks like she is about to hit the back of her head on the pub wall, I see Thornes' hand stretch out heroically, like a famous cricketer to grab her, to save her from hurting herself. Only the cricketer's lightning fast hand misses the ball, and instead comes falling down into the side of her freckled cheek. It hits with such force that I hear something in her face crack. It sounds like bush turkey bones splitting, makes Gordon's blow to her face that night seem meek. Her head spins round, her entire frame pirouetting like a lithe dancer hitting into the wall like it has suddenly been hit by a car. Something that feels like gravel or large rocks haemorrhages inside my head. My head feels all smoky and fiery, like it does not belong to me, like it is a part of these rubbish bins. I am bilious in the stomach but I cannot run forward or turn away. I am stuck. My head is blazing hot yet I am frozen. Just like Dad is above me, pounding away, I am all hot and yet I am frozen stiff. My eyes whirling, I see him grab onto her neck. His large teeth are grinding like you see German soldiers crunching their teeth under their flat, steel helmets in World War Two movies. His neck is muscled right into his shoulders now, like those German SS soldiers when they are about to kill Americans or Hebrews or something, and he slams her head against the wall like it is a piece of soft fruit he has had enough of, but which has enraged him because it has left some kind of bitter-sharp taste in his mouth. Then he stops, mid movement, stonily, like the intergalactic robot he really is, and thinks for about a second, maybe two, changing tack, and this time brings her head down to his knee. About midway down his own steel knee catapults upwards like it is a rocket, hitting her head so hard I hear something explode in there, something like steel shattering and showering all over the wall.

'Bitch! Fucking slut bitch!' He shouts again. 'You've killed me. You've bloody killed me!'

Her head clamped in his world heavyweight champion fists like it is a small ball, for a brief moment he gazes into her tiny, mousy eyes, and for a moment it looks like his own eyes are stunned in a kind of pact of recognition. Like they are seeing things in there, things deep inside of Dusty's closing eyelids, I don't know, like maybe their eyes are a continuum of one. Seeing himself as a teenager lumbering out of home, angry, unhappy, ready to take on the world; she, Dusty, like unwanted cloth, running, screaming, thrown out of the same decrepit house. He turning left, she turning right. Luck? Fate? throwing them off that same stage in different directions. And before long it is too late to uncurve the bends, to traverse the angles. He turns away from those eyes, and screams into the dark, 'Look what you've done. Piece of shit! He can have ya! He can have all that's left of ya!' He is banging her head against the wall like it is one of those soft, springy oblong balls in a boxing gym and he is in a drunken daze.

Even from where I am crouched behind the bins, I can see her eyelids go up and the immense whiteness in her eyes turning brown. I cannot say for sure, but I think there is blood spilling out of them. The syrup is becoming blood. Everything is happening so fast, so quickly, yet I can swear her eyes are searching the dark alley for me. Like she knows, she knows I am there. Cold air whirls inside me like a refrigerator, and yet I am still sweating. The sweat is pouring through my cold body watching what is happening, Thornes breaking her freckled head like it is porcelain. Inside me, inside my cold flesh, my stomach is galloping like a horse trying to get home, thumping hooves on the ground, and yet it is like there is no home, nowhere to go to. And the more I see those eyes, her little elfin eyes lazily searching the alley for me, the more I cannot move, the more frozen I become, the more my own eyes shift to Thornes and see the enormous power in his frame, the giant savagery in his arms, his teeth like bayonet points, and it keeps me pinned behind the rubbish bins like I am a hiding soldier. I have no choice: I have to keep dead still. The truth is, it is like a block of cement is fastened to my chest and I cannot move no matter what I think. The feeling reminds me of pictures of concrete blocks tied to the feet of mafia victims, sinking them down into deep rivers and oceans, their hands thrashing the water with life, and the world spinning like a washing machine around them, seeing my own head being driven into a wall, seeing, as I see coming from Dusty's head, a thick, tarry fluid roaming down my face and neck and shoulders. Seeing that fat cement fist smashing into my cheeks because I let the car tyres down. Because I happened to be caught, caught avenging Mum's bloody beating, my father's eyes glowering, staring red ice at me, a stone fist shooting out of the sky, the baking hot sun above turning it into a bird, a pretty bird, something sweet, that of all the children in the world has chosen me to fly into and peck smartly on the cheek. And my head is lying there twisted backwards on my shoulders by that bird, like it is going to fall off my neck, except a peck from a second pretty flying bird brings my head hurtling forwards, in the opposite direction. The pretty birds fly off and blackness spins around in my head, my head now lying cosily twisted in the brown backyard dust; and I lie there unable to move on the warm earth, wondering why. Later, much later, waking in Mum's arms, one of the few times I have been there, that I can recall really being there.

Hearing her voice like sweet comforting sugar: 'Everything will be OK, my little mate. Don't worry, Gray, everything'll be OK, son. We won't let him get away with this. I love ya. I love ya too much, my little mate.'

And then hearing her sugar voice turn to pepper, screaming at the long, shattered man standing in front of her.

'Get the hell out of me sight! Get the fucking hell outta here! And when ya calmed down and thought about what ya done, you take him to the hospital. You take him!'

The one side of my face, wrapped in her bony arms, feels like it has dropped four centimetres lower than the other, like the bones in there are no more than chicken neck gristle that has been chewed too much on the one side. And he just stands there, this long, remorseful man with the muscly back, who has slapped us, me and Gordon many times, this time dishing out to me what he has dished out to Mum for years. And not even Gordon can protect me. He is eight. I am six. This man who can take us up to Mt Moon, who can take the time to share with us a cold but sacred moment of peace. And Mum is sitting there, over and over, calling him 'a useless piece of shit'. I can feel him, the cement block in here, in my chest, and I cannot move, cannot so much as budge. Seeing Dusty's head sagging, no longer a part of her neck, it just hangs there, a throwaway doll's head torn from its collar, a plastic toy thwarted in a fit of childhood rage. Standing now, only because Thornes holds her there, in a standing position, finally letting go of her like she will stand on her own two feet and apologise. Maybe? Only she just slips straight down, hitting the ground, a splatter of thin yellow jelly.

# 28.

SOMETHING SORE AND AGITATED MEANDERS in Thornes' eyes. I can see it, seeing him wander around her like he is trying to identify a corpse, stiffly holding his crotch, bending down, rickety, feeling first himself then her pulse, her wrist that he once held so gentlemanly, so majestically, now hanging limp in his stained hand. He puts his thick square head to her nose, listening like she may be trying to whisper something to him. A last thank you? A word of sorrow? And then he is standing at her side, pacing, shaking his hands in the black air, feeling his crotch as though something in there is missing, as though searching, doing up his zipper, easing the zip with large, lumpy hands over that delicate material, shaking his boxer hands again, that certain bloated pride in his face extinguished, looking about him like a burglar now, afraid, suspicious, and then running, first in a slow jog that is coupled with a limp, just like mine, I note just like mine, and then he bursts into a sprint, right past me, intergalactic Phantom shadow passing into the thick night.

I pick myself up, noting how easy it is now without him there, and move my limbs at will, quickly walking over to Dusty, thinking what I will say to her, how I will console her, how I will apologise and pick her up and carry her home or to Ruth's Place or the bridge—or somewhere. Anywhere. The hospital? As I approach, I curse myself for being such a whimp, a coward, such a bleeding wuss, no good to anyone. But I will make up for it now, I swear, take Dusty in my arms and tell her that she is alright, wipe the blood from her nose and face and do whatever she wants me to do, carry her wherever she wants to be carried — to Sydney if that's what she wants! I bend over her, even in the dark, expecting to look into two thankful eyes, to hear her little voice calling my name, see her precious little pink lips moving, but all I see is a face, grotesquely still, silent, covered in a thick brown-red slime, like it is a painting torn in half. Her nose looks skew, like it has been smashed in two, and points to the side of her face. Her eyes are closed, red and lumpy, her naked shoulders covered in the same red slime as her face. Her hair lies there long and dead, no longer blonde any more, but rather brown and badly highlighted. The spikes on her crown are thick and flat. Next to her, her shoulder bag lies alone, like a child abandoned.

When I call her name there is no reply, not even a flicker. Her little lips are squashed and cracked open and look like they will break if she opens them to speak. I think for a moment I see them quiver, but it could be the quiver I feel in my eyes as they peruse her body. I close my eyes, a scrappy grey cat shrieks, glides past us and accelerates through the alley. I catch such a fright, for a moment I think it is Dusty come back to life. But she just lies there still like the earth.

Some drunks, loud, laughing, saunter out of the pub. They stand there, just outside the alley, and I panic, thinking maybe they have seen what has happened and are waiting for me to come out of there. Or maybe they are planning something — and are about to suddenly come running in to the alley to tackle me? But they just continue to stand there and laugh and talk, and I put my ear to Dusty's face like Thornes had done, up to her little freckled face that used to wear above it that shiny electric turquoise-blue hat. I lean forward and place my ear right up to her twisted, broken nose, feeling her blood-soaked mouth wet on my cheek. I am amazed, I feel the tickle of breath. It is such a wonderful feeling, like angels or fairies coming out of there, like I am Peter Pan and she is the beautiful fairy. And then I become stuck, watching the drunks laughing outside the pub, not knowing what to do, what to do now, how I will ever lift her and carry her somewhere, how I will ever get her to walk. I try to lift her, taking her by the watch hand, that she still wears, that Thornes had held her so romantically by, and pull her up, first slowly, then with a slight jar, but she is just like a rag doll, without life, and when I let go of her she just slumps to the ground not even feeling the pain of the thud.

Thinking of what Gordon would do, I decide I have to take my chances — for Dusty — and I run up to the drunks standing outside the pub. I cannot speak properly and hear my voice squeaking and squealing as though in one long clutter of letters, finally pointing down the alley to her limp form.

'Jesus! Lawd!' They shout out, and even in their slobbering drunkenness they are able to suddenly race down the alley, all laughter gone, their hard-earned liquor cash wasted.

I wait around at the top of the alley, unsure what to do. I see one of them on his mobile phone, first thinking it may be to the police and I should run, but then hearing the word ambulance and remaining. It is not even a few minutes before that ambulance is screaming to a halt outside the alley. I watch the ambulancemen, dressed smartly in their black pants, white shirts and luminous yellow vests, looking like a bright new breed of long, slimline penguins as they scratch their heads around her body. And then rush back to the van, bringing back with them a stretcher and oxygen. A mask is placed over Dusty's little face and she is lifted and strapped into the stretcher. With a slight heave the two luminous penguins lift the stretcher and carry her off, the drunks looking on like it is a throwaway carcass being carried from the slaughter. To me, Dusty, our Dust, on that stretcher under the light of the pub, shines like a wounded sports star, perhaps even a reclining Egyptian queen. To me she looks like she is covered in real glory, our Poet Queen. It is like she is in a special hammock being trumpeted off into a special white place. And I swear I will do what I can to save her.

'Think the poor lass's gone...' I hear one of the drunk's say. 'Beat'n to bloody mash, ay.'

And I see Dusty, a glow like a queen around her, being sucked into the white van, into the bright vacuum in there, and then the van screams off as it arrived, ripping sharp dagger sounds into the night, carrying our shining freckled Dust in it, knowing I have to get to Gordon, have to get to him as fast as I can.

# 29.

I WALK THROUGH THE BLACK TOWN, a lone, distressed bat, zigzagging to the bridge. Knowing in the back of my mind I cannot tell Gordon everything, he will kill me, already concocting in my head what I will tell him, what I will miss out, just forget to mention—like what a coward I have been, what a useless piece of dog shit. How I watched everything and did nothing, not one useless piece of shit. And I see in thinking about my version, like I am back in the classroom, except for some brave people like Gord we continually concoct stories to hide the truth even from ourselves; it is our self-comforting wool of pride. The truth is I feel like shit, I feel like killing myself before I even get to Gordon

I guess they won't be getting that apartment like Ruth suggested for a long time now. That is my only consolation. My only consolation for what's to come.

Running and half walking through the streets now, it is so dark and deserted, sort of like pictures you see on TV of small towns where there is always murder an mayhem going down. At every step, at every corner, I expect the shadow of Thornes to step out of one of these dark crevices and trip me up. I look over my shoulder, nothing. I look forward, nothing. Breaking into a run again, a slight breeze smacking in my face, I feel like I am on reality TV.

Back under the bridge, it is quieter now, most of the kids, high as kites, have left. A small circle gathered just above the river, are still drinking and joking and falling over backwards like life is one big laugh. Seeing me, a couple of them call out: 'Yo, Gray.'

'Yo!' I call back. I see Little Danno lying next to them, a curled earthworm in the golden stripes of his black tracksuit pants hugging his skateboard to his side, knowing that if he does not sleep with it, does not tie himself to it, like a husband to a wife, it will be gone by morning. I remember Dusty once, who like most everyone thought of Little Danno as very cute, running a hand across his long straight black hair and shaking it, saying, 'Hey, cute little homie man, when ya gonna go home?' and he took hold of her other hand, dangling all loose and friendly at her side, and bit it. So hard there were drops of blood and deep tooth marks left on it. She never touched him again.

I find Gordon a bit further along the river. Asleep. On the damp ground next to him, in his arms, Candy's friend, who he said could be mine. See what I mean, obviously a joke. Their clothes lie on their bodies, all dishevelled, like dolls dressed by two year-olds. Just a little above them, I notice another sleeping form, Shooter, asleep now, but probably tired out from the grog and spending most of the night peeping and hoping.

Anxious, breathing sharply, I shake Gordon and call his name into his ear, expecting him to rouse and be ready for what I have to tell him. But he does not move, not a millimetre. I become more violent in my shaking, punching him on the shoulder, hitting him on the back, but still nothing. So I continue, a little bit crazy, like I owe it to Dusty, owe it to her, to tell him now. In the end all I succeed in doing is stirring the sleeping body in front of him, who scowls and looks angrily at me, and then elbows Gordon hard in the chest. For a moment he lifts his head and begins manically, like a rugby league player under tackle, to thrash his fists and kick his legs, only hopelessly in the air like he is having a bad dream, and then it is back to silence, sleep, his own dark consciousness.

Irritated, I become aware that the mozzies are stirring tonight, I can feel them nipping at my hands and fingers and neck. But even their swarming hordes aren't enough to bother Gordon or his 'bride' or any of the others tonight. Even those who are still conscious, just sit there, like the mosquitoes are part of the atmosphere. I sit behind Gordon, fuming. I wish I could just erase my life like a rubber over pencil. Just inebriate it out of sight like Gordon and the others tonight. There is too much scribbled writing on it, I think. I just want a blank sheet.

I give up trying like I always give up, knowing it is useless to try waking Gordon in this state. Actually, even if he woke up, he would be no better than me right now, just a useless lump of shit, of scribbled defecation that is impossible to rub out. I look over to the river, it seems much darker now, like the lights on the overpass and the roadside have been mostly switched off or toned down or shot out or something. No longer the steady glow on the water, just a dull sense of brown and grey, just the memory of glow, afterglow. The truth is you need grog and drugs if you want to see the radiance, if you want to illuminate the glow from below, to make light visible. The eye by itself just so fucking dark and feeble. Inside me, in the flesh, where the bones stick to the red meat, it is worse than this dull glimmer on the river. It is muddy gelatine. It is hard sometimes to understand how someone like Ruth Hannah can believe. Ruth Hannah, so calm, assertive, knowing. How can anyone believe? Because, in the end, what is there to be seen? Mud. Shit, I swear, giving up and sneaking in next to Gordon, close behind him, allowing his unconscious body to provide warmth. It is cold and I am beginning to shiver.

The next morning, late, we wake with the sun spreading over the obfuscating river like nothing has happened, like nothing in the world has changed, like all was a drunken dream. But whether real or unreal, I still have to tell Gordon, still have to bring myself out of my own hangover and tell him. It scares me. I feel like I am about to tell a truth to my father—and he is going to strike me. But I have to.

Gordon, shaking his head, still trying to open his eyes fully to admit the sunlight, listens, stroking his mouth, scratching his head, doing up his zipper. When I am finished he stands up pale yellow in the face like all the colour has gone out of it and been replaced with bleach. The worms are climbing in his eyes now; they are like gunshot slicing through the back of his head and down into his gut. He is choking, his eyes spitting worm blood; they look nightclub purple, tinged with green. He kicks, not that softly, the back of the body that has spent the night with him.

'What the...?' comes back a snorting, wet cry.

He stares down and the body slowly rises from the earth, dusts itself off, and walks away. 'Well stuff ya too, then,' it says.

They raise fingers at one another—game over!

Gordon strides up and down, confused, his bushy hair, wild, untameable, like it is reflecting carnage.

Finally, finally, he says something.

'C'mon buddy. For fuck's bloody sakes! C'mon!'

It is like some force has showered over him, like some tidal surge has burst the banks of the river in him and is pouring straight back out of him. I see in his worm-filled eyes unknown worlds whirling as though through a dirty stormwater drain. And yet still he looks beaten, stunned, like there is a bullet lodged in his head. Like he has to get that bullet out to have any hope of saving himself. I follow him, splashing, delirious, in the wake of a pile of mud and stones and bullets.

# 30.

WE ARE ENTERING ANOTHER WORLD, sliding through hospital doors, lights shining down unnaturally, almost blindingly in a misty-bright kind of way, the smell of the hospital a medicine vial that has been dropped on the floor and mopped up with meths. Gordon sounds breathless, like an animal, standing there leaning with his curly bushy hair and baggy pants into the enquiry counter, the elderly woman behind the counter, so clean next to him, so white and lemon-fresh that she looks like she must spend half her life scrubbing down.

'Dusty... we're looking for Dusty,' he says.

'Dusty? Dusty who?'

Gordon looks at me, like he has forgotten; I know he has forgotten.

'Jones,' I say. 'Dusty Jones.'

The woman peers, like she is solving a mystery, into a large book, and says, 'The one who was brought into emergency late last night?'

Gordon nods, not knowing.

'I'm afraid she's still in ICU.'

'ICU?' Gordon says, 'Where's that? Is she pregnant?'

'That's intensive care, dear. I'm afraid you can't go in there. Are you relatives or something?'

'Her... her... uh, stepbrothers,' Gordon says looking the lemon-fresh woman directly in the eye, as do I.

The woman looks at him, sceptically. 'Only her parents are allowed up there.'

'Will she be in there long?' Gordon asks.

'I don't know dearie. Maybe if you wait around I can get one of the nurses to talk to you?'

'Ah fuck.' Gordon says, and the lemon-fresh woman looks down, biting her teeth. 'Fuck't, fuck't, fuck't.' he says. 'I have to see her.'

The woman's eyes roll. She shakes her head. 'Sorry. Do you want me to get the nurse?'

'Naa,' Gordon says and pulls me aside like we are leaving the hospital or going to ponder somewhere else for a while.

If there is any place we know, it is Ipswich Hospital. Both Gordon and me have been in and out for various childhood ailments, even colds and flues, which Mum used to take us in for, "Cause it's safe an sure—an cost nothing anyway.' And then with me and my asthma and my broken leg that never heeled, you could say I kinda grew up in this hospital. And of course Mum and Dad and aunts and uncles and cousins, all of them at one time or another have spent days in the hospital, bleeding, broken, sometimes near death. In no time Gordon has decided on our next course of action. Find our own way through the sterile, methylated maze.

Of course it doesn't take Gordon and me long to find the ICU ward. And then Gordon takes over, walking with confidence, as though he has permission from the Queen herself to be there. He just barges his way in, smashing open the swing doors. I stop, momentarily, the doors slamming shut on me, peering through the little window on the door, seeing her, Dusty, tubes running from nose, arms, head; the watch that was at the bottom of this nowhere to be seen. Then I gently open the doors and follow. Seeing Gordon already staring, befuddled, into her face that is like a potato gone off, all mauve and yellow and puffy. Her eyes are large, purple-green, like there is a hailstorm in there. They are tightly closed like she is sleeping in a bad, knotted dream. And even if she were awake I doubt she would be able to open them. I wonder if Gordon is even sure this is her. She looks so different. Not the Dusty I remember, with the cute little electric turquoise-blue hat, the blonde fringe across her forehead, the crown of spikes on top of her head. More like someone's puffily sick, overweight grandmother. My stomach hollows and spins.

Gordon goes up closer to her, and it looks like he is smelling her. Her hair, her ears. Her lips.

'Fuck that mongrel dog!' he is whispering in a roar. 'Fuck him dead. I'm gonna kill the cunt for this. I'm tellin ya Gray, I'm gonna kill him dead!'

He takes hold of Dusty's limp arm, the one with no tubes in it and rubs it, rubs it clumsily at first, a little shyly, and then like a child discovering the warm softness of a fluffy toy. Not since he was eight and Dad bashed me unconscious have I seen tears in Gordon's eyes. Now they are filling with them; they look wet and orange. His eyes look like I have never seen them before, so soft they are like two marbles, silky and cloudy, and they stare at her like they cannot remove themselves from her sight, like they are glued into her. Above them, a beam of light shines in from a window, stretching just over their heads like a thick, silver veil, like it is meant for them alone. The only thing that comes to my mind is a song, or a choir in a church, I don't know why; we only ever went to church a few times in our lives, maybe it is from TV? But the voices are so loud and skin-penetrating it sounds like they are coming from the walls. In that light, they look angelic and yet so completely normal at the same time, just like a normal couple in a normal bedroom, except everything is so white in here, and it is like Gordon is bending over her, saying goodnight. And then he moves backwards out of that silver light and I cannot help but think how ugly, how swollen, how out of proportion her head looks. The cement, that concrete block in me suddenly comes back, expands; I feel it pinning me. I am reaching out to her but unable to move, I am a useless piece of gravel. And I see him there, that great big shadow of his, Detective Senior Constable Watno Thornes rubbing her head for a few heavenly seconds, pulling her head into him, and then smashing it against a wall like it is a soft apple, breaking her face on his knee like it is no more than a dry twig. And somehow even when she fell then, she looked better than this. I have seen my mother's face purple and swollen after taking a smack from my dad, from Mick; I have seen my dad's face blue and swollen after being smashed in a brawl, but nothing, nothing like this. This is like a train crash, an accident that you read about where the injured person never looks or sounds the same ever again. Can never kiss again. So much for forever. Eternity is crap. I am glad she clawed so viciously that dull torch in her cat teeth.

Gordon reaches into his pants pocket and pulls out his Mt Moon stone. He tries to show it to her. Like it is their wedding ring.

Like somehow it will revive her, bring back memories, bring her back to consciousness. And when it doesn't work, when she does not even flicker an eyelid, he places it on the white table beside her bed and begins a frantic search through the drawer in the table, eventually coming up with the silver Seiko watch. He looks at it for a minute like his eyes are arcing over massive distances, and then places it in his pocket. As though not satisfied, he dives down again, looking this time under her square, wonder white bed, stretching and finally coming up with her shoulder bag. He scavenges through it, through all those shelves and drawers and files in there, coming up eventually with some paper which has writing on it, which she has written on, and stuffs all the pages quickly in his pocket. Then he goes into the bag again. Digging even deeper this time, right into the bottom of it. Eventually he comes up with a stone, her stone from Mt Moon, charcoal with grey lines shooting out and around like they are still seeking something. He picks up his own stone from the white table and places the two stones in the thick of his palm. He lifts her limp hand and places it over the stones. The sun, that beam of silver light shining through the window is already lower now, a funnel of brown flying dust particles, and it catches their hands like it is a golden sheet entwining them.

I don't know if he is expecting magic, a sudden cure to come out of it, the stones, or even the light shining upon them, but in any event nothing happens. He may as well be holding a broken doll and a stone picked up from any street. But from where I stand at the front of her bed, behind them, I see the beam of dust-filled light shining on them like it is magic; it forms a soft golden canopy around them and in that enclosed light I hear Gordon cry again. His cry is runny and snivelly and at times rasping; it pains in my chest like someone is sticking needles into me, and I curse myself for being so weak and useless. More than anything I want someone to hold me. But in front of me there is only Gordon and Dusty holding onto one another.

Gordon says, 'I love ya, Dust. I love ya. Really, really.' It is like he is casting a hook after fish. And, as before when I heard him say those words, it sounds so strange coming from his lips, like a language we do not speak, made up of words we do not know the meaning of. And yet he repeats it, 'I love ya, Dust. Really, really, I love ya, babe.' And I see that I have never seen anything like this except on TV or in the movies. It just seems so strange when you see it in real life. My face almost goes red. I want to go right up to them and study them, their faces, their hands, their eyes, and see if it is real. Not just a stage.

After a few moments Gordon leans over and kisses the cracked, still faintly bleeding lips and holds the kiss there, holds it, and I am able to examine it, that kiss on her bloated, smashed lips, to see in its deformity if it is real. That it really exists. And I see in front of me something I had never realised before, just how loud love is. Although Dusty is deaf and dumb, unconscious to it, the love between the two of them is so roaring loud you can hear it shouting and hollering all around them. And I wish life could always be like this. It does not worry me one iota if she can never walk or talk again, if she is quadriplegic, deaf and dumb for life. Just as long as we can hang on to her. Hear that hollering sound. In my mouth I taste reality, it is the syrup of her eyes trickling, the orange of Gordon's tears drizzling, and in me I feel as though something is being ripped from my gut.

Gordon's lips move away from her and his head falls back like he is examining a picture he is not sure of. I think, wondering if it is true. If it is all really happening. Wondering what meaning there might be in it. After a while, like he needs to look closer, needs to examine each brush stroke, he bends his head again and allows his mouth to linger again on her blood-specked lips. The thick fluid from his eyes flows onto her distended face like it is watering her, giving her flesh life. In the background I hear a metallic voice crackling like it is shooting from Heaven.

'Jesus Christ! What's going on here? What do you boys think you're bloody doing here?'

And Gordon just turns around, immediately, pushing that metallic voice, that distilled, white-washed flesh, that messenger of Heaven, out of the way, the worms in his eyes a thick string of raging electricity; and I race after him, looking back for the last time at the stones on the table he has left behind, praying in the pit of my stomach, they, those stones, by some occult magic I have heard about from others, seen for myself on TV, will bring her back to life and make us one happy family again. I cross my fingers like I hold great magical powers. Praying, praying.

# 3 1.

SUN SLICING INTO OUR HEADS, saturating our armpits, we walk the streets, the grey Ipswich streets, Gordon kicking the ground like somehow that can change everything; the earth, the cement, the sidewalk, and the bitumen beneath our feet will understand, bring answers. And then we sit in the park at the back of the magistrate's court, near the hospital, in front of the City Council buildings — everything so close to everything in Ipswich — a small town — giving me the shivers, and I say to Gordon, 'Maybe we should just tell Ruth Hannah? Tell her everything, hey? She'll know what to do?'

Gordon says nothing, not even looking like he is thinking or interested, looking more like he is still holding a disfigured head in his hands, imploring Dusty to live. 'Fuck. Fuck. Fuck,' is all he says.

Squinting into the sun, we sit there. And sit some more. Everyone looks out of joint, off beam, slightly out of focus today, sort of like they were born with a missing chromosome or something; this town so full of people with missing chromosomes that it is not funny. Only today, *everyone* looks in need of care, mental care, even the passing magistrate, the passing attorneys, the city council professionals, the prosecutors. Them, them especially.

After a while I try again.

'Ruth will know...'

Like he is doing me a great favour, he squints up to me through the sun and says, 'Naa, bro. Naa. I have a better idea. A much better idea. You're such a goody two-shoes, ya goose.' He sits and thinks some more and then says, 'Yeah OK, Gray, we'll hang out at Ruth's for a while, but you don't say nothin, nothing at all, mate, ya understand? Just like that Dusty's been beaten and shit and we found her in the hospital like?'

I nod, and that's what we tell Ruth Hannah when we arrive at Ruth's Place. But I don't think she the hell believes us. She is upset about Dusty, but upset with us as well, like we somehow had something to do with it; but she doesn't say anything explicit. And on one of her walls there still hangs that Robert Louis Stevenson poster about friendship that I like so much. About the best thing in life we can hope for. An honest friend.

The next day, in the cold morning, we hear Dusty is gone. Yes, died. Not that anyone from the hospital phoned. It is in the local rag that Ruth always gets. And Ruth shows us. The story just speaks about a girl who had run away from home, was out of work, on drugs, maybe a prostitute, and was found beaten and unconscious, her face and head badly disfigured. Died overnight. Police are investigating but have no leads. The story says there is family in Brisbane who have come forward to claim her. Take her back home to be buried. Just another dead-cold story in the local rag.

'Shit! Shit! Shit!' is all Gordon says. All Gordon says all morning. Over and over. 'Shit, shit, shit. Fuck, fuck, fuck.' And I see a triangle shatter, like one side has been ripped out like the wing from an aeroplane.

There's just a single line now, a line between me and Gordon, and that line is not looking straight. Gordon cannot speak to me through it. He holds his feelings in his chest like his bones will eventually burst out of his throat. The line between us is like a faulty antenna that just delivers bluhrrrg and crackles and fuzz. I say I am going to the toilet. But go only because I want to be alone. I cannot show my feelings here, in front of Gordon. I could in front of Ruth, but somehow not in front of Ruth and Gordon. So I go to the toilet. And in there something in my throat bursts like the bones in Gordon's chest. I cry and hold back a howl, swallowing it in my chest, reaching for my puffer because the feelings in there are squashing my lungs and I can't get any air. I sit back on the toilet seat and beat my chest. I don't know why. I just do it. Maybe I saw someone do it on TV once? I'm sure I have seen very sad people in the Middle East do it. Women. Even men. I don't want to be like them, but I can't help myself. I just do it, beat my chest like a mental case before I can even think about it, and by the time I do, I feel better for having done it. And then I wash my face off so Gordon can't see, and slip out of the bathroom.

Later, I am surprised to walk past the bathroom and hear someone crying. I know it is him because we are the only two left in the house now. Ruth said we could stay behind because of Dusty. She knows how we feel. She doesn't seem to care anyway, knowing the house is about to close down. And then I hear his voice as though garbled under a tap of running water, muffled, half drowning, 'Fegk! Mthe feygkr! G'd. Fegkky'ncnt-pic-pic-pic!'

He comes out of the bathroom, unashamed, his eyes pink, and says, 'C'mon, Gray. C'mon buddy, we have things to do.'

And I follow him out of the house.

At the first public telephone booth Gordon steps in and as I follow, he says, 'Now just be quiet, mate. Just keep ya gob shut.'

He lifts the receiver, drops a coin in, dials, listens for a while, and opens his mouth widely, like he wants every word to be heard. 'I want to speak to Detective Senior Cuntstable Thornes,' he says, pronouncing the name and title very deliberately. 'Oh, yeah... no, it's Gordon Morrow here. Yes, just tell the Cuntstable it's Gordon Morrow. Yes, yes, I'd like to now. That's right — Senior Cuntstable Watno Thornes! Yes, it's bloody urgent, mate!'

He winks at me while he waits. Then he is back on the line. 'Uhh, Mr, sir... I mean Cuntstable,' saying that word deliberately again, 'it's Gordon here. Yeah... I'm fine. No, Cuntstable, I'm just callin 'cause I have some information, mate. I want to like repay ya for not pursuing me an me little bro like. Yeah, yeah, I have. No, I'm sure it'll interest you. Naa hey, this's different, mate, I mean Cuntstable. It's big... V big, man. I seen it with me own two eyes, dude... Drugs, loads an loads of em, mate... being buried in plastic bags... right there by the river. Yeah, that's it, mate, big time hey... heroine an E an M an L an stuff. Plenty of it, mate. You'll be a hero man. Yeah, yeah, I can take you there anytime. Of course. Naaa, like I can't do that. Just you, Cuntstable. Just you... otherwise... well, afterwards you can do what ya fuckin like. It's all yours... it's up to yourself, mate. I'm just tellin ya for now. Yeah, yeah, meet... yeah, at three... yep, that's good by me, mate,

V good by me… by the bridge… ya know where the homies hang? Yeah, of course. Cheers, mate, cheers, Cuntstable!'

Gordon replaces the receiver and winks at me again.

'I think ya got me drift,' he says. 'We're in business, bro. Just one thing, if he has anyone with him, anyone at all, we say there are two stashes, and you the hell take the other copper for a little walk upstream, ya understand that? Good… an just tell him to start digging. Yeah, buddy, anywhere… yeah, yeah… where ya like that's far away enough! Just keep him diggin, mate. Yeah, that's it like, with his bloody hands, or whatever, for as long as you bloody can. Can I trust ya on this one, bro?'

I nod, firmly. Again. Feeling completely uneasy. Eager to help, to be a part of Gordon's plan, justice, but seeing myself when it comes down to it, freeze. Unable to get the image out of my head — of an icicle, a cement block. Me, a useless piece of gravel dog turd. I want to tell Gordon what I see, but instead swallow the putrid air.

After the call we just hang around in the city, then buy some fast food and a six-pack and go down to the river. In the heat of the day, we eat, drink, and wait. Gordon is sweating, his hair is all over the place, like electricity, and the ends glint in the sun. The only other things we have with us are a small garden spade we bought cheaply on the way, from Coles, and a heavy star picket that Gordon picked up from an old torn down fence that we found lying in an old derelict house.

We are sitting away from where the other kids usually hang out, and far down the embankment so that we cannot easily be seen from the road. After we finish our food and down the beers, Gordon gets up and walks along the river with the star picket like a cowboy waiting for high noon. After a while he strides up the embankment a little way, picks up a dry branch and places it upright in the ground. He places the star picket next to it.

'This's for you, Wattie Thornebag,' he says more to himself than to me.

Then we walk back again, only further than where we were sitting before, to a place near the bridge, I presume where he said we would meet Thornes. We sit and wait, partly in the shade of a gum, but mainly in the sun. Gordon's forehead is sweating profusely. He looks cool though.

Just after three, Thornes trundles down the embankment. He

is dressed in a black-collared t-shirt and smart blue denim jeans.
He looks like an off duty wrestler rather than a real detective. His
movements are slow and laboured, like the weight of his flesh is
too much for his dinosaur skeleton. His chest is bursting out of his
t-shirt.

As soon as Thornes arrives, Gordon stands up and starts to
walk and Thornes and me follow. I notice Thornes' knuckles in
the thick daylight, they are red and swollen. Walking next to him,
I feel like a dirty cockroach. I feel like spitting on him, or calling
him names. But I know Gordon would kill me. I don't know if I
really could anyway. I hate no one in the world more than him,
and I tell him that, in my mind, without looking at him. I feel like
tying him down and torturing him. Skinning him alive like I have
seen them do in Japan in the movies. I want to see him scream.
And bow before me. And bring Dusty back.

'Hey, Cuntstable, mate, d'ya have a wife?' Gordon says out of
the blue, carrying the little garden spade like we are part of some
women's voluntary river gardening association or something.

'Shit yeah!' Thornes replies. 'What's it to you anyways, Mr
Morra?'

'D'ya love her?'

'Hey, Mr Morra, you surprise me, I didn't realise you were
interested in such things. Yeah, mate, since you're so interested,
'course I love her.'

'Ya sure?'

'Look, Mr Morrow, my friend, I'm not going to say this again,
I'm not here to play games. It's got fuck all to do with you, mate.
But, yeah, of course I love her.'

'So, like what was it with Dusty, man? Why d'ya need to beat
up on her?'

'Hah Gordo! Now I see, now I see. So that's what you think?
Let me tell you this, matey, if you've brought me here in connection
with that piece of... I'm gonna knock ya block off right now!'

'Naa, I'm just mentioning it, sir, Cunstable. Just very
interested.'

'Listen, matey, I'm sorry for you about what happened to
Dusty,' he says suddenly lowering tempo, turning to the mustard-
brown river and then back to Gordon, 'but let's get this straight,
here and now, Dusty's got nothing to do with me or me wife.
It's about stealing and robbing and dishonesty, that's what it's

about. She was a slag an ya know it! I think you should actually be thankful, mate. She's not the sorta lass I had in mind for you boys.'

I feel like spitting again. Right in his face. Taking a bazooka out of my back pocket and shooting it at his head. Like they do in Iraq. I can see Gordon stretching his fingers around the spade. His hands look pink and lumpy, like they are bloating.

'What's it got to do with you, anyhows, who we hang with?' Gordon says. 'You may be a big copper hey, but you're not our bloody dad? We can hang with whoever we like.'

'Then don't ask questions, buddy. Keep ya nose out of it!'

Gordon's eyes look yellow in the sun, like they are luminous. 'Did ya hurt her?'

'OK, so that's it, Mr Morra. I'm going to thump ya one, now, and then I'll look for this so-called drugs shit in my own time. If they even exist!'

'Gray saw ya… doin things.'

'Gray? Fuck Gray!' The dinosaur skeleton looks angry now, like it is stiffening, the flesh bristling, shooting off sheets of anger. 'The only thing Gray wanted, and I think ya know it, mate, was a piece of the action for himself!'

'Piece of the action…?'

One of those world heavyweight champion fists comes raining down like lightning on Gordon, grabbing him by the scruff of the neck and then tightening on his collar. Whatever his plan, it looks like Gordon has blown it. I just want to shout to Gordon, 'Let's spit on the useless turd and make a run for it.' But it is impossible right now, in the current circumstances. Even I can see that.

'OK, OK, I'm sorry,' Gordon says, curling his squeezed neck. 'But I know ya beat up on her. I know it for a fact.'

'You know shit, Gordon Morrow. Believe what ya like,' Thornes says looking straight into Gordon's wild, spinning eyes. 'I'm not a liar. Like you. Dusty meant nothing to me, mate. And Gray wouldn't know from shit!' He looks down, as though discovering Gordon's ears beneath the mattress of hair, brings his head up to his face, and breathes into Gordon's ears. 'I stopped Dusty to question her about the alleyway bashing and robbery — that bloody assault you know you were a part of, Mr Big Man Gordon Morra — and Gray run like a bloody baby.' He looks at the red, murky river and then back again. 'Now am I gonna thump ya, good an solid, here and now and then come back to arrest you and your little squirt brother here for doing over that old feller... or are we gonna get on with it?'

Gordon's eyes bounce my way. And then back to Thornes, sort of changing his whole demeanour, suddenly looking up to Thornes, his head twisting upwards to Thornes' forehead and past that into the sun, all humble like—I guess especially seeing as Thornes still has that steel rugby forward grip on his collar. And is twisting his head downwards.

'OK, OK, let's get on with it,' Gordon says. 'Maybe ya done us a favour, mate. Maybe ya did in the end. And leave me fucking neck, OK!'

'OK, OK then, Gordo, and no more about that Dusty stuff. Or, I swear, I'll arrest yers both, now!'

Thornes lets go of Gordon, stretching his fingers at his side like he could draw a six-shooter at any moment. Gordon breathes out relieved, long and slowly, like a fan shutting down.

'Just remember who you two fucking are, mate. And what you've done,' Thornes says.

Gordon rubs his neck, gawks over at the river, at the mud that seems to hold up the sun, but says nothing. He clutches the little garden spade in his right hand like it is heavy beyond its size and he is a famous Maori warrior.

A few more steps, and Gordon says with emphasis, 'Hey mate. Here. We here, *Cuntstable*.'

'How d'ya know?' Thornes says.

'I marked the spot, mate, d'ya think I'm a fucking dingbat?' Gordon looks up, but passed Thornes, at nothing in particular. And then points down with jumpy eyes. 'Here, in line with this tree, just by this dead branch. I seen it all, mate, just here. I seen it goin down. They think no one seen em. But we owe ya, Cuntstable, so I'm showin ya. Though, of course,' Gordon rubs his neck as though suddenly in pain again, 'some payment wouldn't go down the wrong way?'

Thornes glares at Gordon. 'Never mind fucking payment, Mr Morrow. If it weren't for me, buddy, you'd be in gaol by now. And ya little brother here, in an institution, I can tell ya that! First I wanna see this fucking stuff.'

Gordon says, 'I'll show ya everythin when ya start diggin.'

'Not me, mate, you!'

207

'Then the deal's off.' Gordon turns like he is no longer interested. 'C'mon, Gray, bro, let's split. Do what ya want with it, *Cuntstable*, I fucking good as showed ya the spot now anyways.'

Thornes looks Gordon in the eyes, and they stand there like that for a minute, eye to eye, toe to toe, super-duper heavyweight champion versus the future super heavyweight champ.

'I'm telling you now Gordo, lad, if there's nothing under this ground, I'll break every bone in ya fucking body. And don't call me *Cuntstable* again... right?'

'Whatever,' Gordon says. 'But I'm telling ya, far as I seen it's not far below the surface. Lots of it man. You gonna thank ya lucky stars, mate.' Gordon points his round black worker's boot to the exact spot.' 'Start diggin... Cuntstable.' He says that word again, but softer.

# 32.

ANNOYED, DRY TUCKS CRINKLE IN THE FLESH around Thornes' neck; you can hear his teeth grit and his nose snort like a boxer. But he takes the little garden spade from Gordon. It looks lost, like a wingless sparrow in his hand. Slowly he goes down on all fours. He checks us first, pink veins in his eyes, tightening his fists. Then like a road worker with completely the wrong size shovel, or more like he is the road worker's sick, oversized young son spending a day off school with his dad, he begins to pound the earth. He is lucky, or maybe it is Gord and I who are lucky, the ground is very soft from recent council re-plantings, and as he becomes more comfortable with the ease of it, the ease of movement of the soil, so he begins to relax and deepen his concentration. Even enjoy it, I think, just the physical labour of it.

'Here, I'll help ya,' Gordon says after a while. Thornes nods and Gordon leans over to get down into that soil with him, stretching as he does so, backwards, stretching backwards and to the side, but quickly, with magical speed like I have never seen him move before, and in that one gymnastic movement like a famous Kung Fu maestro he grabs the black star picket and brings it hurtling down on the back of Thornes' head. It is like a work of art, Gordon's movement, his turning and arcing and slicing through the air with the star picket. And as it cracks down on the back of Thornes' head the star picket pings like a musical instrument. I observe the sharp edge of the instrument tinging right into the soft of Thornes' bone head, just above his thick neck. It sticks there for a second and then falls to the side, and a sliver of red blood slowly begins to trickle from the soft, bald flesh. Eyes shocked and rolling, he falls over.

'Useless cunt! That's for fucking with Dusty!' Gordon shouts, new super heavyweight champion of the world, Thornes out for the count, beaten, Dusty's memory avenged.

I smile, shocked and cold inside, colder than I would have expected to feel, sort of like my own blood is draining from my skin, leaving my stomach biliously hollow. But something in my mind is proud of Gordon. I wish Dusty could be here, to watch him, and Mum and Dad, even Mick the prick, to see what Gordon has done. That he learnt something from family. That he is taking responsibility. That he is willing to defend his family through anything. And then the coldness in my skin turns colder still, to ice, like someone has switched off all the electrics inside, spotting Thornes' big, Phantom head turn, his eyes like shining white globes staring at Gordon.

'Fucking little scumbag!' he tries to shout, but the voice trickles like a whisper.

At the same time, his brilliant white globe-eyes spinning like jet balls, he makes a lunge for Gordon's feet. But Gordon manages to move out of the way, slightly down the embankment, a boxer fleet of foot. Still holding the star picket, Gordon's eyes heave heavenward and he strikes again, only this time he misses the target, the big square baldhead, and instead strikes Thornes across the back, between the shoulder blades. Thornes grunts in pain, or anger, I don't know, but grunts like a pig, a wounded wrestler, and makes another dive for Gordon's ankles. I feel the cold whirring inside me, the blood cells pumping hollow in my face. It is like things are going wrong, awfully, freakily wrong. Like whatever Gordon planned is fouling up. I see Gordon managing, just managing to jump, avoiding Thornes' awkward dive. In the same movement, this time, to my relief, feeling my face warm, Gordon manages a blow with the star picket right on target — directly across the top of Thornes' rock head. Blood spatters and my stomach folds. I think even Gordon catches a fright, because I see his eyes shut quickly like an insect has flown into them. Only as he blinks he loses his balance, and don't ask me how, as he is falling over, Thornes, his face smattered in the thick maroon liquid that has already worked its way round to his doughy cheeks, manages to grab hold of one of Gordon's ankles. Once he has hold of the ankle, it is like he comes alive, like a man rescued, sparks of electric reinvigoration lighting his face. He tugs, hard, making sure that Gordon is brought down, pinning his ankle to the ground. Through shortening breath, I see Gordon's face looks white, unbelieving, and then suddenly like someone has switched on a machine, he turns into a wild man, pummelling Thornes with his fists in the head. His movements, the battering motion of his fists, are like a demented person that you sometimes see on the streets of Ipswich, out of control for no good reason, ramming into a parent, a carer, cursing and smashing things. You can see from Gordon's rolling eyes he is not in control, just going crazy. The blood from Thornes' head, I see, is staining Gordon's knuckles so that it looks like he is wearing rubies on his fingers. But Gordon is striking from the ground, at an awkward angle, and even I can see that against the World War Two, German hard head of Thornes, the blows are not that meaningful or sharp, and Thornes just keeps holding onto Gordon, onto his leg, his clasp like tight steel handcuffs. And all the time he is trying to pull Gordon towards him, I think so that he can tuck Gordon under his body and smother him. And he is screaming and ranting at the same time: 'Little fucker! Little fucking shithead scumbag!' The veins and blood in his baldhead are running down his neck brown like the Bremer River.

Eventually the super heavyweight boxer turned wrestling champ has success, and I feel my stomach completely ice over. He manages to heave Gordon into his torso and roll on top of Gordon's struggling body. I feel like I am suffocating just watching Gordon kicking and pushing and punching for his life. I am going to fall over, I know it, the inside of me is hollow and yet like cement churning, watching as they pummel one another and roll down the embankment, Gordon's face full of thick red rivulets and blotches of brown soil that mingle with the sprigs of blood that flow from Thornes' broken skull.

They roll like that, like they are enchained, somehow bonded together, two people whose play has spiralled out of control, two overgrown kids who at bottom love one another, their faces red like clowns, not even trying to stop themselves, just angry and yet happy to roll on like that, over and over, entwined in one another's arms, all the way down the embankment, across the grey cement walkway, until k'plossh! – k'plossh! like two naughty children, they merge with the mustard-brown river, the harsh sunlight sparking like opals around them. They are treading water now, spitting out brown grime, World War Two heroes, just like on TV, Allies and Axis facing one another, deep in the water, throwing punches that mainly hit the air, shouting, spitting, heads bobbing in and out of the muddy water. I don't know if it is a lucky blow, but suddenly Gordon's nose cracks and blood spurts from it. I shudder, and in my armpits I feel a thick gush of sweat that turns to frost. I am boiling hot in the blazing sun and yet everything inside of me is frozen just like I feared. Like something in me is dead. With each blow that Thornes lands, each time I want to run forward to help Gordon, I feel like something in me dies. Like Dad is smashing me.

I see Gordon, his splintered, bloody nose, looking at me, peering at me over the brown, mud water, only I am grabbing for my puffer, trying my best just to breathe, seeing those eyes pleading, crying, insistent, Thornes' fists thrashing around that plea, seeing Dad's eyes shooting rounds and rounds of bullets into me, cracking into my cheek. Mum screaming at him to get out, 'Just get the hell outta here!' And now Thornes has Gordon around the neck and he is screaming like a madman, 'I'm gonna kill ya! I'm gonna kill ya, fucking little arsehole!' And he is forcing Gordon's head under the water, and there doesn't seem to be enough coming out of my puffer for me to catch my breath; it is like the cement in there is hardening, growing too block-hard, and the puffer cannot melt it, cannot break cracks big enough in it to allow even the faintest glimmers of oxygen through to my lungs. My father looks so big, so massively big, just standing there, like a bear in front of me; I wish I was never born. I gasp down a breath, a real wheezy breath, angry with myself, angry at my lazy breath. Angry at being born, that bit of dirty sperm of his that won the race to give me oxygen, only to spend the rest of his life suffocating it. I am so angry I pick up the star picket and charge down the hill wanting only one thing—to drown myself. Seeing as I stand there for a moment, at the very edge of the river, Gordon's eyes turning white and upwards, his head submerging in the mustard-brown water, Thornes' thick World War Two fingers squashing his head, pushing it under that water, and I take the picket, but without thinking, like I am Moses parting the Red Sea, as though I am commanded by God or something, and smash it over the big, square red skull that is still so profusely bleeding the blood is pouring off in cupfuls into the river. And without thinking I slam down again, feeling in me Dusty, Gordon, Dad, Mum, feeling in me a kind of love and hate and anger at the same time, and the possibility of... I don't know... something I have never felt before and cannot name.

Thornes looks at me after the last blow, turns that hard, World War Two square head to me, like he is surprised, taken aback, deeply astonished and disappointed. And I think he is somehow, miraculously, like you see in those Chinese martial warrior movies, going to fly out of the river and grab me, smash a bony fist into my face, throttle me, drown me, but then it is like his thoughts have gone somewhere else, something else has taken his attention, and he turns his head back to Gordon but with less zeal, like he is barely remembering what he is doing, and I smash down with the star picket again. And again he looks at me, and this time I see Dad's shame, his sorrowful begging eyes before Mum and me in her arms; only this time the eyes look so shocked they do not even bother to sit right in his head, they just somehow become upturned and out of place, all red and then white, and his head slips on that thick, bulky neck of his like it is very, very tired. A refreshed Knight of the Roundtable, Gordon's head appears out of the brown slime like it is that shiny sword, that great shiny sword we imagine coming to save us, and his hands grasp the thick head in front of him. But rather than a knight, they push down softly like a priest, a holy priest in charge of a baptism, and I see in Gordon's eyes a moment of unknowing, a moment of that same, I don't know — love? — hate? — anger? — pride? that I had just witnessed in me.

The water is still now, thick and muddy and still. Gordon is looking into it like a diver, still holding onto Thornes, like he and Thornes are trying to cipher that water, what is really beneath it, seeing the light down there that he often speaks about. For a while they remain there like that, searching, divers in a slow, still, meaningful dance, eyes penetrating directly below, and then it is like Gordon's head rolls in confusion, unsure what to do next because he has never done what comes next before.

Now instead of two divers in solemn adventure, Gordon is desperately treading water, holding up this massive, separate weight, this huge rock, screaming for me to help. I lean over the edge with very little strength and Gordon has to do most of the heaving from behind, pushing Thornes out of the water. The sun above us is dying, stroking the river red, and I see a baptism gone horribly wrong.

We, Gordon and me, are helping the afflicted now, pulling and shoving his super heavyweight body onto the walkway. He lies there, shaped like a generous wad of child's dough, fat and limp. It is like the earth has expelled him but cannot quite shake him off and Gordon starts pumping at his chest, hitting it, shouting, 'Fuck you! Fuck you! Mother fucking cunt!' Nothing happens. The dough just lies there, rolled from the earth, a child's hand unwilling to disappear. Just a useless piece of wet, yellow plasticine. Gordon looks for a minute like he is going to do something I could never in my wildest dreams imagine, something I never thought he could even fantasise doing. But he does it, he actually does it; he brings his mouth down onto Thornes' fat, cracked white lips and kisses them. Breathing his angry breath into Thornes' gargantuan mouth, just like we've seen on TV rescue shows. Only there is something different in this because it is so close up it is real, dead set real, and because it is Thornes, big, fat Thornebag whose iron hands have bashed the soul from our Dust. And then Gordon stops, just stops, his bleached lips trembling and quavering, putting his ear to Thornes' mouth and nose, waiting, listening, like a voice might come out of there.

Gordon looks up into the red sun that is being swallowed by silver-white clouds, by that looming white City of Heaven, and says, 'There's nothing down there. Nothing. Fucker! Motherfucking fucker! Fucking piece of shit! We fucked, Gray. Fucked! We better get the hell outta here. Now everyone is dead, even us.'

I look down. I have never seen a dead body, not this close. Usually they are on TV or in the movies. And not counting Dusty's which, though grotesquely limp, still somehow looked alive, full of pained possibilities. I stare into the lumpy eyes, half open like they are staring back at me with dry jelly fat in them, somehow staring out and yet not looking right at me, but rather through me, through my cold head. The sweat has drained from me, dried cold on my skin. It is like an icy shower has washed over my body and my fingers and toes are numb. My breath is shallow, short, sore. It pains to breathe. Death, I see, like love, is loud, very, very loud. Has a loud emptiness that bounces from the dead body into the onlooker's flesh and bones. Like it is telling you something

214

that you cannot understand. Only the person down there is not the person you knew. Already not the person you knew. It is just something, just something else… a stone, a black ghost of the person you knew? It is freaky, warped. Chilly.

Was I actually a part of this? Did I help bring about this death? I have to pinch and ask myself. *Cunt! See what ya made us go an do!* My own voice screams involuntarily in my head. Guiltily, like we ruined a good life.

Gordon, I think seeing what I see in my head, lays Thornes out straight like he is a heavy sleeping bag, straightening out his big, lumpy body, parting his wrestler legs slightly, but then ponders for a moment, changes tack, and proceeds delicately, and then with an unforeseen struggle begins to open the giant zipper. At first I am horrified, unbelieving, and then I see what is on his mind. I am witnessing my brother Gordon's Court. His open air justice. It scares and amazes me, and I have to keep telling myself he knows what he is doing. This is justice. This is reason. Pure and simple, under the bridge, no frills truth. Gordon lifts and peeks below the elastic of Thornes' shiny black boxer shorts, which are shiny just like Mick the prick's, and gives out a slight, a very slight smile, seeing what is in there. He grabs an old twig from the ground, you can see not wanting to touch it, the thing in there, that torch of darkness that I had witnessed, and pulls it from beneath the shiny pants. It has a bandage around it, white and brown-red with stains, like it belongs in the Bremer. The sight turns my stomach like a cold tumble dryer. It is just like the rest of him now, a lump, just another lump on the body. Only this lump makes my head hollow and dizzy, and I see Dusty, that brown liquid pouring from her throat sending the entire world into chaos and mayhem.

Before we leave, I squeeze one last look into Thornes' half open, jelly eyes, seeing in them powers that still confuse me, that no longer belong, that are not there, yet still, still, even as we move off, cast their shadow over us. A shiver twists caterpillar hairs down my spine. Maybe yes, maybe after all, it is all a bit unreal? And yet I know this, this I know for a fact, we are on the run again. We have blood dripping everywhere from our hands.

# 33.

GORDON IS STILL SOAKING WET AND I CAN SEE FOR THE FIRST TIME his fingers are trembling like he has Ross River Fever or something. But he doesn't say anything, doesn't say a word. Only looks straight, so straight ahead his look tells me he is actually looking behind, into the back of his head. His eyes are deep pink and baggy underneath. He has a cut on the bridge of his nose that is red, but he doesn't mention it or let it bother him. We walk down the river a fair way and then he chooses a place, without saying anything, and just sits there, in the very ends of the dying sun, in the dry smell of the bush on the embankment, the sky looking like it may soon storm, and still he does not saying anything.

When he is mostly dry, but shaking with cold, he gets up and I follow him up the embankment, leaving the river and the bloody baptism behind.

Like vagabonds we lumber our way through the city, past the magistrates' court, the city council buildings, even the police station, like it, that ever watchful brown brick eye on the city, where Thornes dwelt, is not there, does not exist, never did exist, just walking, like in a ghost town, not saying anything. It is like some invisible energy is carrying us. We could walk for kilometres, for days, for weeks, something just keeping our legs going. At the other end of town, at One Mile Bridge, by Leichhardt Park, where we had done that house job with that wuss lad Reno, we walk into the park. The day is thickly clouded now, a little blip that is the sun drowned in sparkling green and purple lightning, around the lightning a rolling thunder that rumbles like God's angry voice. It is everywhere around us, the loud thunder and sparkling lightning, but Gordon doesn't seem to care, and we just sit down on the embankment, among the trees and brush, at the curve in the river where the Bremer comes around and moves off in some or other direction, into more mud.

The river looks black and swollen, part of the black and luminous green cloud jungle that is everywhere around and above us... and I hear Fat Deano's voice next to me again, just like on that day he left us, ordered out by Gordon, drilling in my ears... *My nan always says, the river does not swell with clear water.* I feel it now, just like he said, looking into that river, the darkness, the mud in that river swelling inside me.

Gordon, looking down into the black river, says, 'Fuck Gray, I dunno. I just dunno mate. If there is a God, like Ruth says, I sure as hell can't see Him. Can't even get a glimmer through this brown fucking bloating mud. Or maybe it's that He *can't* see us? I dunno mate. I just dunno.' He scratches his head, like it hurts, with his red-marked hands. 'It's just too thick man, everywhere, wherever ya look, it's all fucking mud. We fucked, dude. Fucked. We got rid of that fat dickhead, and now we more fucked than ever, bro.' He looks at me for a minute, hard, then soft, and says, 'Ya done well today, Gray, ya know that, ya done bloody well mate. I always told ya, man, you no wuss. No wuss at all.'

I want to hug someone. I just want to feel the touching flesh of acknowledgement and warmth but know that won't happen. Instead I follow Gordon's thoughts into that rising river and feel like I am drowning, like I am in that river with Thornes right now. I have done something I thought I was never capable of—I have broken through concrete—and yet I am drowning, and know I will soon be dead. My head is spinning, it is like there is a hole in there, a wild maelstrom, and it is squeezing me down.

'Shit, Gray, you look white as a ghost, man,' I hear a distant voice. And then it is like my head is fighting, will do anything to stay above the water, and there is this huge urge coming from my stomach to reveal myself, to confess. And in front of me is this bishop, at any rate this priest, and he is saying, 'Fuck man, what's wrong, bro? Speak to me, mate. Speak to me, for God's sake. You can say whatever ya want. It's me, ya bro, man.'

And suddenly I am speaking like I am possessed by a poltergeist, spilling things out of my mouth, telling Gordon, 'I wanna come clean man. I dunno, I just wanna come clean.'

'Yes, yes,' the priest is saying. 'Talk to me, mate. Talk.'

And I say, 'I just want to go back to school like Mum an Mr Goss and everyone says, even Thornes, even dickhead Thornes. Like Mum says maybe I can be different. Maybe I can. Maybe I can even get a big house for us one day, for all of us like. For Mum as well.'

And the priest looks into my eyes, and says, 'Don't let me hold ya, Gray. Like Mum always says, you belong to you. I don't want it any other way. I'll never tell anyone what really happened at the river. Although I'd love to, mate, I'd love to.'

Relieved and angry that everything in the end will have to be covered up, like it always is, I say: 'Tomorrow, Gord. Tomorrow first thing I'm going back, man. I'm going to school and I'm gonna make something good.' I look into Gordon the Priest's eyes and I feel completely and utterly lost. I am afraid.

And Gordon the Priest says, 'Look at this for a minute.'

He draws the silver Seiko watch out of his pocket, the one that was stolen, that Fat Deano nearly killed for, the one that Dusty wore with such pride, that is like an engagement ring and a death trap at the same time, and says, 'This is what it comes to mate. This is what it all comes to.'

I look up at him, confused, and he stands up, gazing through the weeds and bush in front of us, down into the swollen black river below, and throws the watch, but high, high into the air. After a few seconds you hear it, rather than see it in the darkness of the day, the silver watch dropping into the muddy water—ka'sshlop! And he just says, 'That mate... that's what it comes to.'

We sit there in silence after that, like in a holy temple or something, thinking.

After a while Gordon says, but very quietly, almost to himself: 'Maybe I'll just commit suicide.'

Something in me, I don't know what, my chest or my stomach, just thrusts. 'Please Gord. No, don't man. Don't say that Gord.'

'Naa... just joking mate,' he says and laughs, slapping the back of my head. And I laugh too, relieved. 'Like fuck,' he says.

I am left confused, not sure what he means. We hear that word going around all the time, under the bridge, in the shelters, at school, it is like a rite of passage, to have tried it just once. And then there were those two last year who went all the way. It sort of rips like a blunt knife through you, knowing, like Dusty's own shiny blue bangles, how close it can get. But I see Gordon as different. Willing to stick it through. Now I am not sure. Everything lately bites that deep. I cannot trust what I see before me, it scares me. I could not face Thornes' death square in the eye on my own. Gordon, I see in that river in front of us, is capable of anything. The fronts of my knees give a jolt and something I cannot understand keeps shooting through my foggy skull.

Night falls, just pitches, like tar rolling all around us. The thick green clouds drift past a game, striving half moon, swallow it, mercilessly, suffocating it like there is no room for both in the sky. You can no longer see the river at all. We can hardly see ourselves, knowing with our eyes we will soon, again, see everything. But it takes a while to adjust. Even for us it takes a while to adjust to the dark. Especially when the night is this dark. And when we can see again, when our eyes are accustomed, we see that we do not really want to see, we are tired, dead dog tired, just like you see cowboys on the run in the movies, desperate to get away yet ready to shut their eyes and keep them shut for days. Like them we have been through a treadmill, as Mum would call it, a treadmill, and somehow we have to keep on moving. I have seen now, for sure, the loudness of love. Of death. The cold, hollow pain that seeps into everything around it. Even Dusty, barely clinging to life, unconscious, did not look at peace, her spirit somehow twisted, lying in that alley, her feet flicking like they were on automatic, in a kind of hell. Even in hospital, still as a post, she did not look at peace.

We just lie back, Gordon and me, stiff, unable to do anything, and even in our sleep, this deep, dog-tired sleep, the damp begins to creep into our flesh, through the toes in our shoes, through our fingertips tied into our shirts. There is no defence from the damp, the rising cold from the river. And then hard apples are falling out of the sky, suddenly falling out of nowhere, spinning and twisting into our faces, first one, then two, then three, smack, smack, smack, whipping like cane toads across the cheeks, and we wake at the same time, seeing that we are not dreaming and it is not apples, or cane toads, but hail, hard fucking hail; there is no mercy, no mercy from the storm. Thornes' revenge? It crosses my black head. Is this Thornes' revenge? Do the powerful—the rich and the powerful—ever get caught out like this? In open storms?

I am confused, half dreaming, angry, Gordon pulling me up by the hand and running with me like we are children all over again, little children at a park, running from an unforgiving parent, the dark black sky, into the toilets in the children's playground in the picnic area above the river. It is open. Fucking open. We cannot believe our luck. Shelter. We enter a single toilet cubicle and I take a deep drag on my puffer, needing clarity in my lungs, and then Gordon and I snuggle in, on the floor, close up, hugging one another, at last hugging one another, and go to sleep again, a grin on my face, as I lie between the warmth of Gordon and the cold of the whitewashed wall.

A single shard of golden light cuts like a long knife into the toilet, waking Gordon and me. It is a clear day, the hail and rain dried up and sucked back into the sky, and in that single slice of sunlight we see a sign that maybe our luck is in. We walk out of the toilet and it is like I can see for kilometres and kilometres ahead of me; everything looks so blue and clear.

I grab onto Gordon's arm, and say: 'I don't care what happens, mate. I'm comin with ya.'

He looks at me through that wild, woolly hair of his and smiles. Then laughs, 'You're good value, mate. Good fucking value. I love ya, bro. I fucking love ya.' I let go his arm, a child astonished, but he just looks away like he too is astonished, cannot believe what has leapt from his throat to the reality of air, and just says, 'C'mon Gray, let's get the fuck outta here. Head out to the Moon for a while. Sort things out.'

And while Gordon is immediately mulling in his head, thinking out our next move, I am feeling my heart thumping like something in me, some heavy burden has been released and we are at the beginning of something new and essential. It is a strange thing but the fact is when you're in trouble life comes alive. It is electric. Things happen. Suddenly everything is real. Even if it drives you crazy, I love this feeling. I love Gordon. It is better, much, much better than going back to school.

We walk quickly, making our way home to Sadliers Crossing, grey clouds unfolding again, smudging the sun. Under that struggling sun, that messed up yellow speck of round gloss, the air is brisk, like it had been all night, and we feel the damp still in our clothes as we walk through the suburbs, passing through

West Ipswich, neat rows of dark-brick housing commission homes abutting paint-flaked small Queensland railway cottages like our own. Knowing everyone is asleep, still asleep, and it gives us a kind of superiority knowing what we have done and no one awake to even know we are at their doorstep, crossing their paths, striding openly through their pasty morning breath streets.

Thankfully, when we arrive home it is too early, far too early to find Mum's or Mick's bleary eyes ready to question us. We sneak straight into the garage and wheel the bike out and down the road, out of earshot. Gordon has to work hard at getting it to kick-start. He looks tired, exhausted, like the last thing he wants is to spend half an hour struggling to kick-start the machine into motion. He curses and swears with each heaving kick. Until finally the bike takes and he revs the engine, screaming to the sky above the stuttering roar, 'Ya bewdy. Ya fuckin little bewdy.'

The fresh air gliding past our faces, it is like taking a shower after a day on a work site, completely invigorating. Just holding onto Gordon, sitting on the back there, is all I ever want in the world, wondering if Dusty would ever have replaced me, if they really would have moved into their own place without me. Already I am missing the closeness of my head against her delicate flesh, her brittle bones, knowing that Gordon feels it, feels it even more harshly than I do, that I am no substitute for Dusty. Feeling Mum and Dad still with me, like they are a gap in my life, like they are the fantasy of reality, like they are the actors on a stage, and I am reality, my life—opening my eyes to catch the full force of the wind in them, feeling Gordon's thick back, knowing it is not hers. Thinking that maybe, just maybe, for once, I have chosen right.

# 34.

AT MT MOON GORDON SEEMS RENEWED WITH ENERGY and takes us
further in than we normally go, towards the drier, less rainforesty
western side. He lies down, and I lie next to him on the coarse
montane heath; it is like he wants to hurt himself, wants to feel the
punishing toughness of nature on his body. And he lies there, just
lies there, the coarse bush pricking into us, looking up at the grey-
white clouds, saying nothing, absolutely nothing. I fall asleep
and wake up to find Gordon already sitting up, but like he is in
a trance, like something in the mountain has taken possession of
him, snap-frozen him, his hands lying palm upwards in his folded
legs like he is holding up a holy book. His eyes are staring straight
out, focused on who knows what? Like there is no recognition —
not of what he is looking at or from what may be looking back at
him. It is like two people meeting briefly and intimately at a party
yet walking by one another in the streets only days later without
knowing one another. His breathing is shallow and intermittent.
I try to follow his gaze, to reach that point on which it is focused,
find what is there, that holds him so intently, yet so unrecognisably.
I stare and stare, and think I finally see it, a little pointy grey head
with black comic book bandit-like eyes peering our way. At any
moment I expect Gordon to break out of his trance, jump up and
chase the thing, the little endangered rock wallaby, throw stones
at it, as he usually does up here. But it is different this time, and
when he realises I am seeing what he is seeing, he says, 'It's just
like us, you know Gray. Just like us, the bugger. No different.'

He stands up slowly, deliberately, and reaches into his baggy
pants pocket. He draws out a crinkled piece of paper. I can see

by the childish scrawl on it, it is one of Dusty's poems that he had taken from her bag in the hospital. He opens it, looks it over once, twice, then proceeds to read it aloud, as though from a stage, as though to me as well as the rock wallaby. He reads slowly, with great concentration, as though not wanting to get a word wrong, but he also reads softly, as though not to disturb the little endangered rock wallaby, so softly that I have to stretch my neck upwards and prick my ears like a rabbit to hear him. "Getting By," he reads, mouth round and dry:

> '...If we get... badly hurt we sometimes... squeal
> If we're desperately... in need we... sometimes steal
> If we not... being bashed... by big fat mugs
> We... sitting round... takin all sorts... of drugs.
> If we not... hoonin round
> Or running... up the... death toll
> We at pubs... or discos... full... of alcohol
> There are... some things... that we do
> That... turns people... off too
> And we wish they could... understand, man
> That we live... our lives... doin the best we can.'

He looks ahead into the bush, at the comic, robber-head of the little rock wallaby as it turns away and hops off. It is like the wallaby specially waited to hear that poem, and then, having heard it, has coyly turned its head and run off back into the brush. Gordon is staring ahead now, only now definitely at something that is not there, like he is seeing something he has not seen before, like maybe Dusty's death has brought him closer to something new. And standing there, as though in a frozen daze, he repeats the words on his bedroom wall,

> When a man finishes
> he is only beginning
> and when he stops
> he is as puzzled as ever

They are the sacred words that have probably been completely torn off our wall by now in some rough and tumble of the new stream of visitors who take up and fill our house. And I wonder as he finishes saying those words whether his life, to him, feels like it has finished or is just beginning, or whether it has just temporarily hiccuped, or whether it has really grown more confused than ever.

'One day...' he says, 'one day...' and just stops there.

# 3 5.

WE HEAD STRAIGHT BACK TO RUTH'S PLACE like there is a red line with batteries in it drawing us there. When we arrive there it is like a wake. Or rather a funeral with a grey party atmosphere. Everyone is moping around, especially Little Pumpy, who is wandering around like he has lost a pet mouse and doesn't quite know where to look for it. They are all packing their few belongings, making arrangements where to go—home, friends, relatives, other shelters, who knows? The fact is Ruth's Place is closing down. Well that is, she can no longer take in kids, until she has successfully re-incorporated or something and re-applied for government funding, and she does not know when that will be. The girls especially are hugging each other and hugging her, saying for the hundredth time it is not her fault and that Ruth's Place is better than all the other shelters in town. They tell her loudly and repeatedly she means more to them than their own mums—and that they hate everyone everywhere for doing this to her. One day they will get back at them. I doubt it. But who knows with some of them? There are more than a couple of loonies among them. They offer to help Ruth around the house—a first—and even swear they will go and talk—make that scream—at the Prime Minister if necessary. Again, I doubt it. But who knows, that's something most of these girls sure know how to do—scream. But Ruth Hannah just smiles, awkwardly, that lower lip scowl of hers fudging true appreciation. Little Pumpy says he will give up school now; he doesn't care about anything because no one else cares. But Ruth, between encouraging sentences to everyone else, is trying to pull him back on track, telling him she'll be just fine, her shelter will re-open soon, and the most important thing he can do with his life right now is to keep going to school. She is trying to convince him that being at an aunt's house, out in the sticks in Kalbar for a while, will not be so bad, may even be a good thing—because then maybe he won't be distracted from school and will see more of his mum, who is very busy with other things at the moment. As most of us know—like trying to straighten out—kick the grog and dope habit and things.

'Like I care,' Little Pumpy says.

Ruth just scowls. And tries again.

Gordon has decided to tell Ruth everything. She is still the only one we can trust, and he concedes maybe the only one able to give us some decent advice. Ruth does what she often does when she first sees us, makes us have a shower, clean up and put on some new clothes. When we have done that, had dinner, giving thanks for the food—a final, final thanks—and, as she puts it, has thanked God for the time 'You have allowed this house to be a home for so many,' she meets Gordon and me in her study downstairs.

Gordon sits there, in front of her desk, rocking on his chair, which she immediately tells him to stop doing, while I sit very still, wide-eyed, just watching them both. As he said he would, he tells her everything—minus, of course, how drunk and stoned he was on the night Dusty was attacked and a couple of other details. He says that we had met Thornes—whose brutal murder, she informs us, she already knew about through her own sources, before it even hit the morning papers and TV news—cruising the area under the bridge that we often hang in. He says we tried our best to be friendly, like we always do with Thornes, but in the circumstances that Ruth knows something of now, an argument broke out over what really happened. Gordon then goes into strong detail about what I saw happen on that night, and Ruth bites her teeth and grinds her jaws like she needs something enormously sweet to chew on. She looks seriously troubled. Like she has taken an arrow.

Eyes now steering directly into Ruth's forehead, Gordon says that Thornes became extremely nervous and heated when confronted with the evidence—which is no lie, of course—and without warning lashed out and punched Gordon in the nose.

Something of a lie. But Gordon points to his badly cut nose to prove it. Not only that, Gordon says, as he tried to defend himself with an old star picket he just happened to find lying on the ground, Thornes managed to push him into the river. Sort of true. Thornes then jumped in after Gordon and tried to drown him. Sort of true, sort of lie. Ruth's eyes roll and flicker and Gordon clicks his nose to show her it is still dislocated. He points to his eyes to show her how purple-red and puffy they still are. Ruth's eyes start rolling faster. Now comes the really good part. In his version of events, Gordon makes me out to be a hero. Of mammoth proportions. The little brother who, uncaring about his own life, and seeing that Gordon is about to be drowned in the crushing strength of Thornes' almighty hands, just, only just in time saves his life by hitting Thornes over the head several times with the star picket.

Gordon looks at me and smiles and winks in full view of Ruth as though he is pinning the Victoria Cross to my breast. I beam and my shoulders straighten. Bloody awesome. How many people have big brothers like that? He says without his 'little bro's massive strength and lightenin thinkin' he would have had no chance against the intergalactic metal-head Thornes, and, in short, if it were not for me he would not be here to tell his tale. He then goes on to say how we both even tried to save Thornes' life by hauling him out of the river and giving him artificial resuscitation. True for Gordon—bullshit for me. I couldn't have given a rat's. Was anyway back to being dead set scared. Remembering that kiss of Gordon's on Thornes' bloated, cracked white lips. Yuurrggh! I shiver. Still shiver. Wishing it was all like Shakespeare said—an act. Then Gordon says, quite honestly—I can see it in his rocking eyes that he must have been thinking a lot about it—the biggest surprise was that Thornes never pulled his gun on us. He concludes, before Ruth can opine anything, that it was probably because it must've fallen out of his pants in the river. Actually, that was the strange thing, we never saw a gun on Thornes at any time, but of course Gordon doesn't tell her that. I feel over the moon with pride. Hoping Ruth feels the same.

Instead, Ruth breathes in sharply like it is another razor cut on her brain. She looks let down, somehow so deeply disappointed she looks at odds with herself. Instead of pride in us, it is like a bloody gash in her head she does not want to carry around with her. Definitely does not want it to stick around to become a scab.

It makes me quiver. Remembering those staring, fat, jelly-white eyes. Maybe that is what she is seeing, too? I'm not keen to ask.

'I'm going to be perfectly frank with you blokes,' she raises her voice into one of those assertive tones, 'the best thing you can do is tell the truth—just like you've told me.' She eyes us squarely. 'But this time you have to tell it to the police. I think this time you have a lot of evidence that shows you only did what you could do. You defended yourselves. More than that, you discovered that our famous Detective Senior Constable Watno Thornes was not by any means as clean or caring as he made out. Was a temperamental hunk of harsh human being unfit to be a juvenile cop.' Her eyes stare out at Gordon like they are in a confessional, like she is one of those Catholic priests in a box with diamond-shaped shadows over their faces that you see on TV. 'I think if you tell the truth, lads,' she goes on gravely, 'the whole truth that is, they will believe you. And even if they don't, even if they don't, and you fellers end up bagged with Thornes' death, I think in the end a jury will believe you. Because in the end, fellers, it is not just the police you will be telling the truth to, it is ordinary people. It is yourselves. And when you tell yourselves the truth it is like being in the company of God. And in the very end that's all that matters. The truth will give you peace. People will notice. And you will be at peace with yourselves. That… that's the most important thing of all. Being at peace with yourselves. You can spend your whole lives on the run; but it'll catch up with you eventually. Karma has a terrible habit of doing that.'

Gordon's eyes pin themselves to her forehead like she is a high priestess. He sits there for a while, not saying anything, physically with his jaw chewing over her advice. Karma. No one wants karma. It always sounds so frigging bad. Opposite of awesome. Gruesome? I shiver. Seeing karma somehow coming up behind my chair ready to grab me with its long fingers round the throat. I wheeze and grab for my puffer. Behind Ruth I see now she has changed the poster. This one shouts… *I could not say I believe. I know! I have had the experience of being gripped by something that is stronger than myself. — Carl Gustav Jung.*

God! I think about that one. Sounds, in that instant, like karma gone crazy to me. Like karma is a ghost. I look back at Ruth, a little bit scared, continuing to weigh her like I fully agree with everything she is saying. It seems to me, right now, there

is something definitely wrong with that poster on her wall—
and whoever this Carl Gustav Jung feller is. Because 'knowing'
doesn't make any difference, at any rate from what I've found.
I mean, just knowing karma or something is going to happen,
doesn't mean it will. For definite. He says he has been gripped by
something stronger than himself and that's how come he knows.
Well, I mean, I've been gripped by lots'a things much stronger
than myself—like Dad an Mick the prick an Thornes, an even
some schoolteachers like, and I know nothing more than anyone
else. To be honest, I have also been gripped pretty strong by some
very powerful drugs. And seen things. But it helped shit. Not a
thing. Seems to me, doesn't matter what you've been gripped by,
knowing means nothing. Maybe, I think for a second, to give that
Carl Gustav Jung feller a chance, knowing what was down there
in the Bremer River was what helped Gordon in his death-battle
with Thornes? I dunno, I dunno… The reality is, if I wasn't there,
outside the river, me, yeah, breathless, cowardly turd shit me, I
think it's true, he would've drowned. And the truth is I'm still
scared shit of things stronger than me. Anyway, that's what I'm
sitting there thinking while Gordon considers Ruth's advice. I am
also thinking how I much prefer Ruth's Treasure Island one about
friendship. That means so much more to me… *We are all travellers
in the wilderness of this world, and the best that we can find in our
travels is an honest friend.* That's real; I feel Dusty's white shadow
pass hollow inside me.

Eventually Gordon shakes his head, and says, 'We'll have to
think, Ruth mum. We need time.'

Ruth turns to me and I stiffen.

'Yeah, we'll have to think, mum.'

'Well then, whatever you choose,' she says in a soft, kindly
voice now, like grandmas you see talking sadly to their grandkids
on TV, 'whatever you choose… you have to promise yourselves to
make a fresh, clean start.' Her eyes loom like white clouds between
us. 'I don't care… even if you leave town and never come back
again… the main thing is this… you have to promise yourselves
to turn a new leaf, find work, go to school, think ahead.' She turns
deliberately to me with that frown on her lower lip that is hard to
know if she is looking angry at you or is just maybe considering
her own bitterness. 'Gray, you especially, you have got to go to
school, mate, and get an education. Out of everyone I know here,

well, except for Gordon,' she winks and smiles at him, 'you're the most capable. You can make something of yourself, mate. But you have to believe that yourself first. School will help you do that.'

'Yeah,' I say, and look down at my shoes, feeling tremendously embarrassed.

'Don't think too long, lads, you know Ruth's Place is over.' Her lower lip uncurls and turns into a quavery dance. 'The first thing you fellers should do is go home. That's my real advice. But make up your minds quickly, because the longer you take to come clean the less the authorities are going believe you when they do eventually catch up with you. And they will. I know they will. They always do. And remember, always remember, the truth is a very powerful tool.'

*And lies,* I say to myself, *and lies are even more powerful.* But I look at her with a face full of agreement. Like I've learnt to do when I'm lying. The only truth, as far as I've seen, and this is no lie, is that we sometimes need to lie. There is this constant need for lies. To avoid trouble. To find grub and money and shelter when you need them. And, for the lucky ones, I guess, to get ahead in this world. Like the bloody kids up the road at the big white-walled grammar school in their neat little school ties and straw boaters. Gordon looks at me, flicking the whites of his eyes upwards like fried eggs being turned. I need to know from him where we're headed. Hoping, hoping with all my heart it's not to the bloody cops, like she says.

# 36.

THE NEXT MORNING GORDON TELLS RUTH WE ARE A STEP CLOSER to going to the police. I shiver, and so does she, but she with relief that she has convinced someone in such deep trouble as us to do the right thing. You see emanating from her Ajax clean, fresh white face that thing like she 'knows', like along with that Carl Gustav Jung bloke she has it perched in there, right in the middle of her glowing face, like she has been gripped by something very powerful and stronger than herself. Something we cannot see. She stands there beaming. Like God is all around her.

'That's wonderful fellers. Absolutely the best and bravest thing you lads can do. Get it all out in the open. I am very happy. I think you will be the better for it. All will end well, you'll see.' Ruth smiles like we are her prizes, and hugs us. She promises we will see her again.

'I am a phoenix,' she says, whatever that means.

And suddenly, after our meeting with Ruth, everyone in the house is hugging. I think it is the most I have ever hugged in my life. I feel warm and fresh like white bread toast. And dizzy.

Outside the house, getting on the bike, Gordon says, 'Fuck the truth. They'll never fucking believe us anyways, dude. Not when it's one of their mates that's the fucking dickhead murd'rer. C'mon bro, hop on. We may as well come clean — some other fucking place.'

Suddenly I am hot and my heart is pumping excitement. Gordon has made a decision and it sits like a lotus flower right there in the middle of my stomach, spreading magnificent white petals into my chest. I don't like the thought of gaol, having to sleep with strange people, away from Gordon. Even court cases, which you have to go through to get in or stay the hell out of gaol, give me the creeps. It's like being on a platform. Being stared at by strange, sleepy-eyed people while you are cross-examined and made to look like an idiot. I know some people on TV make it look easy, but I just go chilly and hollow inside like a windsock just thinking about it. Getting away is the right thing to do. Something inside, something inside my stomach and chest just tells me Gordon has made the right decision. It is our best and maybe only option. I feel so light and happy with the decision I can cry. Maybe we are being led by a stronger force?

We go home to collect some clothes, and I suppose in our way to say goodbye to Mum.

'Ya haven't been to school again,' is her greeting as she opens the front door for us, cigarette in hand.

'I have, I was there,' I shoot back.

'That's not what Mr Goss tells me. And it sounds like the coppers are lookin for yers both!'

I look around, not knowing what to say, trying to gather breath.

Gordon butts in for me. 'Gray's going back to school, Mum. Today. Promise.'

I glare at him with eyes that could kill and he half winks at me and I know everything is alright. He is telling me the truth while he is lying to Mum. Awesome.

'And ya better find a job, young Lord Morrow,' she says to Gordon, an ultra thin laser beam of white smoke streaking from her nose as she breathes and talks at the same time.

'Yeah, that's exactly what I'm doin, Mum. Getting me things and goin up north. They told me at Centrelink, there's plenty work up there, in the mines.'

'And how exactly ya going to get there?'

'Train, Mum. That's why I'm here. Getting me things like, and then hop on a train. To Rocky. Or thereabouts.'

We are still all standing at the door.

'OK, ya better c'mon in then, boys,' she says, her eyes more awake now than the half-closed state they were in when she first opened the door. Smoke is still billowing like sea foam around her head.

Mick, we see, is in the lounge, a couple of mates with him, sitting in the couches. They are all shirtless, white and hairy, and buttering cold toast. It looks like juice, but I can see — and smell in the air — they are washing it down with rum or something. They've probably been on a binge.

'No work today?' Gordon says to Mick.

'I'd shut me fucking trap if I were ya, mate.' Mick turns like he could draw a Luger on Gordon. 'You only ever come home when you're bleedin hungry, don't ya!'

Gordon mutters something, probably like 'Get nicked' and Mick turns again, 'What ya say? What ya say, mate? I wanna hear it. C'mon, what ya say? Say it loud, so we can all hear it. C'mon!'

Gordon opens his mouth like he is about to repeat exactly what he had said, and Mum jumps up from a chair.

'Jesus Christ fellers, take it easy! Gordon don't mean no harm, Mick. He just come by to say g'bye. Me boy's off north, to work in the mines.' She looks hazily proud.

'That'll be the flipping day,' Mick laughs. 'He couldn' even find a job on the mines here.'

'Well maybe, Mick, but that's because there's only one bloody mine left in the town,' Mum snarls. 'Not like in Dad's time, when this town was so bleeding full of coal mines you couldn't breathe for the black dust. Even then there weren't enough work to go round.'

'Well, he can't even get a job in a shop,' Mick says. 'Not even a bleeding thrift shop, never mind goin up north!'

And Mum immediately looks at Gordon and then the two men in the room, red, rock wallaby eyes darting east to west, anything to avoid a clash, and says, 'Gordon, these're Mick's cousins here, from down south, Sydney ways. Benno an Chris. An these are me two boys, Gordon an Gray.' She heaves her chest.

'How ya goin, son?' They both look up at Gordon and don't even bother to look in my direction.

'They're in yer beds for a couple of nights,' Mum says like she is rubbing a hand over a shirt to ease out the creases, 'but that won't worry ya now ya going up north an all that?'

I notice now she is sitting in a thin, almost see-through nightie and it embarrasses me.

Mick bursts out laughing, making a show of it for his so-called cousins, eager to take up where he left off. 'Yeah, there's plenty'a work up there alright, but will he find it? Not Gordo. Not bloody Gordo, me lad. Not on yer life. I give him two weeks, Ange, two weeks, and he'll be back on ya doorstep again, begging for a meal.'

'I wouldn't beg yers fer nothing. Even if I was starving in Sudan or somewhere,' Gordon says, eyes glowing with thick, red worms in them.

'Cool it will ya, Mick,' Mum says, 'the kid's off in just a few minutes. For once in yer bloody life just say g'bye nicely. Wish him luck.'

Mick just looks away, takes a sip from his glass like it's water, and then like he is having second or third thoughts, turns back.

'What the hell happened t'ya face anyways, Gordo?' he says, and before Gordon can even begin to reply, he says, 'Get roughed up in a fight, hey? Yeah, don' tell me, there was ten of the fellers and only you an young string bean here.'

The three men laugh. Mum frowns and inhales on a cigarette, deeply, like it is coming from a special oxygen tank, like she needs it to breathe.

Gordon speaks through his eyes. 'As a matter'a fact that's dead right, Mick. Only there were five of em and they was all coppers!'

Mick laughs, 'Just listen to him. Can ya believe a kid like this?'

And Mum says, 'Christ Mick, you can be cruel.' She turns to Gordon. 'Maybe ya better have that nose of yers seen to before ya go, son?'

She actually gets up, in that thin see-though nightie of hers, holding a cigarette, and takes a close inspection at the gash on Gordon's nose, blowing bits of slowly exhaling smoke into his eyes. The smoke, rather than her inspection, makes him pull back. She holds his arm sort of like she doesn't want to show him she means to. But I can see she does.

'I will, Mum, promise, soon as I get up there,' Gordon says.

She sits down again. I feel relieved, it is harder to see through her nightie when she is sitting down and there is not so much light on her.

'You can have your bed back in a coupla days, Gray,' she says to me. 'In the mean while you can just bring a mattress in here hey. The main thing is that ya get to school, mate. I'm telling ya, Gray, if ya get to school you'll be right son. Maybe one day ya'll even get rich. Like them kids up the road at the Grammar place. Anyways, I'm relyin on ya, son, to get us a big house in Brisbane one day.'

'Yeah, Mum, of course.' I feel so embarrassed I could climb under the couch in front of everyone.

Despite the dry hoarseness in her voice, I see a little white-clouded glimmer in her shrivelled red grape eyes and I feel strongly that I want to touch that spot in her. Behind the blackness, I see, there is still a kind of kinship in her; I can feel it closely sometimes. I want to hug her through those eyes.

Gordon marches into the bedroom and I follow directly behind.

Immediately, among the rubble of Mick's cousins' clothes, he says, 'Fuck em. Fuck em. Fuck em dead.'

His poster has been ripped right in two, half the paper hanging curled over on the wall, the only words visible, barely, a couple at the very end... *puzzled*... and... *ever*. His Rambo poster just has a neck with a red bandage around it.

'Shit! Dickheads!' he breathes, and starts packing a small backpack he pulls out from the bottom of the cupboard. 'Just pack a bag like ya goin to school, mate,' he says to me. 'They won't know the fucking difference. They never fucking do.'

The room hasn't felt like ours for a while, but now it really feels like an island floating away from us, like something we never knew, never dreamed and slept in. It's almost scary. It contains so many other shadows now, and even though Mick's cousins' clothes are all over the place, it seems empty. It feels black and hollow like an abandoned hut in the bush. Nowadays we wouldn't be surprised to walk into our bedroom and have to say to someone we've never met before: 'Excuse me, d'ya mind if we come in?'

Nevertheless, despite everything, I am excited. Actually busting inside. My heart is humming, screaming like a field full of summer cicadas. I even wish we could actually tell Mum the truth — that we are going away. Not coming back for a long time. Leaving all this crap behind, maybe *never* coming back. But, of course, I have to remind myself... Mum would never understand. I look up into a dim light beaming right into us from the old, dilapidated bedroom window. It is like that light in the hospital shining in on Gordon and Dusty. Only it is dirty and brown.

When we come out of the bedroom, all packed and ready, Mum says: 'There's some Anzacs in the kitchen, Gray. Grab a couple an some fresh bread if ya like. I would've had some fruit ready if I knew you'd be here an goin back to school today.'

'Thanks, Mum,' I say, and just look away from her.

And then she looks at Gordon.

'What's happened with the lass? Dropped her already?'

'Yeah, dropped her already Mum,' Gordon says. 'Dropped her dead!'

But she doesn't seem to get his meaning, and just says with some pride in Gordon, 'An if she drops by here, I just let her know ya workin up north, hey?'

'Yeah, just tell her I'm up north, Mum. And not to bleeding follow me up there.'

'OK, well then, sounds like ya really and truly dumped her then,' Mum says. 'Can't say I'm too unhappy, son. I think that girl knew too much. Give us a hug then. Or ya too big for that now, too?'

Gordon saunters up to her like she is someone he is meeting for the first time, and hugs her, like ice. I imagine her hard skin on me, and feel lukewarm.

'What ya doing with the bike?' she says.

'Keeping it safe in the garage. What d'ya think! And don't let him use it.' Gordon points with his eyes to Mick, who, looking at his two cousins, raises his middle finger and says under his breath: 'Fuckass.'

For once Gordon just curls his lip and chooses to ignore it. We make our way to the door, and as we open it Mum calls out to me like there is a rush of light in her voice, 'Enjoy school, Gray. Have a good day, mate.'

It sounds just like an ordinary mum, so everyday, so like an ordinary family. Yet to me it is like sunshine. I feel myself reach for my puffer.

We slip through the front door — on our way to Sydney — feeling the fresh air and freedom upon our faces.

# 37.

SYDNEY IS A BUZZ. Sleeping in the park under the big bridge here, meeting new people, seeing new things, filling with new ideas. The Sydney Harbour Bridge. It is such a big bridge, such a big park, surrounded by trees and masses of water, it makes Ipswich look second rate. We are making new friends so quickly, it almost seems unreal. Even more than unreal. Surreal. And it almost becomes surreal, I mean really, really surreal when one of the kids, baseball cap facing backwards, a bit drunk, says to Gord: 'So, dude, who's the beanpole fucking cripple always with ya?' Gordon just casually steps back and then smashes the kid right in the face so that it knocks the baseball cap right off his head and the kid has to be carried like a wounded soldier to a tap and have the blood rinsed off his face. After that I become immediately more acceptable, even being told, forever being told, like everyone is my mum, or dad, or uncle, or aunt, where to go, which hospital to get my puffer medication from, how to survive without it. It is a new beginning, new friends, new hope. Turning a new leaf. Just like Ruth said. Just as Gordon promised.

There is even a little kid around, about twelve, actually two or three of them, just like Little Danno, carrying skateboards everywhere and screaming out, especially when they are pissed, all sorts of rubbish that even sounds a bit like Little Danno's hip-hop warcry: 'IIIIIII... meeeee... weeeeeee...' And everyone is a hip-hop artist, ready to show their stuff and play their music at the soonest opportunity. Everywhere, in each face, we look for and think we see Fat Deano and Kelly; we even compare, openly, some of the new people we meet with them, but unless they are very carefully disguised, there is actually no sign of them. It is a real disappointment to us. We really, really wanted to catch up with some familiar kids from back home, 'homey-homies' or something like that, who we know deep down like. And somehow we expected to find them here. They both always wanted to head for Sydney one day. But no one here has even heard of them. They have just vanished off the face of the earth. Maybe they have even separated and gone their own ways? Beamed up into another universe? Who knows? Freaky. No doubt they will turn up some day. Probably dead, knowing them. Specially Fat Deano. Knowing him. So much like a swelling river, no wonder he was saying that. And I am thinking of Gordon's wall poster, I don't know why, I don't know why, but it seems so apt now, like we have passed through a thousand lives and need to reconsider, recalling the words that I know always, always run through his mind: *When a man finishes/ he is only beginning/ and when he stops/ he is as puzzled as ever.*

Maybe start again, at home? I think. Like as if. Like as fucking if. Praying for a parallel universe, another universe, knowing it will not come. I'll be patient, wait for Gord to decide. Something strong to grip us—like that Gustav Jung bloke says. Things happen. They do. They always do. You can't force em; they just happen. Life just pushes you on. And then before you know it you're on the run, making life-saving decisions again. Feeling the goose bumps swell on your flesh. That's life. Real life.

A couple of weeks after we are in Sydney, Gordon wakes up late one morning and says, 'Maybe we should call Mum. Just to let her know we're OK like.'

I nod, actually smile, I have been hoping he will say that one day, too afraid to say it myself. Who knows why? I hate Gordon thinking of me as immature. It's bad enough he has to stand over me like a henchman.

We go to a telephone booth and reverse the charges. Hoping, I think praying Mum will answer.

'Where the bloody hell are yer?' I hear her shrieking through the black plastic receiver, like we have called a megaphone. 'Ya know if Mick answered he wouldn't have accepted?'

'Yeah, Mum. We just wanted ya to know we're OK like. In Sydney. How's that?'

'What the f —'

'Sydney, what's wrong with Sydney?'

Something garbled I can't hear — then, 'And what about Rocky, Emerald, work up north?'

'Naaa, I tried it, Mum. Wasn't so good. So now I'm tryin Sydney.'

'An what about Gray, we been searchin all over for him. Everyone is. Calling all over… an the police an his headmaster…'

'He ended up with me, Mum. But he's good, Mum. Real good. We'll be fine. Promise. Back in Ipswich soon. Promise.'

'And… is he with ya now? Can I say hello to him?'

'Hi Mum,' I shout into the phone, grabbing half the receiver.

'I hope ya got ya prescription, Gray? An ya know yer mum loves ya… an Gordon… we been worried to death over yers.'

Hearing Mum's voice so close to my ear, I sense a quiver in me, feel it rattle down my throat into my stomach like a call that rings out but never gets answered. Like a drop of syrup from Dusty's eyes. Emotions scream in me like a hot field of yelling cicadas. Like we used to hear them arguing and ranting, despite the peace out there, at our secret place, Mt Moon.

'Thanks Mum,' I say for some stupid reason. 'An don't worry I have my puffer prescription and everything. An I think about ya…' And then I move my head away from the phone because I feel my stomach or my chest or something in me is going to unravel and rip. I am fighting with my eyes to keep them dry.

In the background there is a faint but distinct detonation.

'Angel, tell em to get their fuckin asses back here! The whole bleeding town's lookin fer the buggers!'

'Mick says to come back,' Mum echoes in a calmer way what he is saying. 'There's always place for you lads here. Ya know that.'

Gordon looks at me, and then the phone goes click, and both Gordon and me are left hugging the plastic receiver like it is an animal or something we once loved and has breathed its last. Gordon doesn't even bother to put it back on the hook as we walk out of the booth. Just leaves it dangling there, a beast hanging. I guess to show someone. To show someone we've been there. What it comes to.

A large half moon shines in the sky, all golden white and speckled grey; I guess the cheese inside gone off a tad, like in our fridge at home. It rocks above us, half full or half empty, I don't know which. A bad sign? Maybe I'm just getting paranoia? We have been in Sydney for a good three weeks or so now, mainly sleeping under the great harbour bridge. Tonight, not for the first time, we are getting drunk as hell, and stoned, Gordon taking deep inhales from a bong and both of us sharing some tablets one of the kids says is speed or something. Despite the so-called speed, we are getting so hungry and thirsty it's like we haven't eaten for days, and no one seems to have any bread. One of the kids suggests something we haven't done for a while, Gordon insisting we try to rather hang out for Centrelink. But having second thoughts, because Centrelink might dob us in.

In any event, the call has come, a decision has been made, and it feels right, like exactly the right thing to do. At any rate something inside us just tells us it is right. Sits well in our stomach and chest, so to speak. So we follow one of the kids to this house he knows, and that he says will be easy to get into. From the outside it may not look as big as some of our Ipswich houses, much more cramped looking, made of brick, and joining right next to another house. But it is perfectly painted, not a speck of flaking colour or rust or mould, and it looks sort of upper class. Like fashionable semi-detached houses you see in movies of London. Yeah, I think London at any rate. Rich and comfortable like Mum says I will one day be if I go to school. Like our rellies that we never met.

Like the kid said, getting in is easy. Inside we immediately feel at home, or if we don't, which I don't for a while, I actually feel a bit spooked, like bigger forces than any of us are looking down on us, we make ourselves feel at home by starting to dance and pulling at curtains and table cloths and drawers and things. Just like in Ipswich. When we have discovered the liquor cabinet and taken a good few gulps, the cold shivers, that feeling of spooks and stuff, drifts off completely. Only this time we get pissed on malt whiskey and gin and French Benedictine liqueur or something that is rich like syrup. It reminds me of something I don't want to think about. And just carry on sipping and passing the bottles round like they are water bottles dished out at half time in a footy game.

After a while Gordon sits down with me on a couch that we sink into like it is a warm fireplace, only built from woollen fluffy stuff, and does not burn. It is like the couch Mum imagines for us one day, I'm sure. I'm sure this is the one!

And like Dad, I mean like a father, just like an ordinary, caring father, Gordon says to me: 'Fuck Gray, this is it, man. This, the things that make us forget about the bloody world, that make it all worthwhile, mate. Makes a dude feel like a king.' He takes a deep sip from the bottle of malt whisky and passes it on to me.

I make a mental note to write that down in my journal. What he has just said. And another thing that passes through my mind, passes through it like a golden arrow, seeing the moon hanging up there, half empty or half full, I don't the hell know, outside the window. And it is this: They say, at any rate I heard it said at school and other places often, that the darkest hour comes before the dawn. Well, if that is really so, I am thinking with that golden arrow shooting through my head, maybe Gordon and me are lucky. Maybe Gordon and me are very, very lucky and the moon is actually halfway full — because the truth is, we still have a ways to go to get into that darkest hour. For the moment we do not have much, we're out of money, have no home, no rellies, no bike any more, but we're still the hell enjoying ourselves — and Gord has never mentioned suicide again. And that's cool. Way, way cool. Everything seems like the dawn. Like the only thing hanging in the sky is a halfway full moon. I love it. I love it. I love it.

This is our dawn. Our swelling, filling moon. Me and Gord. And we haven't even passed through the darkest hour! Just together here, in the middle of the night, in the darkness, lying together on a warm couch, having a good time. Getting so smashed that Gordon turns to me, hugs me, and says, 'I'll look after ya, Gray. No worries, mate, I'll always be here for ya.' Or words to that effect. I love the feel of his bear-like embrace around my body. I think it is the first time I have felt it since I was small. I feel like we dinkum are in a theatre or something. I just don't want the curtains to shut, and have to go home. Knowing he must be getting very, very smashed. Or lonely. Missing Dusty, I'm sure. Knowing I am. Fuck, I am. Which reminds me, I'd like to… no, no, I definitely will, send a snapshot back to Mum. Of Gord and me under the Sydney Harbour Bridge, just to show her how well we are, how two brothers can be family. I think she'll understand. I think she tried, once. I really do. Seeing, in the end, as we all come to see, there is no choice, we cannot write our own scripts, can only try to change it, and in the end, mostly, the only way we can do that is by forgetting. By getting out of our wee little trees. By getting so high the world looks so small like we can fit. Small like Ipswich Square on a Saturday morning, nothing more than long beards and little dots of fuzzy grey. I see Detective Senior Constable Watno Thornes and Dusty right there in front of me. The scene is like a thick paste, it keeps coming up; it is like I need to burn it or cook it to smithereens or something so that it will soften and unstick and eventually smoke off, right out of my brain. But even with all this drink in me, and tablets and stuff, it sits in my head like my head is a dinkum freezer. It will not diminish, it will not go away. It is frozen there. I search my head for the defrost button... and find my feelings for Dusty are among the only feelings I ever had. And I want to hold onto them. Even with Thornes forever frozen there next to her, standing like a giant ugly cane toad in front of her, strangling her, muddying the image, it is almost comfortable. It is almost real.

...Yes, life has begun again in a new place and Gordon, his hair wilder and woollier than ever, looks renewed, bright, enthusiastic for the first time in weeks as we rummage through the house throwing cushions and blankets and sheets and tipping beds and chairs... not to mention smashing glass art nouveau lamps, that even we know are art nouveau, and other ornaments and things. We throw them against the walls like they are eggs, enjoying watching them crack and smash into thousands of little new art nouveau designs on the floor. And like Little Danno, one of the kids that are like Little Danno — I swear, it must be an art form — is shitting right there in the middle of the lounge floor, and then painting the walls with his delicate little fingers in difficult to comprehend but beautiful brown and light brown and almost yellow patterns. The lines run thick and deep in parts and then thin and shallow, and sometimes all over the show in spirals like a circle that can never find its end. This kid is an artist, a genius, the best I have ever seen, even better than the Ipswich kids, but no one in the world will ever know that. No one. It is all just a spiralling circle like this kid is painting, sometimes the lines so thin you can hardly see them, can hardly make out they are there, lose direction, and sometimes thick and heavy so that they almost ache, throb and then wither, starting all over again. A puzzle, a circular puzzle. Of shit.

In this luxurious house, it is so snug and warm. Just so comforting to be under a rich roof in the dark again, messing up things that in the blackness look so decent, so perfect and perfectly still, that in the daylight have this knack of blinding us, of making us feel small like annoying flies or mosquitoes or cockroaches or things dirty and creepy. In the back of our minds, Gordon and me, Dusty a glimmer on the brown water under the bridge, receding. A glimmer fading, fighting, as Gordon would say, to find the surface. To come to the top, and dazzle our eyes. She withdraws like the smell of eucalypts, that loud, dry smell at the heart of Mt Moon which passes into memory like drips of Benedictine syrup as we make our way through the green brush, back down the sandy hill, to home. Or Ruth's Place. That is no more. Nothing quite tangible. Nothing, nothing forever. There is no choice in that. None at all.

Maybe one day, one day, we will be caught. Maybe one day we won't. Images of Thornes' big, square, rock-like cranium, eyes half open or half closed, as the case may be, I don't know, a star picket smashing over his doughy head; sweet mouth, sweet love, sweet family, a spotted brown bandage around his gravelly, yearning, filthy torchlight; a truth in there, our truth, which no one will deign to listen to. Which no one will ever hear. Was it ever real? I don't know. What I do know is this, that it's time to throw away my journals, so many lost and about the place anyways. I mean, shit, what are they worth? Gordon is right. What does it all come down to? ...'That. K'plossh.' Nothing more. And then, at random, it starts all over again... Fuck! The water looks so much clearer here, so much warmer under the bridge, in Sydney, almost turquoise-blue, like here at last we might see through the mud, see what lies on the other side, what lies at the bottom of it all... Maybe one day, if I go to school here, I'll have a big house in Sydney even, like Mum says...

## Other Fiction @ IP

*Back Burning, by Sylvia Petter*
*ISBN 9781876819422, AU$28*

*The Buggerum Intrigue, by Paul Sterling*
*ISBN 9781876819682, AU$30*

*Easter at Tobruk, by Michael O'Sullivan*
*ISBN 9781876819405, AU$30*

*House of Given, by Bill Collopy*
*ISBN 9781876819378, AU$30*

*The Dispossessed, by Andrew Lansdown*
*ISBN 1876819308, AU$27*

*Secret Writing, by Michael O'Sullivan*
*ISBN 1876819294, AU$27*

*A Ticket for Perpetual Locomotion, by Geoffrey Gates*
*ISBN 1876819286, AU$27*

*The Diggings Are Silent, by Wendy Evans*
*ISBN 1876819243, AU$24*

*After Moonlight, by Merle Thornton*
*ISBN 1876819227, AU$25*

*Another, by Joel Deane*
*ISBN 1876819251, AU$27*

*For the latest from IP, please visit us online at*
*http://www.ipoz.biz/store/store.htm*
*or contact us by phone/fax at 61 7 3324 9319 or 61 7 3395 0269*
*or sales@ipoz.biz*

LaVergne, TN USA
11 December 2009
166765LV00006B/28/P

9 781876 819804